THE DOCTOR MAKES A CHOICE

by Elizabeth Seifert

D1316843

THORNDIKE PRESS · THORNDIKE, MAINE

Library of Congress Cataloging in Publication Data:

Seifert, Elizabeth, 1897-
  The doctor makes a choice.

  1. Large type books. I. Title.
[PS3537.E352D564 1986]   813'.52   86-22974
ISBN 0-89621-753-1 (alk. paper)

14188448

438 p.; 22 cm.

Large Print edition available in North America by arrangement
with Dodd, Mead & Company, Inc.

Cover design by James B. Murray.

THE DOCTOR MAKES A CHOICE

For
Doc and Nell
Sandra and Johnny

THE DOCTOR MAKES A CHOICE

CHAPTER ONE

He was a tall man, lean and muscular. His dark hair swept thickly across his head, his brown eyes were brightly alert; his strong-featured face was that of a thinker, a man eagerly receptive to ideas and emotion. He was interested in everything that went on about him, and those who passed or saw him were attracted by that interest, and responded to it.

Even in the crowded corridor of surgery, the busy people looked up at his approach, and paused long enough to look after him. Of the dozen patients who lay, sheeted and waiting, on stretchers, of those who guided the carts, or carried IV bottles, or walked briskly, this man alone was dressed in a dark business suit; he walked with the assurance of familiarity, he threaded his way swiftly between the carts, glanced knowingly down at the moaning woman on one of them, brushed past the rack of tanks without disturbing a thing, and was aware of nurse, patient, orderly without speaking to any of them.

'If this were my hospital,' thought Jock, 'I wouldn't allow me to go through here.'

When he reached the elevators, his finger touched a button as a thing which he had done many times.

The elevator came up; two green-swathed men came out, said, 'Good morning, doctor,' to Jock, and went down the hall. Jock stepped into the elevator, touched a button, the doors slid shut, the mechanism hummed softly.

At the next floor three people got in; at the next, two more. Jock Askew saw them, and his mind acknowledged their presence; he moved back against the far steel wall to accommodate them; yet, in a sense, he did not *see* them at all. They had their business in this hospital, just as he did. But his business was not theirs.

A doctor, he was here on personal matters. He had just been with his father; later, he would go again to his room, and sit beside his bed—but not as a doctor. Today the things he must think about were thoughts which any man must give to the matter of his father's illness, his breakdown, his collapse. His possible death.

Jock leaned his shoulders against the steel wall, felt the elevator move, heard the other occupants talk—it was sure a cold day. Winter had come early. No snow, though ...

And he thought about his father. A week ago,

Jock had been summoned; he had been here with his mother for five days. His medically trained mind told him what had happened to Jim Askew, what his condition now was, and what could be expected. But—personally—what would this collapse mean? To Jim? To his wife? To Jock himself?

The elevator stopped, two people got off, two more got on. Jock's eyes flicked across the heads; six people were now in this steel box. So far as Jock knew, they had never been close together before, and they never would be again. They had nothing in common, except that they were human beings, and, for one reason or another, today they were going down in an elevator of the Brownlee Memorial Hospital.

Jock felt the jar under his feet. The others felt it and looked at each other, wide-eyed. The elevator had stopped. Not at a floor landing; they were somewhere between the fourth and fifth floors, and the gate did not open.

One of the women gasped sharply, the man nearest the door slapped his hand against the latticed guard. Jock straightened, said, 'Excuse me,' and reached his long arm to touch the emergency button with his forefinger. Nothing happened. Jock looked up at the ceiling. Yes, there was an emergency hatch.

'We'll just wait,' he said deeply. 'A fuse has

13

burned out, or something of that kind.'

His bright eyes surveyed his companions. There was a man in white garments; obviously he worked in the hospital as an orderly or attendant of some sort. There was a woman in a tailored robe. She'd be a patient being sent to some place for examination or treatment—tests, perhaps. There were three people, a man and two women, who, like himself, wore street clothes.

And now all six of them did have something in common. Anxiety. They had trusted themselves to an automatic elevator, which, one of the women said, no one ever really trusted! And now they were stalled somewhere in the narrow tube of the elevator shaft. The light was on, the fan whirred air to them, yet the place suddenly seemed stifling. The man at the front shook the gate, and began to shout. The emergency button which Jock had pressed showed red on the floor indicator.

'They'll send help to us,' he said deeply.

'When?' cried one of the women, her voice shrill with rising terror.

Jock looked at his watch. Like many medical workers, he wore it on the inside of his wrist. 'We've been here ninety seconds,' he said calmly.

The man in the white jacket sat down in the

corner and clasped his hands around his knees. 'Me,' he said cheerfully, 'I'll catch up on my sleep. I never get enough of that.'

Jock grinned at him. He remembered the days when he too would have snatched this extra free minute. 'Orderly?' he asked, his deep voice vibrating in the small space.

'Yeah. It's a dog's life.' The chap was cheerful about it. He probably was a good orderly.

'I don't think anybody gets enough sleep these days,' said Jock; talk would ease the tension, he hoped. Their difficulty would be noticed, a phone message would already be going down to the busy maintenance rooms of this big hospital.

'I'm supposed to be down on the second floor,' said the woman in the blue robe, 'for blood tests. Maybe they'll wonder where I am, and ...'

'You have someone sick on the seventh floor, haven't you?' the woman in the red hat asked the man at the gate. 'I've seen you in the hall.'

'Yeah. My wife. I don't think there's much wrong. The doctors keep her here, just the same. You don't catch any doctor admitting he doesn't know the answers.'

The orderly opened one eye to look up at Jock. He had spotted the watch.

Jock was smiling. 'I've seen *you* in the halls,

15

too,' he told the woman in the blue hat.

'Oh, my, yes. I half own this hospital.' She was a plump woman, with a ready smile. 'Some of the family is always in. I feel funny when I don't have to come here every day. It's my son, now. Fourteen. He broke his arm playing football in the street. I have told him a hundred times not to play in the street.'

'Did a car hit him?' asked the woman in the red hat.

'My, no. He just fell over his own awkwardness, and the thing broke.' She laughed comfortably, and the others laughed with her. Yes, it helped them to talk to each other.

The lights in the elevator blinked off, and on again. In the second of darkness, the woman in the blue robe screamed softly.

'They're working on us,' said the orderly.

'I was on my way down to buy Johnny out,' Blue Hat said, talking calmly. 'My husband said not to bring him home if he cost more than he's worth.'

Again, everyone laughed.

'I come every day,' said Red Hat. 'If I don't show up tomorrow, they'll miss me, and ask what's wrong.'

This time the laughter was uncertain.

'There's a woman in the room with my mother,' said Red Hat, inconsequentially. 'She

16

won't get well very fast for worrying about things at home. She's got a grown daughter—evidently she lives at home—but that woman—the sick one, you know—gall bladder—she worries all the time. When the girl comes to see her—*Girl!* She's twenty-nine—Mamma must ask a hundred questions. Did the laundry go out? Did the laundry come back? Did Papa eat a good breakfast? Did Amelia—that's the daughter—did Amelia go straight home from the hospital every afternoon? She is not to be out alone after dark, and she is not to buy a winter coat until Mamma is well enough to help her pick it out. *Wheee!* What a woman! Can't let her girl grow up!'

'I can't stand mothers who want to breathe for their kids ...'

The women chattered happily on this subject. Jock leaned back against the wall. He could have told tales of his own mother, loving, possessive ...

Beyond the eddy of talk which the women had stirred, the man began again to shake the guard lattice. He cursed below his breath. 'Damn hospitals!' he groaned. 'I hate the things. They're in business, but it's one business where the customer has absolutely no rights!' He turned to face his companions. 'My wife is one of those customers—she's just here for examination and tests. The first thing they did was put her to bed, then nothin'. Absolutely nothin' for six whole hours! Nobody came near her. We had to pay for her room before we could go upstairs. They don't trust us, not for one thing! Whole set-up is crazy. They give her a sleeping pill at night, then wake her up at five in the morning to wash her face. Does that make sense? I ask you!'

He was indeed forgetting his anxiety in his talk. The orderly was looking at him, and grinning.

'And the food!' the man continued. 'It comes in cold, and looks like a bricklayer's helper had mixed it in a hod. And you get it at certain hours whether you want it then or not. Maybe you're used to your dinner at seven. When do you get it in this hospital? Five o'clock. Only it's supper. You get your *dinner* at eleven A.M., and you eat it then, or not ever.'

'This hospital is no different from others ...' Red Hat attempted.

'I know that, Ma'am.' The man turned on her, his face flushed with earnestness. 'I've talked to my friends. All hospitals do the same way. Take visiting hours. Two to four on some afternoons, seven to eight at night. And no exceptions, unless you're dying. Then your closest relative can come—so he can pay the rest of the

18

bill, I guess, as you get carried out.

'My wife's worried about herself, and she'd like folks around to talk to. God knows she can't talk to the nurses. They switch in, switch out—and you could be bleeding to death, or breaking your heart, for all they care. They're sent in to give a shot, and that's what they do give. Sometimes, they don't even *look* at my wife while they're doing it!

'But you pay a fortune for this sort of service. Two people in a room, eighteen dollars a day, with shots and medicines and the doctor bill extra. *Doctors.* They got plenty of them around—but they don't care, either. They come in—maybe four or five of 'em at a time—they talk about the case; they talk across the bed. Not *to* my wife, but about her—and she can't understand a damn word they say! When she asks one of 'em to explain, or I ask, they don't tell us a thing. I tell you, it ain't the way to do!

'I'd move her, but like I say, other hospitals do the same way. I've inquired—' His eyes met Jock's.

Jock was smiling.

'You think that's funny, Mister?'

Jock shook his head. 'I don't think it's at all funny,' he said heartily. 'And you're right—all hospitals—most of them, at any rate—do just as you say. I've inquired into the situation myself.' There was a firmness in his voice, and something in his face ... His five companions looked at him with new interest.

'You haven't said why you were here, sir,' said Red Hat.

'Oh—I'm a visitor, too. I'm here to see my father. Dr. Askew.'

A flurry of interest swept the group. The orderly looked up. 'The boss,' he breathed. 'Might-a-known.' He made a move to stand up.

Jock's hand on his shoulder pressed the man down again. 'Rest your feet,' he advised. 'This won't last forever.'

The women were telling each other about 'Dr. Askew.'

'He took out my husband's appendix five years ago,' said Red Hat. 'He's a wonderful doctor.'

'... fine man,' said Blue Robe. 'I've read about him in the paper. How's he getting along, sir?'

Jock shrugged. 'There isn't much change from day to day.'

'I hope he won't be sick long,' said Red Hat.

Jock nodded acknowledgement of the hope. His father would be sick as long as there were days for him. A big man, a fine man, a 'wonderful doctor'—but now the tree had fallen.

Around him, in their small box, the others were talking busily. At first they spoke of his father, and of the things they knew about him—he was 'head of this big hospital.' Which he was. Medical Director. He had been, for years.

The man at the gate attempted to soften his words of criticism. Jock murmured something about his being right. Hospitals *were* in a rut of habits and practices, many of them no longer useful.

While the others talked, Jock gradually drifted into thought—about his father, up in that high bed, guard rails up, the sick man's eyes bloodshot and bewildered, his trembling voice no longer one of authority. Dr. Askew's assistant, and his second assistant, were running the hospital and doing his work.

But Jock's mother made all other decisions. That Dr. Jim was not to be moved out of the apartment, that only a few of the staff doctors should come in to see him, that he should have no other visitors—just now— No, certainly *not* the Chaplain! Jock's father cried when he got emotional, and Emma could not stand that.

She had decided that Jock should come home, and she had decided that he must stay ...

Jock sighed. His mother. A tall woman, with a back as straight as a flagpole, her white hair beautifully dressed, tinted to a faintly blue silver, her tailored clothes immaculate, her jewellery restrained, but always in place. Ear-rings, a single strand of pearls, a pin of some sort, and two rings.

Had she always looked just this way? It seemed to Jock that she had, and yet he must remember her as a much younger woman. He himself was forty-five. Emma had been twenty-two when Jock was born, with Jim eight years older.

He remembered his father as a younger man, with sandy hair. Now he was bald.

But, in his earliest memory, Emma looked as she looked now, tall, strong, and handsome. Kind, in her own way. She had done literally everything for her only son. She wanted to continue to do everything. She ...

Jock's ear lifted to faint sounds in the elevator shaft. He could hear them, with his head against the wall.

When nothing happened, he let his thoughts go to Anna. His heart hastened its beat, and the shadow of a smile lifted the corners of his flexible mouth as his mind winged swiftly across the mountains to the wooded slopes of the California hills. He stole a glance at his watch. They'd been 'in' for fifteen minutes, and the noises in the shaft were resuming again. Perhaps he heard men shouting ...

Three-thirty here; that would be one-thirty

22

at Tree Valley. If the day were fine, Anna would be out of doors, eating her lunch on the sheltered lower terrace, perhaps. Perhaps someone would be with her. One of the technicians from the Foundation, or a teacher from the town school—no, not a teacher on a week day. But there would be someone!

On the table there would be a salad—some sliced meat, perhaps some crab—tall glasses of tea—hot or cold—crisp wafer cookies, and a bowl of fruit.

Anna would be curled up in the high-backed chair, her glossy head dark against the blue cushion, and whoever was with her would be talking while Anna listened.

Anna was wonderful company; everyone said so. Yet Anna did not talk much. She was not silent, but she listened more often than she talked. It took people a time to realise this.

Sunlight would filter through the leaves of the tall trees, there might be a breeze, or there might be fog. Anna liked to wrap up and sit outside in the fog. She said it was like having a dream become alive, palpable, and real.

Down below the house, but still among the redwoods and the ferns, Jock's associates would be at work, phones would ring, and the consultation rooms would be busy. If the day were fine, men would sun themselves about the pool, the tennis court would be in use—patients would walk along the paths under the tall old trees.

Perhaps one might go as far as the house, and Anna. She would welcome that one, her eyes gravely smiling; she would offer a chair—and some tea?—and a chance for the visitor to talk, quietly and unhurriedly.

Jock closed his eyes and breathed deeply.

Back there his own office and desk would be empty, his own voice would be missing in the consultation room. Yet the work would go on without him. Good work. He and Anna had built the Foundation to that end. They had laboured valiantly. And it had all been worth while. The work was good. Jock regretted no step which had brought that attainment to him.

No, not even Iris.

The children, yes. But not Iris. She—

Jock's nerve ends jumped to attention. Blue Robe had begun to cry, like a child suddenly giving way to tension and fear. Quickly, the orderly was on his feet. 'Oh, now, Ma'am ...' He looked appealingly at Jock.

And Jock made his try. He put a comforting hand on the woman's shoulder, he pointed to the escape hatch. 'If we were in real trouble, they'd have sent a man down the shaft to help us up and out.'

'I couldn't get through that size hole,' said Red Hat in dismay.

This made the others laugh, and Blue Robe dabbed at her eyes, gulped, sobbed, and tried to smile. 'I didn't want to come to the hospital in the first place,' she declared.

'They'll be good to you, and take care of you,' said Jock.

'How do you know?'

He laughed a little, and shook his head. 'Well, if it were my hospital, *I'd* be good to you.'

'Are you a doctor?'

'Yes, I am.'

'He's Dr. Askew's son,' said Blue Hat.

'Are you going to do your father's work while he's sick?' asked Red Hat eagerly.

Jock sighed. His mother would like to hear his answer. 'I'm not a surgeon,' he said quietly. 'And I'm afraid not the man my father is.'

'You could be, maybe, if you'd try,' said Blue Robe encouragingly. And Jock's mind clicked with satisfaction. Her thoughts had been taken away from her momentary panic.

Jock told about the sounds which he had heard, and this gave the others plenty to talk about. What was going on, they speculated. What would be done? How would they know ...?

Jock was free again to think—about Iris, and the children.

Iris, whom he had married when she was eighteen. He had fallen in love with the pretty girl who had hair like corn silk, smiling blue eyes, and pretty teeth. She danced well, and thought Jock was *wonderful.* And they had married—too soon, too young. They immediately had two babies. Betsy and Jamie. Betsy, blonde like her mother, and Jamie dark.

Jock thought of them now as he had known them last—Betsy about five, and Jamie three. Just babies still.

He had not seen them for years. He could have. Iris had custody, but she would have let him see the children. Only, he'd been far away, he'd been proud, hurt, and stubborn—and, finally, he had feared what the interjection of himself, an unknown father, a second father, might do to the strangers who were his children. By then, life had taught him to think on all sides of a subject.

He remembered with a stab of pain how they had looked and sounded in their half-hour of play before going to bed. Betsy tenderly putting her doll to bed, Jamie playing roughly with a stuffed animal ... Their water-clear voices still echoed in Jock's ears.

Could he see the children now? On this trip?

26

At the age they were now, twenty-two and twenty, it surely could do no harm. If any sort of an opening presented itself, he would see them. For he had missed that part of his life. His work, Anna—those things were very good. But there were two bruised spots which had never healed. The hurt he had had to do to his parents, and what he had done to lose his family. If he could ever go back, even a short way ...

He straightened, and shook himself. He was, in his own fashion, as bad as Blue Robe. Emotional. He was letting his whole life pass in review, like a drowning man snatching at memory.

The five others in the elevator were exchanging names, now, and even addresses. Jock readily said that he was Dr. James Askew, Jr., but commonly called Jock, and that he lived in California. No, he didn't know many people in San Diego, he lived near San Francisco, he—

The lights went out, came on again, and there was a humming sound; the elevator shuddered a little, and began to move, down a few feet, then up—slowly—or it seemed slowly. One could not tell, really. The emergency light went off, and the elevator stopped with the indicator marking five.

The door slid open, and for a second or two, no one moved. In the corridor two overalled workmen, the hospital Administrator, a curious aide looked at the people who had been imprisoned.

'Goodness!' cried Red Hat, scrambling for the door. 'I thought I couldn't wait to get out of this thing!'

The others laughed, and followed her, streaming into the hall, chattering. They talked to the people in the corridor, they talked to each other. They would never forget *this* experience, they promised themselves and each other.

They would not. They would remember the friendliness; they had been in trouble together, and in that trouble they had found comfort in their common humanity. Those things, they would remember.

'I hope your father gets well fast, doctor,' each one said to Jock.

Then, smiling, they scattered. The women towards the stairs. Nothing, they told each other, would get them in that elevator again. The man in the brown suit sheepishly followed the orderly who was telling the Administrator to front for him. 'I've been warned to be on time, or else!' The two men disappeared into the next elevator.

The Administrator detained Jock with a word of inquiry about his father, a brief expression of regret about the elevator, and the supposition

that Jock would be staying around for a time?
'If I can do anything for you—'

'Yes, sir,' said Jock. 'I'd surely call on you.'

CHAPTER TWO

Jock went down to the main floor and got his topcoat from the closet of his father's office. He would walk to the hotel, rest for an hour ...

His mother could not understand why he insisted on staying at the hotel, nor why he must go there to rest. But Jock was deeply conscious of his need to be separated somewhat from the hospital and his parents. He despaired of ever making Emma understand this need. If she loved a person, she wanted to crawl into that loved one's pocket, into his heart and mind, and dwell there in continuous companionship. She so loved Jock. Didn't he love her?

Jock shut his eyes in pain, and, pushing through the glass doors, he went out into the crisp, damp cold of the November afternoon. Across the Boulevard, people were skating on the beautiful rink which had been built since he left the city. There had been many changes in that time. Three new hospital buildings in the Group, and Brownlee itself had expanded.

Well, why not? Things had not stood still for Jock.

Indeed they had not.

He thought of the way in the elevator his thoughts had skimmed across the main events of his life. He must remember to tell Anna that she was warmly prominent in that review. Anna ...

A week ago Jock had been with Anna and a few of their friends, in his home, seated before the fire on his own hearth. The evening was foggy, and the fire's glow was welcome, its warmth enjoyed. They had eaten a good dinner; Anna had done delicious things with a boned pork roast; she had stuffed it with chestnuts and roasted it to a crackling, rich brown. Her salad was supreme; she had spread garlic butter on rye wafers, and had made a custard with a bright garnish of loganberry jam.

After the meal, everyone was feeling replete and in a pleasantly jovial mood. There'd been four or five of the Foundation people present; it was not a party, except that Anna had the gift of making any gathering seem special, and yet casually intimate, too.

That evening, these friends had gathered by casual invitation; they had eaten heartily of doctors understood, and Minter explained to his wife.

'Hardening of the arteries, dear. It progressively shuts off areas of the brain, causes pressure, and anxiety.'

'A change in personality,' contributed Dr. Keys. 'This is not the first attack, is it, Askew?'

Anna had held out her hand to Jock, and he had gone to stand beside her, his face troubled.

'No,' he said, 'for the past couple of years—Father thought he had had a slight stroke, and he probably did. It's affected his eyes, and he drags one foot a little when he walks. When he—did—walk ...'

'Do they think?' asked Frances fearfully.

'No,' said Jock. 'Oh, I don't know. I didn't talk to the doctor. I talked only to Mother. They'd evidently put Dad under sedation. He had an attack of some sort while eating his dinner this evening. She was with him, and the experience was hard on her. She wants me to come home.'

Anna's fingers tightened on his hand. 'Of course you must go,' she said firmly.

'There isn't a thing I can do.' Jock brought a small, cushioned bench to the side of her chair and sat down. The three doctors were sitting on the deep couch, Frances Minter in the pink armchair.

34

good food, they had moved on to the living-room fire. Anna curled up in the round, chintz-covered chair; Jock remembered that behind her, reflected in the wide window, there had stood a large pot of blooming geraniums.

Minter had been there that night, and his wife. Applewhite, and Keys ...

After dinner, they drank coffee or brandy—or both. They talked of Foundation matters, gossip mostly. Small, intimate anecdotes. Minter said that men came bigger these days, and in the future they'd do well to buy bigger beds. Of course, said the women, that would mean special linens ...

And the phone had rung.

Jock was inclined to ignore it, but Anna told him to answer. Kim would still be clearing away.

Jock had grumbled something about husbands being more expendable than house boys, and the other men had laughed at him. And, laughing, too, he had gone to answer the telephone.

Immediately he wished that he had not.

For his mother had been on the other end of the line, with word of his father's collapse.

Jock had never heard Emma sound so shaken, so frightened. 'He—Jock, he's so *bad!*' He hasn't been too well, of course. You know that.

31

But this evening—oh, it was at dinner! He couldn't get up from the table, and the way he looked at me—and he couldn't talk. And his eyes—he looked so *strange*, Jock!'

Jock had sought to calm her, to reassure her.

'Didn't you know that this sort of thing would happen, Mother?' Jock himself had told her that it might.

'Yes—but not before my eyes, Jock! That was so *bad!*'

'I know, dear. But help was close. Or were you at home?'

Yes, they had been. In the penthouse apartment which Dr. Askew had occupied since coming to Brownlee, in the thirties, as Chief Surgical Resident.

His mother had urged Jock to come home.

'Mother, I can't do a thing your doctors there can't do. They know more than I about these things.'

'But you're his *son*. He needs you, and I do.'

'Is Father conscious?'

'They've given him medicine—and he seems quiet now, and asleep. But he will be conscious, of course.' That was said in Emma's usual firm way.

Jock was doubtful about going to St. Louis, to his father's bedside. 'He won't want to see me, Mother,' he attempted.

'Why, Jock—'

'No, he won't. Not under the circumstances.'

'He's sick, Jock.' His father was mortally sick. Did Emma know that?

'I won't decide now,' he told his mother. 'I'll call you in the morning.'

She had talked for a few minutes more, urging, insisting that he come. 'At least, come, Jock,' she concluded. 'Then you'll know for yourself how things are. It isn't only his sickness, dear. *I* need you.'

Jock did not want to go; he had gone through this before. He sat for several minutes beside the telephone, and considered his reluctance. But if his mother did need him, had he any choice?

Torn with emotion and with indecision, he went back to his guests. It was then that he noticed the geranium, and the chair in which Anna sat. He supposed the chair had been there since they'd built and furnished the house. But that evening he became acutely aware of its enveloping roundness, of the patterned chintz which covered it. There were great rose-coloured poppies, and some daisies, some gold-coloured grasses or leaves—all on a white background.

Looking at the chair, gravely Jock told his friends of his father's attack. The other

'You'd be a comfort to your parents,' said Frances.

'Now, that's the easy thing to say,' Jock told her. 'But as a matter of truth, under the circumstances, I truly think it would only upset Father to have me come in.'

'Oh, Jock,' said Anna.

The men, the doctors, waited for him to explain.

'My father,' said Jock, reaching for a cigarette, lighting it, carefully putting the match end into the blue ash-tray. He hadn't wanted a cigarette; he smoked very seldom—but he did want something to do with his hands. He was finding himself greatly agitated by the news which his mother's call had brought to him. He had thought himself prepared for this—or some—development. But now that the word had come—

'In recent years,' he began again, 'my father and I have been opposed on various matters. He wanted me to be a surgeon, you see, not a psychiatrist. He—well, anyway, take my word for it. He won't want to see me. With him helpless, and me on my feet.'

As he told this, Anna watched him gravely. Her enormous eyes had never left his face.

'But, now,' she said at this point, 'you still must go to St. Louis. For your mother

35

needs you.'

Emma had said that she did. But ...

'Father has a 500-bed hospital at his disposal.'

'What comfort is there to a 500-bed hospital?' demanded Anna.

The men had laughed, and Jock with them.

But Anna was quite serious; she repeated that his mother would need him at such a time.

'So does the Foundation need me—at any time,' said Jock.

The Foundation was not a small project. Its buildings, its work, its personnel—Jock had established the centre himself, and had carried it on to its present form, each detail a matter of his personal decision.

'And you,' he went on. 'Don't *you* need me?'

'Always,' said Anna readily. She looked around her, at the living-room, and their friends, and beyond that room, at the dining-room, which was like an indoor garden; perhaps her mind touched upon all of her home, which she and Jock had built together. She took a deep breath. 'I can take care of the Foundation and of myself,' she said firmly. 'For a time.'

Jock laughed, and shook his head. Anna was as tiny as a doll, as fragile and exquisite.

'Well,' she declared, 'surely the staff can take care of the Foundation! Can't you?' she asked the three staff men present.

'Well—' said Minter.

'We'll do our best,' said Applewhite.

'He goes away on other business,' Anna argued with them.

'Oh, yes. And if he'd stay away this time for just a while ...'

'Well, of course!' said Anna. 'He'll have to come back. Because you'll be needing some of his ideas.'

That was a stock joke around the Foundation. Some of the men claimed that Askew came into every staff meeting with the declaration: 'Gentlemen, I have an idea!'

He did say that, often enough. But the Foundation had been built on his ideas! He hadn't had them all, but it was his idea which had started the thing and, yes, kept it growing, too. So—he was needed. Though he did leave occasionally, and he could leave now, for a while.

He could leave Anna, too, for a while. She told him so after their guests were gone, and she and Jock were about to go to bed. They had gone out on to the porch to watch their friends leave—and now they stood looking out upon the trees, listening to the winds in their tops.

'I'll be able to manage,' she told Jock, tucking her hand through his arm. 'I can do that better than I could handle your staying here on my account.'

Jock had pretended to be puzzled by that statement. But she knew that he understood her. He always understood her. She just rolled her big eyes up at him, and shook her head.

'Will you go with me?'

'No.'

It needed no words. His marriage to Anna had never been accepted in St. Louis.

He sighed about that, and touched her arm, guiding her towards their red front door, and the stairs which led up to the bedroom floor. 'I'll phone for a reservation,' he said as they climbed.

'You are not grieved about your father?' she asked a half-hour later. She sat on the side of her bed, slim and pretty in a sleeveless, Chinese pyjama suit of gleaming green silk.

Jock considered the term. 'I have been *grieved* since I first knew that this illness was upon him,' he said thoughtfully. 'Now—death will be a merciful thing. He can't work any more, you know. Not if I interpret Mother's message correctly. And my father will find it hard to face life without his work. At times his illness will cushion his realisation; at others, he will protest against it. This—Anna, my darling— this is not an easy way to die.'

'Are there easy ways?'

He smiled at her. 'Yes,' he said quietly. 'Yes, there are.'

He still did not want to go to St. Louis, and his reluctance was becoming a guilty burden upon him, for it seemed that indeed he had no choice. His mother's need—Anna's insistence. He slept poorly, and the next morning Anna drove with him to the city and to the airport and, while he weighed his bags, she said that she would pick up his ticket. She was making much of her role of taking care of him, of being efficient and self-reliant. Jock smiled as he took his bags from the car. He folded his topcoat over his arm; the day was sparkling clear here in California, but he would meet with truly cold weather in Missouri, even if he stayed only a few days.

When he joined her, Anna gave him his ticket envelope with a smile which made him open the thing and look at its contents.

'I brought a round trip,' she said. 'I wanted to be sure you would come back.' Her black eyes studied his face. Swiftly her finger touched the cleft in his chin, and she smiled bravely.

Too soon, the flight was being announced. Jock touched Anna's arm, then drew her close to his side as they started for the ramp. 'I'll come back soon,' he promised, clutching at his hat when the wind caught them. 'I don't want to go. I'll *want* to come back!'

'We'll both remember that,' she said, lifting her face for his kiss.

At the plane door, Jock turned to wave to the slender girl in her light coat; the wind lifted the ends of her black hair, her teeth flashed white in a brave smile, but her dark eyes were those of a lost and fearful child. Jock tried to look the reassurance which he could not speak. He wanted to come back; he did not want to go.

And now, a week later, he still was in St. Louis, held here. No longer could he doubt that he was really needed.

His thinking had taken him down the avenue, into the hotel, and up to his room. He sat now in an armchair, and looked across the room at his own face in the wide mirror of the dresser.

He confronted the mirrored image of himself as he would have faced a patient who had come to the doctor, asking to be told the why of his feelings and behaviour. Could Jock, the physician, to any degree help himself? Could he analyse himself? His purposes? His hidden compulsions?

He considered the image seen in the glass. It was the head of a tall man, a large man. The skin was smooth, a little brown still from the western sun; a healthy red glowed in the cheeks. The hair was thick, dark brown, and coarse, difficult to keep smooth without dressing, and Jock seldom had time to do more than comb his hair, or run his fingers through it. The hairline was good, with a modified peak on his broad forehead. That forehead showed some wrinkles; in forty years, this man had done his thinking and his feeling.

The eyes were brown, and somewhat deeply set. The brows were thick, and each angled upward. There was an expression of intensity in the eyes, a brightness, an eagerness.

The nose was straight and narrow, the mouth was neither large nor small, his lips were well-chiselled, and firmly held. The upper lip was deeply indented between nose and mouth, and there was a cleft in the firm chin. The jaw was well-defined, but not hard.

Like many faces, this one had its differing sides. The right side, seen only, was smooth, even tranquil in its quietness. But the left— here the lines were deeper, the mouth was more heavily bracketed, the eyebrow did not arch quite so far; that half of the face was of a man who could be deeply concerned, even agitated. Who grieved and loved, strongly, who strove for the things he wanted—and would fight to attain them.

Which man was Jock Askew? Which man must now face Jock Askew's life, and make his decisions?

For half an hour, Jock sat in the chair, thinking, and yet trying not to think. He should rest for this brief time away from the hospital, away from his father, and his mother.

A man was a creature alone. That was one philosophy.

'To know for whom the bell tolls.' That was another.

And both were true.

Certainly his father was alone these days, fighting his battle, alone in his fears, his hopes, and his anxiety. Yet his illness was like the casting of a stone into water; the swimming circles touched many people. Emma, of course, and Jock, his son. And, touching Jock, it extended its wave clear across the country to the Foundation and the people who worked there, or came there for help. The water lapped against Anna. Here in the city again, Dr. Askew's illness touched the life of every member of the hospital personnel; who would replace him, who would do his work? It touched many lives outside of the hospital—the man on whom Dr. Askew had once performed a delicate intestinal operation and now would come back for a needed second one, if

Dr. Askew could do the surgery. He could not, and the patient must seek help elsewhere, and the doctors he sought would then be touched by the falling of this one tree. By the casting of that smooth stone. And each one touched must make some decision because of the effects of that stone's casting.

Jock must make his decision. Or was he already caught in a trap, where his own reasoning and decisions would make no difference? If so—if he thought it were so, should he get out *now?* Quickly and ruthlessly?

When Jock returned to the hospital, his determination was fixed to tell his mother that he must return to California at once. He went in through the entrance of the Pavilion, a section of rooms and suites set aside for the wealthy sick and injured, people who could pay for privacy and luxury, for special care. Just now there was quite a bit of arguing going on within the profession about 'pavilions.' But anything so well established by custom and precedent would continue in Dr. Askew's hospital! Jock could be certain of that!

He touched the elevator button, with a reminiscent smile. Had Blue Robe had her tests? And walked up to the seventh floor again? Before the elevator came, he was joined by an

43

elderly woman, her daughter and a nurse.

'I can tell you one thing,' said the older woman; she wore handsome furs, and her cheek was as soft as a rose petal. 'I am *not* going to undress and go to bed! That's all nonsense in my case. I'm not sick. I'm going to have minor surgery at noon tomorrow. I'll lie down for that, but twenty hours ahead of it I am not getting into any bed!'

Jock saw the nurse exchange glances with the daughter.

'Now, Mother—'

'Hospitals do that to *cow* a person,' declared the matron. 'They get you flat on your back, into one of those horrid shirts, and they think they've taken the fight out of you! Well, I'll show them!' The elevator came, and she marched in.

Jock followed the women, shaking his head. This patient, too, would go to bed. Immediately. He'd bet.

The Medical Director's apartment was on the top floor of the Pavilion, and the elevator made the journey without mishap. Fine thing, thought Jock, if the *Pavilion* elevator should cut up!

Having reached his destination, he stepped out and crossed the corridor to the closed white door; his mother must have been listening, for she opened the door even as his hand fell to the knob.

'Oh, Jock,' she said, as if grateful that he had come.

He looked at her anxiously. 'Is something wrong?'

Emma shook her head. 'Nothing new. Come in, dear. Hang your coat in the closet. Is it cold out?'

'Cold enough. Not bad. Mother—?'

Every effort had been exerted to make the apartment look unlike a hospital dwelling. Emma redecorated at intervals; now the living-room was done in warm, rosy-brown tones with touches of clear yellow. The carpet was pale green. There was a gas-log fire on the small brick hearth, books and bits of pottery glowed on the shelves beside it.

'You seem more worried this evening,' Jock told his mother, sitting down on the couch, and picking up the folded newspaper.

Emma sat in the soft-cushioned armchair, but she did not relax. 'You know what a bad night your father had,' she said anxiously. 'It was— very bad, Jock.'

'Yes, dear, I know. You should have let the nurse handle it.'

'I know. You told me to close my door, and

get some rest. But, Jock—'

'Look, dear.' Jock laid the paper aside, and turned to face his mother. 'Father is going to have bad nights, from now on. You must face that fact. In his sort of illness, the nights seem to be especially difficult. There are some reasons for this, but generally we doctors don't understand that phase.

'But his nights will be bad, his fears will seem worse. He'll protest more. He might even do things that will hurt himself, or you. That is why we insisted on a male nurse, at night.'

'He wouldn't take his medicine; he screamed and fought. And he—he cursed me. His face got red, and his mouth twisted to one side, and—'

'Mother.'

Emma nodded, and stopped talking, twisting her handkerchief between her fingers. 'I've never heard of a case like this, Jock,' she said faintly.

'They occur, many times. Sometimes in homes where hospital care and nursing are not available. An illness like Father's has been known to kill strong women. That's why I urge you to use the cushion which is available to you. Move him downstairs, let the nurses and the intern take care of him at night.'

'But, Jock ...'

'You would not be unfeeling. If Father were himself, and advising a patient's family, he would say the same as I do.'

'But he knows me; he knows I'm there. That must be a comfort to him. He finally went to sleep, and he's slept since, though he's awake now. And he clings to me so, Jock. That's why I think ...'

Jock glanced at her, and he felt his lips press together. Now his mother was leaning towards him, her face intent.

'That's why I think,' she said again, 'that this would be the time for you to tell your father that you'll stay here, Jock. That you will take care of that little—matter.' The lawsuit, she meant. Characteristically, she avoided mention of it as such.

Jock's face settled into deep lines, and seeing the frown, his mother rose and came to sit on the couch beside him, to put her hand on his arm. 'Jock, dear,' she said firmly, 'he *needs* that reassurance. I'm sure that trouble is on his mind. He'd feel, as I do, that you could help him, and you cannot refuse to try! You must remember how much your father and I have done for you. We gave you a wonderful education, and you could have worked here with Jim, risen in your profession ...'

'I've done all right, Mother.'

'I'm glad to hear that.' Her ringed hand was shaking a little. 'You went off on your own, and I am glad if you have done well. But now the time has come when you can help us, and you surely will acknowledge that you owe us that help. As our only child, you—'

Jock took out his handkerchief and touched it to his lips. 'I seem to owe a lot to many people,' he said quietly.

'Yes,' his mother agreed at once. 'You do. There's your father, and me. And then there's Iris—and your children.'

Jock was startled, and shocked. He stared at his mother, unbelieving. That she should bring in Iris—and the children—after eighteen years! And the way—

He put the handkerchief away. 'I must mention Anna as well,' he said coldly. 'I owe her a great deal.' He got to his feet and walked the length of the room. 'And then there is myself. Don't you recognise that claim?'

His mother looked at him oddly. 'I just don't understand you, Jock,' she said.

'You have not understood me for some time, have you?'

'I have not seen you for some time!' Now she spoke sharply. 'Not for any length of time. And now—the man you are now is a stranger to me! You don't seem to be a part of our family any more. You don't think and act as if you belonged to us.'

'I'm sorry, Mother. For all that has happened. Not just now, not just Father's illness. I wish many things had not happened, or that they could have happened differently.'

'If you are sorry, you have a chance to change some of the things you regret, to correct them. You could stay on here, Jock. After—after that other thing is cleared up, there would be good work for you to do.'

Jock clasped his hands together, tightly, achingly. 'Yes,' he agreed. 'If—as I assume— you mean for me to try to fill Father's shoes, it would be good work. Or it could be. But the point is, Mother, it is not *my* work. I am not a surgeon, and I am not needed as one here.'

'I wasn't thinking of the surgical work. Your father has been leaning heavily upon Dr. Barnaby and the other men he has trained. After all, Jock, he is seventy-five; he's not been *doing* a lot of surgery for the past five years.'

'Well, then Barnaby and the others can carry on for him now. He'd be much more confident of their ability than he would be of mine. He knows I'm no surgeon.'

Emma smiled patiently. 'Your father has been Medical Director of his hospital for a great many years, Jock. Brownlee is his life's blood.

You could carry on *that* work of his. I am sure the Board would be glad to let you step into his place. Can you say that that would not be good work?'

'No,' said Jock slowly, 'I couldn't.' Not any more than he could deny the claim which his ageing parents made upon him. He had never lightly turned his back upon his family.

'I am afraid, dear,' said Emma, softening her tone, 'that now you cannot consider yourself first.'

Jock said nothing.

'Jock?'

He stood against the window draperies, and visibly summoned his strength, his will. 'Mother ...' he said desperately, 'I'm sorry about the lawsuit. I'll do what I can to handle that. But as for staying here and trying to do Father's work—you *know* the differences there have been between him and me in the past!'

Mrs. Askew mournfully shook her head. 'I know there never should have been those differences, Jock.'

'No. There should not have been. And I am truly sorry that they did exist.'

'But now ...'

Now the differences were still there.

'Now,' Jock said slowly, 'Father is sick. But I don't believe the reasons for our differing have

50

vanished. I—'

'Jock!' Again her hand stretched towards him. 'You *wouldn't* quarrel with him now!'

No. He would not.

'Will you make me just one promise, son?'

Jock's eyes lifted to her face.

'Only that you think this over. Soberly and honestly.'

Jock nodded. 'Yes,' he agreed. 'I can promise that I'll think about it—and of course talk to Anna.'

Emma Askew slapped her hands sharply together, and blew her breath audibly between her lips; she was exasperated, impatient with her stubborn son.

Jock smiled at her, shaking his head. 'Anna is a big part of my life, Mother,' he said quietly. 'You must face that fact.'

'I'd face it more easily if I did not remember that Iris once was a part of your life, too, and—'

'She withdrew from my life.'

Iris had broken their marriage, not Jock. Emma Askew had never acknowledged that truth, but it was a truth, just the same.

'Iris,' Emma was saying, 'was very young— and you had done some foolish things.'

'I'd been foolish,' Jock agreed, 'and not grown-up enough myself to pay my debts.'

'I don't know what you are talking about,'

said Emma.

She did know. But she had never been one to face facts if those facts differed from her own ideas of the way things should be.

For the care of his father, they had put a hospital bed into the room which had once been Jock's. Across the hall was his parents' larger bedroom and bath. At the end of the hall was a small kitchen, and the terrace where the family sometimes ate their meals.

The nurse rose when Jock entered, said, 'Good evening, doctor,' and then glanced at the man on the bed.

The head had been elevated; James Askew lay propped on several pillows, his hands tautly grasping the side rails. He was a large man; in health, he was florid. Now his colour had a bluish cast which troubled his doctor-son. His eyes were red-rimmed, his lips trembled when he looked at Jock. Already he had lost weight, and the skin of his throat hung in limp folds.

But he recognised Jock.

'How are you feeling, Father?' Jock asked, lifting his wrist. The pulse was irregular.

'I'll stay with him,' he said in an aside to the nurse. 'You might go get your supper ...'

'All right, doctor. Thank you.'

She straightened things on the long table set

against the wall, and then went out. She was a capable woman, in her thirties. Not pretty, but fresh-looking, and kind. She had asked for this duty. For many years, she had been one of the o.r. girls, and she was devoted to Dr. Askew.

Jock pulled up a chair, and sat down beside his father's bed. He hoped his mother would stay out of the room, but he would bet that she was lingering in the hall, hoping to hear what might be said.

Dr. Askew was looking at his son, wanting to speak, but not quite having the strength.

What must it be like ...? thought Jock. Conditioned by the life he had led, brought now to this state, what did a man like Jim Askew think, and feel? So far as a man so stricken could think and feel.

Quietly, Jock spoke to his father of the chilly November day, and told of the little mishap in the elevator.

'It was only a blown fuse. The people were wonderful. No one got really panicky. In fact, it was interesting to see how each did react. We went into that elevator as strangers, we came out knowing each other very well indeed.' His deep voice was calm; Jock knew that his father comprehended little of what he said.

The sick man lay gazing at his son's face, and

53

now tears began to run down his cheek. He moaned a little, and Jock took tissues and wiped the tears away.

'I—got mad,' said his father, his voice high and weak. 'Last night—I—'

'Well, there was no harm done.'

'Why do I do that way?' the old man asked pitifully. 'I don't mean to—' He *was* old. Suddenly Jock admitted that fact. His father was an old man; his strength and his skill were gone. Now Jock was the stronger; now decisions must rest with him.

This made his son feel odd. His hand warmly pressed his father's arm. 'You're sick, Father. And a sick man—'

That Jim Askew should ask such a question! *'What makes me ...?'*

'What—what can you do for me?' (There was not much that anyone could do.)

'These things take time. You know that.'

A weak gesture of that white hand. 'I know nothing,' the motion said.

Jock bit his lip, and tried to think of something to say. His own strong, virile presence was no comfort to Jim Askew. Jock, in his dark suit and tie, able easily to stand and walk and think and talk, gave no ease to the sick man, his bare throat scrawny above the hospital shirt, his temples sunken, his eyes confused.

Now his father was trying to speak again; his hand clutched at Jock's arm. 'Will you stay, Jock?' he asked. 'You can. You know—my hospital. You know my work.' Perspiration beaded his forehead, his nose, and his cheeks. Jock wiped it away. 'It was good work, Jock.'

'Yes,' said his son firmly. 'It was good.'

'Jock.' It was his mother's voice, behind him, softly firm. She had come quietly into the room. 'Tell him that you will stay.'

Jock took a deep breath, and gazed at his mother. Choosing to consider only that Jock was her son, Jim's son, and that Jim was ill, she would try to force him—

Not finding the right words to say to her at this time, Jock turned back to his father.

But the sick man had fallen asleep.

Gently, Jock disengaged his hand, turned away from the bed, and walked out of the room. Emma followed him.

They ate dinner together, Jock firmly refusing to talk further about staying in St. Louis. He had promised his mother to think about the matter, and he would think, though he already knew that he could not, would not, stay. Oh, long enough, perhaps, to handle the immediate problems, but then he would return to California, to Anna, and to his own work.

After dinner, he went downstairs, and smiled as he looked about him at the dark, carved wood of the entrance lobby, at its elaborate elegance. As high as his shoulders, the tall wainscoting was of green veined marble; above this were hung portraits, deeply framed in gold, of the original John Brownlee, of his wife and of his son, now Chairman of the Board.

Jock nodded to the young woman behind the desk and went over to look at the doctors' register. His father's name was still where he remembered it when a small Jock had had to stand back, legs braced, and look up, and up, to trace the letters.

This hospital had been his home since childhood, and though he had changed, here all was much as he remembered it from that time.

And as through a glass darkly, his thoughts went back, and back again—to the boy he had been, to the youth, and the man.

There echoed in his ears the things that had been said, and his limbs remembered the things that had been done. His heart remembered both joy and pain.

Walking slowly, Jock went down the hall to the library. There he would be able to think, undisturbed, of the things that were past, and carefully consider the matters of the present.

CHAPTER THREE

Jock selected a chair, and turned it so that he could sit with his back to the room. On the wavering crown-glass of the window pane before him, there immediately appeared pictures. Of the little boy, Jock, of his father and mother. His father had been a large man, usually dressed in white. At one time Jock thought all fathers wore white shoes and sharply creased white duck trousers, long open coats, or short, buttoned ones. Sometimes his father wore soft white clothes that hung like sacks upon his body, and a tight white cap which hid his hair. But his skin was always ruddy, and clean, his brown eyes had twinkled or were keenly intent on what his small son had to tell him, or show him.

Jock had played on the terrace outside of their apartment, that terrace carefully protected with a heavy stone balustrade. Jock's earliest memory of punished naughtiness was when he had been caught pushing things through that railing to fall down, and down, upon the lawn of the hospital, or upon the heads of those who might, unwary, be standing below. He remembered his father had talked to him earnestly of the impact that a small iron truck could make after falling ten stories.

'My first lesson in physics,' thought the man in the oak chair. 'An introduction to Galileo and the equation of falling weights.'

His mother had punished him; she had taken all small toys from the shelves in his room. He remembered that, too. His father, in white, holding the small boy on his knee—and the bare spots on his toy shelves. Like most small boys, Jock had liked little things, miniature trucks and tiny animals.

He had been taken, regularly, for walks in the park and allowed to play there on the grass. Children were deliberately brought into contact with him. He lived in no 'neighbourhood'; he had no brothers or sisters of his own. Companionship must be provided for him, and it was.

He went to a school which also conducted a summer day camp. The station wagon would pick him up at the Pavilion entrance each morning and return him there each night. This had been an expensive school, and the other children were from rich families in the city. At that time Dr. Askew was Chief Surgical Resident of the hospital, but he was not a rich man. Jock knew now that he had not been. But his parents had sent their little boy to a school where he could be among children, where he could play with children, as well as learn with them.

It had been a good school, somewhat on the progressive side; it had encouraged individualism and ingenuity. Later, did his parents regret those things which their son had learned?

The camp had been the best. It was out in the country, in a wooded area where a small boy could cut down a tree, and did. A small tree. Where he could play in the little creek, and for one whole glorious summer could work like a Trojan to dam the waters—and flood the dining hall! He could play and work with other children at the camp, or he could sit on the stream bank alone for long hours and dream. He could even take a bundle of sandwiches and wander off into the woods.

He could also learn to play baseball, and to square dance with the little girls, and make fudge. He could build a fire and learn not to cry when his tin can full of stew tipped over into it.

He could break his arm; and, when his buddy, running, plunged through the plate glass of the school door, Jock Askew, ten years old, could hold his fingers tightly around Noah's arm, and keep the blood from spurting ...

Maybe he had saved Noah's life. His father thought that he had helped, and praised him. He had let Jock come into the emergency room and watch while he sewed up the gash in Noah's arm.

'Some day you'll be doing this kind of work yourself, Jock,' had said Jim Askew.

'Sure I will,' had said Jock.

Emma asked her son if the blood had made him sick. He hadn't known what she meant, and his father had laughed.

After the two accidents, Emma Askew had wanted to send the boy to another school, one where they'd watch him more carefully.

'You can't keep him from getting scratched!' cried Jim.

But she had tried. Jock was not allowed to have a bicycle, nor a jalopy such as other sixteen-year-olds wanted, and got, and painted with girls' pictures and strange slogans.

'I look forward to the day when he brings home his first black eye.' Jock had heard his father say that, laughing, to one of the other doctors.

Jock looked forward to that day, too, but

it had never come.

He remembered the trips he had taken with his parents. 'Jock's trips,' they were called. From his position of manhood he knew that those trips were other and apart from the convocations and clinics which his father had attended, alone.

Jock's trips were carefully planned, their destination thoughtfully determined. In the early fall, his mother would begin to plan where they would go during their winter vacation. No sooner were they back from old Mexico, or Bermuda, but what she would again bring out travel folders and begin to stack magazines on the living-room table, looking forward to their summer trip.

They went to Canada and to New Mexico; they went to Yellowstone, and to Yosemite. They took Jock to Washington, and dutifully showed him the proper shrines. They hadn't camped out at Yosemite, and Jock never did get to go to Coney Island, but the trips were very nice.

So were his friends—very nice. The boys and girls with whom he had gone to school were an average lot of youngsters. The only handicap lay in the fact that Jock lived in a hospital; there was no easy running in and out of Jock's house.

One must be invited, and brought up in the elevator to play in Jock's big room, or, under Emma's watchful eye, out on the terrace.

Jock went to the homes of his friends—but there, too, informality was lacking. For Emma must be told that he would play at Noah's that Saturday afternoon; she would walk with Jock, down the two blocks, and when he was ready to start home, Noah's mother would phone to Mrs. Askew.

Had all that ritual been necessary? By the time he was six, Jock knew the hospital, how to operate the elevators, where he could go, and where not. At twelve, he might have been trusted, on his own.

But still, in Emma's way, he had made friends. Noah Green, particularly. The guy had looked Jock up in California just last summer. He'd immediately fallen in love with Anna, and declared that if ever Jock didn't treat her right, she was to get in touch with him.

'You should have your own wife,' said Anna, her eyes glowing, 'and a family!'

'It's you or nothing,' had said Noah, staunchly.

They had enjoyed Noah. A night or two ago, he had come to see Jock, and they had talked quietly in the apartment living-room. Jock must see his friend again before leaving. He—

Let's see. Where was he?

Schools, he guessed. Was it his father or mother who had decided that he would attend a public high school, and one of the local universities' pre-med schools? It could have been both of them.

Their decision had left Jock with them—and ready to enter the medical school where his father taught, and for which Brownlee Memorial Hospital served as a teaching medium. It was a good school, though there were things to be said about a boy breaking somewhat with his family while still in school.

There were other things to be said about the desirability of a son's staying too close to his father, when that son was about to follow his father's profession.

Still, at the time, Jock had liked what was going on. He had liked the big public high school after the guided, selected experiences of the small private school. His mother had worried some about his adjustment.

But Jock had needed no adjustment as such. He soon found that other clothes would make him a part of the high school picture, and he got those clothes. He was big enough to play football, but he had no inclinations that way. He did play tennis, and was on the swimming team and, in his senior year he was student manager of the football team. That had been fun, and their out-of-town trips took him away from his parents for the first time in his life.

He made new friends, and had a number of girls. In pre-med that sort of experience continued, though he soon learned to be cautious about the friends he brought up to the penthouse. At the University, with the usual counterbalance between town and gown, Jock had worked hard, and had fun—a large part of it away from the campus.

Then had come med school, and after that his internship and his residency. But before those things—

Now Jock got up from his chair, and walked around the room. He walked through the stacks, and looked, unseeing, at the books ranged upon the shelves.

Did all families nibble away at the individualities of their children?

Did their love always stick myriad pegs into the homeground to which they affixed their Lilliputian threads, myriad too in number, binding the loved one, holding him, unless—until—in one great lurch, the bonds should be snapped, and sent flying?

Jock took a flat, red book from the shelf, and

brought it back to his chair. Holding it open in his hands, he sat looking out at the scattering of lights in the park. And beyond them at the darkness of the night. For a long time, he sat looking out at that darkness, across the city—across the years.

Thinking of medical school, Jock now felt stirring in him again a bit of the excitement which had bubbled like wine in his veins those days, to know that, at last, he was about to become a doctor, himself, a man who could, like his father, and his grandfather, heal the sick, comfort the dying, and bring life into the world.

Jock had never had any other dream. He would be a doctor; he would wear white, and walk the halls of a hospital—some hospital—not too different from Brownlee.

'You'll take your father's place,' some of the more sentimental personnel had used to say to him at that time.

But at that time, Jim Askew was a young man. He amply filled his own place. And Jock did not ever think he wanted to be a surgeon, though he said nothing of that around home. He was too busy studying, working, and having such fun as med students can manage.

During those years he married Iris—and had

his first quarrel with his father.

Medical school had been made somewhat hazardous for Jock because the other students insisted that he got special favours through his relationship to Dr. Askew. Those favours extended, the meds claimed, to the piece of meat Jock got for lunch, and the sort of questions asked him in the pit.

Jock denied that favours were given.

Looking back, he still doubted that any standards had been eased for him. Dr. Jim was well-liked, and he could do a lot—or not—to change things for the men who were associated with Brownlee Hospital. A matter of scheduling, some sticky questions asked at a meeting. But Jock doubted that many favours were given to the son of Dr. Jim Askew, a damned good surgeon, and Medical Director of Brownlee Memorial.

Perhaps the faculty did expect Jock also to be a good surgeon, and sometimes coasted on that expectation without making the boy prove himself the hard way, but beyond that ...

It was the other students who told Jock not to bother applying for an internship.

'You've got it made already, boy.'

Jock had questioned that.

'Well, sure you have. You'll go into Brown-

66

lee and nestle all soft and cosy under Daddy's wing.'

'But I've asked for a position affording future specialisation in psychiatry.'

'Oh, yes,' had said his chief tormentor, a chap named Brandt who had certainly done med school without any favour. Now he was practising here in the city, and was making a big name for himself—perhaps because he *had* waited tables and worked for an undertaker in order to get his education.

That day, twenty years ago, Brandt had leaned back against the wall, closed his eyes, and asked, 'Does Daddy know you wrote down psychiatry, Jock-o?'

Jock had not discussed the matter with his father. 'It will be all right with him,' he declared. 'He'll want me to do the thing I want to do.'

'Oh, yeah?' asked Brandt. He'd been peeling an orange. The smell of it remained with Jock, and tainted his memory of that unhappy time. 'Want to bet you'll end up interning at Brownlee? And while it's a good shop, it is conspicuously lacking in any psychiatric service.'

Suddenly Jock was frightened and furious. His father couldn't—and if he could, he would not! He fumbled for things to shout at Brandt, and he advanced upon the young man ready to do battle on the subject. He might easily have got that first black eye then and there, but Brandt was not having any part of a row with Askew. 'I'm not fighting the Big Shot's son!' he had assured the bristling young man who stood above him. 'And you don't need to believe a word I say. These things will all be revealed to you, sonny.'

Well—they had been revealed. Jock had never liked Brandt, and it was largely because the man had known before Jock did how his father would feel and act.

At the time, Jock went on and sent his papers to the Intern Exchange. He did not want to do surgery, he couldn't ever be as good at it as his father. But he did have a feel for psychiatry. He had recognised that feel when the subject first came up for study and exposition to the students. He made his decision then, and he stayed with it.

He was truly right for that branch of his profession. He had suspected it then, just as he knew it now. Then he wondered that all the students had not felt the excitement, the challenge as strongly as he did. But a good many had not.

Jim Askew had not. He scoffed at the idea of psychiatry as a proper field of endeavour. He would not listen to Jock's arguments. 'Get in your year as general intern, and you'll have a better idea of the work you want to do,' he advised. 'Don't try to make *any* decision now.'

'But, Father—'

'Look, Jock. I know what I am talking about. I can help make you a great surgeon—I can't do a thing for you in psychiatry. Leave that to the soft-fingered Joe's, the ones who can't make the grade otherwise.'

'I'm not *good* at surgery, Father.'

'Well, of course you're not! No graduating medic is good at it. We don't want him to be. We want him able to be taught. But you do your first year in general, and then come on my team as surgical intern and resident; I promise that you'll get good at surgery.'

Jock had stood staring at his father. 'I'm to intern here?' he had asked feebly.

'Well, sure. What did you expect? How else do you suppose I could be sure about the surgery thing and your prospects?'

Jock had been sick. Disillusioned. That his father, whom he loved to the point of worship, would so oppose his dearest wish, and negate his decision for his life as a man.

Emma had always made decisions for her son. From the choice of a necktie to the girl whom he would take to a dance; Jock had come to expect decisions from her; he had learned some-

69

what to brace himself against Emma.

But his father—from the time he had taken his little son by the hand and explained the instruments in a white enamelled case, Jim had led Jock, he had inspired him and trained him as a boy who would become a doctor.

Granting his father's disappointment that Jock was choosing to go into another branch of medical service, granting that Jock should have talked this thing over with Jim sooner, and repeatedly, Jim should have been more reasonable.

He should not have claimed his son as intern in his own hospital; it was not likely that the placement bureau would have happened to send Jock home—especially since he had indicated psychiatry. But Jim had arranged for the internship, and he would continue to arrange Jock's life and work, or—

Or else, his manner said, he would not continue to subsidise Jock and his family.

And by that time—

Then, and now, the disillusionment which had come to Jock Askew about his father had been a bigger thing in his life than his marriage to Iris. If Jim Askew would have *talked* to his son about the matter, if he had seemed ready to listen to his son talk—but he had not, he was not. He had brought a son into the world, he had carefully raised that son and guided his life to a certain purpose of his own, and he was not going to be thwarted in that purpose by any half-baked notions of a grass-green medical student!

Jock had married Iris while in his second year of medical school, a foolish thing to do, a wrong thing, for both of them. The marriage had had no firm foundation of need and performance of its own.

Two children had been born of it, Betsy, and then Jamie, and they too became a part of a picture, of a carefully set scene. Jim and Emma were generous to the little family, they provided the young people with a home and a car, they bought clothes for the children. It was generous, and loving, but it was wrong.

In Jock's senior year of medical school, Jim Askew was made Medical Director of Brownlee Memorial Hospital. He was already one of the city's leading surgeons. And Emma Askew had been glad of the appointment because it would assure a place for Jock.

She said that—and then Jim Askew proved the truth of what she had said.

That was one of the things which Jock Askew must think about on this night in the hospital library.

Another thing was his marriage to Iris. Whether he wanted to do it or not, he must go back and think about how it had happened, and about what had happened to the marriage.

Had he married Iris because he loved her? It was hard to remember, exactly, with so many years between, so many things that had happened.

Now Jock sat alone with his thoughts. In this huge building, its roof sheltering hundreds of other people, he sat alone, and in his loneliness, he thought, agonisingly, back, and back again ...

Had he loved Iris? Yes. Of course he had. There had been love—young love—and excitement, surely.

He had known Iris for some time; she had been one of the little girls in his dancing-class; he met her again when his father bought a horse to secure him exercise, and then sent his son out to the stables to exercise the horse which he was too busy to ride. Iris too rode—and talked to Jock—and invited him to 'come over.'

Jock had known other girls better than he did Iris. Those girls had been more fun—but none of them had possessed the sweet wonder of Iris Desmoyer. Her hair was a pale gold, her skin was pink and white, she spoke softly, and shyly; she was a nice girl, and really pretty. She made a boy, a man, feel big and strong. And a guy liked to feel that way.

When the time came for the debutante parties to include the girls with whom Jock had gone to school, and the boys—three boys to every girl was the desirable ratio—Jock was invited to all the affairs. He went to some of them, at his mother's suggestion, and at nearly all of those he attended he met Iris, danced with her, and liked her.

Soon he began to be paired off with Iris for the more intimate parties. 'Bring Iris, will you, Jock? We'll swim and have cocktails, and then dinner ...'

Soon he began to ask Iris if she were going to a certain dance, or to a week-end house party; he'd pick her up, and they'd drive down, or out—or in—together. 'O.K? Swell!'

Of course they were young. Too young—but no younger than a lot of the crowd who were being married. Iris was bridesmaid for several of her friends—and Jock was asked to usher.

Even as a second-year medical student, Jock set no precedent; there were other married students. They were unusual, in those days, but not impossible. Of course they had to have family help. Or the brides 'worked their husband's way through school.'

Not Iris. Though her family was not rich, Iris was too much of a 'lady,' born and bred, to work for hire. She served her half-day at the Junior League tea-room; she did several things for sweet charity—but hers was a sheltered life. Nothing ugly or very realistic had ever touched it.

Jock remembered that his mother had mentioned this quality to her friends, as if Iris's hothouse fragility was something to praise and cherish. 'You don't see that sort of lovely girl often enough these days.'

Emma could never have been like Iris. Was that why she had admired her so much?

A month or two of their being paired off led Iris to expect Jock to take her places, to do things for her. She would call him and ask him to drive her into the city for some yarn, or to meet a train. Would he stop at the Library and pick out several new books for her mother to read? She had such a cold ...

Medical school did not allow much free time for errand running and party going, and there inevitably came a time when the Dean spoke to Dr. Askew about Jock's work. Jim spoke to Emma, and together they had a conference with their son.

Jock remembered every detail of that conference, brief as it had been.

He had been somewhere for the evening, and had come in—not too late. As had been his practice since little boyhood he went in to kiss his mother good-night. She was propped up in her bed, a net over her silvery hair, glasses on her nose, a book in her hand. The blanket was a deep pink, and its colour reflected upward so that his mother's face looked flushed. Jim was sitting in the armchair, in his shirt-sleeves, listening to a late news report on the radio.

Jock had kissed his mother, and she had held his hand, moving so that there was room for him to sit beside her on the bed. 'Visit a while,' she suggested.

'I have studying to do.'

'How's the work going?' Jim had asked.

'Not too well, I expect,' Jock had said readily. 'My adviser says I need to study more and dance less.'

'That sounds like good advice,' said his father, snapping off the radio, then turning so that he looked directly at Jock.

'Jock studies,' said Emma, patting Jock's hand.

'But not enough, Mother,' Jock said quickly. 'Med takes hours and hours of book-breaking. I tried to tell Iris tonight that I'd have to cut down on the parties and dates.'

'Iris, eh?' mused Jim, his eyebrow arching.

'And what did Iris say?' asked Emma, smiling.

'Oh—well, of course she said it would be all right with her, but just the same she expects me to take her to the Meyer ball next Saturday night, and to the Symphony on Friday, and—'

'And you want to do it,' laughed Jim.

Jock grinned, and nodded. 'But I have to study, too, sir!'

'Yes, you do,' Jim agreed. 'Does Iris realise that?'

'She says she does, but Iris doesn't know much about med school and stuff. She's—well—she's just a girl who likes fun.'

Jim seemed to ponder the situation. 'I don't suppose you want to break off clean with Iris?' he asked.

'Oh, no, sir! I mean—well, it wouldn't be fair to her. She's done nothing. And I—well, no, sir, I couldn't break off.'

The suggestion was preposterous!

'Jock.' His mother sat more erectly in bed, clutching her woolly jacket together with her hand. 'Could I ask you a question that may be none of my business?'

'If it's none of your business,' suggested Jim jovially, 'you'd better not ask it.'

But Jock was saying, 'Of course, Mother.'

And Emma listened to Jock, though she threw a rueful smile at Jock's father. 'Well,' she said, 'I thought I'd just as well ask what your plans were with Iris.'

'Plans?' asked her startled son. 'Goodness, Mother, we can't afford things like *plans*. It's going to be years before I earn a dime.'

'I know all that,' said Emma. 'But I wonder if your father and I couldn't help you a little. I mean, if you're preoccupied with Iris to the point that you can't study, you might never earn that dime. So—if you could settle down and be with her—'

'But, Mother—'

'It's just a suggestion, Jock. But I think it could work out. Studying medicine takes a long time. Your father and I know that, and we know too that young men want to marry. We'd hate to see you give up your studies—'

That night Jock had been too stunned to say yea or nay. He had taken the 'suggestion' across the hall to his own room—and probably had not got a thing from the books he spread before his eyes until two in the morning.

The next day, his mother had suggested that he could at least talk the idea over with Iris.

And Iris of course was all dewy surrender and happiness. Oh, she did love Jock! And they could be married during a vacation—he'd have a week in the spring, wouldn't he? And then, every night he could study, and she would watch him, and—oh, wasn't it *wonderful,* Jock?

It had been wonderful, he guessed. Yes, it had been.

The days sped by like a whirling ball—the ring—the announcement party—the pre-wedding parties—the little apartment two blocks from the hospital—the wedding.

A small wedding, as such things went. Three bridesmaids. A reception at the Country Club, a week's honeymoon at Sea Island—one of the staff doctors had a winter home there.

It was about then that Jock stopped worrying about money. He couldn't afford a diamond ring, nor a trip to Sea Island, but his father could, and—so what?

They were a 'nice young couple.' Iris made a picture-book bride, and the little apartment was stacked with wedding gifts. Iris too was an only child. Her mother, and Emma, congratulated each other on their ability to keep the children close. Both applauded the match because it assured an appropriate mate with the right background, and because the marriage made the young people settle down. They had not heard, and would not have heeded, Margaret Mead's claim that such a marriage is premature imprisonment of young people before they have had a chance to explore their own minds, or the minds of others.

After the honeymoon, Jock became accustomed to eating Sunday dinner with her parents. Genteel folk, the Desmoyers, who served a scanty meal on Dresden china and Irish linen and mahogany, and treated Iris and Jock as if they still were dating.

Yes—they married too young. Jock Askew, at 23, was not to grow up for another ten years. The anthropologist was right. 'A man who does not support himself is not yet a man, and a man who lets his parents support his wife is likely to *feel* he is not a man.'

It was all a part of a picture—their pale yellow and violet wedding, the week at Sea Island, and their return home again, brown and laughing, Jock determined to get down to work. Like children they were delighted to be married, to play at keeping house, to be independent.

They were married at Easter, and Betsy was born on the last day of that same year. Eighteen months later, Jamie came along.

How had Jock felt about being a father? Oh, indeed, he did remember that!

He was happy, and proud, with a full, rich sense of completion. He was, he supposed, an average, normal young father; he fussed about Iris, made a nuisance of himself with the o.b. service of the hospital, and he cherished the babies. He had always had a strong sense of family; his own children carried on the feeling. He liked doing things for the kids, such time as he was at home. They were his in a way that went beyond possession. They were a projection of himself, of his body, his mind, his consciousness as a person. Planning for Jamie, he began to understand his father's dreams for himself.

Iris's parents had viewed the precipitate acquisition of a family with distaste. *They* had been married for ten years before *they* had a child. But Jim and Emma were delighted. Jim stood at the nursery window and looked at his grandchildren quite as proudly as did Jock. Whenever Emma brought the children home, she showed them proudly to the hospital maids and nurses; she could be counted on as a baby sitter whenever Iris and Jock wanted her. Their delight pleased Jock. It made up somewhat for his failing Jim in not becoming a surgeon.

CHAPTER FOUR

In no position to be independent, or even to dwell upon his disagreement with his father, Jock put in his year as general intern at Brownlee Hospital. When time came for his specialising internship, the staff men agreed that Jock had not any aptitude for surgery. He would make a good doctor, but not in that field. They persuaded Jim to accept the fact. And a compromise was reached.

Jock would specialise in internal medicine; that was a good field; the internist worked hand in hand with the surgeon. Nothing was said, then, about psychiatry.

Jock worked hard at his job, and he became a fair internist, with the determination to become a better one and, some day, a psychiatrist.

Two years after he got his M.D. Jock became a resident at Brownlee Hospital. This meant a salary, so that he could somewhat pay his own way, and he did pay it—somewhat—insisting that Iris be economical. He was economical himself, though his parents were still generous. They talked of building a house for the 'kids' at the edge of the city; Emma began to plan on Betsy's school—a private one.

By that time Jock was working too hard to notice things like straws. For it was about then that he began to have what Anna called his 'ideas.' During his two years as resident at Brownlee he did have one idea that he remembered.

He had worked hard for those two years. The thing he was doing was a compromise, but he had just sense enough to know that the knowledge he was storing up would later be helpful to him. He was popular in the hospital—he hoped in his own right. Of course he was still Dr. Jim's son. No one called him anything but Jock, or, formally, 'Doctor.' There was just one Dr. Askew in that hospital, and Jock agreed with the conviction.

Now Jock smiled wryly, looked at his watch—surprised to find that it was only eight o'clock. His thoughts had covered so much time, he would have expected it to be much later!

All right. Let's see—

Oh, yes. Ideas.

Perhaps he had had several—more likely a few—while he was resident here at Brownlee. He tried to picture himself as he had been then—and a few pictures did come up of a tall, earnest young man in white jacket and ducks, bending over a patient in an oxygen tent, walking swiftly along the halls, going into surgery—into conferences—making grand rounds with the students. And most vividly of all, a picture of himself standing at the floor desk one morning, waiting to speak to Dr. Askew about a young girl who had measles but who also seemed about to need an appendectomy. Jock wanted his father's opinion on the blood count, and the extent of the emergency ...

By then his father was beginning to lose his hair. Jock remembered exactly how Jim had looked, standing in the corridor, talking to a patient ready to go home after being in the hospital for a check-up. The sun glistened on Dr. Jim's head; his face was pink and smiling, his white clothes without a wrinkle.

He called the patient by his first name, and extended his hand. 'Good-bye, Jerry. Come and see us again some time.'

'Not if I can help it!' said that Jerry, with conviction.

'You'll be back,' the surgeon promised. 'You busy chaps have to find some way to catch up with yourselves. And after your week here, you do feel better, don't you?'

Jerry settled his coat on his shoulders, and

jutted his chin. 'I may be better physically,' he conceded. 'But a week in your damned hospital, Jim Askew, has left me an emotional wreck!'

Jim laughed, and patted the man's shoulder as he went into the elevator. But Jock had a question for his father.

'What did he mean, Dad?'

'These successful businessmen,' said Jim, 'are spoiled babies. They hate to confess to physical ailments, and they come into the hospital with a chip on their shoulder. They don't want to undress, they don't want to be put into a high bed, they don't want breakfast at seven, or supper at five—and when you fight against a thing for a week, Jock, your nerves take a beating. And—oh, yes! They particularly hate enemas.

'Now! What's *your* problem?'

Jock stated his problems, and the child was taken care of. But Jock kept thinking about 'Jerry' and the thing he had said. 'A week in your damned hospital has left me an emotional wreck.'

In the weeks that followed Jock paid especial attention to other businessmen who entered the hospital for check-ups or rest. And he came to the conclusion, after three months of observation, that these executive types often showed up an emotional disturbance not handled by the physical examination and its resultant treatment.

Jock became excited about his findings; he made copious notes, he cross-filed the data. Was there some physical manifestation common to all?

There was not. One man was underweight, several men were overweight, several were normal. Some slept well, some did not. Some were bachelors, some married—happily and so-so— some had family problems.

No, the fault could not be pinned down that way.

Then—why again? Was the hospital to blame, as Jerry had suggested? After three months, Jock decided that it could be, somewhat.

So he began to look at the hospital, and what it did to the 'healthy' man admitted for five or seven days of routine work-ups. Men who came in with emotional disturbances had different ones on leaving. Well-adjusted men left with self-confessed jitters. 'The heebies.'

So—what did the hospital do to them?

Jock became fascinated by his inquiry—and his ideas on what could be done about the situation.

Even now, Jock could see his pages and pages of reports on the subject; he could hear echoing in his ears today the youthful excitement of that young medical resident.

A hospital, he decided, was not a fit place in which to be sick. Under the influence of its implacable routines and procedures it was an even worse place in which to be 'well.'

And the thing that interested Jock just then was why those routines must be implacable. Why couldn't they be adjusted for the individual patient?

When he begun to ask why, he soon met the answer to his problem.

Good or bad, the routine already set up could *not* be changed, the individual could *not* be considered as an individual, because no one in the hospital had the single, over-all authority to change things. Jock, in his capacity as internist, could eliminate the hated enemas, but he could not tell the diet kitchen to serve meals at 'odd' hours of the day, he could not tell the nurses—

There was no one with enough power to make changes, desirable or otherwise.

Of course, the Administrator was *supposed* to be in charge of the hospital as a whole. But let him try to tell the business office, or the Medical Director, what to do, and see what would happen. His authority would be ignored, and his attempt at any degree of discipline could not be enforced. That's what would happen!

The Administrator had to contend with too many groups within the hospital organisation, each with its own jealously guarded goals, its own jealousies of other groups. There was, at Brownlee Memorial, a Board of Trustees. The Brownlee family—son, granddaughter, grandson—were predominant on that Board; and no one on the Board was a doctor. The Board was entrusted with the business and financial problems of the hospital. What a nurse said to a patient was no concern of theirs. But the Administrator must make his financial report to that Board, he must listen to what they said about economy and conservation of time, personnel, and supplies.

Second, there was a medical board, of which Dr. James Askew, Sr., was the head—or Director. This board was all doctors, and their job was to establish and enforce the medical policies of the hospital, as well as to defend each other's professional status in the community.

Next, there was the nursing staff, which was entrusted with the nursing care of the patients, and which was headed by a Supervisor. Her interest was in the care of the patients, but she also had to establish an order of work and routine which would get the most out of her 'girls' without killing them.

Last, there was the housekeeping staff, and

on it people who were remarkably low-paid, with little opportunity for job improvement. Bed changing, meals, cleaning and renovating—those things were all scheduled, and it was better to stick to schedule, lest chaos result, and nothing get done.

Having made these determinations, Jock was far from through, or even discouraged. He became more interested, and more determined, to find a solution. He stayed longer at the hospital than his duty required, he came earlier, and was at home less. He went about the hospital, observing procedure, asking questions, making notes, comparing instances, always gathering his careful evidence towards such conclusions as it would seem justifiable for him to make.

The hospital personnel began to notice Jock's presence in strange places at strange times. 'Goodness, Jock,' said Mrs. Stone, the executive housekeeper, 'I fall over you everywhere I turn!'

'We have a spy in our midst!' declared Pete Henderson, being very funny in the doctors' lounge.

Jock did not like Pete Henderson. Now, from his position of years and experience, Jock could decide why, as a younger man, he had not liked the popular, successful young surgeon.

Part of it, of course, was explained by the fact

that Henderson *was* a surgeon, and successful. Pete was actually all that Jock's father had wished his son might be. Each time Jim would praise the young staff man, Jock would wince, feeling that Jim was turning the knife in the wound of disappointment and failure.

Iris liked Pete. She thought he was cute, and that he was fun. He belonged to the good clubs, he went to the proper parties, and when the Jock Askews would show up on some golf club's veranda or at some party, Pete was always gallant and attentive to Jock's pretty wife. So—Jock had been jealous of the guy on that count.

Pete was a bachelor; he could afford to be gallant to a lot of ladies, especially the young married ones. He lived like a rich man, and probably was rich. Ten years older than Jock, he had a big practice, and he was popular in the right circles.

Jock made an effort to remember exactly how Pete had looked on that day when he called Jock a spy. He had striking features, pale blue eyes, dark blond hair—an expressive mouth, a square jaw tapering to a boyish chin; he moved with an easy grace. At social gatherings, or in a relaxed mood, he became smiling, genial, even jaunty. At work, the man was attentive and sober. A lot of people liked Pete Henderson.

Jock did not.

And after the morning he spent in the man's o.r., he thought he had cause not to like Pete. Perhaps Pete knew what Iris's husband had seen and heard that day; perhaps he feared the 'spy' in their midst. Certainly Jock was putting *that* case down in his records!

Today Jock could still quote his report of that morning in Dr. Henderson's operating room: 'Immediately after the first operation of the day, the scrub nurse contacted the head surgical nurse and gave her a broken bit of matter, apparently a surgical tool. The head nurse called Dr. H. in from the dressing room, showed him the matter, and suggested that an X-ray be made to determine if any had been left in the patient. The doctor examined the substance and declined to have an X-ray made; when she repeated her opinion, he seemed determined against it, saying that the patient would not be able to pay for X-rays which he, as surgeon, would not order as necessary. He dismissed the incident, saying that the matter would be so small, anyway, it couldn't harm her.'

The 'matter' might have been small, the occurrence insignificant, but Pete Henderson did not like knowing that there was a 'spy' in the hospital. Jock felt sure that he would not again be permitted to observe in Dr. Henderson's o.r.

And yet, with a case like that—and other cases—changes should certainly be made! More excited by the day, he went about seeing the changes that needed to be made, and deciding which ones could be made!

His determination was set firmly into a mould when the hospital rustled over word that Henderson was involved in a malpractice suit.

'They'll sue anybody with a dollar,' Jim Askew dismissed the charge, 'and Pete's making lots of dollars these days.'

'Could the family have a case?' asked Jock, anxiously.

'Oh, Jock—why do you suppose we all carry malpractice insurance? Anybody can think they have a case against a doctor! If you give sulpha to one of your pneumonia patients, and it affects his kidneys, you're probably "guilty" of malpractice. A jury would perhaps declare that you were, and order a large sum paid to the patient's family.'

'But, Father—'

'This thing against Pete—a matter of esophagus block, or some such—it's the same situation, Jock. The patient, and in this case the patient's family, does not know the whole picture. They don't understand what it is necessary to do—'

'Did Henderson ever try to make them understand?'

'They've gone to court. He'll have a chance to testify.'

'I don't mean now. I mean before surgery, or, if there was an accident of some sort, and I presume there was, did he try to explain to the patient's family just what happened?'

'Oh, Jock! A man as busy as Henderson ...'

Jock bit his lip. 'Yes,' he agreed, 'he's busy. But I've been thinking, Father—'

His father was exasperated, and showed it. 'It's my opinion,' he said sharply, 'that you are doing too much *thinking* these days about matters that won't get you much of anywhere.'

Jock was too enthralled in his project to let a bit of rasping bad humour stop him from saying what he felt must be said to the Medical Director of a big hospital. If he could make his father realise ...

'The trouble may be, Father,' he said slowly, 'that all of us get so rushed, so absorbed in our doctoring, that we forget the patients.'

'What are you talking about?'

Emma and Jim had come for dinner with the young people that evening. Now Emma and Iris were at the rear of the apartment putting the children to bed, and busily talking.

Jock and his father sat in the living-room, the

lamp light mellow, a cup of good coffee at hand. Jim Askew was smoking a cigar; Jock sat on the couch, his hands clasped between his knees as he leaned forward to talk to his father.

Jim thought he talked nonsense. Of course the doctors considered their patients. They considered little else!

But Jock sat shaking his head.

'Not as people, Dad. Not as individuals. And certainly not as *sick* people who need, at the time of their illness, a great amount of thought and interest and care. They need it, but they don't get it when they are sick in a hospital!'

'Oh, Jock!'

'They *don't!* They should— Why, Dad, you and I both know that patients have been complaining for years about the thoughtlessness, the inadequate care—yes, and the mistreatment—which they encounter in a hospital.'

'Now, Jock—'

'Yes! One case, or two, could be a matter of spoiled babies, or crackpots. But not all the complaints we hear, and the equal number we probably don't hear. And there's another thing: what has been done, what have *you* done, as Medical Director, to look into the matter? To see if the complaints are justified?'

'Just what would those complaints be?' asked Dr. Askew, his tone acid.

'Well—let's take a patient about to undergo surgery, scheduled for nine o'clock on a Tuesday morning. A tonsillectomy, say. What do we do? We tell our man to come to the hospital at three on Monday afternoon. And he does. Jittery as a cat, fearful of all the white he sees in the corridor, shying like a skittish horse at any cart he may pass. And, first thing, a nurse tells him to undress, put on a hospital shirt, and get into bed. Right?'

Jim nodded, looking at the ash on his cigar.

'Right! There's no real need for him to go to bed, and certainly no need for the shirt. He could change to his own pyjamas. He could even stay in his street clothes—for all that will be done to him! An intern will come in for the history, sometimes necessary, sometimes not—but interns have to learn to take them. A nurse will take his temperature and pulse. A technician may come for a blood sample; he may even get a shot. He eats a light supper, and gets a sleeping pill. But there is no good reason to put him to bed at three in the afternoon. He certainly doesn't rest!

'I asked a nurse or two why this practice was followed. And do you know what I was told? That "we like to have them ready right away, so that when the doctor comes he can examine them." '

'And you don't find that reason enough?' asked Jim.

'No. For what kind of examination do you give on the evening before a scheduled operation of that sort? Or any sort? You talk to the patient, you look at his chart—maybe you take his pulse. You don't do more, do you?'

'Well—I go in for the patient's sake, to boost his morale, as much as anything. That's what you're advocating, isn't it?'

'Attention to his needs, yes. And of course you should go in—and be as warmly interested as possible. But couldn't you do that for a man still having the dignity of his own clothes? Personally, I believe a small change like that could go quite a way to relieve the rancour so many patients feel against the hospital and its personnel.'

'And you think that's desirable?'

'I'm sure it's desirable. And necessary, too. If we are doctors in the true sense ...'

His father sighed heavily. 'Oh, Jock,' he said wearily, 'you're talking nonsense! Hospital routine has been established over a long period of trial and error. We've developed the best possible, the most efficient, system that we can have. We ...'

For another ten minutes they argued the question, both interested, each sure that the other was seeing the situation in a very narrow and short-sighted way. Their voices lifted, and back in the bathroom small Betsy said that Granddaddy was *mad.*

'Oh, no, dear,' said Emma. 'He and Daddy are just talking shop.'

'Every resident,' declared Jim at last, 'feels and acts like a new broom. He must come in and set things a-right in the hospital! All the old nurses, he decides, and the old surgeons, are muffing the jobs.'

'Now, Dad—'

'All right, then, what *are* you saying? Do you know what kind of day I had today? Five major surgical problems, and an emergency. My back aches, my hands are sore—my feet are killing me—and nobody would think I could get through such a schedule, but I did! And the reason I did was because the o.r. girls and the orderlies—bless 'em!—kept things coming right at me. No motion lost, no time lost. We worked like machines, and we did a damn good job of every item that came under the lights. Colostomy, duodenal ulcer, gut resection, pinned a hip, corrected a hiatus, and, as a climax, a seeping appendix. The works, Jock, the *works!*

'And before we saw the cases, the girls had them in shape, and they took care of them after they left o.r. And what let us do that? Routine, my dear boy, practice, careful assemblage—'

'And six shiny new automobiles came off the assembly line,' said Jock, his tone grave.

Jim Askew stared at his son.

'You didn't have—you don't speak of—one *person* in those six jobs, Father.'

'Well, of course they were persons. Good grief, they bled and reacted! But I had to concentrate on the *problems*, Jock. You don't know what my job is!'

'I know you are a fine surgeon, Father, and kinder than most to and about your patients. But you still talk of a surgical day in terms of a factory production line. And—well—I think that hurts the work you do, that the hospital does!'

'And you could change it!'

'I'd like to see some changes made. Being that young broom, you mentioned, I think the patient could be made the centre of all hospital interest, and made to feel that he is. That, along with his clothes, he need not feel he loses his entity, his individual personality, the minute he comes into our fine, big hospital.'

'And you know how to bring that about?' Jim Askew's eyes were cold. He was not a man to take criticism of the work that he had learned to do so well. His hospital was dear to him, and to have a grass-green pipsqueak—

Jock knew what he was thinking. But he would say some of his things anyway. He got up and walked the length of the room, his head down, thinking. He was shocked at his father's reaction, at his opposition. It repeated the shock he had felt when his father had refused to let him intern in psychiatry. Could Jock never disagree with his father? If he could not, why? Because Jock was Jim's son? A 'boy,' who would never be able to catch up with his father and acquire the status of manhood's judgment and responsibility? Would Jim like it if he thought Jock went along with him on every point just because he was Jim's son? No, Jock didn't think he would like it. And, anyway, couldn't this, and other differences, be matters between two *men?* Though maybe it was such a matter.

Perhaps Jim Askew was disappointed in Jock as a man, quite apart from his being his son. Perhaps he wished that Dr. James Askew, Jr., would be the typical university-oriented, career-type doctor like Pete Henderson, not apt to become stickily involved in the personal side of his profession.

Jock came back to his seat on the couch, and looked at his father. The cigar was half-smoked by then, and Jim Askew was getting restless about the turn of the evening. He'd be happy if the women would come back, or if Jock would talk about something else.

But Jock still had a few things to say, and having got into this discussion, he'd better say them. 'The first time I began to think about all this,' he said slowly, 'I decided that the emphasis on staff convenience rather than patient benefit grew out of the faulty organisation of most hospitals.'

'You did, eh?' said Jim Askew.

'Now, Father, you need not take this as a personal attack. If you could bring yourself to listen to what I have to say, and consider the thing impersonally—'

'I'm afraid I can't do that, Jock. It should be no surprise to you that I am a medical director, and—'

'But that's one of my points. You're the Medical Director, but there are several groups in the hospital organisation with as much authority as you have, and often that authority conflicts with yours. *That's* the fault I have in mind. The doctors must listen to the Board, the Board must listen to the Supervisor of Nurses—or quarrel with her—the Administrator can baulk all three of these groups with a clampdown on money allowed— You know I'm right!'

Jim pursed his lips and shrugged his shoulders. 'Doctors have been griping about Boards, and nurses about doctors, since Hippocrates. I wasn't there, but I'll bet on it.'

'So will I,' said Jock. 'But, Dad, can't you see—if you stop to think about it—that when the members of a hospital staff are too concerned with their own problems and dissatisfactions they may—and do—lose sight of the patients' emotional needs? And even though your recovery rate is high, even though the patients' medical needs are ultimately cared for, that same patient leaves the hospital feeling that the individual staff members are unfeeling and callous.'

'That brings us back to the matter of time and efficiency.'

'It does. And to your day in surgery. Which you likened to an assembly line.'

'You used that word, not I.'

Jock laughed, and nodded. 'Yes—' he agreed. 'Though it is a fair analogy, isn't it? Not only for you, but in my department, too. In fact, the idea was first given to me by a chap who came in for a routine work-up. I laughed when he said it to me, but since then, noticing what is going on, I've stopped laughing, Dad. I think the fellow was too correct to be funny.'

'Tell me what he said, and see if I'll laugh.'

'He was a clever chap—an electronics engineer,

as a matter of fact. And what he said went something like this: "The general emphasis in hospitals today is on efficiency and the skilful application of therapeutic methods." '

'What's wrong with that?'

'Let me go on. He said that if we consider a hospital as an organisation engaged in the production of health, patients may be compared to the raw material in a modern factory. That our raw material must be fashioned and refashioned to approximate as closely as possible the criteria of "health." '

'He got wound up on his thesis and pointed out that patients are conveyed to their rooms on wheels; they are processed through routine channels and are stored in neat beds to await the application of medical and nursing techniques in which they are acted upon, but never are expected to participate. In many hospitals, patients are labelled—with wrist band, and chart notation, with a code number—'

'Now, Jock—'

'Dad, do you ever speak of a patient as the "hip in 43"?'

'Well—names—'

'Mhmmmn. The names become lost, the people become lost. And we end up with my engineer's "product." Do you think that's good?'

'I think I get a hell of a lot of work done!'

'Yes, so do I. But, Dad—'

'Oh, let's drop it, Jock. The women would never understand what we're talking about.'

The 'women' had come into the room, and the talk went to other things. Jock was called to the hospital, and while the matter came up again with his father—Jim was guilty of speaking obliquely, sometimes sarcastically, about it even in Staff meetings—that particular discussion had ended there.

Jock couldn't talk to his young wife about his new interest and ideas. Iris Askew, married for nearly five years, mother of two children, was as pretty as ever, and as softly unaware of the world and its problems.

'Don't talk shop to her, Jock!' Pete Henderson protested one night during the intermission of a symphony concert. 'Look at her! She's a doll! Literally, she is a doll.'

Iris liked being called a doll; she liked Pete's calling her that. She dimpled, and flushed prettily, and thanked Dr. Henderson for rescuing her from Jock's seriousness.

Jock had said nothing. Perhaps he didn't really mind not being able to talk to Iris; perhaps he hadn't expected her to understand.

Was it before that concert, or after it, that Jock became aware of Sue Jordan? She had been

Supervisor in the Pavilion just about as long as Jock had been resident internist of the hospital.'

He still vividly remembered Sue. She was a tall young woman with smoothly brushed red-blonde hair, a clear skin, and beautiful blue eyes. She was an excellent nurse, and a fine person. She had humour and understanding—Jock liked her. His memory of her formed a series of pictures.

The first was of a day when Jock had been working at the chart desk and a phone inquiry had come in about a chronic they had. Did she ever get out of bed, or some such question.

The nurse in training had answered the phone; she did not know the person by name, and said she didn't think Mrs. Fordyce *was* a patient—

Jock had looked up alertly. Miss Jordan had got out of her chair. 'She's in 3-A, Miss Dawson,' she told the girl quietly.

'Oh, yes!' said Miss Dawson. 'I didn't know her name.'

'Yes, sir!' she said into the phone, 'she gets out of bed some days. Yes, sir. Thank you, sir.'

Miss Dawson put down the telephone, and Miss Jordan suggested that a nurse, even on temporary duty, might do well to learn the names of the patients on her ward.

'Especially in the Pavilion,' said Miss Dawson, entirely agreeable to the suggestion.

'On all wards,' said Jock's deep voice from behind the chart desk. 'They have feelings about that, practically everywhere.'

'Yes, doctor,' said the trainee vaguely.

Miss Jordan lifted an eyebrow at the resident.

'I'm fast becoming a one-man committee on restoring individuality to the patient,' said Jock dryly.

'Could you enlarge your committee, doctor?' asked Miss Jordan. 'I've had my own nightmares about rows of beds filled with clothing-store dummies.'

That was the beginning.

After that there was a bond of understanding between Sue Jordan and Jock Askew. If they heard an intern ask another, 'What about the tests on that gall bladder in Bed 6?' Sue would wink at Jock. If she heard an orderly ask another if he'd 'done the guy in 267,' Miss Jordan would rebuke him sharply, and her rebuke would be reinforced by the resident.

It was an easy step for Jock to talk to Sue about the other failings which he encountered in hospital procedure. She agreed with him that failings were there, and began to suggest ways in which changes could be made; sometimes these suggestions were so impossible of realisation that they became absurd, but the nurse and the resident enjoyed their jokes.

Jock liked Sue. He knew that he still would like her. Those days, he saw her constantly at work, and even a time or two away from the hospital. One day, driving through the park, he passed her as she walked briskly in the crisp autumn sunlight, her blown hair shining; he asked if she wanted a lift; she countered with the suggestion that he walk a mile with her. 'It may seem like compounding felony to our feet, but it feels good to strike out and *walk!*'

Jock parked his car, and walked her mile— and back again to his car. She then accepted his invitation to stop at the drive-in for a cheeseburger and coffee. Enjoying the refreshment, they talked. Jock found her an interesting person. She could talk on all sorts of subjects, her family, city politics, the state of the world, and about a popular song that was downright ridiculous.

A week or so later, at Sue's instigation, Jock tried to spread out his notes and records at home so that he might whip up a paper to present to a meeting of the city medical association. He asked Iris not to touch the things; he could not do the whole job at one sitting.

The first time he left them, spread out on two card tables at the end of the living-room,

Iris stacked the papers neatly, without any regard for subject matter, and put them on top of his chest of drawers. 'The kids would have made confetti out of them,' she told Jock, reasonably enough.

'And that's how far I got with my paper,' Jock wryly told Sue.

She agreed that Iris was being reasonable. But—

'We have only a four-room apartment,' said Jock.

Sue was thinking. She supposed there was nowhere in the hospital—

There was Jock's old room in the penthouse apartment, but with his father unsympathetic—

'I'll tell you,' said Sue. 'I have a place. It isn't much, but I'm not there a lot. You could spread out there for a few days—long enough to get your notes lined up anyway. I'll bring you a key.'

Jock himself brought up the matter of speculation and talk should he take that key and go in and out of Sue's apartment at will.

Sue laughed, and gave him the key.

Over a matter of days—it couldn't have been for more than two weeks, could it?—Jock couldn't remember, he had gone to Sue's apartment several times, sometimes for half an hour, sometimes for longer. Sometimes she was there,

106

often she was not. He spread out his notes, he scribbled on a pad of yellow paper—he talked things out with Sue when she was available. The whole atmosphere had been one of casual friendliness.

He would go to the apartment, slip out of his coat, get a Coke from her refrigerator, and settle down to work. Sue might come in, change her uniform for something casual, sometimes a blouse and slacks, once a tailored housecoat—she would be going back to the hospital in a matter of four hours. Sometimes she would work, iron, or wash her hair—things like that.

Once she brought crackers and cheese and sat with Jock—there was nothing beyond friendship and a mutual interest in what he was doing.

He could tell his father that on the day when Jim brought up the matter of his going regularly to Sue Jordan's apartment.

'Now who told you about that?' asked Jock, in innocent curiosity. Who would be interested, he meant.

'You might have known someone would see you going there, and talk,' said Jim impatiently. 'Haven't you a bit of sense?'

'I didn't know I'd need that kind of sense,' said Jock, beginning to realise what his father had in mind.

'It was a silly thing for you to get into, Jock,' said Jim, 'and with one of the hospital nurses, of all people!'

'Now, just hold up,' said Jock. 'You've got on the wrong track, Dad. You see, I had this paper I wanted to write—'

'What paper?' asked Jim.

Could Jock tell him? Not with any sympathetic understanding to be expected.

'It doesn't matter, what paper,' said Jock. 'I wanted to write one. I can't spread my notes and stuff out at home; the kids get into things. If I used the library here at the hospital, I have only odd minutes, and I'd spend them getting things together, and putting them away again. Miss Jordan understood my difficulty, and let me use her place. Most of the time she hasn't been there.'

'But you have a key to her apartment?'

Jock sighed. 'Yes. I have a key. And you—and your spies—can think what you damn please, but—'

'You could ruin Miss Jordan's career, son.'

'I hadn't thought of that.' Jock had not. 'I won't go there any more.'

He had to go once more to get his papers. He never had written that paper, by the way. He had to tell Sue what his father had said; she knew for herself what he had suggested.

She tried to laugh, but she was too angry, too hurt. So she wept a little, and called a few names.

And Jock had said what he could think of to say.

But at the end of the week, when he learned that Sue was leaving the hospital, he was too angry to trust himself to speak. She had a good job, a better job, at another hospital—but the whole thing made him sick.

Even today he wished he could have thought of some way to 'make it up to' Sue Jordan.

CHAPTER FIVE

Jock was so stunned at whatever had been said or done to Sue that for days he stayed away from his father, knowing that he could not trust himself to speak temperately. He made foolish plans of asking for a residency in the hospital to which she had moved—of leaving for some place, away from his father and his spies.

He did not, he remembered, quarrel with his father about Sue. Her name was not mentioned again between them, nor her absence from the hospital. But it was only weeks later that he did come into open conflict with Jim on the matter of the changes which he—and Sue—would like to see made in the hospital.

Now Jock shifted his weight in the hard chair, and smoothed his hands over the flat red book, wishing that he might avoid the remembrance of that quarrel of eighteen years ago. He could not. It had been too big a thing in his life.

At the time, he tried to conclude that the place and the occasion made the quarrel so bitter, but now he felt that it had come as a climax to many disagreements with his father. Jock was deviating from the pattern which his father's hopes had laid down. When that deviation showed up in public, Jim's defeat became evident to the world. Jim could not take that revelation, nor, scarcely, could his son.

The thing happened at a staff policy meeting, and from Jim's point of view there could have been no worse place for it. Jock was into the matter before he knew just what was happening. Someone—later he learned that the idea was Jim's—someone had proposed a limiting of visiting hours in the children's ward to two days a week—an hour in the afternoon, an hour in the evening—

'Except for the mothers, of course,' had said Jock, almost indifferently.

110

'*Not* excepting mothers!' cried Jim Askew.

Jock looked up; he was tired, and had been slumped down in his chair, catching up on his rest. 'But, sir—' he said, not believing his ears.

'The mothers make all the trouble we have in the pediatric wards!' said Jim. 'The children cry when they come, they cry when they leave ...'

'Would they cry if the mothers were allowed to stay?' Jock asked quietly.

By then several men were ready to speak, and did speak—on both sides of a subject which, in eighteen years, was to become so nearly settled as to seem foolish even to consider.

But then it was heresy to point out that hospitalisation could be a devastating experience to a child. It was even worse to say, as Jock did say, after some minutes of wrangling on the subject, that children should not be hospitalised at all, if that were in any way possible. 'Keep them at home,' he declared. 'And if you can't keep them there, take them home as soon as is at all possible.'

The meeting had ended with Jim Askew walking out of the room, red as a beet, his eyes blazing. That same afternoon, the new visiting-hours regulation went up on the bulletin boards, and all pediatric wards fell under the ruling.

When next Jock encountered his father, Jim would not speak to him.

That evening Emma came to the apartment and asked Iris to let her talk to Jock alone. Iris looked somewhat affronted.

'It has nothing to do with you, dear,' Emma conciliated her.

'Iris may as well stay,' Jock put in. 'I think I know what you want to talk about, Mother.'

But Iris decided to leave. She went into the bedroom, and closed the door. Jock gazed at his mother, waiting.

'If you know what it is I want to say, Jock,' said Emma, 'why haven't you—why don't you act sensibly of your own accord?'

'Mother ...'

'You are not acting sensibly, dear. Not when you persist in angering your father, upsetting him, defying him, before the other staff men.'

'Am I not to have any opinions of my own?' Jock asked her. The question had become a big item in his life.

'But why should your opinions differ from your father's? Certainly his years of experience would lead him to form wise opinions and make the right decisions.'

'Sometimes years of experience put a man into a groove of habit, Mother. He—'

'Jock!'

'Yes, Mother?'

'I don't want to argue with you. I don't know where this arguing streak has come from lately. You never argued as a child! But I came here tonight to tell you to stop it. If you have those differing opinions, for heaven's sake, son, don't you have sense enough to keep them to yourself? Don't say the things you do, and don't *do* the things that you know upset your father. Haven't you a lick of sense? Don't you realise how well situated you are, both as a man and as a doctor?

'In the hospital, your position is assured, and it is a good position. Then think of your home here, your family, the things you have. Don't you realise, son, how much your father does for you, and will continue to do?'

'If I keep my mouth shut?' asked Jock.

'Well, not that—but don't get so radical, Jock. Sometimes he feels that you seek ways in which to disagree with him.'

'I don't, Mother. But I have been investigating things which I am sure Father has not had the time to look into. If he would just listen to me—'

Emma sighed. 'My advice would be to drop your investigations, Jock. Do your work, enjoy your family—and stop trying to change the world. Now, promise Mother?'

But Jock would make no promises. He would say that he was sorry if his father was upset. Yes, he would try to avoid arguments. And, yes, of course he loved his mother, and his father, too. And was grateful to them.

His mother had gone back to the hospital, confident that she had made Jock see the error into which he had fallen. And Jock had meant to keep his promise not to quarrel again with Jim. Of course some changes would be necessary ...

By the next day word of his quarrel with Jim during staff meeting had permeated the whole hospital. Jock was aware of that from the minute he checked in, and he at once determined to refuse to talk about the affair. Let Jim explain, and draw conclusions. Jock would attend to the job, and ignore all attempts to draw him out. When he encountered his father, his manner was carefully as usual.

It was little Beulah Stone who broke down his defences. Mrs. Stone was executive housekeeper of the big hospital. She supervised the maids and the men who did the heavy cleaning; it was she who said when a certain corridor should be scrubbed and waxed. She herself was not above wiping a steamy window, or getting down on her knees to see if a stain could be removed without making a hole in the floor. Jock had known her all his life; she was a tiny thing, as brown as a berry, with strong, kind hands, and a pair of bright brown eyes—the eyes of a cunning animal. It was hard now to think of her as dead.

That morning, meeting Mrs. Stone on the stairs, it did not occur to Jock to be watchful of *her!* For what could she say that he might resent, or need to ignore?

She was coming down, her arms full of pillows. Jock was going up, three steps at a time, and they met on the landing.

'Hi, Beulah!' Jock greeted her, meaning to go around her and her pillows.

'Oh, Jock!' said the housekeeper. 'I've been wanting to see you.'

'Yes? Make it fast, sweetheart.'

She backed him into the corner of the landing. The stair wells were enclosed, with fire doors at top and bottom. Others used the stairs, but a moment or two of privacy was a probability.

'I'll make it fast,' said Beulah. 'But I feel I have to say this to you, Jock.'

'Oh, oh,' said Jock.

'Now listen to me.'

Jock braced his shoulders against the rough plaster of the wall. 'Yes, Ma'am,' he said docilely.

'As you suspect, I've heard about the quarrel you had with your father, Jock. But—wait a minute—*this* is what I have to say! And it will probably be different from what has already been said to you.'

'I just don't want to talk about it, Beulah.'

'I know. I know how much you admire your father and truly love him. I know that. But just the same, my dear, it is the opinion of this old lady that the time has come—and passed—when *you* should make a change. I mean it, dear. You should leave this hospital, stop working with your father.' She peered at him anxiously over the top pillow.

Jock gaped at her. Her grey head bobbed with her conviction. 'Yes, you should, Jock,' she said again. 'It's time you should be on your own, making your own mistakes, and knowing your own success, too. You're young, you have a life of your own to lead, and you'll never in the world do it while you stay here in the shadow of your father and his reputation. He's a wonderful man, of course. But no shadow is good for a young man to live under. And then there's your mother, bless her. You're only eight to her, Jock, and she'll never let you be any older; she'll never let you grow up and express your own ideas. Do you understand what I'm saying, Jock, dear?'

Jock understood. It surprised him that she would say it, though she was right. He would always love Beulah Stone for her bravery that morning.

That morning, Jock thanked the housekeeper and promised to remember what she had said. He did remember it. He had even considered ways of doing what she advised.

He would like to make a change; he should have made the move before this. He would apply for a position in some other hospital. But there he was stymied. He would apply, and tell of his experience at Brownlee Memorial. Immediately a letter of inquiry would come back to his father, the Medical Director.

And the fat would be in the fire. As it might have to be—sometime.

Financial considerations made it impossible for Jock to consider private practice.

He began to read the ads in the medical journals. Isolated towns needed doctors, and offered inducements—a home and guaranteed income. A clinic building and a home and guaranteed income. A small hospital—

In any case, he must finish this year at Brownlee, and that meant months of working as he had been working, but now alert to the differences between his ideas and his father's, always conscious of a need to seem to go along with the Director's theories and practices, to keep his mouth shut, to ignore the openings made by his father—and others—for an argument.

It was a frustrating way for a man to live and work. Jock had always been popular, and well liked. Now he truly realised the extent to which his father's position had smoothed the way for him in his profession.

Jock surely must make that change soon— but until he did, he must work on at Brownlee, frustrated or no. It was not good, but it was natural, that he should take his frustration out upon those who must endure his short temper, his need to strike back.

He made life miserable for Iris and the children.

In the 'pit' he acquired an unenviable reputatoin. 'Watch out for Jock,' the student doctors would tell each other.

Both sets of victims were helpless against him.

No wonder his family—

And he hoped that the young doctors-in-the-making did not remember him too bitterly. Probably they did not. The pit was a proving ground for all medics. Jock had served his turn in the place. The pit, it was reasoned, was a pre-taste of the lonely decisions which any doctor must make, and for all his life. If the candidate came there to present a case, listing his patient's present illness, his chief complaint, detailing the past history, and habits—and finally explaining his own diagnosis, and out-lining his plan of treatment—the student would expect to be bombarded by questions from the men who sat upon the circling rows of benches. Faculty and fellow students would quickly spot an oversight, indecisiveness, slipshod think-ing—and in those days, Jock Askew was the quickest and most merciless of them all. He made life, and the study of medicine, very tough for the men of that particular class. The hospital, and the medical school, noted that he did.

And later thought an explanation of his mood could be found in Iris's behaviour and action.

But Jock had been almost too preoccupied with himself that winter to notice Iris's chang-ing mood. If it had changed. He didn't know. He really did not. Looking back, he could not remember just how things had been between him and Iris those months. He remembered his short temper at home, and the time, or two—or three—when he had been impatient with the children. But if there were indications of what was coming, he had not seen them.

The night that Iris asked him for a divorce,

he was both bewildered and shocked. *Why?* What reason did she have? Was there another man ...?

'There is another woman,' she told him. She was nervous, obviously, and just as obviously determined to see this thing through.

'What woman?' Jock asked her.

And she mentioned Sue Jordan, Jock's visits to her apartment, the key which he had given back months ago.

Of course Jock told her that she was crazy! Of course he said that he would not listen to such nonsense! A divorce, indeed! What about the children?

'What about them?' Iris asked him. 'You've paid little attention to them lately.'

'But I'm a busy man, Iris!'

'And cross when you are at home,' she reminded him.

'I'm sorry.'

She mentioned Sue Jordan again. Had his mother and father told her about Sue? She would not have known of that small interlude—it could not even be called by such a *name!* The whole thing was rigged. Ridiculous!

But she still insisted that she wanted a divorce, quietly if possible. If not—

And Jock had told her that he would let her have the thing, quietly. Should he get out at once?

No. She had already taken the children to her mother's, and would go there herself, now that she had talked to Jock.

She had the whole thing planned; there was nothing he could have said or done.

His parents thought otherwise. They were horrified at the situation. Why had he let Iris leave? What did she want of Jock that he would not give her, or do?

'She just said that she wanted a divorce, Mother.'

'Did you try to persuade her?' asked Jim.

'There weren't any points for argument or persuasion, sir.'

Had they expected him to beg, to make promises? And of what?

'Don't you care?'

'Of course I care. But the idea is not mine.' It was then that he thought of Pete Henderson. Pale-eyed, petulant—Pete had the face of a boy. But he was also a man of striking grace, and good looks. He had money. Success. Of course! Henderson was the snake in the grass! Jock looked alertly at his parents.

But before he could speak, Emma mentioned Sue Jordan. Did Jock suppose ...?

'Iris mentioned her,' Jock confirmed. 'But you both know that was nothing. I suppose somebody could build it into an item, if they wanted to, but—'

'I don't think you should allow Iris to go through with this, Jock.'

'What can I do, Mother? Fight her in court?'

'No—I suppose not.'

A man, he found, was pretty damn helpless in a thing like that, unless he did want to raise a stink. For the sake of the children, Jock would not fight.

It was wrong. All of it. But Iris got her divorce, and custody of the children, with Jock having the right of 'reasonable visitation.' He would contribute to their support.

When his parents rebuked him, and deplored the break-up of his marriage, he said that he was sorry.

'Sorry!'

'You seem to blame me. But—'

'Couldn't you have worked harder for your marriage? Weren't you at all fond of Iris and the children?'

'Nobody asked me that in court.'

'Now, Jock—your father and I feel terribly about this. We had done so much for you. We had made the marriage possible, and we were good to Iris and the children.'

They had been; their generosity had been great—but all their gifts had had strings tied to them. Apron strings.

Now again, and still, Jock thought about those strings. Just tonight Emma had reminded him that she and Jim had been generous, hoping, wanting to keep him close to them. They loved him—

He loved them, too, of course. But somehow the strings had changed his love for them. Could not a son take things from his parents and yet remain his own man? If he could not, something was wrong. In the gift, in the giver, or in the receiver. Perhaps in all three.

When was the time to stop that particular wrong? At the beginning, of course.

And Jock was the one who should have refused to be tied. He had not refused, and it was wrong.

He was sorry for many things. Without being able to do much of anything to stop it, he had been truly sorry about the divorce. Now he had Anna, and his good work, but he was still sorry about that failure in his life.

Especially he was sorry to have lost his children.

Now, the father of those children sat in the quiet library, chin down on his chest, thinking about his children as they last had been his. Small children, sometimes naughty, sometimes enchanting. Always with a claim upon a man.

Sweet Betsy, and little Jamie who might, too, have been a doctor. Though Jock would never raise a son to be his own image, to cast his shadow along that of his father!

How had Iris raised them? And Pete Henderson?

For Iris had married Pete within six months of her divorce, and the break with Jock had become irrevocable.

Bitterly sure that Pete, his money and success, had been the first cause of the divorce, Jock did not exercise his right of visitation. He would not go to see his children in Pete Henderson's home. The break was complete.

By that time, by the Christmas of 1941, war had come. Noah Green enlisted at once, and Jock had wanted to, though of course he could not have gone with Noah. If he could have, would he have been the one to step on a land mine, and lose half of his face? Would he have adjusted to that loss as well as had Noah? How long had it taken Noah to make such an adjustment? Even after the plastic surgeons had finished and left him with a blank expanse of skin and muscle—and no eye?

It did seem as if every man had a task of shaping himself to the things which life brought to him.

Jock had identified his task slowly and

reluctantly.

Jim had said that he need not rush into enlistment. He was needed at home as badly as he would be in the South Pacific, or France, or Africa, or England.

So Jock did not 'rush.' And now he must wonder if he had 'gone in' when Noah did, how things might have shaped up for him. They would have been different, surely.

For, along about March of that next year, Jock would not have been around to quarrel again with his father, and finally.

The divorce, and the war, had somewhat dulled Jock's enthusiasm for hospital reforms. He had not given up the fight, but more pressing involvements had pushed those matters into the background.

But along about February, when the hospital began to realise the shortages that the war would bring, Jock got out his notes and became interested in fitting the things which he thought should be done into the circumstances which had come to the hospital.

With personnel reduced, he argued, why couldn't ambulatory patients be served a simple, all-purpose menu in a dining-room on each ward? This would eliminate the menu presentation, the preparing of trays, and the carrying of them to each bedside, and the carrying away again, too. It would also permit meals to be served at more nearly normal hours. Breakfast at 7.30, luncheon at 12, dinner at six.

Jock would try it on his wards, he decided. The nurses were dubious, but the dietician said he could try. If the patients liked it ...

The patients did like it. They liked having a chance to visit with the other sick people, to exchange symptoms, and gossip about the nurses and the doctors. It took no longer to prepare a table and chairs in the sun room, and serve the meal there, than it did to serve the patients individually. The patients ate better.

'But it should be a *hospital* rule,' worried Miss Timmerman. 'See what you can do in staff conference, Jock.'

'It's a matter for the Administrator,' said Jock.

'But the doctors have to agree. You know—the Administrator can give out any number of orders, and everybody will obey them except the doctors.'

'Oh, now—'

'It's true!' said Timmerman. 'Look! In every elevator there is a No Smoking sign. And who smokes in the elevators? *Only* the doctors. And the Administrator cannot do one thing about it! So—'

'All right,' said Jock. 'I'll bring it up.'

And at the next general staff meeting he did present the matter, making some introductory remarks about shortages, the need for the doctors to hold the line firmly against bed-pan detail, and then he went on to tell of his experiment which seemed to be working very well on the diagnostic and medical wards.

He was half-way through before he caught the look in his father's eye. He hesitated, then set his chin, and continued. Could the plan be recommended by the staff as routine procedure?

The other men were interested, some were enthusiastic, some waited to see what Dr. Askew would say.

'It's an idea,' said Jim. 'I didn't have the thing on my agenda, but I welcome emergency items. Of course I don't think it would work. These are no times to make radical changes in the work hours of the kitchen help, or to change routines on the wards. But, thank you, Jock, for giving us a little humour to brighten our days. Now, the next item for consideration is—'

Jock sat there; he heard what was said, he knew what was decided upon, what tabled or refused.

He went out of the meeting, and hunted up Maude Timmerman. 'Dust off your trays,' he said. 'The Old Man turned his thumbs down on our idea.'

'But, Jock—'

'You try talking to him.'

'Jock, I am sorry.'

Jock gulped. He was sorry, too. And he lost no time in seeking out his father—before Jim could or would send for him.

Jim was waiting for him, cold rage in his eye. Belatedly, Jock realised, appalled, that again he had opposed his father in public. Before the only public that mattered to the Medical Director.

Jim would not listen to anything Jock wanted to say; he had only one thing to say to his son. And that amounted to an ultimatum. 'If you can't agree with my way of doing things, Jock, there is just one thing for you to do.'

'Yes, Father,' said Jock. 'You will have my resignation at once.'

He had not looked at Jim when he said that; he did not see him again before leaving the hospital. Perhaps Jim regretted—Jock didn't know. His father was right. Jock must leave.

Perhaps he had done wrong to make the break. Perhaps he had done wrong to persist with the 'ideas' which he knew Jim feared, and would refuse.

Perhaps Jock had done the only thing he could do. Perhaps, even, it was the thing Jim wanted him to do.

At any rate, it was done—seventeen years ago. Though it had torn Jock into fine shreds to leave the hospital, to leave his mother and father. He had always had a strong sense of family ties, and for years after he left St. Louis he was homesick, tempted a hundred times to return, to beg forgiveness and acceptance.

Perhaps he would have returned at once, but he went immediately into the Army and was sent to a variety of posts, none of them within hundreds of miles of home. He wrote to Emma, he kept her informed of his whereabouts and his well-being. She wrote to him. Perhaps, during those war years, she had even been proud of her son, a Captain—a Major—in the Army Medical Corps.

For three years Jock knew another life, the emergencies and the crises when he was in a line hospital, the gruelling hard work, the heartbreak of a back-of-the-lines Base hospital, and the regimented, routine work of a Post hospital in the States. It was all hard work, and it was good work. No surgeon, Jock did surgery; he did everything that he was told to do; he liked it, and had sense enough to value the experience he was getting.

Those years were passed with the accrued feeling familiar to all men who serve their country in time of war—that his past life as a civilian was a dream, and his future stretched no farther than tomorrow's sick call or casualty list.

When the war was over, Jock was in California, and he stayed there. His Army Service had removed the necessity to ask his father to recommend him for a job in some hospital other than Brownlee. His residencies at Brownlee were on his record, but his war service was there, too. After getting out of uniform, Jock could pick and choose the place where he wanted to work. He had saved some money, but he again accepted a residency, this time in a hospital in southern California.

He chose it because it was a progressive insitution. In that hospital, he was nobody's son; he had equal staff rating with any of the men there.

It was a fashionable hospital, well equipped, and imaginatively operated. Jock was popular. He was older, his manner assured. He had the brow and nose of a thinking, proud man. His mouth was firm in preoccupation, light blazed behind his eyes; his lips were cross-hatched with lurking smiles. When he got his first idea, and mentioned it to the Director, he was listened to, and given permission to sell the idea to outsiders. He did sell it, going to the big movie studios first, and then to other large corporations, to present his story.

Executives, he said, were perhaps the most expensive part of any organisation's assets. They should be cared for, and preserved. 'Don't let your valuable men get sick, and even die. See that they are checked regularly, and any warning, physical, signs heeded.'

Jock held conviction in his voice and eyes. His idea caught on. His hospital came to have a regular list of executive Big Shots and, in time, of movie stars, too, who would come into the hospital, stay a week, be carefully checked, and advised.

Jock watched these patients carefully, adding to his old notes, seeing the old signs appear, and some new ones. With the permission of the Director, he began to make changes in the hospital.

The same changes which he had advocated to Jim Askew worked in this hospital. A patient coming in for a check-up—and, gradually, any patient—was not put to bed unless it was necessary; he was not treated as a very sick person unless he was sick. Instead of draping him in a muslin bag, he was allowed to wear his own clothes, not only as a symbol of dignity, but as an image of his own social importance.

A movie star, put into a muslin jacket and a droopy terry robe, must exert tremendous effort to impress the hospital personnel—and himself—with his real identity. But let him wear his foulard pyjamas, his tailored silk robe, his ascot, and the exertion was not necessary. He could answer questions, be examined and tested just as well in his own clothes. Unless bed rest was a consideration, no patient was put to bed on admittance.

When the patient undressed, his street clothes were kept close by and available. He was allowed to keep his personal belongings without having a staff member fingering through them, listing them, and carrying them away.

His autonomy was maintained as much as possible. He was informed about his progress, and the exact state of his temperature and blood pressure. Those things, Jock felt, were enormously important to the patient, even if he didn't know what the data indicated. In time, Jock's hospital allowed its patients, except where a mental condition indicated otherwise, to chart their own temperatures, weight, and so on. The patients liked this, feeling that they were taking an active part in their own therapy.

The operational routine of the hospital was altered; the patient's time of waking, washing, eating, sleeping, was flexible. Certainly it was not determined by convenience in nurses' work shift. The wards were organised to let the patients take their meals at any time they desired within a range of two hours; sleeping hours were also patient-determined unless some special reason indicated otherwise.

The changes took time to effect, and to be accepted by the hospital personnel. Some few patients mistrusted the changes. But most of them liked the new regime, and they spread the word of a hospital where a man could be treated like a human being. A local paper carried a feature; a popular magazine and the bulletin of a big drug company told the story.

Patients came from distances that constantly increased; the top brass of a huge insurance company, of an aircraft industry, of an investment company came in for annual check-ups. Gradually the check-up business became the biggest item in that hospital, and Jock devoted all his time to that service.

He had many high-priced, high-powered organisation men under his jurisdiction. They entered the hospital, they went through the ritual check-up and observation. Their physical needs were detected, analysed, prescribed for.

But their emotional needs gave Jock new things to think about. Again he began to make notes, and keep records. At the end of a year he was pretty sure that the men who came to him, to the hospital—aside and apart from their physical condition, which often was found to be good—could bring a head full of emotional problems.

The hospital had no means of giving its clients an emotional check-up. Was there any place that would so examine these busy men, and try to help them? If there was not such a place ...

Jock found himself with new ideas, new plans, a new challenge. If emotional problems existed, it surely was as important to detect and handle them as to correct any physical disturbance. A guilt feeling could cripple a man as surely as hypertension or a malfunctioning gall bladder.

But there Jock's training and ability ended. He wished he had studied psychiatry, had had more of it, had specialised in it. Diagnostics was good, but it was not enough. Not for Jock.

CHAPTER SIX

In the quiet of the library, someone spoke aloud, and Jock straightened in the oak chair, looked at his watch. It was ten o'clock. He got up, his limbs stiff from long sitting. He took his books back to the shelves, spoke gravely to the attendant at the desk and went out.

In the corridor, he hesitated, but only for a second or two. Then he strode to the elevator, went up in it, and swiftly along the corridor of surgery; all the operating rooms were locked for the night. He softly opened the apartment door, hoping that he need not disturb his mother. But she was waiting for him.

'I just came for my coat,' said Jock. 'Is Father ...?'

'He's a little restless. Not bad. He asked for you.'

Jock went to the door of the sick-room and looked in. The nurse rose and came to him; Jock talked to her for a minute, his voice low. The man on the bed made no sign that he was aware of Jock's presence.

'I think he'll sleep,' Jock said when he returned to his mother. 'You'd better get to bed, dear. I'll come back in the morning.'

'For breakfast, Jock?'

'Perhaps. But you eat when you get up. Good night, dear.'

He kissed her and left, his coat over his arm. His mother had wanted to talk; but Jock was not yet ready. For now he must think about Anna.

He kept her face before him as he walked the

short blocks to the hotel; he went upstairs, ordered a drink sent up, some cheese and crackers. He undressed, and in robe and slippers, sat down to watch a newscast, to eat and drink, and to think again.

Anna.

It was ten years ago that Jock first saw Anna. He had gone to Di Trapani's Restaurant with some friends—he didn't remember who they were—and had become aware of a girl with straight dark hair who stood on the edge of the raised platform, remote and cool in a white frock, while the band played itself into a frenzy, a man sang excruciatingly, and a pianist crashed and swayed, then dwindled into a twinkling arpeggio. Then the girl in white became the centre of a gleaming spotlight. She stood just where she had been, still cool, remote—and a man *ached* to touch her, to warm her. Grave-faced, she finished the song, acknowledged the applause with a stiff little bent-knee bow, and sang again. Her voice was sweet, her eyes were big, her mouth was childish, rounded in song.

Jock listened to her, watched her. The next night he returned to the restaurant, and the night after that. He went alone. He learned her name—Anna Heath—and while she may not have been so famous herself, she was singing with a famous band. Jock ignored the band, as best he could. He came only to see Anna, to look at her. Gradually he became aware of another man who, like himself, was always there, and alone. He too watched Anna. That man was Luke Fogarty, a composer, a pianist of some skill—and he was in love with Anna Heath. George Di Trapani, aware of what was going on, had told this to Jock, and asked *his* name.

Jock read every news release about the girl, and nearly always Luke Fogarty was mentioned. She was his protégée, it was said; he wanted to marry her. He wanted to write a musical comedy for her; he would marry her. Anna was twenty-two, single—part American Indian—she had Oriental blood ...

The stories were partly true, partly untrue. But the fact of Anna stood out bright and clear for Jock. He went back again and again to watch her, to hear her. When the band moved to Las Vegas, he went there for the week-end. And it was there that Luke Fogarty spoke to him, coming to the small table, asking if he might sit down, and doing it without waiting for permission.

'I'm Luke Fogarty,' he told Jock. He was a very tall, very thin man, with a face pleasantly like that of a horse. He spoke with a flat, nasal drawl which Jock thought he exaggerated. He wore handsomely tailored clothes, and carefully let them assume the rustic charm of a gunny sack.

'I've noticed you coming to hear the band,' he said to Jock. 'I gather that our Anna is the attraction.'

Jock smiled at him, and asked if he wanted a drink.

'No. Like you, I have to space my drinks to last the evening. Because I am hanging around, too, brother—and I happen to have the inside track. In other words, Anna is my girl.'

'Oh?'

Luke Fogarty flushed. And Jock saw him do it. Ha! he thought. He just wishes she were his girl. And so this Fogarty character was in no better position than was Jock Askew.

Jock would stick around.

He did.

Later Anna was to call it a romantic court-ship, and maybe it was one. Jock had known only that he must continue to see the girl, to know her, and if at all possible, to have her for his own. Afterwards, Jock reminded Anna of the money it had cost him, the time—the sleep lost—the damage to his brain and liver from the drinks he had had to buy.

'But it was worth it?' she would ask him gravely.

It was worth it.

The second week of the Las Vegas engagement, Anna smiled at the tall man whose melting brown eyes watched her so intently. Using that smile as encouragement, Jock spoke to her the next day when, after a long wait, he saw her come into the hotel lobby. She talked to him for a minute. She was glad, she said, that Dr. Askew enjoyed their act; they would be in Las Vegas for six weeks ...

The next week end she had lunch with Dr. Askew, and when she left him, she reached up and shyly touched the cleft in his chin, smiled at him with her eyes, and went into the elevator.

The 'romantic courtship' continued for that entire six weeks—Luke Fogarty had dropped out of the picture. Probably to attend to his business, thought Jock, guilty about his own affairs, but stubborn, too.

And, after an engagement at Palm Springs—during those three weeks Anna spent all her free time with Jock and the affair made the gossip columns—Anna said that, yes, of course she would marry Jock.

She loved him, so why shouldn't she marry him?

The wonder of it could still bemuse Jock. But he had seized upon his luck. They were married at once, and returned to Los Angeles, where the wonder of Anna continued. She was a spunky girl, and straight thinking. She was a constant delight and surprise to Jock. Without one backward look, she had given up her career, and Luke—who had been a good friend! He had indeed wanted to put her into a musical comedy; it would have meant a tremendous success for her. That same musical ran for three years on Broadway.

But Anna had chosen to marry Jock, and having done that, she was determined to make him a good wife. The only cloud on their happiness was her grief that she had not been able to give him a child. This continued to be a living sorrow to her, though Jock had done all that he could to reassure her. He loved her dearly, she knew that, and returned his love, but still she could not express that love in a child. For no child came.

In an effort to show her that there were additional ways to express themselves, Jock talked to her about his work, and made it the centre of their life together. Anna was interested. She read widely in an effort to understand the work he did, she made his ideas a part of her own excited ambition. It was Anna who encouraged him towards the study of psychiatry.

He remembered the first time she had said to him, 'If you need to know psychiatry, can't you study it?'

'But—'

'All right! You are thirty-five years old, and you have a wife to feed. But you also have these good ideas which should be carried out! You have come to a place where you need psychiatry to continue the work you have started. Are you afraid to go on, Jock?' She was not a great talker, but when she did speak, a man listened.

Though he tried to tell her that she would be out of place, her interest in his work made her like to go with Jock when he was asked to speak at some medical meeting.

'You followed me, and listened to me. I want to go, Jock.'

And go she did. She had gone to one such meeting, where Jock was asked to speak on what were still called his 'radical ideas on hospital reform'—and it was after the meeting that she began to talk about psychiatry.

The State Medical Society meeting was held in the northern part of California, and Anna had loved the countryside there, the forests, the cooler, brisker air, the fogs that rolled in from the sea.

'I would like to live here some day,' she said to Jock. 'Among the tall trees.'

'In one of the National Parks, no doubt?' Jock teased her.

'Near one of them,' she said serenely.

Just as serenely, she went to the meeting where Jock would speak. She sat there, dark haired, wide eyed, tiny among all the men. There had been a few women, of course, doctors, anaesthesiologists—Anna looked like nothing but the speaker's wife. She wore no hat, her black, straight hair framed her intent face; her suit was red, with a white blouse—

Jock talked, for the umpteenth time, on the reforms which he had instituted in the hospital where he was resident diagnostician; he talked about his reasons for wanting the changes.

'Few patients,' he said, 'complain about conditions in the hospital while they are still in the hospital. Most of their bitter resentments are expressed weeks, and even months, after they have gone home. That repression alone is not a good thing, psychologically speaking.'

He mentioned the fact that he knew no more about psychology than most internists. Then he went on: 'There is a psychological reason for that repression, I believe. When a patient enters a hospital he is sick and frightened. Even when he is well, and comes in only for an examination, he is frightened. He feels helpless, no longer able to express his own independence. If he is sick, or thinks something critically wrong may be discovered, he knows that he is threatened, in the hospital, by unknown forces, and that his very survival is dependent upon others. Emotionally, he reverts to the status of a child, an infant. This regression means a tremendous psychological shock to all adults, and hospitals do not recognise that shock, or, if they suspect it, they make no effort to ease it. Instead they increase the patient's sense of inadequacy. They take away all symbols of his personal identity; his clothes, his jewellery, his money are counted and carried off. He is given bedclothes which do nothing for his self-image; he must give up his upright position, the symbol of his strength and his status as a human being. His sense of privacy is violated; all persons who belong to the hospital, with that belonging expressed and emphasised by white coats and uniforms, have unlimited access to his body.

'He has no control of time, because of the hospital administrative scheduling of activities; he is denied knowledge about himself; temperature, respiration, and so on, become matters for a secret record ...'

It was a talk which Jock had made many times. Anna was to hear him make it again. And again.

But that night, after they went to bed, planning to get up early for the drive home, she asked, in her calm, logical voice, 'Jock, why aren't you a psychologist?'

'Because I am a doctor of medicine.'

'Aren't some doctors psychologists?'

'They become psychiatrists.'

'Don't you want to be a psychiatrist?'

'Yes.' He told her of his old wish to intern and specialise in the field.

'Why didn't you do it?'

And he tried to tell her about his father's dream for his only son.

She listened; she was getting to know his parents, gradually, at a distance of two thousand miles.

'But why don't you become one now?'

He mentioned a reason or two—age—his responsibilities. But he also said that he really needed to be one to carry on the sort of diagnostic work he was doing.

'Every big brass that comes in to us, Anna,' he said, sitting up in bed and talking eagerly, 'brings an emotional problem with him to the hospital. I know it is there when I first see the man, but my limitations are such ...'

'In the hospital, you mean, they do not treat his emotions?'

'We don't even discuss them—not as such. No. We'd need a special department, or some special hospital, where the man's emotions, and his inner person, could be examined.'

'Could you make such a hospital?'

How could he ...?

She was sure that he could establish such a place. Why not?

That was the first of it.

Within a year plans were being made—a location was selected—details were discussed and decided upon. With the money which Jock had saved, with the money that he and Anna denied themselves by not spending it on things they needed, some acreage was bought in a wooded valley northwest of San Francisco. The manner and means of securing patients were considered. Admissions would be arranged through the same corporation heads who had been arranging for the physical check-ups, but referral should come through the medical directors of hospitals making the routine check-ups. There would be mental and emotional evaluations by the staff psychiatrist and psychologists ...

Here Jock felt stymied. Where to start? With himself? With a building? With advertising his project, and selling it? He did start there. He talked to conventions of doctors, and of industrialists. He appeared before board meetings; he talked to the men he was still examining and diagnosing in the hospital. He spoke of a place where an executive could get emotional understanding—

'Where is such a place?'

'In my head. I have plans.'

'Well, get to it, Doc. Get to it!'

He was asked to discuss his present work, and his ideas for his 'unit,' at a national medical convention. Jock always called his establishment a 'unit.' He would not use the term hospital, or institution, certainly not sanitarium. It was to be a unit in the over-all medical picture. It had a place, there was need for such a unit.

The convocation was to be in St. Louis, and Anna told him firmly that he must go there and make his talk.

'And you must certainly go to see your father and mother while there,' she said firmly.

'Will you go with me?'

'Not this time.'

'Anna—'

'They don't know me, Jock. They will be kind to me when they know me.'

'I'll not go without you.'

'Yes. Because you need to make your talk. The hospital here wants you to go.'

She was right. So Jock went to St. Louis.

146

His talk was successful, the discussion of it was lively—his father came up to him, and asked him about the thing. Was it really to come about? Just what would it do? Psychoanalysis?

'Not a couch in the place,' said Jock, laughing. He was glad to see Jim, their old easy friendship seemed to be present. Would Jock come to the apartment, his father asked.

Yes, he meant to. He wanted to see his mother.

'Let's go over now,' said Jim. 'You can skip this luncheon and the paper by Goldblatt.'

Jock nodded, glad to go with his father.

The convention was being held in this very hotel where Jock now sat. He and Jim walked to the hospital along the same route which Jock was now using between the two places.

Jock went up to see Emma, and she was tearfully glad to see him. She patted his arms, held him away to look at him, and hugged him again.

While the three ate lunch on the terrace, Emma kept smiling at him. Jim asked about the work Jock was doing, and nodded. Diagnostics was a fine field.

'He's got a notion he wants to open his own hospital, Emma,' he said indulgently, to his wife. 'Tell her about it, Jock. And me, too. I'm as interested as a man can be.'

Jim Askew had aged in eight years' time. His hair had thinned, his eyes looked a little rheumy—and he seemed glad to see his son. He listened intently as Jock spoke of his prospective 'unit.' He sighed with envy when Jock described the land he owned, the deep, still woods, the little flashing river which bisected the grounds.

'Won't this take a lot of money?' asked Emma.

Jock looked at his father, and smiled. Both men smiled. 'Yes, Mother, it will take some. We'll start small, and hope to grow.'

'You will grow,' said Jim. 'You may even get rich. With the world full of organisation men having, you say, emotional problems.'

'They do have them, sir. I imagine all men do. But your big organisation man has them where it hurts a lot of other people.'

'That's right. As a sawbones, I don't know a lot about this mental aspect, but I guess it's there. And I still think you'll get rich.'

He was friendly, he was interested, and Jock thought he was sincere.

'If you're convinced of that, sir,' he said, only half-seriously, 'perhaps you'd like to go into the project with me.'

Jim was startled. What did Jock mean?

148

'Well, as Mother suggests, this thing will need some working capital. I thought perhaps you would—'

'No,' said Jim Askew. Flatly, and coldly. Jock felt his cheeks go hot.

'Is that why you came to St. Louis?' Jim asked. 'To hit me for money?'

Jock rose from his chair. 'I came to address the convocation—by request,' he said stiffly. '*You* invited me to come here to eat lunch.'

'And you asked for money.'

'When you showed interest in the unit I plan to start, I offered you a chance—I'm sorry if you misunderstood.'

His father looked old. Jock became more concerned with the way he looked than with the fact ...

'What makes you think you can run a hospital?' Jim demanded. 'Or a *unit*. You've never taken a step alone in your life! You've always had someone behind you, giving the orders. The army, the hospital where you are now resident, or me.' His voice rose and his colour deepened. 'I don't see how you have the *nerve* to ask me for money, and help, Jock,' he said crossly. 'You've gone against me at every point. You left the hospital here and went to California—you married an Indian—'

Jock gasped. And almost laughed. 'Oh,

Father!' he protested.

'I read it,' said Jim Askew. 'She was a night-club singer, and she is part Indian. I've seen her picture.'

Jock took out his billfold. He could show his own picture of Anna. She was dark, and grave; her hair was straight, and black. His parents probably would have rejected any second wife Jock might have chosen for himself, but if they would accept Anna enough to get to know her...

Jim refused even to look at Jock's picture. 'She is not an Indian,' said Jock. 'Though if she were—'

But Jim went abruptly into the apartment. Jock tried to talk about Anna to his mother. They were not to take publicity material too seriously. If they knew Anna—he wanted them to know her! 'I love her very dearly.'

Emma said little—and Jim was back almost immediately with a cheque in his hand which he placed on the table. It was for five hundred dollars. Jock looked at it. He went around the table and kissed his mother. He glanced at Jim. 'Good-bye, Father,' he said quietly. 'Whether you believe it or not, I am glad that I could see you both.'

He went away, leaving the pink cheque, fluttering, upon the table.

On his way home, Jock determined that he would not tell Anna what had happened. He would say only that he had seen his parents. But Anna read him too well, too clearly. She got the whole thing from him, his humiliation, his disappointment.

'I'd never realised that it would be so bad to be an Indian,' she said thoughtfully.

'They don't know you!' Jock insisted.

'Nor Indians,' said Anna. 'But they hurt you very much.'

'Yes. I—I miss them, Anna. It is not right to be separated from one's parents, unless they are dead.'

'That is true.' Anna had been raised by grandparents: her mother had died when she was two, her father in the first year of the war.

'I know my father is not well,' Jock told his wife. 'I think Mother knows that he isn't. She may not have acknowledged it, but she knows. She didn't say a word to either of us about my unit.'

'We won't let this stop your plans,' Anna told Jock. 'You didn't count on getting help from your father...'

No. Jock had not.

'I think, don't you, that we could get help to start your unit?'

Jock didn't know ... 'I'm in no condition now

to ask for it,' he confessed, ruefully. 'Perhaps I could start with the hospital here, and we could start with one building—get a resident psychiatrist—'

'With you so many miles away?' asked Anna. 'No! *You* will be the resident psychiatrist. You must be!'

'But, my sweet—'

'You are already a doctor. Could you not take some training? How long would that take?'

'Oh, a year's residency would start me nicely.'

'All right. You will take a year's residency. I will get me a job—'

'Not away from me.' Not singing in a night-club, Jock was thinking, where Luke Fogarty would have access to Anna, with his glamorous suggestions of a career.

'Where would you have to go?' Anna asked thoughtfully, 'to become a psychiatrist?'

Jock laughed, not so much at her question as to her acceptance of the fact that a year would do it.

'There are hospitals here—in Kansas—in the East.'

'Let's stay out here. I'd get a job in the hospital office—'

'Singing?'

'I can type—and meet people—'

Jock kissed her head and was thankful for her

serene manner of facing the problems of life.

And she was right. For Jock did leave the hospital, and went into another one for a year's concentrated work in psychiatry, discovering that he had been learning a good deal about the subject in the past ten years; he attended lectures at the medical school; he read—and Anna worked at the hospital office. It was not a bad year, at all. It gave them time to think about their project, to level off some of the experimental rough spots.

Other men in Jock's new field become interested in what he planned to do, and helped him so that he learned a lot in that year's time. Another thing that helped was that he knew exactly what he wanted to learn, and he could work to that end without waste.

Among his friends there were several who wanted a part in the thing which he projected. Some offered money, an advertising firm earmarked ten thousand dollars towards his enterprise. A lawyer advised him to incorporate. This was done and the Tree Valley Foundation became a fact.

Others among his new associates wanted directly to help. 'Give me a job, Askew,' they asked, and meant what they said.

Gradually the thing began to shape up, and the promise of the future became ever more exciting. Anna never once faltered in her faith, nor let Jock doubt. He soon realised that he would be able to pick and choose his co-workers; he knew he would get patients. He told himself that he must go slowly, and he did. They would start, then finance any growth out of earnings. There would be no waste.

He continued to call his project a unit, refusing all emotion-charged words and terms as applied to it. His fifty acres of pleasantly wooded hill and valley, the silver river that crossed it, looked like any beauty spot of northern California. His first building—the clinic building, that was never so called, just the 'main building'—might have been some vacation hotel. Here were the examination and consultation rooms, and here about half of the patients were housed. Later, cottages were built; by now they had four of these separate buildings which could each comfortably house eight men. In their early years Jock and Anna lived in one of them. And Anna had done most of the cooking for the first patients. They started with four ...

Never had there been any signs of the mental and emotional problems of their guests. There were no barred windows, no guards, no locked doors. By now their capacity was sixty guests, and that capacity was usually filled.

Among the full-time staff of seventy-five, the seven doctors and four registered nurses never wore white coats or uniforms. The atmosphere was one of gracious country living without the resort-hotel frills and pressures.

Looking back, Jock could still wonder at the way the Foundation had grown. The other staff men had come in on their own, the gamble had been their own. Their faith in the project had made the thing work as much as anything else.

There was no chief, no boss. Jock's idea had started the project, but the carrying out of his idea made the Foundation important. An idea by itself could be like a bead of morning dew upon a branch, to be burned off and forgotten before the sun was an hour old. It had to be seized upon, implemented into something real and usable. Jock was not inclined to over-estimate his initial contribution.

'A good thing for my ego,' he told himself, wryly, late that November night in the St. Louis hotel.

Behind him and the rest of the staff, notably Anna, there were years of hard work, interest, and some fun. Along the wooded mountainside the buildings had taken form, roads constructed —and patients came. Guests.

A few executive-type men, of their own initiative, sought a Tree Valley emotional inventory; from Jock's past lists of companies and corporations requiring regular check-ups for their key personnel, he drew a steady stream of candidates for such an inventory. Routines were tried, and developed into what seemed to bring the best all-round results.

Before his arrival, the patient's colleagues and his family supplied background data. Securing those data had been one of the most important details which the Foundation had worked out.

The typical patient was asked to arrive in time for Sunday dinner; he stayed until Saturday afternoon. During those six days he went through a thorough going-over with the staff psychologists and psychiatrists, but there was no hint of psychoanalysis. There were no couches; upon departure the patients proudly told about that. Only once had a high-priced—and high-strung—TV star discounted the value of his week's examination because the usual gimmicks were lacking. He was the exception.

Patients were treated with consideration and understanding. There was only one strict rule; everyone had to take daily walks over the surrounding hills and through the woods.

The Foundation was a good place to work, a good place to go for an emotional check-up. Jock rubbed his hand over his hair, and thought that he himself would like to take refuge there immediately. Just at the minute he'd make better patient-material than staff.

He thought again of the details which had brought the project to its present recognised success. Qualification in psychiatry had come all but automatically to Dr. James Askew, Jr. There had been a few mistakes; now and then some ground had been lost, but, as Anna said, they had started right with the location, and the rest came of its own good will and performance. Or so it seemed, looking back over the years.

Jock's and Anna's home, built against a mountain slope, seemed no more a matter of effort—looking back—than had been the discovery that the ocean could be seen on a clear day. Trees were cut down, or trimmed, and the view became a matter of individual search and triumph for the patients.

The one and only disappointment of those years, it now seemed to Jock, was that Anna had no children. Unlike the Shah of Iran, Jock would not cast aside such a wife, but, to be honest with himself, he had missed that side of his life—and Anna knew it. She knew they both lacked the feeling that children would have given, that they were building towards the future.

When Jock returned to California, he would

try to speak again to her of adopting children. This always depressed Anna; she thought it meant a confession of her failure. When he went home, Jock would try to make her see it as a means of by-passing a road block.

And he meant to go home very soon. Perhaps he should call Anna right now and tell her so.

CHAPTER SEVEN

Confident that he had done his thinking, and made his decision, Jock went to bed, and lay there, wide-eyed, staring at the lights upon his ceiling, listening to the noise of cars arriving and departing in the drive below; now and then a woman's clear voice would rise above the general sound. In the corridor outside his door, two men laughed, and a woman spoke rapidly; someone in the room next to his took a shower and tuned in the late show on TV.

And Jock lay listening, and thinking still. Four years ago he had made his speech to the 'head shrinkers' about his Foundation, and about the psychiatric reasons behind malpractice suits. Six months later, two representatives of a large insurance company came to see him.

Their firm dealt largely with hospital and professional casualty insurance. The company had written his own policy. These men, both high in the executive echelons of the firm, said that they knew about the talk which Dr. Askew had given at the recent convocation. They had secured transcripts of that talk, and now had sought out Dr. Askew on the chance that he could be of help to them.

They were, they said, forming a team which would investigate the large, and growing, number of malpractice suits being filed against doctors and hospitals. They believed that Dr. Askew belonged on that team. Would he be interested?

It had taken a bit more than their asking him to serve. The men had stayed around, talking to Jock, and to the other staff men of the Foundation. They met Anna. They said that they felt Jock had stirred up a good lead in what he had said about patient disgruntlement after hospitalisation.

The longer they stayed and talked, the more interested Jock became in their project. Of course he spoke of his duties to the Foundation—he could not be away indefinitely—

Could he manage to be away occasionally?

For special investigations? Say, to trace down the emotional cause of some specific suit on file—with the hope that errors which had been made might be avoided in the future, so that some lawsuits might never happen again.

'And then we could drop our insurance rates against you medics.'

There was another aspect which appealed to Jock. He still wanted to help the *patients,* to remove some of the hazards for *them.* As a matter of truth, the whole idea appealed to him, and he thought about it deeply, talked about it to his staff.

'Why not give it a whirl?' asked Sam Minter.

'I flatter myself that I'm needed here.'

'Well, you are,' said Sam, 'but for the ultimate good—'

'The absences would be spotty,' said Applewhite. 'I mean, you'd come and go, wouldn't you?'

That would be the arrangement, if Jock took on the assignment.

'You could certainly get along without me for a part of the time,' mused Jock.

'We've done it before.'

'And without disaster,' Jock agreed.

'If you'd always come back,' said Minter. 'You see, Jock, we can substitute, and do. But we're not *you!* We haven't your feel for man's inner turmoil. We haven't your feel—or is it a bird-dog's nose?—for the little, immaterial things in a guy's background which cause his emotions to ferment. In conference, you're always the one to put your finger on the obviously unimportant.'

The other men had laughed, but Jock knew what Minter meant. He had been seeking out such weak spots for a long time; also, he wanted to improve the over-all hospital picture if he possibly could.

So he decided to join the investigation team. (Before he was done with it, he was heading and directing the operation.)

The decision once made, Jock became excited and interested in the project. To determine and correct any faults which might lead patients to file lawsuits. If the lawsuits were justified, changes should be made in the doctors' habits and practices. If the lawsuit was not based on actual damage done, the team would seek to find out what made the patient, and his lawyer, think that he had been hurt. At first, Jock concentrated on the second item.

His enthusiasm became so great that he found he must budget and limit the time he spent on his team work. But on his trips away from the Foundation, he did accomplish rewarding things.

Often Anna went with him—to be sure, she said, that he would not become so absorbed in tracking down a clue that he would forget his obligation to the 'boys' at home.

Jock did many things, found out many things, and reached some valuable conclusions. Thinking back over the years this project had taken he remembered certain highlights. Not always in sequence as they had happened, but as they now popped up in his mind.

He already knew that changes in hospital procedure were possible, but during the investigation he decided that changes would be made, in the older and more firmly established hospitals, only when the patients revolted against their customary treatment, and began to make trouble for the hospital. That was, for Jock, an exciting minute, to know and declare that every patient bore the responsibility for seeing that he got good health care in a hospital by making firm demands upon the medical personnel who were paid to provide him with that care.

Jock could remember the team discussion of that point. And their acceptance of it as elemental.

Jock thought about the team with which he had worked. Three other men and one woman.

He had quarrelled with them, argued hotly, and they had become his staunch friends by the time they made their final report. Jock urged the team members, in tracing down the cause of some individual malpractice suit, to probe deeply into every hospital experience in the patient's background. If he were suing a doctor for mistreatment, had he ever been hospitalised? Had he been hospitalised during the treatment for which he was suing? Usually he had been.

Jock, a psychiatrist, reasoned that the anger which the patient was evincing in a medical-malpractice suit could have started with some hospital incident. This investigation brought about a fruitful inquiry into patients' attitudes towards hospitals. All and any patients; all and any hospitals.

At Jock's suggestion—it was then that he was made directing head of the team—eight hospitals were selected from the files of the insurance company. Eight hospitals in different parts of the country, all of similiar size and service. Completely out of Jock's control, Brownlee Memorial was one of the hospitals designated. In four of these institutions—Brownlee one of them—patients frequently sued the staff or attending physicians. In the other four, the doctors were rarely sued.

The survey was to determine how the 'bad' hospitals differed from the 'good' hospitals in their treatment of patients. Each team member was given one good and one bad hospital for a probing investigation; Jock was to oversee the progress of their work, and to check on points where a team member asked for verification, or where Jock had one of his 'ideas' that might clear up a foggy point.

The investigations made were painstaking. It took months for the team members to look into a hospital's functioning. Immediately, differences were discovered between the good hospitals and the bad, but Jock's evaluation showed him, quite soon, that the differences were only comparative. He rechecked that point for himself. Patients fared worse in the 'bad' hospitals, but the 'good' ones fell far short of what he, the team, and the patients, thought a hospital should be.

In the bad hospitals, the investigators found excessive charges made for drugs given to the patients, and in one case they found that patients were billed for drugs which they did not receive at all. Medical reports in these hospitals were not entirely reliable, and in some cases the records regarding abortions and deaths had been falsified. Instances of medical incompetence were discovered and verified.

A hospital employee told one of the investigators that a staff member, a physician, wanted his partner to give the anaesthesia for a scheduled tonsillectomy. The partner had previously given anaesthesia, but had no special training. The hospital administrator refused permission and the staff doctor went over his head to the surgery chief who reprimanded the administrator for trying to prevent it. The partner-doctor's M.D. would permit him to give anaesthesia, and to be paid for doing it. The operation took place and during the surgery the child died in cardiac arrest. The report did not attribute the death to the manner in which the anaesthesia had been given, but the parents were suing the doctor who had arranged for the surgery.

The team member wanted Jock to investigate the case more completely, but he did not, since the case involved Brownlee Hospital.

He was too closely reminded of the malpractice suit which had been filed against Pete Henderson when he first began his nosing around Jim Askew's hospital. He accepted the team worker's report as being adequate.

Tonight he thought about the matter, wondering if he could now seek a means of looking up the records on that case. As a matter of personal curiosity, he'd like to know all the details as they were written down.

But, no, he couldn't do that.

And what he *should* do, was to go to sleep. It was past midnight, and tomorrow would be a rough day. He turned away from the lights which filtered through the window blinds.

Gross violation of professional conduct did not show up in any of the good hospitals investigated, but in both types of institution, the patients complained about visiting hours, the food, unaccustomed routines, and the lack of real interest and attention from the nurses and other personnel. Too-large bills, not being told what was wrong with them—

Jock yawned.

And did not go to sleep.

Malpractice. Insurance. Lawsuits. Justified, and without any basis of justification. A big problem, a growing problem.

The increasing number of lawsuits was truly alarming. Medical associations were conducting their own investigations. Many—most—doctors protected themselves against malpractice suits by special insurance policies.

In former days the premiums had been modest, and the protection adequate. But within the past few years the suits had so increased in number, and juries had allotted such large sums for damages, that premium rates had

had to be increased. In some cases, the companies were refusing to issue policies. Some surgeons were refusing to perform certain high-risk operations, fearing costly lawsuits if results were not satisfactory.

So, the investigating team had looked into that situation. Jock's team of psychologists and sociologists—and himself a psychiatrist—tried to find out why patients sued doctors. If they could unearth some basic causes, preventive measures might be taken, and the number of lawsuits would be minimised.

They looked at the hospitals, and at the patients who had been involved in such lawsuits. And—they looked at the doctors.

Jock sighed, and sighed again. He closed his eyes and tried to think of other things. He put his pillows one on top of the other, and punched them into what fleetingly seemed to be comfort.

He sat up, fumbled for the lamp, and lit a cigarette. For he had now come flat up against the brick wall of 'that case' in Brownlee Hospital. When it had first come across his desk, he had groaned at the inevitability of it. He remembered that earlier suit against Pete Henderson which had been filed shortly before Jock left Brownlee, and which had been settled out of court, as this one had been last year.

By Jock's own rules, the team members were to take certain cases selected and provided by the three big insurance companies now joined on the project; they were to look at and talk to the patient involved, and his family; they were to look at the hospital, and the doctors and personnel involved.

When Pete Henderson's case came up, Jock knew that this time he must refuse to check the matter. His associate had obtained the hospital records; he had made his report on Brownlee as it was then operating; there was little difference from the hospital which Jock had known in 1942.

Then, though reluctant, Jock assumed the task of talking to the family of this child, masking his name and profession when he did so. He was a representative of the insurance company, he explained, making a survey of cases which had been involved in lawsuits of a medical nature. Yes, he knew that there had been a settlement, but would the mother of the injured child talk to him? He showed his credentials, and talked reassuringly of the purposes of the investigation.

Almost anyone would talk to Jock, and this mother was no exception. Her child had been grievously hurt; the money which she had received in no way compensated for the loss of eyesight. 'I knew it wouldn't!' she said tensely, 'but I had to do something! It seemed— You see, that doctor treated me like a dumb person. If he had explained what happened—he didn't. Maybe he cared, but he didn't *act* as if he cared. And all he said was that the result was unfortunate! Why didn't he *tell* me?'

'Did you ever know?'

'Yes. Ether had burned her eyes. But that Dr. Henderson— Do you know him? He has eyes like ice. And he acted— It was not knowing what had happened that frightened me, you see. If Dr. Henderson had acted differently, I don't think I would ever have sued.'

There it was. Down in simple language. And the testimony was repeated so many times that the team's report eventually had been: 'A malpractice suit is evidence of a breakdown in the doctor-patient relationship. The suit is often the result of a particular kind of relationship where the doctor and patient have not understood one another and where each has, in his own way, been unable to face, realistically and directly, the feelings that arose in the relationship during the treatment of illness.'

Well! That should be that! Jock could turn off the light, smash out his cigarette, and go to sleep!

Only, he did not.

Whenever he had come to St. Louis, Jock made a point of seeing his mother, and of not avoiding a meeting with Jim. The two men were polite, even somewhat friendly, towards one another. They were not at all close.

And yet Jock knew that his father was interested enough in his activities to check on Jock's work, his whereabouts, his participation in the insurance company inquiry. Eighteen or so months ago, when Jock was already working up his final report on the investigation, Jim Askew sought out his son during still another medical meeting. This one was a gathering of diplomate surgeons, and Jim was a big shot in such a group. Jock again had been asked to talk, this time on the psychological hazards that children met during the surgery.

'... *and* the hazards of the necessary hospital experience.' Jock added to his topic. He told of the material which had lately come into his hands on the matter of unsatisfactory doctor-patient relationships. 'If we could make people feel better emotionally during and after a hospital session,' he said, 'we would immeasurably increase our recovery rate and cut down on the malpractice suits. There are many simple ways to secure this better relationship where children are concerned.

'One of them is by a wise use of mothers.'

He was aware of Jim Askew's presence in the audience. Big, florid Jim stood out in any assemblage.

'For years,' Jock said calmly, 'I have been urging hospitals to let mothers stay with their children, to carry as much as possible of the home environment and security into the hospital with the child.'

He went on to tell of a little boy scheduled to have eye surgery at ten o'clock one morning. He must enter the hospital at 6 A.M. Why? Because that was a hospital rule. A good rule? A bad rule? A necessary rule? Just a rule. The child entered at six.

The nurse came around to give the boy a shot—coyly described as a 'mosquito bite.' It was no such thing, and the kid knew it would not be, but he up-ended obediently. The nurse slowly shoved in the needle, the boy squirmed, the thing hurt like sixty, the nurse fought him—the needle bent to a 90-degree angle—and when it was finally withdrawn—the boy then in screaming hysterics which set off the four other children in the ward—the mother was grateful that the needle had not broken. What did the nurse say? That there had been no danger, needles were made better these days.

There was laughter across the room. Jim Askew laughed. His son did not smile.

171

Then he pointed out quietly that the nurse might have—but had not—shown concern for the child's pain, and the mother's fright.

He went on to say that the child was taken to o.r. at ten, and the mother sent downstairs to wait. She would be called when he was returned to the ward. She was not called. At one-thirty she went up again on her own, and in that condition of nerves she spent a wild afternoon with five children, her own blinded with bandages, the other four recovering from tonsillectomies. She found the hospital care poorly organised, slipshod and totally without compassion. When the children cried, which was their only way to summon help, their cries were ignored. She attended to her son herself, but the other children went largely untended. Their mothers had been told that they only upset their children, and should go home.

At seven, when visiting hours were over, this mother was also forced to leave. When she begged to stay, the intern called her overprotective. She left, and came back at seven the next morning, without permission, and found her child lying deathly quiet, sucking his thumb. When he realised his mother had returned, the boy cried pitiably, though he was not normally a nervous or clinging child. She took the little boy home.

'The wound of that hospital experience will stay with the boy, and with his mother. I don't know if she sued or not.

'Now this sort of thing happens all the time in good, hospital-accredited institutions. It is an everyday case. Shall we see what changes could be made to improve things for mother and child, and not hurt the hospital?'

There had been more to his talk, of course, other cases cited, discussion from the floor, arguments—

Discussion and arguments continued at the luncheon which followed the talk.

Jim Askew wedged his chair in at the table where Jock sat, wanting to continue the argument. He said that he well remembered Jock's wish to have mothers come into the pediatric wards, and completely disorganise the place. Of course, for that morning's talk, Jock had hunted for exaggerated, or at best isolated, cases as his examples—

'I did not need to hunt,' said Jock coldly. 'The tonsillectomy I used, sir, happened in your own hospital.'

Jock should not have said that. The men all knew they were father and son. But the case *had* been Pete Henderson's, and the case *was* one of Brownlee's.

To cover his blunt, and instantly regretted,

accusation of Jim, Jock had gone on to speak briefly of the team and its findings. 'Our conclusions seem so easily arrived at, and our recommendations seem too simple to carry out—

'Over and over we find that patients who have filed malpractice suits will also say that they would not have taken legal action if the doctors had treated them like human beings.

'Oh, now, Jock!' cried Jim. 'They come in giving us carte blanche— "Do everything you can, doctor, spare no expense or effort." And when they leave, they get their bill—and then sue us because it's bigger than they really want to pay. That, and their untrained decision that the operation was unsuccessful, are the two causes for malpractice suits. Deny that if you can.'

'I can't deny it, and I won't,' said Jock pleasantly. 'But we have also determined that it is not only the bill but the doctor's attitude which has offended your suing patient. Maybe you can't change the cost of your surgery and hospital care, but I am certain you can change the attitude.'

'We don't have time to cosset patients!' said one of the men.

'Then you don't have the time to take their cases, sir,' Jock told him.

Although ready to argue, the men were interested in the work he had done, and in the report which he would make. Even Jim seemed interested.

Now Jock did not remember just how much of the report he had given to those eight men, but he did remember where the talk had led. And of course he remembered the report—it had urged a re-examination of the standards set by the Hospital Accreditation Board to eliminate the evils which the investigation had brought out. In addition to physical advances in hospital care, which were good and necessary, the report urged that other changes be made to emancipate the patient from the mistreatment he had been getting.

At that luncheon table, Jock mentioned the board of review, to be made up of experts from the various fields of medicine—psychiatry, psychology—and Jim snorted—hospital administration, sociology and law—

'No surgeons?' had asked one of the eight surgeons at the table.

'Not on that board,' said Jock. 'That board is to examine, evaluate, and use the findings of the investigation which we have made, and, given that material, the board would be asked to suggest changes in hospital administration, medical-staff organisation, hospital-accreditation methods, work-quality evaluation and control, as well as the training and performance requirements for physicians practising in hospitals. This group would continue to serve as a committee to advise on action ...'

He had spoken of the need to establish so firmly a well-known standard of conduct for physicians in hospitals that doctors would no longer be reluctant to call attention to the substandard performance of any colleague. That way, some discipline would be possible. And the whole level of performance would rise.

There was fevered discussion, and a lot of wild-eyed suggestions. They went back to medical schools, and forward to a complete shake up of hospital staffs.

And finally—this part Jock now remembered all too vividly—they came to the point of emotionally disturbed doctors as a factor in patient-dissatisfaction and the resultant malpractice suits.

Jim Askew called his son a blithering idiot. He was very angry at any such suggestion. Doctors, from the time of their registering for pre-med, were psychoanalysed and supervised. They were busy, sure. And overworked—but, by God, they didn't have the *time* to be emotionally disturbed!

Jock looked at his father, and waited.

Some of the other men waited, too, and used their first chance to ask Jock what it was he had in mind. How were the doctors emotionally disturbed?

'Much as any man can be disturbed. In our diagnostic work at the Foundation we find the balanced, undisturbed man a rarity. He may be handling his pressures, but the disturbance is there.'

'All right,' said Jim. 'So we're all crazy!'

'That goes beyond my thesis, sir,' Jock told him. 'But in our investigation of malpractice suits, we did find that many of the individuals concerned, both patients and doctors, were emotionally ill. They included neurotics, and even psychotics. In fact, we finally concluded that the psychological relationship was more important in medical malpractice suits than the quality of the treatment or the question of whether the doctor had made a mistake. We found that the patient's reaction to his doctor often stemmed from a twisted emotional attitude.'

'Damn right!' said Jim.

Jock nodded. 'Equally often,' he continued, 'we found that the breakdown in the relationship arose from the doctor's emotional make-up. The doctor may have deep-rooted prejudices—racial or religious ones. He may suffer from a persecution complex. Frequently doctors are immature, suspicious, and dependent upon their patients for the gratification of emotional needs—though often, of course, on an unconscious level.'

Jim Askew got up to leave the table. The other men, he said, could stay as long as they liked to listen to such talk. He had to go over to his hospital and gratify some of his emotional needs. 'And I'm not unconscious about it, either.'

His friends laughed. But gravely, and sorrowfully, Jock watched his father go out of the dining-room.

It was his first suspicion of his father's changing mind. He was shocked, and startled to think that Jim might be on the verge of some sort of break-up. He hoped that he had done nothing to account for it. He stayed in the city for an additional twenty-four hours; he attended the lectures and demonstrations, wanting to watch Jim. He went to see his mother and asked her how Jim had been lately.

'Oh, about the same as always, Jock. I would like to see him get away for a real vacation this summer.'

'Has he ever talked of retiring?'

'Oh, no. He has an assistant he likes and trusts, and he lets Dr. Barnaby do a lot of the work. But I truly think that retirement would kill your father, dear.'

On that trip, Jock had been planning to go to see Noah Green. He had, in a most cowardly fashion, avoided Noah heretofore. But this time Noah himself saw Jock's name in the paper and sent him an invitation—so Jock planned to see his friend. He almost didn't go, after his shock about his father. He could phone Noah, he thought, and say that he had to leave sooner than he had expected.

But he didn't phone. He went to the apartment hotel where Noah was living, and he was very glad that he had gone.

The guy was simply wonderful! He greeted Jock as if they had parted only days ago. He was big, and hearty, and natural.

Jock was to come in, come in! How was he? 'Let me have a look at you!'

And of course Jock had a look at Noah. One side of his face was blank—the other was the rugged, man-type version of the boy Jock had known and liked.

Noah seemed entirely unconscious of his face. His attitude asked what was there unusual about a chap with only one eye?

And within five minutes he was asking Jock what was on *his* mind?

Did there have to be something?

No, but there was, just the same.

And Jock, the psychiatrist, found himself re-counting his worry about Jim.

'The man's visibly falling to pieces, Noah. Have you ever seen a brick wall crumble, or a tall brick chimney? It begins to buckle and crack, while still holding its shape—and then, all at once, it crashes, and there's nothing!'

'If that's how your Dad looks to you why not do something about it?'

'Well—for one thing there may not be any-thing one could do. Secondly, my father does not have the least respect for me or my opinion on any subject.'

Noah nodded. '*That* is what has upset you,' he said quietly.

Jock stared at his friend. One eye or two, Noah was just the same as he'd been when both of them were boys of ten. Clear-thinking, honest—

'Our fathers get older, Jock,' he reminded the doctor. 'But the remarkable thing is that we, their sons, don't grow. Not mentally. I'm still about six to my father, and you seem to be no older to yours.'

Somehow that had comforted Jock. It was true. Jim Askew wanted a son six years old. He didn't relish having a son who acted like a grown man.

Noah said other things to cheer Jock—and finally Jock called him remarkable. 'Why haven't you married, Green?'

'Who'd want me?' countered Noah, getting up to fix Jock a drink.

'I'd think there might be plenty of girls who would be glad to have a guy like you.'

Noah brought the glass to Jock, the light from the lamp at his elbow strongly illuminating the empty, pink side of his face. 'They'd be glad to have the Green money,' he said calmly. 'But that's not what I asked. I said, who'd *want* me?' He sat down with his own drink.

'You don't seem to be letting it bother you.'

'No, it's not bothering me. But of course it bothers everyone else. "My face, I don't mind it, because I'm behind it ..." ' And the truth was that Noah didn't mind a face that jarred others.

The guy was indeed wonderful! When he was in California last summer, and had come to see Jock, the men at the Foundation had wanted to put Noah Green into a glass case.

He hit it off with Anna at once. Jock hoped that the guy could find a girl like Anna. Not her, of course. Jock's life was built around his little black-haired wife. He wanted her, to talk to her, to touch her—

With a mighty heave upward, Jock reached

out for the telephone. He would talk to Anna! Even if she scolded him, he needed to hear her voice.

She did not scold. She was glad to talk to him, she said. She was missing him. How was his father?

She said that they had been having fog—and rain, at last. Think of their part of the country needing rain! Yes, things seemed to be going all right at the Main Building. How was Jock's mother?

Emma had never met Anna; she didn't want to meet her. She was consistently reproachful with Jock, even to this day, about his divorce and remarriage.

Every time he had seen Emma, through the years, she had urged him to go see Iris. But he had never gone.

This time, too, Emma was suggesting that he go. Pete Henderson, she said, had died last spring. Iris was now a rich woman; Pete had made good money and had invested it fortunately ...

Would Jock be home soon, Anna was asking.

'As soon as I can,' said Jock. 'There are details here to be cleared up.'

'What sort of details?'

'Well—of course there is Father, and what we will do about him, should it seem that he may live for any time.'

'Won't he?'

'Perhaps not. But he could live for years, not well, not in control of himself.'

'I see. But—'

'No. I can't, and I won't stay here indefinitely for that reason. But the lawsuit is a different thing.'

'What lawsuit?'

He was reluctant to tell even Anna that his father was about to be sued, in open court, for negligent care and abuse of a patient. Not, probably, that he had abused, or been negligent— but to have his name as a surgeon impugned ...

'It's a malpractice suit,' Jock said quietly. 'I don't know the details. A man was injured, Father cared for him—and just before he fell ill, the family, and the man, filed a suit for damages. Big damages. The thing angered him, and—'

'Did it cause his stroke?'

'I don't know.'

'Could it have caused it?' Anna persisted.

'Yes.'

'All right. Go on.'

Jock sighed. 'Well—of course now others must handle the situation.'

'And you're staying on to do it.'

'I must, Anna!'

'Doesn't he have insurance? Your father, I mean?'

'Yes, and normally the company would handle the matter.'

'What company is it, Jock?'

He hesitated. 'Corbett,' he then said gruffly.

'Oh, oh!'

'Now, Anna!'

'I was just remembering that you had worked for them on your investigation.'

'That has no significance now.'

'All right, then, tell me the rest.'

So he told her. 'If he would have let them— But Father was angry about the suit. He said he would fight it, and I think he said it pretty emphatically to the insurance company. Though now—of course—'

'Are you going to enjoy eating crow, Dr. Askew?'

'Anna, please!'

'Well, that's what they want you to do, isn't it? Your mother, and the hospital—'

'I don't know what they want. Or care. If Father was right, and the case can be defended in court—'

'Does the insurance company think it can be?'

'All insurance companies are afraid of juries and their big settlements.'

'And you're not?'

'Well—Father's name should be defended, if it can be. That's what I mean to find out.'

'It sounds to me that you have somewhat been caught in a trap, my boy.'

Jock was angry—mainly because he himself had explored that possibility.

'They are,' insisted Anna, 'hoping to use your connection with the company, aren't they?' She did not identify 'they.'

Nor did Jock. 'No, they are not!' he shouted. There was a long minute of silence in California.

'I mean,' Jock said lamely, 'I would not allow my connection to be used.'

'But you are staying on to handle the case?'

'Yes, I feel that I must do what I can to clear the matter up. Establish innocence and no injury, or make a satisfactory settlement. In any event, I'd hope we could avoid publicising this matter and fastening the charge on Father's name. He has been a famous and a good surgeon. Now he is sick, and cannot defend himself. I must see what I can do for him.'

Anna said nothing.

'It won't take long, my darling.'

'I hope not.' Anna spoke softly. 'I hope not.'

She hung up then, and Jock went to bed, to sleep.

CHAPTER EIGHT

The next morning, his mind clouded with a vague sense of worry, Jock rolled out of bed, turned on the TV for the morning news, showered, shaved, and dressed. He gathered some things to go out for cleaning and laundering, and debated whether he had promised to have breakfast with his mother. No, he'd told her to eat ...

It was still early; he'd eat his breakfast, and take a brisk walk in the park before going to the hospital to tell his mother just how long he would stay, exactly what he would do. Beginning today, he would look at the medical record of the case involved in the lawsuit, he would talk to the hospital personnel, he would see the lawyers, and perhaps the injured man. But he definitely would not, at any time, approach the insurance company with a plea for favour!

The day was sunny, and probably cold. The people down on the street walked at a good clip, and those who waited at the bus stop drew their coats close against their throats. Jock stood at the window and watched them while waiting for his breakfast—and he thought of his trip to the city, just a year ago, when he had agreed to stay at the apartment. It had been a wrong thing; it was more difficult to decide things so close to the problem, and to see its relatively unimportant aspects.

This time—

Jock's breakfast came, and he sat down to eat it, determined to concentrate on the food, and the morning newspaper. Surely he had done all the thinking that the issue required.

His father had now been ill for a year. It was just before Christmas last year that his mother had sent for him, and Jock had come at once because the symptoms had sounded like a stroke.

Certainly his father was very ill. Confused, thick of speech, unbearably anxious about himself. What had happened, he asked.

He wanted Jock to say, and yet he would not take his opinion any more than he would take what the staff doctors told him. What was wrong with his eyes? He couldn't focus ...

The staff men were all somewhat relieved to find diabetes. It gave them something to tell Jim, and to work on.

The diabetes, and the eye condition, were only a part of the whole picture. The hospital doctors knew what ailed Jim. They left it to Jock to tell his father, which he found himself unable to do, mainly because he was sure that Jim knew, too, that his arteries were hardening. That he would get over that seizure, and have others from which he would not recover so completely, until, finally—

But Jim took cheer in the diabetes finding, and submitted readily, even with interest, to the diet programme, to the balancing tests for insulin tolerance. His eyes would clear up, he told Jock.

'But I have to make some plans, too,' he told his son. He had consented to use a wheel chair, until he felt better. He wore pyjamas and a handsome blue robe, with a white scarf. 'I'm not fooling myself,' he'd declared. 'At my age, I'd better not. But you're going to have to help me, son.'

'In any way I can,' said Jock. On that trip there had been no discussion of ideas, or Foundations, or Anna. Jock had come home to help his parents, in the back of his mind a plan to move them to California, close enough to him so that he could watch them both, and see them often.

But his father had other ideas, and other

plans. Jock was to come back to Brownlee Memorial, step into his father's shoes, do his work ...

'I'm no surgeon, Father. You know that.'

Jim had waved his hand in dismissal of the protest. 'Barnaby's here to take over as surgical chief,' he said. 'But the hospital—you could be medical director. After you're settled in, substituting for me, I'll step down, and you can take over.'

Jock could have done that. He could have put on Jim Askew's shoes, and walked in Jim's paths. He could have lived and worked again in his father's shadow, with Jim checking each thing he did, advising—controlling each thing. There would be no *changing* Jim Askew's hospital, no shaking up of the staff, no alteration of routine and rules. Still, Jock could have done what his father asked.

Emma had added her plea. She sensed what was in his mind, and she made promises. He'd be given a free hand, she said. His father, as Jock must know, would not be capable even of supervision. Jock could, and should, humour him. Adjustments would be made. The Jim Askews would probably move to a near-by apartment, one with maid and meal service. Jock could occupy this penthouse. His name would mean so much here in the city.

By then his Foundation should be well enough established so that it would run itself. And surely Jock wanted to help his father? To give him a sense of security and satisfaction?

Neither Jim nor Emma—nor Jock—had mentioned Anna.

But he had refused to return to Brownlee Memorial Hospital. And his father had continued, nominally medical director, nominally chief surgeon. Gradually going down hill, physically and mentally.

Jock was sorry. But one man could not live another man's life. Ever. Jock had refused to try to do such a thing, knowing that it was right to refuse, yet grieved and suffering a sense of guilt that he must hurt his parents. Jim had been coldly furious. He would not speak to Jock again before he left for California.

Jock tried to explain his refusal to his mother. She would not really listen to him. 'There's nothing more to say, Jock,' she said coldly. 'You'd better go back.'

She was right. And he had gone home.

On this summons, he had not wanted to return.

But now he was here, with decisions to make again, though his father would no longer be able to direct or advise anyone.

His father now was seriously ill. The hardening of the brain arteries had advanced rapidly. He could die at any minute. He could live for years. Just now he was extremely weak, though he did have his periods of frenzy. Those circumstances would continue, and worsen. Jim Askew's family would need much in the way of patience and wisdom and understanding. They must sacrifice much, and also come to judge the proper limits of sacrifice.

Knowing those things, Jock had spent the past twelve hours doing as his mother had asked, thinking about the present situation and about the events which had led all of them to this critical minute. Now his thinking should be done. He could eat his breakfast, take his walk, and go to his mother with his decision. He would stay long enough to try to dispose of the malpractice suit. Then he would go home.

Jock set himself a two-mile walk. He knew the park well, and its distances. He needed the exercise and, walking briskly, he could smile at his determination not to think any more. He had often marvelled at the suggestion of some hypnotist that his subject make his mind a blank. Jock would make no fit subject for hypnotism. His mind always swarmed with thoughts, associations, memories, and plans.

He could walk away from the hotels and the hospital group and think about the people he passed, the traffic, the fine homes along the park edge. He noted some changes, not many. St. Louis was an old and conservative city. It had grown slowly into pleasant ways, and was content to remain as it was. Pleasant.

But when Jock turned to go back, and the hospital buildings loomed before him against the early morning sky, he'd found himself thinking about his problem, and the solution of it. He wished he had Anna here at his side to listen to him talk, to offer one of her wise, and not-obvious suggestions. Her mind was different from Jock's; his swarmed. Hers was a clear, uncluttered path. She could have helped him now.

What, he wondered, would she say to him?

He tried to imagine a conversation he might be having with her, if she were walking beside him now, wearing her straight red coat, perhaps, with a white scarf over her head. Anna disliked hats, and never looked quite at ease in one.

Her head would be at his shoulder, and she would listen when he said that he had reached his decision. He would not stay. The lawsuit taken care of, he would try to make his parents come to California; he wanted to be near them.

But he would not stay in St. Louis.

And Anna—'But should you stay and do your father's work, Jock?'

He would stare at her.

'Could you stay?' she would ask then.

Jock had considered whether he should stay with his parents; he had thought about not wanting to stay—but the possibilities of staying—

Could he stay?

He had missed his family. Since that first day when he had left his home—and every day since, to some degree—he had missed them. He truly loved his mother and father. More than most grown men did love their parents. Jock remembered, in his earliest work in psychiatry—before that! In his war service, he had been shocked to know that some men tenderly cherished their mothers, some clung to them, some admired and feared their fathers—some hated them. Only the lucky few could honestly know that they loved the man and the woman who had given them life, and had raised their sons to manhood. Jock loved his mother, and he loved his father, and in spite of some unfortunate happenings, he loved them still. He regretted the things that had driven them apart. His success in his work had never wholly compensated for his failure to please his parents—

whom he loved.

'Had you known the separation would hurt, would you have done differently?' That would be Anna's sort of questioning, again, and why shouldn't he answer her?

'I couldn't have done differently,' he would have to say. 'I couldn't have stayed and worked with my father, since I disagreed with him on so many points.'

'Now, if you stayed—'

Yes. Now if he should stay on and substitute for Jim Askew in the office of medical director, Jock might—he *could* do the things that he had wanted to do, years ago.

Brownlee had not changed, though probably both Board and staff felt they had a modern, up-to-the-minute hospital. In 1910, John Brownlee and his family had spent three million dollars on building this hospital—an enormous sum in those days. At John Brownlee's death, and through the years, the endowment had been increased, and the family continued its close interest. John Brownlee, Jr., was now Chairman of the Board. Mrs. Mary Beth Brownlee Hudson, a daughter, was an active member, as was her lawyer son, Brownlee Hudson. They were all jealously proud of the hospital, but the recent investigations made by Jock's team told him that they did not have as good an institution as they thought. Physical improvements were necessary to the patients' welfare, but they were not all that could be done for those same patients. If it were Jock's hospital—

He coughed, and shook his head. What had Anna been asking him? What he would do, if he stayed here, even for a time.

He would make changes in this big hospital. He would fight the family and the Board and the staff—and he would end up with a hospital where the patients would be the first consideration. This hospital would no longer be a 'rat race,' where a lot of patients was the chief aim of the administrative office. It would be a hospital where running those same patients through as swiftly as possible would not be the prime motivation, where—

Jock could make a good hospital out of the physical plant at Brownlee, and he would enjoy doing it. Let him be honest about that!

He would, to be equally honest, like to please his father and his mother if he could in any way. This might be the time and the way to pay his debt to his parents, and no longer feel guilty about having left them.

His mother said that he owed a debt to her and Jim. She reminded him that they had done a lot for him, and they had. Perhaps more than they should, and more than Jock should have taken, but that was not the thing. He had taken those things from them, and the debt existed.

Now, their positions were reversed. Now his parents needed him, and he should at least consider their need.

Of course there were other needs to be considered as well. The claims of Jock's work, the Foundation—and Anna. She needed him, too.

If she actually were taking this walk with him Anna would not mention her need, nor her claim; she would not think it was necessary to mention such things. Since their marriage she and Jock had become so much a part of each other that even their love no longer was a matter of words between them. A brief clinging of their hands, a manner of looking across the room, a warm comfort in being close—Jock knew that he was a lucky man. He loved his wife, and neither doubt nor fear entered into their relationship. Jock could only hope that he had fulfilled Anna's love as completely as she had filled his life. From his first sight of her—

He could always see her as she had looked then. The slender, grave-faced girl in white, standing in the light that glared upon the dance band and the platform, herself cool, quiet, poised, and yet not a wooden figure, not one who didn't feel or care. Far from it.

He could think of Anna in a dozen places and circumstances, he could picture her in a velvet dinner gown, or in the jeans she wore when she gardened, in a ruffled challis robe at bedtime—

And always her steady, grave eyes, her swift, flashing smile, her quiet, vibrant voice.

Her longing for children, her hurt that she had not had a child. Thinking of Anna, and her need for Jock's comfort on that subject, Jock thought now, as he often thought—as Anna too must think—of the children he did have.

He remembered them, and pictured them as he had last known them in the home he had provided for them, Betsy about five, Jamie three. Or, when he reminded himself of the passing years, he imagined them as he had seen them briefly ten years ago. He had been in the city and had gone to the penthouse without warning, and he had found the children with his mother. Then Betsy was thirteen, blonde— though not so pale a blonde as her mother. Jamie was dark like Jock, but except for his mouth and chin he looked like Emma. He was slender, and wore shell-rimmed glasses, and had been frankly curious about this 'other father.' Betsy had been on the defensive with him, and the occasion had not been a happy one for all

197

concerned. Jock decided then that he did his best service to his children by not complicating their lives. Iris had married Pete, and he had come into the children's lives so early that he probably filled all the needs they had for a father. Certainly he had supplied them well with material things. Since marrying Pete, Iris had put Jock's support money into a trust fund for the children. She had said that he need not continue to send the money, but he had continued, getting some small traces of satisfaction out of doing it.

Well—Jock sighed, and waited on the traffic light before crossing the Boulevard to the hospital.

When Jock came up to the apartment, it was something of a let-down to have the nurse tell him that his mother had gone to the beauty parlour. At first, Jock would not believe her. His mother had scarcely left the place since his father's attack.

'I know, doctor, but when she said that her hair needed attention, I urged her to go.'

'Sure,' said Jock. 'It's fine that she would go. What sort of night did my father have?'

'Just fair.'

Jock went in to see his father who tried to talk to him, but the effort amounted to little. Then he sat in the living-room and read the morning paper. He made a telephone call and moved restlessly about the room, deciding that Emma had other irons in the fire than the dressing of her hair. She could have been irritated that Jock had not come to eat breakfast with her, as well as over the way he had left last night without really talking to her.

She came in at a quarter to twelve, asked what sort of morning Jim had had, and suggested that Jock take her to Straub's for lunch. She wanted to buy a few things to have in the kitchen, and suddenly she was hungry for one of Straub's sandwiches.

Jock smiled at her and got his coat. He'd let her play her hand out. When the last card was down, he would tell her what he had to say.

She was pleased to be going somewhere with her tall son; they had not had enough of that particular pleasure, she reminded him. Had he seen the flowers which Noah Green had sent that morning?

'Noah is a remarkable fellow.'

'He is, indeed. He does everything a normal man would do. People stare at him, and he doesn't seem to mind.'

'What would you have him do? Hide in a cellar?'

'No, but wouldn't it be easier if he wore an eye patch?'

'It might be, even for Noah. He is not one to evade an issue.'

That discussion took them to Straub's, and up the circular staircase to the balcony. Graciously, Emma greeted the coloured man who had worked at Straub's since Jock's childhood. Emma ordered a chicken salad sandwich; Jock decided upon soup and a Salisbury steak. They would decide about dessert later. Jock looked down into the aisles of the busy store which served fine meats and groceries to the people who lived in this high-income neighbourhood. Its lunch counter and its balcony restaurant also served the hospital workers, the people who were employed in the various shops and professional buildings of the neighbourhood. There were interesting things to see.

Emma seemed to enjoy their outing, and spoke pleasantly to the various people who recognised her. Jock said something about not having needed his morning's walk. 'I'm getting exercise enough standing up for your friends.'

She smiled at him. 'They're curious about my handsome escort.'

Jock studied her as best he could. This was a direct reversal of the mood she had been in, of piteous resignation to Jim's illness, and the resultant burden it would put upon his family.

Whatever her motives, her behaviour gave Jock an opening to make a move that had been in his mind for days.

'If you enjoy my companionship as much as you pretend,' he said, pouring coffee into his mother's cup, 'would you consider coming back to California and living close enough so that I could see you often?'

She looked at him in surprise and protest.

'You shouldn't ask it that way, Jock,' she told him.

'How should I ask it? I've stated the important part of the arrangement. We'd be close together, and I could see you often. You could live on the grounds of the Foundation if you'd like that, or in the town. It would be very pleasant. Don't try to answer me now, Mother, but I wish you'd think about it.'

'You feel a move is necessary?'

'Some sort of move, certainly. Father is not, and will not, be able to carry on his work. You can't stay in the apartment.'

'No-o. But he could stay in the hospital. You suggested that we move him downstairs.'

'Yes, but that would be only a temporary move. Chronic cases ...'

'Do you think he'll live a long time, Jock?'

'I don't know, dear. I honestly do not know.'

She sighed. 'Right now,' she said slowly, 'I

201

don't think we should make any drastic change. He'd understand a move downstairs, but he would be upset if we'd put him into an ambulance and take him any distance. To take him as far as California might kill him, Jock.'

'Now, Mother—'

'If he knew he was leaving Brownlee, it would mean giving up hope of his getting well. And that—your father wouldn't get over that.'

She was right. If Jim—if any patient—lost hope, and the will to live—

'Perhaps we could suggest a convalescent visit to him.'

'Maybe, when he's better, dear. Just now he has the lawsuit on his mind.'

'Oh, Mother ...'

'He does, dear. I'm sure he does. If you could just reassure him, and tell him that you would take care of that—'

'I mean to take care of it. I have an appointment to talk to Brownlee Hudson this afternoon.'

'But—if you plan to leave very soon—'

'I do, but not before we have this thing taken care of.'

She smiled, and nodded, and turned her full attention to the food on her plate.

Jock ate his own meal, saying nothing about his wish to be in California for Thanksgiving, though he meant to get away by then.

When they finished their lunch, Jock followed his mother up and down the aisles of the store as she made her purchases, some soap flakes, some cheese and crackers. A can of fruit juice— Would Jock like a loaf of pumpernickel rye?

He had a largish sack of groceries to carry when they started back to the hospital. 'Don't speak to anyone,' he told his mother. 'I can't possibly tip my hat.'

'Is that heavy, dear? They would deliver it.'

'It isn't too heavy—just mind the hat tipping.'

She smiled faintly and assured him that people would understand.

They went into the hospital through the main entrance, and the receptionist came from behind her desk to speak to Mrs. Askew. Two doctors also greeted her. Jock rested his bag of groceries on the desk edge, and waited.

'Dr. Askew?' someone said behind him.

Jock turned. Standing behind him was Mr. Armstrong, the Administrator of Brownlee Hospital. He was new in the organisation since Jock's day, and this gave both men an advantage. For one thing, he called Jock by his professional title.

Today he had a problem. First, he asked the usual question about Dr. Jim's condition, and

Jock replied.

'I haven't seen him, of course,' said Mr. Armstrong, uneasily. 'But I wondered if his condition warranted my talking to him for a minute or two ...'

'Do you have problems?' Jock asked kindly.

'Yes, sir, I do. And of the sort that I should take up with the medical director.'

'Does my father have an assistant?'

'Not as director.'

'Well, that does present a nice point—for I'm afraid, Mr. Armstrong, that he is in no condition to deal with any sort of problem.'

'Oh. I am sorry.'

'Yes. Dr. McGraugh is attending him, but I think he would confirm this. I wonder—could I be of any help?'

'Well, you just might. It's a ticklish thing— a matter of one of the staff men giving out publicity on a case, and the family disliking it.'

'Oh, oh,' said Jock. 'Well, of course I'd have no authority, but I'll go into the matter with you, if you like. Just as soon as I take my mother and her groceries upstairs. Perhaps you could have the head of your man's service in your office? And the doctor in question, too. We could all talk it over. I'll be right down.'

He told Emma only that a little matter had come up which his father would ordinarily attend to, but that he thought he could handle.

She was pleased. He had known that she would be. He was committing himself to nothing. But he enjoyed the half-hour meeting. He had learned to read men and deal with them. At the end of the session the Administrator praised him. 'You'd make us a good director, sir,' he said earnestly. 'You get your way without anyone knowing what you're up to.'

'I hope my solution was the right one.'

'I think everyone will be satisfied, and I don't believe we'll have the same trouble again very soon. Thank you very much!'

Jock was glad to have been of help, and glad that his experience and training had fitted him for a satisfactory job. He kept his appointment with Brownlee Hudson, and acquainted himself with the details of the malpractice suit. He would, he promised, look up the medical record, and talk to Dr. Barnaby.

'I am sure there was no negligence,' said the attorney.

'I feel confident of that, too,' Jock said. 'But I want my facts. Then, perhaps, I could approach the patient.'

Brownlee Hudson was a small, neat man, with a smooth, oval head, hair brushed close to his skull, neat, small features, a brown suit and a neat tie. 'I—' he said now, hesitated, then tried again. 'Your father would not consider a settlement on any terms. The hospital feels that the insurance company should be brought back into the case, and under the circumstances, perhaps you are the one to talk to them.'

And eat crow.

Jock took a deep breath, and a second one. Then he spoke quietly. 'I would like, first, to explore the possibilities of fighting the case.'

Mr. Hudson did not twitch a muscle. 'The main objective should be to clear the hospital of blame—and your father, of course.'

'Yes,' said Jock, 'that should be the main objective.'

He returned to the hospital at four, and went upstairs. As he went into the apartment, he was brought up short by the sight of a young woman who sat in the big chair, talking to his mother. Pale blonde hair, alabaster skin— Why, it was Iris!

And she hadn't changed a bit! She really had not. He went over to her at once, and said that she had not changed. It was miraculous!

Iris blushed prettily and said how glad she was to see Jock. 'I dropped in to see Nana,' she said in her soft, breathlessly eager way of speaking. 'But I didn't dream I'd get to see you!'

Jock answered something gallant about the pleasure being his. He didn't believe that Iris had dropped in entirely by chance; his mother was too much of a manager. But it made no difference, really. Jock could sit down and talk to Iris, he could be charming to her as to a stranger, and poised. Now he was a man on his own, and successful.

Iris looked the same—she really did! Though she was almost the same age as Jock, and ten years older than Anna, she still looked like a woman in her twenties. Reason told Jock that effort and money had gone into that effect, but the result was good, so why quibble? She was a pretty, blonde young woman; smartly dressed; she talked easily on her own, and responded brightly to what was said. That was new. Perhaps because of the places she had gone, the things she had done as Pete Henderson's wife, perhaps because she too had grown considerably since Jock had known her. Her parents were dead, and she was no longer shadowed by her possessive mother.

What did it matter? Here she was, a gay and lovely woman, who knew how to talk to a man, and build his ego. She talked vivaciously about Arizona, and California, and earnestly assured Jock that she would accept his opinion that northern California was more beautiful than the southern part.

'I've tried to sell the place to Mother,' Jock confessed, 'but with no luck.'

'Oh, we couldn't spare Nana here!' cried Iris. 'The children would be lost! I came today to invite her to go with me to Betsy's for Thanksgiving Day, but she thinks she can't leave.'

'That's her conscience talking,' said Jock.

'I'd not enjoy myself,' said Emma with dignity, 'feeling that I should stay with your father.'

Iris threw her a smile. 'Of course you wouldn't dear. How about you, Jock? Would you like to go? I'm driving up—I'll leave here quite early in the morning—it's seventy-five miles or so. Not really far as you western people figure distances. Betsy insists that Thanksgiving is a family day, and of course she is right. So Jamie and I are going, and you should go, too! She'd love to have you, and I know you'd like to see Betsy; she is a fine little homemaker. You'd like her husband, and adore the baby.'

Jock sat stunned. Iris was beating him with facts, realities not new to him—he knew that Betsy was married, and even that she had a child, but he had never really believed in those things. 'Why,' he blurted, 'Betsy is only a child herself!'

Emma and Iris laughed merrily. Betsy was twenty-two, they reminded him. Twenty-three next month.

'How old is the baby?' Jock asked groggily.

'Oh, she's brand new. Just ten weeks. And such a doll, Jock.'

He sat shaking his head.

'He can't get over being a grandfather!' cried Iris, laughing gaily. 'And I know how he feels. It took me a time to become used to the fact. But, darling—' She stretched her slender hand towards Jock. 'You're surely the youngest grandfather on record!'

Jock took out his handkerchief and mopped his face. 'I think of Betsy as about six!' he said gruffly.

'She's a very efficient young woman,' Iris told him. 'Much more clever at housekeeping than I ever was. She does all her own work—and she sews! And the baby is just precious, Jock!'

'You really must go to see her, Jock!' Emma insisted.

'What's Betsy's husband like?' Jock asked, beginning to feel cross that so much had slipped past his awareness.

'He's an engineer,' said Iris. 'He works for the Government, building dams or locks or something up the river. They'll be coming back to the city in a few months and are planning to build their own home. Nana, haven't you talked to Jock about the children?'

'We've had his father on our minds, dear.'

'Of course,' said Iris, warmly sympathetic. 'But he could go with me to see Betsy, couldn't he?'

'Yes, of course he could. And you should go, Jock.'

He'd been planning to get back to California by Thanksgiving, which was only two days away. But, yes, he could go with Iris, and get acquainted with his family. With Pete Henderson out of the picture, there would be no strain. And all at once he badly wanted to see his children; perhaps a way could be found to join their lives with his again. So he told Iris that he would go with her.

Emma was well aware that his agreement meant Jock's staying in St. Louis for at least two more days. Without mentioning the fact, she visibly settled into the satisfaction of having him there that long; she mentioned various things which he could do for her, and even let him speak of the lawsuit and of his visit to Brownlee Hudson.

'He's worried about adverse publicity for the hospital.'

'And for your father.'

'Yes. Yes, of course. He thinks we should let

the insurance company do the dirty work for us.'

'Could you talk to them?'

Jock frowned. 'I want to look into the case first, Mother.'

'Jock, you do not think ...'

'I don't think anything. I don't know. I have to look up the case record, and talk to people.'

'Not to your father!'

'Oh, no. Unless he himself should bring it up. But since Barnaby probably assisted in the surgery—'

'You'd save time and effort both, wouldn't you, by going to the insurance people and letting them handle all that investigation?'

Jock glanced at her; he had always known that his mother was shrewd. 'Time is important,' he conceded. 'I can't stay on here indefinitely.'

'Then you must go to the insurance company!' said Emma triumphantly.

'If I must,' said Jock, in a tone meant to close the discussion, 'I shall.'

Jock felt somewhat guilty over letting the trip to Betsy's seduce him into delay. Of course he could change his mind about going, though he did want to see Betsy and Jamie—and the baby—but ...

He went back to the hotel, planning to phone Anna and talk to her about the situation. But when he called he was told that Mrs. Askew could not be located at the moment; did he want a delay-call? No—no, he wasn't sure that he would be in the hotel that long; he would call again.

Now, where could Anna be? Any number of places, of course. She did grocery shopping, she walked in the woods, she visited friends— Had Jock really expected her to sit constantly beside the telephone while he was away?

But still feeling abused—and conscious that he did feel so—he went back to the hospital, and up to the apartment—where a small crisis concerning his father delayed their dinner hour. He spoke again to his mother about moving Jim downstairs. 'While I'm here to help you adjust to the change, dear,' he added.

Emma promised to consider the idea over-night. Did Jock think his father wouldn't know it?

'If he recognises the change for what it is, he'll approve.'

Yes, she supposed he would. 'I wouldn't be able to look in on him every few minutes.'

'Which would give you a little rest, perhaps,' said Jock.

'Not if I'd sit up here and fret.'

'Oh, Mother! Come now. What's happened to your clear eye and your sensible mind?'

That sort of talk consumed the evening, and Jock went back to the hotel at ten feeling tired and discouraged.

He had almost forgotten that he meant to talk to Anna until, putting things from his pockets down upon the table, he came across the number which he had scrawled on the memo pad in the afternoon. Good heavens! He had got involved!

He sat down and thought a bit about what he wanted to say. Now his staying for a few more days seemed to concern his father's problems more than his own wish to see his children.

When the call went through, he mentioned those things first to Anna. His mother would need to make an adjustment. 'I can't persuade her that they should come to California and be near us.'

'Did you expect her to agree to do that?' Anna asked quietly.

'Yes, I did. I thought she'd recognise her dependence on me now.'

'I think she recognises it, Jock.'

Jock frowned at the telephone. What did that mean? He pushed the answer away from him. Not having so much as seen her, Anna understood Emma as well as did her son.

He told briefly of his talk with Hudson. 'I'll need a few days to take care of that sticky matter, though I had hoped to be home by Thanksgiving.'

'And you won't make it,' said Anna.

'Well, no. Because, too—' Then, in a rush of words, excitement quivering in his voice, he told Anna about Betsy, and her husband, and the *baby!* He was going to spend Thanksgiving with them! It was a family holiday, and, boy, had he ever acquired a family!

Sounding thrilled, Anna asked a dozen questions, most of them beyond Jock's knowledge to answer. The baby was ten weeks old, he said, and a girl—but he didn't know its name. He didn't even remember the name of Betsy's husband.

'Oh, Jock!'

'Well, all this struck me—the actual realisation of so much family, you know.'

'And you are excited.'

Jock laughed. Yes, that was one word to describe the way he felt.

'I'm excited, too, and thrilled,' Anna told him.

Jock smiled at the telephone. 'To be married to a grandfather?'

She laughed aloud, and Anna's laughter was

so rare, so sparingly given, that he knew that this event was a big thing to her. 'I'm thrilled to be married to *you*,' she told him, 'and not at all worried about the grandfather part. I think there is probably safety in numbers. I mean years, of course.'

'Why, I'm just at the dangerous age!' said Jock, his spirits lifting.

There was a little more of this sort of nonsense, then Anna concluded the conversation by urging him to have a good time at Betsy's.

'But don't eat too much, Jock, dear. I wouldn't want you to lose the cleft in your precious chin.'

His jaw dropped. 'Wha-at?' he asked.

'I fell in love first with your chin, my sweet,' Anna told him gravely. 'I am not sure that I would even *like* a fat man.'

'Oh, for goodness sake!'

He could *feel* the way Anna's head would duck in confirmation of what she had said. 'But you have fun,' she told him, 'and then call me to tell me all that happened. Good night, my darling.'

'I'll be home soon ...' said Jock, but Anna had broken the connection. Jock sat on in the armchair, thinking about her, and what she would be doing, how she would look at that minute, how she must really feel about his being a grandfather ...

Not his side of it. But the fact of the baby, and of his two children by Iris, when she had not yet given him any child.

Another woman would have been jealous, and resentful, and shown it. Not Anna. There probably were some wishful thoughts in her mind just now, but she was truly thrilled by the baby; she truly wanted to be told about Jock's Thanksgiving with his family.

CHAPTER NINE

Thanksgiving turned out to be an almost springlike day, with moisture condensed upon the roadway, and misty sunshine across the countryside. Iris asked Jock to drive her long, slick car, and he gladly agreed. It was, he said, a selfish but good feeling to get away from the hospital.

'I thought you doctors enjoyed the atmosphere of hot rubber and ether.'

'When at work, we don't notice it. When not at work, we're as restless as a member of any

216

patient's family.'

'I see.'

The day started on an informal note. Iris wore a checked coat over her jersey frock, and no hat. Jamie wore a sports jacket. Jamie was not well, being in the process of recovering from an accident. He didn't want to talk about it, he said, and during the drive Jock respected his wish. The slender, dark boy sat in the back seat, and seemed absorbed in a book. Jock now and then would glance up at what he could see of Jamie in the mirror.

'How badly was he hurt?' he once ventured softly to ask Iris.

'He really doesn't want to talk about it,' she murmured.

So Jock drove on.

The day went swiftly. Betsy's home was a pretty grey frame cottage built on a slope overlooking the river. There was a yellow flower box under one of the windows; two yellow ceramic jars stood beside the front steps.

Betsy was bathing the baby when they arrived; she had dinner under way, she told them. Betsy was a slender young woman, with thick, honey-blonde hair. The baby was a picture child, whose enormous blue eyes gazed calmly out at Jock from under the folds of a pink towel. Betsy's husband was in his thirties; his name was

Stephen Pope, and Jock liked him on sight. He liked Betsy, too, not aware that such an opinion was beyond a proper fatherly feeling.

The day was busy; the baby was put to bed, dinner was set on the table and eaten, Stephen showed Jock the plans for the new house in the city. He had a large desk in the second bedroom, with t-squares and large flat books scattered about.

Jamie sat in the chair in the living-room and continued to read his book, answering questions put to him, but not contributing much to the day. Jock was not sure that he 'liked' his son.

Betsy's home was furnished with items which Jock recognised as being parts of the Desmoyer home, the mahogany table, the silver hollow ware, the Picasso crayon study over the couch, the couch itself.

A lady's home, Jock told himself. His daughter, Betsy, was a lady, as was her mother. Well-bred, graciously at ease. Though she seemed ready to work harder than Iris had to make a home, and care for her child. She and Stephen would make a good thing of their marriage, Jock was comfortably sure. He mentioned the trust fund to Iris, and suggested that it might be used towards the projected new home.

Betsy was delighted. 'Seems you've been a good father right along,' she said frankly, and

Jock laughed, though wryly.

'There's a fund for Jamie, too,' he said, glancing at the boy.

'I'm only twenty,' said Jamie, 'but if Nana can be believed, I've ruined my life.'

He limped when he walked; he was much too thin; but—

'Suppose we talk about that,' Jock suggested.

'Not just now, dear,' murmured Iris, and Jock glanced at her. The wifely term had slipped out without her knowing it. In a swift flash, Jock wondered how Pete Henderson had fitted into such domestic scenes as this one.

'I'd like very much to know what happened to you, Jamie,' he firmly told his son. 'I may not have another chance—'

'Tell him,' Betsy urged. 'It was pretty bad—' She looked intently at Jock. 'What do I call you?' she asked.

'Jock would do,' he suggested. 'If Pete took over my title.'

He was able to be matter of fact about their situation. Iris was inclined to be embarrassed by such details, but the children followed his lead.

'Jock, then,' said Betsy sensibly. 'We were fond enough of Pete, but you're different.'

Iris had gone over to Jamie, and was trying to get him to use a hassock for his foot. 'He was hurt in a plane crash,' she told Jock, seeming to think that a brief account of the accident would suffice, and that the boy need not be asked to dwell on the matter. All day she had been babying the young man.

'How did it happen, Jamie?' Jock persisted.

Jamie looked up in protest, and took off his horn-rimmed glasses. 'I goofed,' he said bluntly.

'Oh? How was that?'

'I was learning to fly, and it proved that when I was ready to solo—I wasn't. I pancaked, and the thing flipped over. Cost Mom four thousand bucks to pay for the plane.'

Iris made cooing sounds of assuring him that the money did not matter.

'Were you hurt too badly to go up again immediately?' Jock asked in a matter-of-fact tone.

Everyone turned to stare at him, and Stephen Pope laughed a little.

Jock's eyebrow went up.

'The kid was in the hospital for six weeks,' Stephen explained his levity. 'And *that* wasn't funny.'

'He'll never get in a plane again!' said Iris firmly.

'Oh, come now. In this day, we none of us can make that plan,' said Jock. 'Are you afraid to fly, Jamie?'

'No. Not with a smart one at the controls.

I—I don't think I want to try again. But I'd go in a plane. Sure. Like you say, I'd have to.'

Iris murmured something, and Jock's eyebrows drew together.

'How badly were you hurt?' he persisted.

'Oh—my knee and ankle were the worst. Both broken. Hip dislocated, a couple of ribs cracked—a slight concussion. It wasn't good, but I don't think I rated all the fuss the women made.'

That last was said with spirit, and colour flamed into Jamie's cheeks.

'You were terribly hurt!' Iris cried. 'And you aren't over it yet!'

'When did it happen?' Jock asked quietly, his thoughts darting among the facts he knew. Iris was babying Jamie, and, yes, 'Nana' would have decided that the boy would never get over the accident. Both had probably deplored the flying adventure ...

'Early this past summer,' Jamie was telling Jock. 'What really made it bad, sir, was that I was ready for my last year in pre-med, and now—well, I suppose Nana is right. I'll have to think of something to do besides medicine.'

'Why?' asked Jock.

'Oh, a cripple hasn't any business starting in on a career that would take a lot of standing on his feet. A man needs strength and—'

'He needs mostly a will to study hard, and work hard, and overcome his own particular handicaps, whatever they are.'

'But, sir—' Jamie was leaning forward, the glasses dangling between his knees. Stephen Pope watched the two men, father and son, but strangers to each other, with their thoughts and opinions to be explored and identified.

'We all bring our own handicaps to the profession,' Jock said quietly. 'Some physical, some mental—or emotional—'

'You're in psychiatry, aren't you, sir?'

'I am. But it took me twelve years after I got my M.D. to find and do the thing I was best fitted to do.'

Jamie looked down at his dangling hands. 'I'd about given up the thought of medicine,' he said slowly.

'I've told him that there are all sorts of fine things he *can* do, Jock!' Iris said eagerly.

'Not if he wants to do medicine,' said Jock, laughing a little. Iris looked at him oddly—lifted head, shining eyes, his face intent. 'And he can do that.'

'I'd need help—' said Jamie uncertainly.

Jock shrugged his shoulders. 'If you need it, I'd think help would be available.'

'Would *you* help me, sir?'

'Of course I'd help you.'

Jamie got to his feet. 'I think I'll go take a walk,' he announced.

'But, darling ...' Iris protested.

'Let him go,' said Jock. And *he* sounded like a husband. Well, he was feeling very much the father at the minute. Jamie, he recognised, was much as Jock had been at twenty. Young, eager, full of plans--if Jock could help the boy get his M.D.—and he could help him! In many ways. The day might come when Jamie would work with Jock at the Foundation, and in time take over the place. He—

Jock bit his lip, and shook his head, then put up his hand to smooth his hair. No! He must not commit the sin of trying to mould his son into his own imperfect image.

Within half an hour Jamie came back from his walk, looking tired, and pale, but his eyes were at peace. He let Iris fuss over him, she urged him to stretch out on the couch—they'd be starting home before long—

And they did start home by dusk. Jock kissed Betsy goodbye, and said he'd see her again. He lifted the baby and cradled her fondly, his cheek down against the small, fuzzy head. In such a child a man held his future in his hand. It was a precious moment.

'Take good care of her,' he told Betsy, putting

the small creature back into her arms. 'There isn't another like her in the world, and won't be.'

Betsy's eyes were full of tears. 'Oh, Jock ...' she cried. He kissed her cheek again, and went out. Betsy and Stephen and the baby watched him drive away.

'How could Mother have ever divorced him for Pete Henderson?' Betsy asked her husband.

'Jock's a man with a mind of his own,' said Stephen. 'Some women can't take that.'

Betsy nodded. 'I suppose not. But I sure can take him as my father!'

The drive back to the city was quiet. Jamie settled into the back seat, assuring Iris that he *was* comfortable. But Iris kept looking back at him from time to time.

Jock drove at a steady pace, thinking back over the day. His heart and mind were crowded with the events the day had given to him. Betsy—he had mashed the potatoes for her, and she admired his skill—a small thing, but such admiration is a father's due, and his reward. He had had a twinge—several of them—of regret for the lost years, the lost experiences with the children. He would keep in touch now, and see them often. He'd watch the baby grow, and Betsy's other children. He'd see their new home built, and lived in. As for Jamie—

Head up and back, he drove along, and Iris watched him, seeing again the forward thrust of his interest. She remembered that he had looked just that way when he was young, and—

'Did you have a good day, Jock?' she asked softly.

'I had a wonderful day!' said Jock fervently. 'Thank you for letting me go.'

'You're so understanding with the children.'

Had Pete Henderson not been?

'You should have been with them all along,' Iris continued.

Jock looked at her swiftly. Iris sat in the corner of the seat, one foot tucked under her. She looked a little tired.

'We all make mistakes, Jock,' she said softly.

'Yes, we do,' he agreed.

'I'm glad you enjoyed the day. Nana says the greatest satisfaction in life lies in one's children.'

Jock made no comment. 'Nana' and Iris, together, had planned this happening. They need not have been so elaborate. He had wanted to see Betsy and Jamie. And there *was* a satisfaction in one's children! He'd agree to that, too.

'I'll drop you at the hospital,' said Iris when they came to the city's outskirts.

Jock could have wished to go straight to the hotel, but she was right. He must go up to see his mother, and his father. He needn't stay—he had promised to call Anna.

Arrived at the hospital, he roused Jamie, to 'take care of your mother, son. I don't want anyone to think she's driving alone.'

Also to tell the boy to come to see him. Soon. 'I'm staying on for a day or two longer—I'm at the Chase. Of course when I go back to California, you could fly out and see me there, often.'

'Yes, sir,' said Jamie. 'I'll do that. I'd like to do it.'

Jock went up to the penthouse and spent an hour telling his mother about his day. She listened eagerly, but shook her head at the things he had to say about Jamie. 'Now, Jock, there is no point in being overly optimistic. That boy nearly killed himself!'

'We'll see,' said Jock. 'Now! I'll look in on Dad, and then go to bed. I'm sleepy.'

'In the morning—'

'In the morning we'll move Dad downstairs. Hmmmn?'

'If things seem right.'

Jock went back to the hotel, suddenly tired, sleepy, and hungry. That hardly seemed likely after the meal he had eaten at two o'clock, but he called room service and had food and drink sent up to him. He undressed, bathed, and settled down. He would have a long gossip with Anna when he got through to her. She must tell him about her day, and he had much to tell her.

The call went through fairly quickly. Anna was waiting for it. She said that she had had guests for dinner—oh, early—about four—and had sent them home before they were ready so that she would be free.

That, said Jock, sounded like true hospitality.

She said that the conditions had been made clear when she issued the invitation.

'But they came anyway?'

'I promised them a wonderful dinner. And it was wonderful. They ate enormously. I won't have enough turkey left over for a good sandwich.'

She told him items of Foundation gossip, and Jock enjoyed that. Anna had a clear-eyed way with gossip; not much escaped her, but she brought to the items no rancour or personal bitterness. If Frances Minter was having trouble getting a hat for her projected trip to New York it was because the hats were absurd, not because of any physical failing on Frances's part.

Anna told about some of the guests at the Unit; she told about Clancy's latest idiocy. 'And now, my dear, tell me how Grandpa got along.'

He laughed at her epithet. No doubt the word had been spread around the Foundation?

'Completely. They are burnishing the wheel-chair to meet your train.'

'Won't need it. I never felt younger.'

'Humph!' said Anna.

'I mean it, my dear. I've a brand new future opening before me.'

'Well, that's nice. Tell me—'

So he told her about the baby, her enormous blue eyes, her sweetness; about Betsy, and the mashed potatoes; but mostly he told about Jamie. He described the boy. 'He's dark—no, he doesn't look like me, except for his colouring. He's very thin, but he's not been in good physical shape—and he cuts his hair in one of those flat-top things. I do think they rob a man or boy of his individuality. He wears heavy-rimmed glasses, but I suspect that he does that partly as a defence.'

'Jock!'

'I am telling you, dear. You see, several months ago the kid was hurt. He was trying for a pilot's licence, small plane, and the thing flipped over. He was thrown out, and his right side was hurt, patella crushed—that's the knee—ankle broken, hips dislocated—he walks with a cane. I'll look up the record on his case tomorrow to see what we have to work with.'

Anna made murmuring sounds of inquiry.

'I am telling you,' Jock insisted. 'Or I shall when I get the thing sorted out in my mind. Let's see, where was I? Oh, yes. Jamie's injury. I think he was pretty well smashed up, but my main effort will be first, I think, to get the boy to talk to me freely.'

'He will.'

'It isn't just like a patient, Anna. The relationship comes between us.'

'Do you think he likes you?'

'I believe I can establish some rapport. It's odd, your asking me that. For when I was first with Jamie today, I decided that I didn't like him. He was broody, and self-centred. Gruff in the face of Betsy's efforts to entertain us. That sort of thing. So I made a real project of finding out how he was hurt. His mother thought he shouldn't dwell on the matter, but I persisted, and discovered that his main injury lay in the fact that he was sure his crippling would knock out his plan to study medicine.'

'Oh!' said Anna.

'Now, what does that mean?'

'That was when you started to like him.'

Jock laughed. 'You're all wrong. That was when I saw what outside forces were working on him. People were telling him that he was an invalid, that his life as an active, able

229

person was over—and the boy was inclined to accept their verdict, and sink himself and his ambitions into a slough of despair.'

'My goodness,' said Anna.

'Well, I feel sort of purplish-prosish.'

'You know, Jock, it isn't much like you to decide that you like—or dislike—a person on sight.'

'I can only remind you again that this was my son, not a patient.'

'And that's different? Yes, I suppose it is. So what did you find to say to him?'

'Oh, not much really. Except to point out that every man went into the study of medicine with some sort of personal handicap, and then to plant in his mind that, with help, Jamie could go on with his studies and get somewhere desirable.'

'You'll have to be very careful, won't you, with that help?'

'I don't understand.' Jock sat frowning at his reflection in the mirror.

'Well, I meant,' said Anna, 'that you'd have to be—*careful!* I was thinking of all your mother did for you, and the obligation she feels you are under because of it.'

Jock still frowned. He could see himself doing it, and he felt like frowning. 'I wouldn't say the two situations were very much alike,' he said stiffly.

'They won't be, if you're careful,' Anna replied.

'I'll certainly try to be careful,' Jock told her. He knew that he was resenting her warning, her feelings that he could—or would—do to his son the things his parents had done to him. Though, of course—

'I've found,' he told Anna, 'that it is only when a child is mature—and that maturity comes darn late, sometimes!—that he recognises the full measure of his parents' efforts for him.'

Anna said nothing.

'But,' said Jock, 'there is a security in the knowledge of the continuity of one's blood. That is what I owe my parents, that security. That too is what I owe to Jamie and Betsy, and now small Lucy.'

Anna still did not speak.

During that entire day Jock had felt the pull between himself and his family as they appeared to him. Betsy's warm response, Jamie's real need—the baby, and what she promised Jock in the way of delight and interest ...

Of course Anna could not share those feelings. She must now be feeling an alien, an outsider. Before Jock could think of something to say to her, she asked him to tell her more about the baby. She wanted details, and Jock gave them to her, though he realised that Anna was jealous of his new-found wealth. She couldn't have a 'precious' baby, named Lucy, with enormous eyes and a well-formed head.

'How is the—the grandfather?' Anna asked, her voice shaking a little.

'Oh, he's in fine shape,' said Jock heartily. 'In fact, he's wonderful. Lonely, but wonderful.'

'I am, too,' said Anna faintly. 'Do you think you'll be home by Christmas, Jock?'

'If not, you must come here.'

Anna said nothing.

'I seem to have many things to do here, Anna. The lawsuit alone will take time. Perhaps it could be defended in court, and won. If not, the insurance company must take over, though I'd not want my name to be used with Corbett to effect a quick settlement favourable to us. But first of all, I must be sure of what was done—you understand that?'

'Ye-es,' said Anna softly.

'Then there's the problem about Father, and now Jamie. It will take time, Anna.'

She did not speak.

'*Anna?*' His voice sharpened.

'I'm here, trying to realise that you want to stay in St. Louis.'

'It isn't a matter of wanting—and you could

come here, be with me.'

'No.'

'Look, Anna—'

But she would not yield to his urging. He tried to persuade her. She need not be with his parents, he said. She need not *see* them! Though she would like Jamie—and Betsy. But she would not agree to come. He could stay, if he wanted to—

'I do not *want* to!'

'Good-night, Jock,' she said in her grave way. And the phone clicked in his ear.

The next morning Jock woke with a vague feeling of dread. He tried to analyse it, and decided that it was partly due to his plan to look up the medical records of the malpractice case, and partly to the move he meant to force his mother to make. Of course it would be hard for her, but with Anna feeling as she did, he could not stay in St. Louis much longer, and the change would be easier with him there to care for the details.

He dressed quickly, and reached the hospital in time to have breakfast with her. That pleased Emma, and she chattered busily to him about a dozen things. Jock listened, commented, and watched her.

'Now,' he said, when the last drop was gone

from the coffee pot, 'I'll go in and see Father—'

'He had a restless night, dear.'

'And so did you?'

'Well—yes. You see, he got out of bed, and—'

'Yes.' Jock patted her shoulder, and went across the hall to the sick-room.

His father was ready to talk a little, in a rambling sort of way. He was not angry, or defensive, and the chart showed that a tranquiliser had been given.

Was Jock taking care of things? the sick man asked.

'Everything is in good shape, Father—'

'Barnaby—'

'Don't worry. Barnaby is taking full care of the surgery department. He wouldn't let me on the floor.'

Jim sighed, and tried to smile, and his eyelids drooped. Jock beckoned the nurse into the hall.

'I'm going downstairs and arrange to have my father moved down to medical,' he told the woman. 'Then I'm going to move my mother to a near-by apartment hotel. The strain of nights like last night are too much for her.'

'Yes, doctor. Will she go?'

'I think so, if I stay around until she's accustomed to the idea.'

'She's lived up here for so long ...'

'It never was a good idea. And, for all we

know, she may enjoy the change.'

The nurse smiled anxiously. Jock told her what to do to get his father ready. 'I'll speak to Dr. McGraugh of course.'

'Yes, sir.'

Jock stuck his head into the living-room to tell his mother that he was going downstairs, and withdrew it before she could do more than look up and get ready to speak. Now that he had started this enormous project, he meant to carry it through.

He walked the length of the surgery, passing the usual carts and their attendant orderlies and nurses; he pressed the elevator button, remembering the day when the elevator had stuck.

Where was that assortment of individuals today? Red Hat, Blue Robe, the man in the brown suit? Did they have any thought of Jock Askew? Then *he* would have said that Jock would be back in California by now. Only—he was not. Frowning, he thought of Anna's stubbornness the night before. But—he did *not* want to stay in St. Louis! Perhaps he should have left by now, but he should have stayed, too. Right at this minute, his mother needed him. And by now, his son did, too. Jock's pulse jumped at the thought of having a son who needed him.

Downstairs, he went first to the Medical

Records library, asked for and got the file on the case for which Jim Askew was being sued. A crushed hand—the initial injury was described, the diagnosis was there—the treatment and progress report—the discharge from care—the prognosis—

The man's name was Maxim Yglesias. He was a migrant fruit picker, and could speak no English.

For a long minute, Jock sat tapping the folder with his fingertips. Then he returned it to the librarian, and went on to the Administrator's office.

Mr. Armstrong said that he was glad to see Jock. He called him 'Dr. Askew,' and Jock noticed that he did. He noticed that he responded to the name, and wondered again at all the changes his father's illness could so quickly make.

'I'll not take much of your time, Mr. Armstrong,' Jock said, 'but I am advising Mother to have my father moved down to a room on Medical. Dr. McGraugh had already suggested this, and she objected. But I think now she is ready to agree to it. Providing, of course, that a room is available.'

'We'll see that one is available, doctor.'

Jock sat down. 'I know you can't keep him indefinitely, a chronic—'

'I believe the Board would want to make certain concessions to your father, Dr. Askew.'

'As my father gets better, or worse,' Jock continued, 'other changes may seem advisable. These cases are distressing—'

'Always, for the family.'

'Yes, and one wonders how much the patient knows and retains. But just now, it seems that my mother rates a lot of our consideration. When my father has a bad night, she has one. The days are not too easy. And—my mother is not young. She is younger than my father, however, and this illness need not kill her.'

'That's true.'

'I've suggested moving them both to California to be near me, but she has refused that completely. So I must make other arrangements here.'

The Administrator waited, not seeming at all busy, or hurried, though reason told Jock that a dozen things must be pressing upon him.

'To move Father is our first step. Then—I am advising Mother to give up the penthouse apartment.'

Mr. Armstrong alertly tightened his attention.

Jock smiled wryly. 'There never should have been such an apartment here in the hospital, sir.'

'Space was not at such a premium forty years ago—Jock.'

'No, it was not. And my father was never one to change his routine or his ideas. So—well, anyway, you'll be getting that space back. I'll establish Mother comfortably close by.'

The Administrator studied his visitor, his face thoughtful. 'These changes will mean tremendous adjustments to your parents.'

'They will. And—could I ask you, just as soon as I get Mother moved—to convert that apartment into something useful to the hospital? To do it at *once!* I used to think a recovery room could be made of it.'

'It could!' said Mr. Armstrong eagerly. 'Right up there at surgery—and we do need one!'

'Yes, you do. I don't see how you operate without one—no pun intended, sir.' Jock was smiling.

Mr. Armstrong waved off the suggestion. He was already making plans for the recovery room.

'I'll stay around,' Jock promised, 'long enough to get Mother settled, not only into a new apartment, but to the routine of going back and forth to visit Father.'

'That would help her,' said the Administrator. 'Er—Jock, this is not impertinence—but is your mother financially able to live in

238

one of the hotels close by?'

'I intend to go into that matter with her. There must be a guardian appointed for Father, and I'm going to suggest a financial manager for them both. I am sure that Mother has not been handling those matters. There are several items which will need my attention. That's why I am staying on. As for your question, sir, she'll be able to afford it, with or without my help. But I truly expect to find that Father has invested his money over the years wisely enough so that she will be taken care of. And he, too.

'For another thing—I am trying to see what can be done about the lawsuit which threatens my father's name.'

'I hope that can be handled,' agreed the Administrator.

Jock nodded. 'Are you familiar with the case?'

'Only enough to make me think that some lawyers have got hold of an ignorant man.'

'Oh?' said Jock, making a mental note.

Mr. Armstrong leaned back in his chair and gazed at Jock. 'I wish,' he said slowly, 'that I could see you move into your father's office, sit at his desk, and direct the medical affairs of this hospital.'

Jock laughed a little.

'You seem to be good at such things,' Armstrong told him earnestly.

'The hospital will need to appoint a new medical director,' Jock agreed, 'but wouldn't Barnaby—'

'Dr. Barnaby is a busy surgeon. I'd like to propose your name.'

Jock shook his head. 'Oh, no, sir! I have my Foundation, and I should be getting back to it. I'll stay here only until I have my parents' affairs settled.'

'But in that time, could I ask you ...?'

'Why, I'd help where I could, sir. If I could. Of course the staff and Board would have to approve.'

'I think we could quickly get their approval. Your reputation is well known for the work you did for the insurance-companies evaluation.'

Jock's eyelids dropped. 'Known, but not popular.'

'Among some of the older men, perhaps. It still was good work.'

'Thank you.'

'Could I broach the matter to the staff?'

'As a fill-in, only while I'm here on other business. If you want me to do that ...'

And so it was done. Within days, Jock found himself acting medical director of Brownlee Hospital. His name went up on the call board. 'Dr. James Askew, Jr.'

Emma was so pleased by this development that it softened most of the rough spots involved in her moving to the hotel. She took her own living-room and bedroom furniture, and her chief comment was that she was enjoying a change in the cooking.

Jock found himself glad to have work to do. His days would scarcely have been filled with the unpleasant tasks of appointing a guardian for his father, and persuading his mother that his school books should be discarded.

He spent two days making a tour of the entire medical organisation of the hospital. One of the older Supervisors said that it looked natural to see Jock with a clip board again. 'But where's your white coat, Jock?'

'Now, look. You're to call me "doctor." I have three white hairs, see?' He bent his head down to show her. 'And I won't be wearing a white coat because I won't be doing any professional doctoring.'

'But why not?'

'I am helping Mr. Armstrong out by being a temporary medical director. And that's all I'm doing. Cramer, do the water jugs get sterilised regularly?'

She stared at him.

'I'll want them sterilised. With steam! And I want it done every day.'

'But they don't get dirty ...'

'They get filthy dirty! I'm sure that any staph infections which we may have could be traced to the patients' water bottles. Now, remember! That's an order. Steam! And another thing. No—dry—mopping!'

Miss Cramer was no longer smiling. She sailed down the corridor, her cap quivering with indignation.

Well, Jock had suspected that there was a job to do. He'd been biting his lips sore to find that everything *was* much the same at Brownlee as it had been when he was a resident there. The routines were the same, and the effects. Dr. Barnaby, a good surgeon, was genuinely shocked to find that Jock would object to a patient's being called the 'ulcer in 24.'

'I not only don't want to hear it,' Dr. Askew said to the men who were making grand rounds that morning, 'I don't want it done. The patient has a name. Use it. He doesn't like to be called an ulcer, or by the number of his room.'

'Do you think that's so important, Jock?' Barnaby asked anxiously.

'I think that it is tremendously important.'

Some of the personnel agreed with him, some did not. But his attitude was so intense that his orders were carried out. At once Jock found himself tremendously interested in the work which he was doing. He told Anna that he was.

'How about that cleft in your chin?' she asked.

'What? Oh. Well, I'm working hard now, dear. No more shining the seat of my pants.'

'Shall I send you some clothes?'

'Oh, no. If I need anything, I'll get it.'

'We miss you.'

'Well, I miss you, too.'

'I hope the hospital appreciates what you're doing.'

Jock laughed. 'The feelings are mixed,' he told her. 'I'm going to establish gripe sessions.'

'Oh, Jock! That's what you did in the Los Angeles hospital, isn't it? You sound too much as if you were enjoying your work! I think you've always wanted a crack at that hospital, and now that you have it I don't think you'll ever come home!'

'Yes, I shall. I'm getting ready to have the hospital staff select its Medical Executive Committee, and when that's working they won't need me as a director.'

'What about the lawsuit?'

'I haven't done much on that this past week, but I'll get that cleared up, too. The man was a Mexican.'

'Is that important?'

Jock laughed. 'It could be.'

Anna was right about one thing. He *was* motivated to stay in St. Louis at least partly because he had been given the opportunity at last to make some changes at Brownlee. He himself had recognised the motivation, and been a little disturbed by it.

But still—if he helped the hospital it would be worth a month of his time.

Setting that month as a limit, he dug in at once, and ferreted out a lot of things, some big, some apparently inconsequential, but all of them amounting to an enormous whole. The personnel were both fascinated and horrified by the things he did, the places he went, the changes he made.

Within his first week, he established his gripe session, and named his Executive Medical Committee which he selected with the help of Mr. Armstrong, and the approval of the Board. On it there was a doctor from each service, but not necessarily men of the same rank in the hospital. They would, he said firmly, draw up their own set of simple rules; they would do it at once. 'While I am here.' And in due time, they would select their own Chief, his term to be decided later.

They would endorse and share in the gripe sessions.

'Just what are those sessions, Askew?' Dr.

McGraugh asked him. He was fascinated by this young man, as firm in his decisions as his father had ever been, but more receptive to ideas and suggestions. In fact Jock listened to everybody. Jim had never been one to allow argument or even discussion.

'Come to a session and find out,' said Jock to McGraugh.

'But how—'

'The first one is set for tomorrow night at seven-thirty. We'll hold monthly sessions after we get established. Tomorrow I'll submit, for the hospital staff's approval, a gripe committee.'

'Where are you going to put all those gold letters?' drawled a young doctor.

Jock smiled at him. 'The letters will spell out "Joint Committee for the Care of the Patient," ' he said softly.

'You can't lose with that,' agreed the young man. 'Who can come?'

'Everyone with a complaint about the way the patients are treated, the hospital run, or— well, everyone with a complaint.'

'Where you gonna put all them people?'

Jock made a note on his pad. That youngster was good material. Name: Dr. Dees, resident in orthopedics.

The gripe committee was organised and Dr. Dees was on it. At first, meetings were held once a week, and the small conference room would be crowded. Dr. Askew sat watchful in an obscure corner. Attending were six or seven doctors, a dozen nurses, and some lay personnel. One of the doctors might frown over a letter from a patient. One of the nurses would make doodles around the page of a typewritten suggestion she wanted to present.

'I've decided that we're here to cuss each other out,' Dr. Dees defined the purpose of the meetings.

'Yes,' said Dr. Askew. 'Sharing your gripes will probably make you find ways to run this hospital more harmoniously.'

'I'm for that!' said a red-headed nurse.

Jock's eyebrow went up.

'No, doctor,' she said boldly. 'Brownlee Memorial has not always been harmonious.'

'That could be because you have not worked as a team.'

'We have not. It's been every man for himself. Some of our doctors treat nurses like uniformed custodians!'

'And I've known nurses,' countered an M.D, 'who treat staff doctors like interfering busybodies who have to be tolerated, but not very well.'

The gripe session was on its way. Jock nodded, and uncapped his pen.

CHAPTER TEN

Those were busy weeks for Jock. The lawsuit, his mother's affairs, and the hospital's, left him little time to think about himself. He was shocked one night to have the ringing telephone waken him about an hour after he had fallen asleep, and to hear Anna's voice ask him if he was all right.

'Of course I'm all right.'

'How should I know? I haven't heard a word from you in a week.'

'Oh, Anna—'

'A week!' she said firmly.

Her husband was shocked, he was contrite. All he could say was that he had been busy.

'I am sure of that. How are things going?'

'Slowly. I've been talking to the hospital personnel about the malpractice case. I can't ask Father, right out, you see.'

'Hadn't the insurance people talked to him?'

'I don't know.' Stiffness cracked in his voice.

'Do you have your father's hospital the way you always wanted it to be?'

Jock began to laugh, then he frowned. 'I have recognised my motivation,' he said slowly.

'Is there something to be troubled about?'

'Oh, no. It is just one of the claims made upon me here.'

'I know. Do you see much of Jamie?'

'I see him often, but seldom for long at a time. I've been busy—but I said that, didn't I?'

'Yes, you did. How is your father?'

'About the same.'

'Don't use doctor-talk to me!'

Jock laughed. 'But he *is* about the same, Anna. And will be. Some days he is more alert, others—well, those times are not good.'

'And your mother?'

'Oh, she is adjusting. She sits with Father twice a day, she has made friends at the hotel who find ways to divert her. Her old friends are being kind. She seems inclined to do a little housekeeping. For instance, she cooks her own breakfast, and mine, if I'm available.'

'And you are?'

'Sometimes. She rates a little extra attention just now.'

'When are you coming home?'

'I don't know. If you would come here—at least for Christmas—'

She said nothing.

'Anna?'

'I don't think I should come to St. Louis, Jock.'

'Aren't you being a little stubborn?'

'Aren't you?'

He gave his head an impatient shake. 'If I seem stubborn,' he said starchily, 'I believe I can rationalise my position.'

'So can I!' said Anna spunkily.

Jock tried to persuade her, to argue his side, and she refused to say more than that she could not, possibly, come to St. Louis. Finally, she hung up, and Jock lay in the half-dark, disturbed by their near-quarrel.

But he couldn't quarrel with Anna! They never had.

Why hadn't he called her? Surely it couldn't have been a week!

He was busy. His mother, the hospital, Jamie—he must see more of Jamie. If the boy didn't come around, he'd look him up. Snapping on the light, he scribbled a reminder on the night table memo pad.

At noon the next day, he called Jamie; Iris talked to him, saying that the boy had not been too well, but that he had these spells. 'I suppose they are to be expected.'

'His medical history indicates that his injuries have healed, Iris.'

'If a thing is down on paper, you doctors

insist it must be so.'

'I thought maybe he'd have lunch with me.'

'He hasn't much appetite ...'

'Can't he come to the phone?'

'Oh, yes. Or you could come here to see him.'

'Yes!' Jock said quickly. 'I'll do that.'

'Right away?'

'Can't I?'

'Yes, of course. I have an engagement, but—'

'I'll come another time to see you.'

'You do that. I'll tell Jamie you're coming.'

Jock approached Iris's home with some odd feelings. He knew in a general way where she lived, a few blocks from the hospital, on a street of fine town houses. Iris's home was one of the older houses, the grounds enclosed within a low brick wall, the entrance marked by urn-topped posts. The old bricks of the house had been painted white; the verandah was at the side, the upper one screened, the lower one paved with mossy flagstones.

The classic white front door opened into a wide and gracious hall; Jock was led up a flight of curving stairs to what was really a drawing-room. Its air was one of eighteenth-century elegance.

'Did Iris and Pete buy this place furnished?' Jock asked Jamie when the boy wheeled into the room.

'I don't think so,' said Jamie, 'but I really don't know.'

'It's a charming house, and this room is beautiful.'

Jamie looked around as if for the first time. 'Yes,' he said vaguely, 'it is.'

Jock brushed his hand across the mahogany table, noted the dull-green damask couches which flanked the marble fireplace. There was a handsome mahogany highboy, a drum table—two crystal chandeliers—several armchairs in red and white toile print—a reading table with a book of old prints open upon it.

As he came back to sit on the couch, Jock touched the wheelchair. 'Why this?' he asked his son.

'Mother thinks I'm under less strain when I use it.'

'Do you need it?'

'Oh, no. But I do all sorts of things because she wants me to. Nana got this chair for me.'

Jock made no comment. 'I thought you might like to eat lunch with me, then go to see your grandfather.'

Jamie looked interested. 'At the hospital?'

'That's where he is. We could eat lunch anywhere.'

'I don't have much appetite.'

'I do. I am ravenous for one of the Chase's

shrimp salads.'

Jamie looked up alertly. 'They do make good ones!'

'Let's go get one.'

But Jamie looked troubled. 'I promised Mother not to overdo.'

'With a doctor at hand, how can you get into trouble?'

Jamie laughed a little, got up out of the chair, and walked, limping, across the room. 'I'm getting my coat,' he explained to Jock.

While he waited for the boy to return, Jock looked at some Dresden figurines.

Jamie had his own car, and they used it. The salads were like bouquets, with a circle of pink shrimp set into petals of tomato sections, all surrounded with a ruffle of lettuce. The dressing was perfect. They talked about the prospects for the Hawks that year, and the idea that St. Louis might get pro football. They went to the hospital, and up to see Jim Askew, who recognised Jamie, and wept a little, which embarrassed the boy. But he handled the matter well enough. Jock stayed around. And when the visit was over, he took Jamie down to his office.

'I'm sitting in for your grandfather while I'm in town,' he explained. 'Have a chair while I look through this mail.'

Jamie 'had a chair,' and after a few minutes Jock glanced at the boy who had been gazing at him fixedly.

'Something wrong? Mayonnaise on my chin?'

'No, sir. I was thinking about you.'

'And?' Jock tilted back in his chair. He so wanted this boy to *talk* to him!

'Yes, sir. The way you were with Grandfather upstairs. He's very bad, isn't he?'

'Yes, Jamie, he is. It is hard for us, too, to see a strong man fall to pieces.'

'Well, that's what I meant, sir. You didn't seem at all—well—revolted.'

'I wasn't revolted. He has lost his ability to control some of his reflexes. So he drools a little, and his nose drips. He speaks fuzzily, and without much control of what he says. But those are physical symptoms of cerebral arteriosclerosis, much as your stiff knee and bothersome hip are symptoms—signs—of your skeletal injury.'

'Yes, sir. But—'

'Your injuries are not revolting,' Jock said gently. 'But they disturb many people. Don't they?'

Jamie thought about that. 'Other than me, you mean.'

'Of course. You're not disturbed at all, any more. You're used to the situation, you've accepted it.'

Jamie nodded. 'Then you are talking about Mother—' He glanced at Jock questioningly.

'Mhmmmn. And me, when I first saw you. The nurse upstairs who tried to help you today.'

Jamie nodded. 'I see the likeness. And you're the same about it as you were with Grandfather. You—you were so *patient* with him, sir!'

Jock sat for a minute, not speaking.

'I'm a doctor, son,' he said at last. 'And a doctor who deals with death for any length of time learns that, however long an illness may last, it is a small part of the eternity which awaits. One can afford to be patient.'

Jamie sat back, digesting this thought. 'You are the most *understanding* person I have ever known!' he blurted. 'I wish I could always be around you!'

'You're my son.'

'And I'm glad of that!'

Jock smiled. 'But you are a person in your own right, too, Jamie. You know that.'

'I used to know it.'

'You still know it.'

'Mother ...'

'I know about your mother. I know about all mothers. I presume you're familiar with the phrase "the silver cord." '

'Yes, sir. I consider it a foul idea.'

Jock laughed. 'It isn't, really. Often it is a beautiful idea.'

'Not when the thing strangles you.'

'No. Then it is not beautiful.'

'I love Mother, and I want to please her.'

'Of course you do.'

'She didn't have an easy time with Pete, you know,' said Jamie bluntly.

Jock lifted his hand. 'Don't tell me.'

'But—'

'I was to blame for some of your mother's hard time, you know.'

'I'll bet many times she's wished that she could have your dependability to lean upon!'

Jock said nothing.

'Well—anyway,' Jamie continued, 'ever since I had this accident, it's as if I'd gone back to being a very small child. She hardly wants me to go out of the house alone. And as for my future—I can't see that she wants me to work towards anything! She knows that medicine is out of the picture. She—'

'I'll try to talk to your mother, Jamie, if you like.'

'Would you? Oh, would you?' He leaned across the desk, his manner and voice intent.

'Yes, of course I'll do it. When she said she'd not be at home this noon, I told her that I would come to see her.'

Jock went on with the work of the afternoon, Jamie listening, watching, going with Jock whenever he left the office, and returning.

At four the boy was tired, but happy. 'I feel as if I'd had a day at the circus,' he told Jock when he dropped him at the hotel.

'There are any number of other days. Now. You go home and let your mother fuss over you. I suspect you are tired, and that a hot bath and dinner in bed *would* fix you up. I'll see Iris in a day or two. Tell her.'

'I'll do that. And I'll see *you*.'

'Yes. Certainly.'

Jock watched the small, low car disappear into the traffic, then, shaking his head, he went into the noisy lobby of the hotel. He'd see Iris no later than tomorrow, and as many times after that as it would take to get the woman to be sensible about Jamie.

Late the next afternoon, he did go to see Iris, but within five minutes other callers came in, two smart 'young' women in pretty hats and mink stoles. Their eyes brightened, their low, well-bred voices quivered a little to find him there. After fifteen minutes, Jock left, a glint in his eye when he told Iris good-bye.

'Would you have dinner with me tomorrow night?' he asked. 'I thought perhaps the Boulevard Room?'

She agreed, and he departed, able to smile at the imagined flurry which he left behind him in the Georgian drawing-room.

The next evening Iris wore her own mink stole, her hair like pale sunshine about her head. She was lovely and Jock both saw her as she was and remembered as the girl he had once loved and married.

She talked gayly to Jock about the women he had surprised yesterday, the new Women's Exchange shop, and the latest word about Betsy's baby. Jock listened to her, and considered the changes in Iris since he last had known her. She was now definitely her own woman, freed from the shadow of her girlhood restrictions and her parents' ideas. She seemed sure of herself as a person. Remembering what Jamie had said about Pete, Jock wondered how much of this new poise had come to Iris since Pete's death.

In Iris's eyes, he wondered, had he changed as much as she had? He'd like to ask her that some time.

That night, a large party was being held in the Gold Room, and the hotel lobby was crowded with formally dressed people. As Jock guided Iris towards the Boulevard Room, she stopped several times to speak to friends, introducing her companion simply as 'Dr. Askew,' and trying to keep the conversations brief. But when one especially loquacious old lady detained her, Jock stood aside, his eyes travelling about the lobby, noticing the people and their ever-fascinating ways.

Within minutes his eyes fell upon a big-framed announcement of the entertainment being offered in the Boulevard Room—a singer, a blonde girl in a tight black dress, very bare—and a composer-pianist. Jock made a slight sound of surprise, and walked towards the gold-framed poster.

Luke Fogarty! Of all people! But there he was—two views of the man, where one would have sufficed. Certainly he was no beauty! But he was a well-known performer, and Jock supposed that he rated two pictures. One was a study of his face, the other a view of him seated at the piano. Sardonic, thin as a pipe cleaner—

He went back and touched Iris's arm. 'Shouldn't we be getting something to eat?' he murmured.

'Oh, I am sorry!' she apologised. She said something gracious to the old lady, and tucked her fingers through Jock's arm.

As they passed it, Jock looked again at Fogarty's picture. Would the guy remember him?

'What are you staring at, darling?' Iris asked,

seeming amused. 'That girl?'

'What girl?'

'On the poster, dear. The one with the open smile.'

Jock laughed. 'No, I was looking at the man, believe it or not. He reminds me of someone I know.'

'Oh, that's Luke Fogarty. He's marvellous. He composed "Sunbeams," you know, and hundreds of other hit tunes.'

'Yes. I know,' said Jock, following Iris towards the dining-room.

Jock seated his companion so that she could see the piano. The green and gold Boulevard Room was becoming to her silver-gilt beauty. The golden candelabra gave a soft light and little points of sparkle to the scene. Jock ordered their dinner, and a cocktail, and the girl singer appeared.

'Turn around, Jock,' Iris urged him. 'She's cute.'

'Is she wearing the black dress?'

Iris laughed. 'No, but the white one isn't bad.'

Jock glanced over his shoulder. 'I'll wait for the black one.'

The blonde girl sang three songs, and Jock sipped his cocktail, looked at Iris, and beyond her at the other people in the room. He wished that the lights were brighter so that he could more clearly see the murals of old St. Louis, then withdrew the wish, for if the lights were brighter, Luke Fogarty would have a better chance of seeing *him.*

'I act like a man conducting shady business,' Jock told himself, welcoming their fruit compôte.

'I think Jamie wanted to come with us tonight,' Iris told him.

'Well, he could have.'

She pouted her lips a little, took a strawberry upon the tip of her spoon. 'He has a tremendous crush on you,' she told Jamie's father.

'That's nice. Now, I am sure you should have let him come with us.'

'I will let him, another time. But tonight—I wanted to talk to you about Jamie, Jock. I'm afraid you are leading the boy along a primrose path, my dear.'

Jock choked, coughed, and reached for his water glass. 'Wha-at?'

Iris laughed. 'Oh, not that primrose path! But, darling, you *are* encouraging him beyond all possibility of fulfilment, and I want you to stop it. He's had enough in the way of disappointment.'

Jock looked intently at Iris. 'What *are* you talking about?' he demanded.

She glanced up in genuine surprise. 'But, you know—the way you encourage him into thinking that he might study medicine.'

'Oh, that,' said Jock, beginning to eat again.

'Yes, that. Because, of course, Jock, he can't do it. And he must not try to do it.'

'Why not?'

Iris regarded him in exasperation. He was the picture of calm. Straight-gazing brown eyes, firmly held mouth, determined chin, even the quiet of his strong hand. 'You *know* why not!' she cried. 'He's been hurt! He'll always be a cripple! He's extremely nervous, and—'

'Iris!' Jock broke in. 'Jamie is now twenty, but he's still a boy to you. Have you considered what it will be like when you are seventy, and have to coddle and entertain—and endure—a "boy" of forty-five? A boy as old as I am now.'

Her pretty brows drew together. 'I don't know what you mean.'

'I mean this: if you wrap Jamie in cotton now, you'll have to live with the results.'

'But—'

'He's been injured, and he will always walk with a limp; perhaps he will have to limit the time he can be on his feet. He can't run, but he can walk quite well. He can't pole vault, but I imagine he swims with ease. What I am getting at is this: Jamie has his whole life before him, and he should be allowed to live it for himself as best he can. Part of his nervousness could be due to the frustration he knows, and that you want to doom him to know.'

'But, Jock, your father says a man must be physically strong to be a doctor.'

'Does Jamie want to be a surgeon?'

'I don't know what sort of doctor he wants to be. But even the study of medicine will be too much for him.'

'You're sure of that?'

'So would you be, if you weren't blind.'

'I hope I am not blind.'

'You want him to be a doctor because you're one!'

'I hope that has nothing to do with my wanting to help my son realise his ambition in life.'

'Your word would bear great weight with him, Jock.'

'Then I must be careful what I say, mustn't I?'

'Yes, you must,' said Iris tensely. 'Oh, Jock, please?'

He smiled at her. 'Here's your chop, dear—and I think your "Sunbeams" man is going to play.'

He managed to avoid any further discussion of Jamie that evening, though Iris tried to open the subject several times. They ate their dinner, and listened to Fogarty, who was very good, and who played enclosed in a cone of blue-white light which would probably prevent his seeing anyone more than ten feet away.

Iris enjoyed him very much; and she was only mildly reproachful that Jock, when he took her home, would not promise to help Jamie in her fashion.

'I don't want any part of shaping a man's life,' Jock assured her.

'But that's the point,' said Iris earnestly. 'He isn't a man.'

'He's going to be one sooner than you think,' said Jock, opening the door of her house, and running down the steps to his waiting taxi.

He went to the hospital and checked on his father, and, back at the hotel, he decided to call Anna and tell her about seeing Luke. If she asked him if he'd talked to Luke, and he said that he had not, she would have other questions. Smiling wryly, Jock waited, and waited.

'Mrs. Askew is not available,' the operator said at last. 'Shall I try again later?'

'No,' said Jock. 'Thank you.'

Was Anna refusing to talk to him?

Troubled by this idea, Jock made an effort to turn his thoughts to the problem of his son. Hands off was not going to be good enough. But just how much could a father do? How much should he do?

Had Jim Askew ever pondered such questions about *his* son? Probably he had. Truly, as a man grew older he came to see his parents more clearly, and more justly.

CHAPTER ELEVEN

The next afternoon, Jock was on the pediatrics-orthopedic ward when his signal came in over the intercom. He was slow in recognising it, and the intern called his attention to it.

Jock grinned at the little boy in the nearest fracture frame. 'I'm an absent-minded old geezer,' he told the child.

'Your hair isn't grey,' said the child, grinning back.

'Any day now,' Jock told him. 'Any day.'

What has he got to smile about, Jock asked himself as he went towards the nurses' station. Out of doors, other little boys were skating, or belly-whopping down Art Hill. He was in the hospital, trussed and weighted—and yet he smiled.

There was an urgent outside call for him, the

nurse said, and Jock took up the phone, spoke gruffly into the black mouthpiece.

'Oh, Jock!' It was Iris, her soft voice relieved. 'You are so *hard* to get.'

'What's wrong?' Something had happened to the baby.

'It's Jamie. He's in one of his moods ...'

'What sort of moods would they be? Don't get so excited. I can't understand you.'

'I'm so upset. Well—he gets angry, Jock. And he smashes things. I thought maybe you could talk to him.'

'Will he talk to me?'

'Oh, I'm sure he would. He's locked in his room, and he won't answer me. But if you'd come—'

Jock looked at his watch. 'What happened, Iris? To set him off?'

'Oh, it takes just nothing. I talked to him a little at lunch—and—come over, Jock, and I'll tell you about it.'

'I'll be right over,' Jock said quietly.

He spoke to the floor nurse; he went down to his office and checked with his secretary; then he checked out of the hospital, leaving Iris's phone number.

Not for the first time, he realised his need for a car. His father had not kept, or driven, a car for over a year. Today a light snow was

265

falling, and Jock walked a block and a half before he found a taxi. His topcoat was not warm enough—a chill and pneumonia would help very few people!

He was in something of a mood himself by the time he reached the tall house behind its brick wall. A red-ribbon-tied branch of holly hung from the brass door-knocker. Jock pressed the bell and waited.

Iris herself opened the door, her eyes wide, her blonde hair straying a little from its usual smoothness. 'Oh, Jock!' she breathed gratefully. 'I'm so *glad* you were close.'

Jock dropped his coat and hat upon a chair, and looked around. 'Where is Jamie?'

'He's still upstairs. His room is on the third floor. Let's go in here for a minute.' Iris led the way to a small, wood-panelled room. A fire burned behind a brass screen, and the chairs were of dark red leather. There were book-shelves, a TV set, a portrait above the fireplace.

I'll bet it's called the den, thought Jock, then kicked himself mentally. He was in this house to *help!*

'Would you like a drink?' Iris was asking him.

'You sent for me to help Jamie,' Jock reminded her, 'though I wonder how I could.'

'The boy seems ready to listen to you, Jock.'

'Shouldn't I go up to him, then?'

'Well, I thought we should talk about it a little first, plan what to say, you see, and—'

Jock sat down. 'All right, Iris,' he said patiently. 'Tell me what happened, what's wrong.' He was not going to let her put words into his mouth.

Iris perched on a big, square ottoman, and the firelight shone prettily on her pale hair. She wore a full-skirted dress of silk printed in brown and turquoise blue. Her hand played nervously with the strands of blue beads around her throat.

'Oh,' she began slowly, 'perhaps the whole thing will sound childish to you, Jock. But it was really bad when it was happening. Poor Jamie. This terrible accident has been so frustrating for him. He can't go to parties; he can't skate, or dance—'

'Does he like to do those things?' Jock must remember that he had no knowledge of Jamie as he had been before the accident. How he looked, the things he did, his virtues and faults—

'He loved to skate,' Iris was saying, 'and he was very good. When he was fourteen he planned to be a professional hockey player. Pete laughed at him. Though he skated well, Jamie didn't weigh a hundred pounds, soaking wet.'

Jock said nothing.

Iris's cheeks pinked a little, to realise, be-latedly, that she had mentioned Pete. She'd been careful about that, before.

'Just what happened, today?' Jock asked, glad of his long training in keeping his reactions locked behind his face.

'Well—' Iris clasped her hands around one knee. 'He got angry, you see, and he raced upstairs to his room. And he smashed things. He threw books, and even smashed his micro-scope, which, I'm sure, is his most prized possession. He ground slides and things under his feet, and when I tried to stop him, he pushed me out, and locked the door. He's been up there ever since. And—well—' She fumbled for a handkerchief.

'What set him off?'

'Well—we were eating lunch—and he was dressed in a suit and tie, and I asked him why. Usually, you know, he goes about the house in slacks and an old shirt, a sweater. But today—

'And he told me he was planning to go to the Medical School this afternoon to find out what courses he still lacked to complete his pre-med work, and to see if he'd have a chance to get into Medical School— Oh, it was all non-sense, of course.'

Jock leaned forward to take a candy out of a dish on the low table; he was meticulous about unwrapping it.

'And I decided,' said Iris firmly, 'that the time had come for me to have a sensible talk with Jamie. He can't ever study medicine, and he should face that fact.'

Jock popped the candy into his mouth, and straightened. He had been watching Iris as she talked. She had grown in poise and self-assurance, but she still was the always-sheltered woman, with the instinct to shelter her loved ones in turn.

'I'm only trying to save Jamie more hurt,' she said earnestly. 'He'd start these courses, and not be able to go on— It's better for him to realise now that he cannot study medicine.'

'But why can't he, Iris?'

She stared at him. 'Why, Jock ...'

'What do you know about studying medicine?'

'I—'

Jock nodded, and crunched the candy strongly between his back teeth. 'Yes,' he said, 'you've been married to two doctors. But you never knew what it took to do my work, what I put into it. Did you know any more about Pete?'

Iris's blue eyes widened, and darkened. Tears welled and she dabbed at them with her handkerchief. 'I didn't think you would ...'

Jock stood up, and came over to pat her

shoulder. 'Don't cry. Now. I came over here to see what I could do for Jamie, so I'd better get at that business. I'm needed back in the office.'

Sniffing daintily, Iris stood up. 'I'll take you upstairs.'

Jock pressed her down again. 'I'll find him for myself. Third floor? O.K.'

Jamie's room, he found, was a long, light apartment across the whole front of the big house. A fracture bed stood out from the wall; there were bookcases and stacks of magazines; there were evidences of a dozen hobbies—stuffed birds, a miniature railroad system at the far end of the room; and glass shelves which, now, were stripped clean of the bottles, test tubes and beakers which they had held. His hands in his trouser pockets, his shoulders hunched, Jamie was standing at one of the dormer windows when Jock came in.

'I thought she'd get you here,' the boy said, not turning.

'She was frightened about you, Jamie.'

'I know. But—well—I had to smash things. It—I know it won't help—but I'd reached the point—'

'Didn't it help?'

'At the minute, maybe. But now I'm sorry.'

'Mhmmmn. Microscopes cost a lot. And

you'll need to get another one.'

Jamie's eyes slid towards Jock. 'What for?' he asked sulkily.

'Weren't you planning to go over to the Medical School this afternoon to ask about courses? If you'll drive me back to the hospital, I'll take you to the Dean.'

Jamie turned full about to stare at his father. 'Do you think I *can?*'

'See the Dean? Well, I'm reasonably sure that you can.'

'I meant—'

'Study medicine? There I think you can only try.'

Jamie smiled. 'And how I'd try!' He limped across the room to get his coat. 'I'll clean up this mess when I get back,' he told Jock, locking the door behind him.

Jock took the matter-of-fact line. On the short drive to the Medical School, he talked to the boy about his possibly renting a car. Even for a week or two, he'd find one useful.

Jamie seemed relieved at the treatment. The poor kid had been living under a lot of management and restrictive tension.

They went into the school; the corridor was busy with students; the Dean could see Dr. Askew and his son, and they went right in, Jock watching Jamie, Jamie watching Jock, and the way he had with these people—the way the students had looked at him, the way the Dean treated him now, calling him 'Jim,' then changing it with a wry smile. 'We miss your father,' he said.

'Of course. And here is still another James Askew for you. We call this one Jamie.'

The Dean rose and extended his hand. 'I didn't know about this one,' he admitted.

For the first time Jock wondered if his children had been using Pete's name. There had been no adoption. He had refused his permission for that. Slow anger began to rise in his blood, and he pushed the feeling away. Briefly he told of Jamie's recent accident and the interruption of his plans to study medicine.

The Dean was properly concerned and regretful.

'And our problem is ...' said Jock, stating the problem clearly and concisely. Jamie watched him in envious wonder. If he could ever be so sure of himself!

'Why,' said the Dean, 'I should think most of your difficulties could be cleared up, Jamie. Why don't you go out to the University where they have your records, and lay down a course of study? Even if you can't complete your B. S. requirements by the time classes begin here next fall, you probably could qualify to enter.

I presume your record is satisfactory?'

Jamie's sallow cheeks coloured hotly. 'Yes, sir,' he said. 'I—made good grades usually. And a lot of my scientific credits are already taken care of. This past six months I've been studying German with a tutor. I think I could pass that exam without more work.'

'Good! I'll call the University and talk to the Dean there about you, and put in a good word for the Askew family. Of course, Jock, you'll be in my debt.'

Jock's pointed right eyebrow angled up still farther. 'What can I do for you?' he asked.

'How about—say—three lectures to the medics?'

'Three! You want me to go bankrupt, man? I'd pick my brain dry to give three lectures.'

'Mhmmmn. But you're just about that much in debt.' The Dean winked broadly at Jamie, who still sat there fascinated. 'I want you to talk, one, on the reasons behind malpractice suits. I want you to talk, two, about your Foundation, and the idea behind it. I want you, three, to give us something on psychiatry.'

'You've better psychiatrists on your own staff, sir.'

'Better maybe, but you're different.'

'Now that's a thing to say to a man. When do you want all this lecturing done? I'm leaving the city by Christmas.'

Jamie looked at Jock in alarm.

So did the Dean. 'You can't do that,' he said. 'Can you?'

'If not, there won't be any Foundation for me to talk about.'

'Well, we'll arrange something. Now, Jamie, I hope we'll be seeing you for the fall term of medical school.'

Jamie gulped.'You think I might get in?'

'Did you have your application in here before you were hurt?'

'Yes, sir, but—'

'I know. You hadn't heard from us. And you had another year to go in pre-med. You still have that year.'

'But—' Jamie swallowed hard. 'What about my—well, my limp, sir? Will it interfere with my getting into medical school?'

'You use a cane?'

'Usually,' Jock spoke up. 'And perhaps always will. But physically he's in good shape. He has a good mind, and a true interest in the profession. I've been giving him pep talks to the effect that a physical handicap can be overridden.'

'Jock's been a wonderful boost to my morale,' Jamie said shyly.

'I'm sure he has been,' said the Dean, rising.

Father and son said thank you, and good-bye,

274

and left the office.

'I have to go back to my desk, Jamie,' Jock said when they were out in the corridor. 'It's too late for you to go to the University today, but you should be sure to go tomorrow morning. The Dean will have phoned, and you should consolidate his efforts at once.'

'Yes, sir.' Side by side, the two men walked along the hall, out of the building, and across the parking space to the back door of Brownlee Memorial.

'I'm anxious to begin to study,' Jamie said. 'There won't be anything concrete to do until the semester starts at the end of January, but I might be able to take that German exam. And what with summer school— Oh, I do hope I'll be entering Medic in September!'

'It's up to you that you *do* enter!' Jock said sharply. Then he turned to look at his son. 'I'm sorry,' he said impulsively. 'I shouldn't sound so much like a father.' He had sounded like his *own* father, twenty years ago.

'Why not?' asked Jamie. 'Is that bad? I rather liked it.'

Jock smiled. 'It need not be bad,' he conceded.

'I don't understand, I guess.'

Jock nodded. 'I hope you will some day. Though it is always difficult, and often impossible, to bridge the gap between father and son. A man likes to project himself into his son, make the decisions, guide the young life—and of course the young man wants to guide his own life.'

'But you will work with me, won't you?'

'Only if you want me to, Jamie. That's to be an agreement between us, that I'll go only so far as you want me to on this great project.'

'Do you think I'll make it, Dad?' The name came out without either man realising it. Later Jock was to remember, and cherish the manner of its happening.

He managed to impress Jamie with his interest before the boy went home. 'You clean up the mess in your room,' Jock told him. 'That should take the rest of the evening. And when you go to the University tomorrow, get a list of the books and equipment you'll need for the courses you'll be taking. You can buy them, and start studying. Perhaps my vast experience will help you there. Do you have a stethoscope, Jamie?'

'No, sir, I—'

'Then it's going to be my privilege to get you one. We'll shop for it when we get your new microscope. And for Pete's sake, kid, don't have such expensive tantrums again!'

Cheeks red, Jamie laughed, and promised to

be careful. Jock sat on, thoughtful, for a minute after the boy had left. He'd make out—and Jock would help him. But he would let the boy choose the way! His main pride should be in the fact that Jamie seemed a lad able to make his own decisions.

It was incredible how the days swept along, taking Jock with them. Betsy came home to visit, planning to stay over Christmas. Stephen was doing field work, but he would be in the city for the holiday itself. Meanwhile Betsy and the baby moved into her old rooms on the third floor across from Jamie's quarters.

Jock went to the house often, alone or with his mother. The baby really gave her a lift. She wanted to take the infant to show to Jim but Jock vetoed the suggestion. 'When he gets better ...'

'Oh, Jock, will he ever be better?'

'I don't know. He could be.'

He gave her what assurance he could; he stayed close to his mother, and was glad of the diversion which the baby made. It was good for the family to be together, natural. It was the very meaning of life, this building towards the future.

Very soon, Jock had another talk with Iris about Jamie, and it turned into a very good talk.

She would try to do what Jock wanted, she promised. 'I know now that I can trust your judgment, Jock.' She gazed into the fire. 'I wish that I had always known that,' she murmured. 'It would have saved us all so much.'

They were sitting in the wood-panelled den; the young people had gone upstairs, and Jock must soon be going back to his hotel room. The house was full of the small, remote noises of its family members moving about. A distant door opened and closed, something heavy thudded to the floor. Close at hand, the fire rustled softly behind the brass screen, and there was a faint, pleasant perfume from a bowl of white flowers on the desk behind Jock. Iris wore a hostess gown of dull blue, girdled with a chain of silver links. Her pale hair was drawn back from her face, and held by a carved silver barrette.

'I wish ...' she said dreamily, gazing into the fire. 'I wish—Is it too late to go back, do you suppose?'

Jock turned his head to look at her. 'Of course it's too late,' he said gruffly.

The best they could hope to do was to patch up holes, and pick up broken pieces. Although, if they had been able to talk, fifteen years ago, as they were talking tonight—

'It would please your mother tremendously,'

Iris was saying, still in that dreamy manner. 'And if your father knew ...'

Jock shifted in the big leather chair. 'He knows enough,' he said deeply. 'Things don't stay with him, but he *knows*. Last week he couldn't place me, and didn't know who I was. This morning he talked to me quite lucidly about insurance papers, and some bonds which he'd bought.'

Iris turned to smile at Jock, and she looked exactly as she had done as a young wife. 'Perhaps,' she said softly, 'you and I, Jock, could bring about a change in him. I mean, if he knew that we were all together. You—*we*—have brought him many hours of unhappiness. If we could wipe those away, maybe he would know it, and—'

'It's a fine thought,' Jock told her. 'Mental peace does mean a great deal to a man in Father's condition.'

That same day, Jim had mentioned the malpractice suit. Had those damned spigs dropped the fool thing?

Jock had spoken reassuringly, though he himself had no assurance. He had made an effort to talk to the man whose hand had been injured. But 'those damned spigs,' through their lawyer, and then in person, had refused to see any Dr. Askew.

There was more to this lawsuit than appeared in the brief, and Jock was troubled.

He was troubled about everything concerning his father's condition. It was a daily renewed grief for the sick man's son to look upon helplessness where there had always been great strength. Trying to fill Jim's position in the hospital, making a dozen decisions a day, Jock must listen to the many echoes of the decisions which his father had made, and would make now if he were able. Stopping in to see the sick man, Jock would stand and look at his father and think how opinionated he had used to be, how sure that every decision of his was right.

One day in staff meeting, someone pointed out that Dr. Jim's policies had differed from Jock's.

'Wonder how your father would react if he knew you were serving as Medical Director?' Dr. Brandt asked thoughtfully. 'As I recall, he tried to guide your feet, but you've strayed from the path pretty far, haven't you, Jock-o?'

Jock made a real effort to keep his face unchanged. In med school days, Brandt had been his tormentor. 'I have told my father that I am filling in for him,' he said quietly.

Brandt lifted his shoulders in a shrug. 'Personally, I am glad you are different, son. I don't think much of continuing dynasties.'

'Neither do I,' said Jock sharply. 'And I wish the staff and the Board would select a new Medical Director at once!'

The other men thought he was angry, but he was not. He was being pulled in many directions these days, and the selection of a new Director would cut one of the ropes tugging at his sense of obligation.

He listened to various doctors assure him that he was doing an excellent job, but he knew that Brandt was the honest one. He had been honest twenty years ago, able to see what Jock had been too blind to see. Now Jock also wondered what his father would feel if he realised that the younger Dr. Askew was directing the medical affairs of Brownlee Hospital and trying to settle a damage suit that could not be settled by saying that Maxim Yglesias had suffered no injury.

Jock asked for, and got, a conference of the opposing lawyers, and could only conclude that the problem involved was bigger than Brownlee Hudson realised. After the meeting he tried to tell the man so. 'You'll have to do more than cite cases to prove that similar injuries show similar after-effects. The jury will see only that this one man cannot use his hand.'

'The case must not go to court!' snapped Hudson. 'We must talk to the insurance company, have them explain to these people just what to expect in payment for an injured hand.'

'They are asking payment for further injury,' said Jock.

'Punitive damages!' cried Hudson. 'Outrageous!'

'Not if there was further injury,' Jock pointed out.

Jamie, in another field of Jock's efforts, was showing more satisfactory results. The boy was positively blooming.

'He's like a different person!' said Betsy.

Jamie was different. He was set at the University, and anxious to have his classes begin. He spoke and walked with new assurance; he slept well, and ate well. He began to put a little flesh on his bones. He studied the books which Jock recommended, and talked to Jock about them. He was interested in his future work, but he was interested in other things, too. What sort of Christmas tree they should have, where it should be put. One afternoon, he hunted for his skates, and found them—in the basement where Iris had hidden them out of sight—and he went to the Steinberg rink to see what he could do in the way of skating.

'I wasn't any threat to the Olympic champions,' he said that evening, 'but I find I can get about without a cane.'

'Was it fun?' asked Jock.

'Not at first. But I think it will come easier. Tomorrow I'll bet my joints will scream, don't you?'

'You're cheerful enough about the prospect,' said Betsy.

There was the great change; Jamie was cheerful about most things those days.

'You've just brought him back to life,' Emma told her son. 'I was worried about the boy, Jock. He had no will to live!'

'Oh, he would have gained that. Remember, he was slowly recovering from a serious injury. I came around just about the time he would have changed anyway.'

'Do you believe that, Jock?'

'Well, naturally, I'm flattered to think that I could be here if he needed me.'

Emma had dropped in at Jock's office on one of her daily visits to the hospital to sit with Jim. She had brought up the matter of Jamie. And then with the facility which was uniquely Emma Askew's she managed to turn her praise into material for a quarrel.

She said that he had done a good job with the boy, but she feared that Jamie might overdo, or get too enthusiastic about studying medicine, and then discover that he couldn't manage the rigorous course. 'You'll have to stay in close enough touch with Jamie now to handle any crisis that may come up.'

'Jamie can handle any crisis for himself if you and Iris will consider him a man, not a helpless boy.'

'He can't expect to compete with healthy young men, Jock.'

'He'll compete, and show up well, I am quite sure.'

'Jock, you're just seeking to evade your responsibility. If you don't stand by Jamie now, we'll have another example of your turning your back on what you know is right, and—Good heavens, son, you have to stand up to your obligation here! If ever you are to be a man in your own right ...'

Jock chewed at his upper lip. 'I thought I was my own man,' he said tightly.

'I'm sure you do think you are. But for *years*, you have not considered your obligations to your family. As a *man* must do!'

Jock sighed. Must he go through all the matter of the divorce and the differences with his father? Emma knew those facts as well as he did.

'In a few weeks' time,' she was telling Jock, 'you have been a wonderful influence on Jamie. Whether by instinct or intent, you've said and done the very things the boy needed. But, Jock, you can't stop now! You must not make the mistake you did with your father! *Stay* with Jamie. He needs you.'

'I plan to keep in touch with the children, Mother.'

'Being half-way across the country is not keeping in touch.'

Again Jock sighed. 'I'll try to do what I should do, Mother,' he promised.

'You have enjoyed your family while you've been here, son.'

'Yes, I have,' said Jock. 'And you're right, Mother, I should never have lost touch with my children.'

'Well!' said Emma, standing up, and showing that she was pleased. 'I'm glad to hear you say *that!*'

Jock watched her leave the office, and then sat shaking his head. He would do—what he should do. His decision on what comprised an obligation might not match Emma's ideas on the same subject, but if she took any pleasure in thinking he had made a concession, he'd let her have what pleasure she could these days.

He would agree that he should not entirely abandon Jamie to his own decisions just now; nor return him to the apprehensions of the women of his family. Jock's advice to the boy would seem to be more realistic than that of his mother or his grandmother. Jock had been thinking about the matter and he would talk about it that afternoon when he had a date to go skating with Jamie.

He kept the date, highly dubious about his ability to stay upright on the steel blades. But Jamie assured him that if he had ever skated, the knack would come back very quickly!

Jock shook his head. 'I hope the skates know about that,' he muttered, tying the shoes which he had rented.

On that crisp winter afternoon, the rink was a wonderful place. The lights had been turned on against the early twilight, and a hundred skaters skimmed and dipped—and fell—upon the ice. Children with the confidence and daring of innocence, skilled and graceful teen-agers, oldsters gliding along with the dignity of proven skill. There was Jamie, achieving smooth glides and a skilful turn.

'How you doin'?' Jock asked the boy.

'Only fair. It's smoother than walking.'

Jock nodded, his eyes shining.

'Now you, Dad,' said Jamie.

'Must I?'

Jamie nodded, firmly.

Jock hadn't been near ice since he was seventeen, and now was supremely unsure of himself. He had bought a heavy sweater, and a tight, knitted cap; he did his best to appear confident as he set foot on the ice. 'You'd better clear a wide space around me,' he told Jamie who was skating in small circles close to his father.

'Want my hand?' Jamie asked, enormously pleased that, though stiff-kneed, he was adept at something which Jock would approach with fear and apprehension.

'What good is one hand going to do me?' Jock demanded. 'What you'll need is a fork lift, or at least a wheelbarrow following close behind.'

It was fun. Jock took his first small, fearful steps upon the ice; he fell, and rose, and eventually he skated without stumbling and without falling. 'There must be a time limit on that theory of yours,' he told Jamie. 'My bones seem to have scant recollection of what it requires to stay erect on this stuff.'

Others noticed, watched, and smiled at the father and son combination. A pretty girl offered a suggestion or two; Jamie talked to her about 'our problem,' and they laughed together. When Jock felt that he had earned a break, she consented to go into the pavilion and eat a hamburger with the Askews.

Her name was Jenny, she said—Jenny Woodham. She lived over on Euclid, and was home on vacation from her school in the East. She had red-gold hair, windblown, and a gay, matter-of-fact manner that reminded Jock of Sue Jordan, whom he had once known and liked. She wore red earmuffs and mittens, and a short, knife-pleated skirt with a dark blue pull-over.

Jamie talked to her without a trace of his usual self-consciousness, and Jock watched the two young people.

'Nursing my bruises,' he explained when they asked him why he was so silent.

'We'll get you some more to nurse in just a minute,' Jamie promised. And then he and Jenny laughed at Jock's growl.

When they went back to the ice they found Noah Green there, doing figure skating, wearing a thick white turtleneck jersey, and a long, tasselled white cap. Jock was able to tell the amazed young people who the man was. 'He used to be my best friend,' he said, meaning that they had been boys together, and that the years had intervened.

'What happened?' asked Jamie.

'Nothing happened. We're still good friends.'

'He surely doesn't let his face interfere with his having fun,' said Jenny. 'I'd like to meet him.'

'That could be arranged,' said Jock. 'I'll just go out and fall down in front of him. You're my next of kin, and common decency would make the guy drag me to your feet.'

'Nut!' said Jamie, skating away. 'Come along, Dad. You won't get your sea legs sitting on a bench!'

Noah saw them of course, and before long he had joined their little group, full of suggestions about Jock's skating.

'That's what California does to one,' he assured the young people. 'A man loses all hardiness and ability to cope with the elements.'

'I've never missed the things up to this minute,' Jock confessed. 'How about my quitting now, Jamie, and hieing myself to a really hot Turkish bath?'

'Haven't you enjoyed it at all?' Jamie asked anxiously.

'The fresh air, the company—oh, and the hamburger,' said Jock. 'I've loved *them!*'

Jamie shook his head in despair, and said that he and Jenny would take three quick turns around the rink, and then they would all go home. Jock stayed with Noah, talking to him about Jamie, and explaining what he had tried to do for the boy.

'Iris had him packed round with little embroidered pillows. Mother was sure his life was at an end, that he must always be an interesting invalid.'

'Spare me,' said Noah. 'I know the routine. When are you going back to California?'

'Any day now. I'll have to. Anna's mad at me for staying this long.'

'Not really?'

'She says she is.'

'Then get going, boy! All it takes is a ticket, an airplane—and you.'

'That makes everything sound simple.'

'Have dinner with me tonight?'

'I'd like that, but I'm planning to check on the early evening routines at the hospital. That's how I could take this hour or two off in the afternoon.'

'You're really working?'

'Of course I'm working. The hospital needed quite a lot done to it. It had got to be a first-class rat race. Why, the thing actually made money! And these days no self-respecting hospital does that! Here come the kids. They're cute together, aren't they?'

'Oh, now, let's not add matchmaking to your other attainments, Jock-o.'

Jock grinned.

The young people skated up, flushed and laughing, evidently planning future meetings. Jock raised an eyebrow at Noah, who was gallant to Jenny, and shook hands with Jamie. 'I'm glad I know a few grandfathers,' he said earnestly. 'But, look, son, don't you let this head-shrinker do your thinking for you. He isn't too good at it, you know. I'd hate to be saddled with any problem he'd solve for me!'

Jock, taken by surprise, stammered a protest, betraying some heat.

Noah waited until he was finished, then he spoke again to Jamie, and still earnestly. 'Solve your own problems, kid,' he insisted. 'Jock did. Or I used to think he did.'

Jamie was not sure how much was serious, how much a big joke. 'He's a great admirer of yours, Mr. Green,' he assured the big man.

'He'd better not be,' growled Noah. 'I don't have so many friends that I can afford to throw one overboard. Well—good-bye all! Call me, Jock, if you stay around and have an evening free. Good-bye, Jenny. It was a real pleasure meeting *you!*' He skated away, his hands clasped behind his back, his head tilted jauntily.

'Isn't he wonderful!' breathed Jenny. 'You get so you forget all about his face.'

'That's because Noah forgets about it,' Jock explained. 'And he is indeed wonderful. Jenny, can we drop you at home?'

'Yes. Yes, you can, Dr. Askew.'

'It's Jamie's car. I'm just being fatherly and generous.'

It had been a pleasant, friendly hour, and Jock did not regret having had no opportunity to talk to Jamie about his idea that the boy might like to go back to California with him, finish his pre-med at Stanford, and enter medical school out there. Jamie would have been at least interested; he had asked a lot of questions about the Foundation, and Jock had promised to let him visit the place.

Their talk could take place at any time, though now, with Jenny entering the picture, Jamie well might want to stay right here in the city, go to school here, and see more of the girl. Since she seemed to be such a very nice girl, Jock would like to see that happen, too. Jamie was at the age where a girl should definitely be in his picture.

Not too much to Jock's surprise, the women folk of the family seemed to think otherwise. Jamie was not strong, Jamie must conserve his strength and get his sleep—

Jock, with Noah's sardonic warning in his mind, did what he could to set things straight. Families, he assured Iris, and his mother—and even Betsy—were wonderful institutions, but the idea that they closed their gates at any given minute was a false stand to take. They must expand, and take in new members, or die. Betsy, and her mother, and her grandmother, had better, right now, begin to get used to the idea of a son-in-law in respect to three-month-old Lucy.

The women were astonished, and Betsy laughed at his suggestion. 'It takes a man,' she told the others, 'to set us straight on some things. But of course you're right, Jock. Jamie should have a girl. I wonder if he'd bring Jenny here to the house?'

Jock made a mental note to be around when that happened. Families were wonderful, and worth almost any sacrifice, but they took a deal of staying around and corner-smoothing to make them function properly.

So did hospitals, gripe sessions or no. Of course a month was too short a time in which to expect miracles. Jock must put in more work on that job unless he meant to abandon it before it was well started.

Two days before Christmas he decided that he would not be able to get back to California to spend even the day with Anna, and he called her that night to tell her so, and again asked her to come to St. Louis.

That night she answered his call, but she refused to consider a trip to Missouri, even to meet and know Jamie.

'You'd be so good for him, Anna,' Jock urged.

'His mother isn't?' asked grave-voiced Anna.

'No. I'm afraid she isn't. She smothers him. Of course she means well—'

'And your mother? Isn't she good for him either?'

'No. *She* dominates him. Or tries to. That's why I owe Jamie so much. I've helped mess things up for the boy by staying away from him for too long. It's been a great personal failure in my life, Anna. It seems, from where I stand now, that I've made a great many mistakes. Far too many.'

Anna's voice came to him as softly as a whispered sigh. 'Good-night, Jock,' she said, and the phone connection was broken.

CHAPTER TWELVE

On that same day, Noah Green had met Jock on the street, and the two men went into the Steeplechase for a drink together. The talk was mainly of the work that Jock was doing in Brownlee Hospital. He said he would not get home for Christmas.

The next morning Noah went to the hospital

and asked to see Dr. Barnaby. Yes, he said, it was important.

His manner and appearance were such that within thirty minutes, he was sitting in the Chief Surgeon's office, studying that slender, dark-haired man. And the surgeon was studying him.

Noah acknowledged the professional scrutiny and spoke briefly of his war injury and the plastic repair; then he said that he had come as a friend of Jock Askew, interested in why 'the guy stays on here so long.'

'He was called here by his father's illness,' said Dr. Barnaby.

'A sad thing,' Noah conceded.

'There are problems connected with such an illness, Mr. Green.'

'I understand Dr. Askew cannot recover? So those problems would be self-terminating, wouldn't they?'

The man in white nodded.

'So—what else holds Jock here?'

'His mother seems to need him. And then—there has been his son.'

'I know about Jamie. But most men handle such family obligations along with their other duties. Don't they?'

'Possibly,' said Dr. Barnaby. 'Though in this case, Jock's divorce ...'

'If you're delicately suggesting,' said Noah bluntly, 'that Iris Henderson is a feature in this delay, forget it. She'd not stand a show with a man married to Anna.'

Dr. Barnaby leaned forward. 'Do you know Jock's wife?' he asked intently.

'I do.' Noah's face was shining. 'She's a wonderful person. But Jock still hangs around here—and so I'd like to know why. Is it the hospital job that holds him?'

'Medical Director of Brownlee Memorial is a good job,' said Dr. Barnaby, his lips tight.

'It probably is,' Noah agreed. 'But, doctor, it doesn't happen to be Jock's job. Besides—weren't you Dr. Jim Askew's assistant? Until Jock came, I mean.'

'Yes. I was.'

'Then it would seem to me that Jock might be taking over a job that rightly belongs to you. How about that?'

His cheeks reddened, but Dr. Barnaby said nothing.

'All right,' said Noah, who was enjoying himself. 'What else is in the picture?'

Dr. Barnaby bit his lip.

'If you think I'm meddling,' said Noah, 'I sure am. But to a good purpose, doctor. So break it down for me, will you?'

'This isn't really a privileged communication,' said Barnaby slowly, 'though I would rather not give you the details. However I believe I can say that the older Dr. Askew is about to be sued in court. For malpractice.'

Noah whistled.

'Yes. And Jock would like to do all he can to save his father's name the notoriety that accompanies such a proceeding.'

'Is it in Jock's power to save Jim Askew?'

'It might be.'

'Don't you doctors carry insurance against these things? Is Jock working with the insurance company?'

'I—don't think so.'

'But that doesn't make sense!'

'It seems to make sense to Jock. To clear his father's name.'

'Yes. And he would stay around for that. Well—maybe I can help. I'll see what I can do. And I may meddle a little in your affairs, too, doctor. D'you mind?'

Dr. Barnaby smiled. 'I'd give anything to have this lawsuit squashed, Mr. Green.'

'Hmmmm,' said Noah. 'Evidently, so would Jock.'

Christmas was the great hurdle. Later, Jock was to know that it had been. At the time he met the day with mixed feelings. He should be at the Foundation with his staff, and at home with Anna. And yet, from his present view of things, it seemed that he should be in St. Louis with his family.

Most particularly, with Jamie. He was not more 'fond' of Jamie, but the boy needed him more. Betsy was happily settled into her pattern of life. She and Stephen were selecting a site for their new home, and already talking about the next baby—and the one after that.

But Jamie—his improvement was a visible thing, day by day. He seldom had moody spells now; only rarely did he show signs of nervousness, and flare-ups of temper due to frustration. He brooded still about his appearance— he looked like a goon! he told his family. 'I do! I'm yellow as a pumpkin, I'm thin, my nose is too big. And I have to wear glasses. I limp—'

'And you also talk too much,' drawled Jock from his corner.

Jamie looked around at him. 'Do I?' he asked naïvely.

'You do. Who cares how you look? Who looks at *you?*'

'Girls think the way a guy looks is important.'

'Some girls, yes. But I've not seen any girls fleeing in panic when you pass by. Have you?'

Jamie grinned.

A girl definitely was in the picture for Jamie,

and Jock was sternly holding the women folk to a hands-off acceptance of that fact. Jenny was a nice girl; they had all liked her when Jamie brought her to the house on Christmas Eve. A girl was good for Jamie. A girl like Jenny. The wrong one, of course, could do a lot of harm.

But Jenny was not the wrong girl. She was pretty, fun to be with, and she had a mind of her own. She was interested in the work Jamie wanted to do. She listened and talked as earnestly as Jamie on the evening when they came to have dinner with Jock at the hotel.

Jamie announced that he thought he knew what special line of medicine he wanted to follow. Was it too soon to decide?

'You're lucky if you can decide early,' Jock told him.

'He has a wonderful idea, Dr. Askew,' said Jenny. She wore a suit of black velveteen and a shining white satin blouse. Her hair shone from brushing, and her face glowed with excitement in Jamie's idea.

'I thought,' Jamie answered his father's questioning look, 'that I'd like to study the diseases and problems of adolescence. Is that—would that be possible, sir?'

'Sure,' said Jock readily. 'There's a definite need for it. Pediatrics stops at fourteen. And your patients are not quite adult then, physically or emotionally.'

'I thought,' said Jamie shyly, but earnestly, too, 'that it would somewhat tie in with psychiatry.'

'Psychiatry would certainly help,' Jock agreed, and went on to discuss with the young people the idea which had come to Jamie. Adolescent medicine was a new field, the possibilities were great ...

His son's plans and dreams could change a dozen times in the next five years. Jock knew that. The important thing was for the boy to have an idea—and the will to live for it, to work for its realisation.

All these things focused Jock's interest in St. Louis, seemed to spotlight his presence there and the need for him to solve various problems.

Things were going along smoothly in California. His staff was coping with any small complications. But Anna thought that he should come home, and stubbornly refused to listen when he tried to explain to her that he could not leave!

His father daily needed Jock's reassurance. Jock seemed able to quiet the sick man when no one else could. The hospital staff and the Board needed persuasion that certain changes were desirable. Certainly Anna could not deny that Jock should see Jamie safely embarked on his pre-medical studies, well set into the routine of classes and hours of study. The lawsuit was proving to be a hard nut to crack. If it could not be kept out of court—or successfully defended in court—Jock must be present to do all that he could to protect his father's name! Anna must see that?

Anna thought that *he* was the stubborn one.

But all these things did hold Jock. On the day when he met Sue Jordan on the street, it seemed to him, too, that he had never left the city. They recognised each other on sight, and went into Straub's for a soda, and to catch up. She was happily married, she said, and the mother of two boys.

'You're doing all right!' said Jock.

Sue smiled. 'I am. And you?'

He told about the Foundation, and about his father's illness. Sue looked trim in a suit of green tweed, a small round hat on the back of her head. Jock told her about the things he was doing at Brownlee. Did Sue remember their ideas?

She did, laughing at their youthful optimism.

'I'm still just as optimistic.'

'And as youthful,' she assured him. 'Really, you haven't changed at all, Jock. It seemed entirely right to meet you on the avenue. Are you going to stay?'

'There are many problems to solve before I can leave.'

There were many problems, some of which he was bungling. He should have flown to California for Christmas, and returned. Perhaps he should go there to stay, and make regular short trips back to St. Louis. Or should he decide to stay in one place, and consolidate all his problems? If Anna would just come to St. Louis ... If Jock could persuade his mother to invite her, would Anna come? Possibly not. Her present mood went deeper than resentment at Jock's mother.

But unless she did come, she could not understand the problems which Jock had on his hands!

She would need to see Jim Askew as Jock saw him that afternoon when he went into his room. Of course Jock was seeing him, too, as he had been in the vigour of his youth and middle age, and the impact of the change was tremendous. Now the thinning hair seemed only scraggly; now the full-fleshed face had fallen into sagging folds, and the firmly chiselled mouth was merely petulant.

Jock greeted his father quietly and pleasantly, smiled a dismissal to the nurse, and sat down in the armchair as if he could visit all evening. Jim was in bed, but he had been up. With someone close at hand, he could move about his room. Today he complained about the smallness of the room. Why couldn't he go home?

Across Jock's mind flashed a picture of the apartment as it now was, a busy recovery room with tiled cubicles and bright chrome attachments for oxygen, brackets for the various jars of glucose, plasma and bottles of blood. Rubber gloves, red, yellow, and black, draped the scrub basin; a white-garmented doctor, an intern and nurses moved about; the sounds of that place, and the watchful, intent air of it were not those of the penthouse as Jim knew it.

'You're in your own hospital, Father,' he said quietly to Jim. 'Don't they treat you right?'

Jim made a sound of assent, and discontent, too. 'They won't let me out in the hall.'

There had been some trouble on that point. Jim had to have a male nurse at night.

'They keep the halls pretty full of people and gear, sir.'

'What's happened to the Pavilion?'

Jock looked alertly at Jim. 'What makes you think ...?'

'Can't you answer me?'

'Of course I can answer you. The Pavilion's

just as it has always been.'

Someone had talked out of turn.

At the last staff meeting, Jock had made the suggestion that the Pavilion be eliminated, that the luxury suites there be converted into one-, two-, and three-bed rooms for the critically ill, with specially trained nurses and interns on constant duty. In the present wards, he continued, he would like to establish self-care units, beginning at once on medical, and then moving on to others. Maternity, orthopedic—

'Psychiatric?' asked Dr. Barnaby quietly.

'Certainly!' said Jock at once.

Some heads were shaken, some nodded.

'Would this system mean a smaller nursing force?' Barnaby again. He had come to be the 'opposition' to a lot of Jock's ideas for changes. Well—Jim Askew had trained Barnaby.

'No,' Jock answered him now, 'but we could distribute and train our nurses for more efficiency, and better care of the patients.'

'Do you think it would work, doctor?' asked the Administrator.

'It does elsewhere.'

'There's one thing, doctor. The Pavilion makes money for the hospital.'

'Yes. And I have considered that. But if we make this change, we'll be adding to our bed-count, and we can give better care all around.'

'What happens to the snobs?' asked a voice in the far corner of the room.

Laughter rippled, and Jock smiled. 'I'm afraid they are not our first interest, just now.'

Of course no action was taken on his suggestion. But someone had talked. Barnaby, he gathered from his father's rambling talk. Jock sat and watched his father. Perhaps Jim should be where he could go 'into the halls,' into a day room, or, come spring, out of doors. There were sanatoriums and nursing homes—Jock should look into the matter.

Later that same afternoon, Jock brought up the question with Dr. Barnaby, catching him in the doctors' lounge up on surgery, between jobs. Barnaby knew Jim's present condition completely. Now if he also knew of near-by institutions, he could advise one best suited to the Askew need.

'We're going to have to do something,' Jock said earnestly.

Barnaby drained his coffee cup, and set it aside. 'He wanted to get out of his room last night,' he said thoughtfully.

'I know he did. And someone must have mentioned the Pavilion thing to him.'

'Changes in this hospital would point up the change in him.'

'Those changes are still desirable.'

Barnaby's cheeks reddened. He started to speak, then said nothing.

'We'll have to make some move,' Jock said. 'There's no permanent place at Brownlee for a man in Father's condition.'

'Have you considered taking him back to your hospital in California?'

'Not to it, as a hospital. The Foundation is an evaluation centre, only; we have no wards, or nursing staff. But I have suggested to Mother that they both come to California, that she live close by, and that we establish Father in a nursing home there, or perhaps with his own nurses in a cottage on the Foundation grounds.'

'She objected?'

'Yes. I could bring it up again, though I've a little more realistic idea now of what it would take to move Father.'

'Your Mother can be upset, too, can't she?'

Barnaby also knew Emma. Jock sat nodding. 'Yes. Her whole life interest is here in St. Louis.'

'She's seemed happy to have you around.'

'I know. But we must still make some decision on a place for Father.'

'What about your wife, Jock? Won't she come here?'

'Not willingly, I'm afraid.'

Dr. Barnaby stood up. 'I'll ask around,'

he promised.

For a time, Jock stayed on surgery, changing, and going into Barnaby's operating room, watching the doctors and the nurses as they conferred and prepared to go to work. Dr. Barnaby's glove had split, and the circulating brought him another pair; there was some talk about the amount of powder to use, a new sulpha drug, and the stains on their green smocks which didn't show up until the damn thing had been washed.

Jock heard all this, and comprehended little. He was still thinking about his father. Odd that Barnaby had brought up the matter of moving him to California. Odder still that Jock should now have completely given up a solution which, a month ago, had seemed the only one.

Why had things changed?

'Things' had not. The change was in Jock. Once he would have tried to tie his interests here in St. Louis to those which he had in California. Now he must realise, face, and handle the wish he presently had to separate his life in California entirely from the busy life which he had begun to live in St. Louis.

'I'm like one of those bigamists,' he told himself, solemnly, going out of the operating room. 'One of those chaps you read about in the paper. A wife and two kids in Los Angeles.

A second wife and three kids in San Francisco. I've always thought the arrangement would take doing, and now I am sure of it.'

He did not smile. His face was darkly stern as he went downstairs.

At the desk where he was checking out, he heard himself say to an inquiring, and interested, attending doctor, 'My plans are in a state of flux, I'm afraid. Or perhaps I'm over into a backwater. I can't decide on much of anything until my father's needs are attended to.'

He said that; and going back to the hotel after dinner, he got out stationery and his pen, sat down in the armchair and addressed an envelope to Anna in California.

Mrs. James Askew, Jr.
Tree Valley Foundation ...

He sat and looked at the marks he had made upon the long airmail envelope. An engraving of the hotel building decorated the left corner. There were little diagonal marks of red and blue forming a border around the rectangle. And the address—

Jock did not often write to Anna. Though he had travelled a lot since their marriage, he had usually phoned to her. This was the first

308

letter he had written since coming to St. Louis on this trip. But now— He laid the envelope aside, and dated the sheet of paper.

'10 January.

'Dear Anna,

'I am afraid I do not have good news for you. For I am afraid that I shall have to stay on for a time longer in St. Louis.'

He stopped writing, and leaned his head back against the cushion of the chair. How should he say it? Well—he could use the words he had used to the doctor earlier that day.

'I am afraid ...'

No. That was repeating himself—as being *afraid*. He wadded up the sheet of paper, and started again.

'Dear Anna,

'I fear that I do not have good news for you. It begins to seem that I must stay in St. Louis until my father's needs are more fully taken care of.'

He regarded the five lines of clear, black handwriting. Would it be easier to talk to Anna? Would she listen to him? She would read a letter, and perhaps understand some of it. If he could just get her here!

He would not go out to her, because then his own needs would be watered down by the change in environment, by the distance between himself and his present problem.

No. He must try to write the things he felt must be said. Perhaps he could put his feeling about the children into words, their claim upon him. 'At this late date.' Would Anna read and understand his feeling of guilt? Now, to him, it seemed incredible that he had seen almost nothing of Betsy and Jamie for eighteen years! How stiff and hurt could a man get! Wouldn't Anna be glad to know that all the old resentments had relaxed, and that now he was free to know his children, to love them, and to do things for them?

His pen moved steadily across the page, filling it, and beginning a second one. He mentioned his desire that she would be with him—and her refusal to come. 'For your own reasons.'

There was his father, and the problems which his illness presented.

'I remember,' he wrote, 'that it was you who insisted that I come to St. Louis. Perhaps you did insist because you understood his condition better than I did. I confess I would not have believed all the complications his illness has taken on, all the problems it has created. Though I knew about the disease clinically I did not guess what it would be like for me to have to deal with my father under those classic aspects. I can only guess at Mother's grief and fear for him by the extent to which she leans on me.

'I had thought Father would resent my coming in on him when he was helpless, and I strong and able. There has been little of this. Once he was assured that I would stay, once he knew that I was doing some of his work, and caring for the complex and unhappy details of the lawsuit, he relaxed, and now seems indifferent, generally, to such affairs. He has his troubled times, of course. Often I can subdue his frenzy where others fail. That again puts a great burden upon me.'

Jock held his pen a few inches above the paper, and sat thoughtful. The day had been warm for January, and beyond his open window a light rain whispered and rustled, a little wind blew the fresh smell of it into the room.

'I hope you can see, Anna, that my parents are my responsibility. Mainly because they are less able to cope with their lives than I am. Doing for them I realise my manhood, just as perhaps my son and my daughter will realise their fulfilled destinies as people in some service to me.'

Now his pen moved swiftly, his face was intent. He filled the second page and started the

311

third. 'Deciding to stay on may be a grave mistake. If so, perhaps it will be cared for in the margin for error which life gives to us. But if I left my obligations here, I could be making a mistake, too.

'It seems that I must help my father. My mother is dependent upon me. Jamie certainly is. For each, in his own way, life is being a little too much to handle alone. While you can, I can take this situation. For a time, at least.'

He concluded the letter, picked up the envelope, and almost without noticing what it was he did, he got his wallet from his coat pocket, opened it, and drew out the return airline ticket which Anna had given him in November. Swiftly he folded the letter, with the ticket inside, swiftly he sealed the envelope. There was a job, over and done.

CHAPTER THIRTEEN

The mail at the Foundation came into the main office and was distributed. Sometimes Anna's personal mail was sent up to the house; usually she went down for it. With Jock gone, she had to find ways to fill the hours. Going down for the mail, chatting for minutes with the various people she saw, perhaps stopping off at one of the homes for gossip and coffee, Anna could use up an entire morning or afternoon.

Sometimes, as the days piled up, she wondered how she had filled her time when Jock was at home. Certainly she was being invited out more often now, for dinner, for a Sunday drive along the coast ... She cut and arranged flowers for the house; she sewed, and mended, she bought new things and put them in place; she planned and ate meals; she read and listened to music ...

So where did all the empty hours come from? Not only in the long evenings when Jock would have been at home, but in the morning, in the early afternoon and, oh, particularly at night!

And particularly after Christmas when everyone thought surely he would come home, and had planned on his coming. Anna had so planned. But, lately, she had begun to wonder. Lately she was filling her days with long, long walks in the woods, choosing to go, with Clancy, beyond the beaten paths where patients might be encountered.

The people of the Foundation knew about the empty hours, and her efforts to fill them, but Anna was not a person to whom one talked easily about deeply intimate things. Her friends did what they could. And together they discussed Anna and Jock. Why didn't he come home, even if he couldn't stay? Why didn't Anna go to St. Louis, at least for Christmas with him?

There were answers, but not very satisfactory ones. Surely nothing was wrong between the Askews! If ever, there was a compatible, happy couple, perfectly adjusted to each other's interests and enthusiasms! They liked each other, they worked well together, and enjoyed the same diversions. What had happened? Was *anything* happening?

Anna, to such questions as were put to her, said that Jock was having difficulty arranging his parents' affairs, that his father was seriously ill, that his son had been hurt—

Some of the Foundation personnel had not known of Jock's previous marriage. Now, some of the more romantic suspected a renewed interest in that other wife.

'She can't be better than Anna!'

'She's there, and Anna's here.'

Those who knew about its arrival were pleased that Anna should get a letter from Jock. 'A big, thick letter,' the clerk told Dr. Keys.

'Doesn't he write regularly?'

'He doesn't write at all. But then, I think he telephones to her.'

'Oh, yes, he would.'

Anna picked up the letter around noon that day. She had driven into town to a church service, and stopped at the main office on her way home. She had already discarded her small round hat, and had tied a scarf about her hair. Her suit was of sapphire-blue wool, and the scarf had pink roses on it.

When the clerk gave her the mail, Jock's letter was on top, and Anna looked up at the girl inquiringly. 'He never writes,' she said.

'Well, he did this time. I hope he's all right.'

'Oh, he's fine,' said Anna in a preoccupied tone. She gathered up the little pile of magazines, a bill from the cleaner's, two circulars about January white sales, and an envelope full of soap and detergent coupons. With the letter in her hand, she went out through the glass-doored lobby, and right past her car parked on the gravel drive. She turned slowly towards home, looking at the envelope, at the stamp, at the engraved picture of the hotel. Her dark brows were drawn closely together in a frown. What had happened to Jock?

The sunlight filtered through the tall trees in rays of pale gold. There was a film of mist in the little valleys, thickening above the river.

Anna saw none of this.

The path was so familiar that she could walk along it without so much as glancing down. Once her foot turned on a large pebble, and she looked down at her calfskin pump in disbelief. Why had she worn such shoes to walk?

Once a low branch caught at the flowered scarf, and impatiently she loosed the knot and let the silken folds drop to her shoulders. Her black hair lifted in a puff of air, and she glanced up at the sun. With a breeze, the mist would soon dissipate. It was a beautiful day ...

And she had a letter from Jock.

About half-way home a bench had been built against the bole of a great tree, and Anna sat down upon it, rubbing the foot she had turned. She put the magazines and other things on the seat beside her, and ran her forefinger under the flap of the long envelope.

An animal of some sort made a scurrying sound in the leaf litter on the ground, and Anna tried to find it. If one sat very still here in the woods, the chipmunks would sometimes come quite close.

She looked again at the envelope, and completely slit the edge of it. Slowly she took out the folded sheets of paper, and the ticket fell into her hand. Her black eyes flared wide, she opened it and looked at the printed words. 'St. Louis to San Francisco.'

Her hand began to shake, and she bit savagely on her lip. She was not going to sit out in the sunlight and howl like a cat! Jock's letter would explain—her trembling fingers fumbled with the sheets of paper. Finally she got them opened, and straight.

And then she closed her eyes, not wanting to read what he might say.

She sat so for several minutes, the sun coming through the branches criss-crossed overhead, printing delicate shadows upon the blue stuff of her jacket and skirt. But after a time, of course, she must open her eyes, lift her head—and of course read the letter. She would have to know what it was that Jock wanted of her so seriously that he would write it down on several sheets of crackling paper.

Carefully she placed the plane ticket a-top the pile of mail beside her, carefully, still-faced, she lifted the letter and began to read, not stopping at all, her eyes and mind held fascinated to the things Jock had to say.

Finished, she dropped her hand, and the little breeze riffled the sheets of loosely held paper. Lest they blow away, she folded them and carefully placed them in the envelope. She would not need to read them again. She knew

317

every word by heart.

And she was bewildered by what those words added up to. What was happening to her, and to Jock? What really had happened in St. Louis? His father was sick—there was a lawsuit—his son was young and nervous and getting over the shock of an injury—his mother—

Had Jock's mother talked again about Anna's being an Indian? That charge had become something of a joke between Anna and Jock. Only something of a joke, because the cruelty inherent in Emma Askew's conviction was not at all funny to the girl involved. If she let herself think about it, and this morning she did.

But, of course, Jock would not have let his mother say things like that! There was something more important, something real.

Like his work. Jock was working in the hospital, directing its medical affairs. In talking to Anna about doing that job, he had sounded pleased and excited. Was he also having patients? Were they interesting? He had not mentioned his work in the letter. But it would present a claim, and one which Anna could not deny. As a doctor's wife, she knew that much! She had never claimed to be a proper wife for a doctor, but she had married Jock because she thought that he loved her. And she was sure that she loved him!

She remembered every minute of their ten years together. She remembered the way he had come to the night club in Las Vegas, and had watched her; she remembered when he first spoke to her. She remembered their marriage, and the year when Jock had done his residency in psychiatry, and she had worked in the hospital office—the buying of this land—the growth of the Foundation—the building of their home— Oh, she did love Jock! And had. And she was almost as sure that he had loved her!

He was not a man to conceal his emotions— not from her, he was not. She knew when he was happy, when troubled—and she knew that their marriage had been based on love, and that it had been a good marriage.

Of course she had given Jock no children. And in St. Louis he had the nice daughter and the enchanting baby. The son who needed his father, and had responded to Jock's interest in him. Those claims Anna could not combat, and they probably were the strongest claims made upon him now. They were the 'burden,' the obligation which he would not put upon Anna—because the children were not hers!— and on which he would not turn his back. So that was a claim which she could neither refute nor deny.

But what about her own claim upon Jock?

A claim she had never before imposed. She was there, and he knew that she was there. But always she had let his work, and his interest in that work, come first in their lives. Had she been wrong? Small point in deciding that now.

Now—should she make a personal claim upon him, and what sort of claim would that be? That she was his wife. But Jock knew that. That she loved him, and needed him. But he knew that, too. She was not helpless, she was not ill—nor old. So what sort of claim could she make?

He had said that she could 'take this situation.' Could she? How could she? What would she *do?*

Stay on, she supposed, live in his home, help run his Foundation. Though she was not needed to do that. He had a good staff.

And, besides, she could not stay on at Tree Valley without Jock, and the hope that he would come to her. Soon.

Now tears glistened in her black eyes, slowly she got to her feet and moved on up the hill to her home—to their home. Hers and Jock's. Its walls gleamed in the pearly light, and the thin sunlight printed leaf shadows like lace upon the wall of their bedroom.

Anna stood still on the path, and lifted her face to the pale sky. Why had this come to her?

Why had Jock done this thing to her! He was saying that he would not return. But why? Why? *Why?*

His mother. Only that woman could have worked such a change in Jock.

Possessive, vindictive, sly—deceitful! Anna had never set eyes on Jock's mother, but she knew! She knew! Leaning on Jock, pointing out the need there was for him— Ha! Clever as the devil, that woman! Anna could use the same tricks. But she would not! She would *not!* She loved Jock Askew for his conscience, his reliability, his sense of duty. And she would not exploit those things in him!

The lawsuit! That wicked old man had got himself into a jam. And, though he had never believed in Jock and his work, he—and the mother—were using Jock now to get them out of their expensive mess! Did Jock realise the dirty, underhanded way they were using Dr. Jim's breakdown, and Jamie's injury to—to—?

Now, Anna moved with speed. She whirled into the house, into the kitchen where Kim was preparing her lunch, a wedge of cheese upon the cutting-block, bone-handled knife and fork laid across a fruit-patterned plate. His yellow face looked around in alarm at the vigour of his Missy's entrance.

'Is something mebbe on fire?' he asked.

'Something mebbe *is* on fire!' cried Anna, rushing out to the hall, and running up the stairs, her heels tapping. *'Me!'*

With no trace of her usual calm and serenity, she went into the violet and white bedroom. She stripped out of her suit and blouse and calfskin pumps, she snatched yellow clam-diggers and a striped jersey from the closet, leaving the hangers to jangle and clatter together. She would make plans! She would go down and eat Kim's lunch, and she would *decide* what she could do to get back at those people in St. Louis! Yes, and at Jock!

She ate her lunch—and she made her plans. Frenzied plans, without much sense to any of them. She would go to St. Louis and tell everybody a thing or two.

She would drop out of sight and no one would ever know.

She would go back to her career, become a great hit, and ...

She planned wildly, and spoke as wildly to Kim, to Dr. Applewhite when he innocently came up the hill to ask to borrow her large electric coffee-maker. Mary Louise was having a party that night. Anna surely was coming?

Anna surely was not! She cried this with vigour, then, hearing the shrillness in her voice, she seemed about to crumple before his eyes.

He caught at her shoulder in alarm, and she poured out a jumble of words about the letter, her suspicions, her planned course of action.

The placid, friendly doctor gazed at her in concern and disbelief.

'I'm going to send for Minter,' he decided.

Anna looked at him sadly. 'I don't need a psychiatrist,' she told her friend.

'But—'

'Yes, I've had a shock. But I'll come out of it pretty soon. I won't do any of the things I thought I would do. I'm sorry I startled you, Bill. And I must go apologise to Kim. I really screamed at him!'

'I don't believe it.'

'I did, just the same.'

'Well, if you did, you come on down the hill and talk to Sam.'

She wouldn't go; she was quite all right. And, no, she wouldn't go to the party, either.

Bill Applewhite finally went off, shaking his head in concern. And forgetting all about the coffeepot.

Within the half-hour Sam Minter, and Frances, his wife, came up the hill.

Anna admitted them, her lips thin, her face wooden. 'I expected you,' she told Sam.

'Bill told me—'

'I know.'

Anna led them into the living-room where a fire burned on the hearth, and where she sat and stared at a porcelain bird on the green chest while she told Jock's assistant about the letter she had had from Jock. She even fetched the letter and let Sam read it.

'I—lost my head, at first,' she said soberly. 'I was collecting hatchets, and starting out at a dead run to destroy everyone responsible for this.'

'Jock, too?'

'I don't blame *him*.'

'Why not, Anna?'

'You think a grown man is able to decide things for himself.'

'Or should be.'

'Yes. And to a degree I think Jock has made his own decisions.'

'To stay on in St. Louis for a time.'

Anna nodded, and drew a deep breath. 'That's what the letter says. I have to decide he's chosen the old way of life instead of this way, here with us.'

Frances now was reading the letter. 'It says more,' she announced, putting the envelope down.

Anna flicked a glance at her, not turning her head, just letting her black eyes slide that way. 'It says more,' she agreed. 'And at first I fought what it said. I fought like a cat. I was crazy, Sam! I really was.'

'Good for you,' he declared, leaning back to light his pipe.

'Yes,' Anna agreed. 'Because it got the panic out of my system. And now I have more sober thoughts on the subject.' She still sat like a child, her feet flat on the floor, her hands lightly clasped. And she stared at the yellow and brown porcelain bird.

'What about that lawsuit he mentions?'

Anna told him. The injured man, the lawsuit. 'They want Jock to use his connections with the insurance company to get a settlement out of court.'

'He probably can be useful, Anna. A man would want to defend his father, especially when he can't defend himself. It looks to me as if Jock *has* been needed in St. Louis.'

'He was. He has been needed, Sam. But not *indefinitely*. Because— What about his work? He's serving as a Medical Director in his father's hospital. But that's not *Jock's* work! And what about his ideas? Will he have ideas? Will he have a chance to express them? Jock would be dead without a chance to express himself and the ideas that come to him. And I may just have the job of preventing that death.'

'Anna—'

Now she looked at Sam, her eyes wide and steady below the bang of black hair. 'He's walked out on me. You're reminding me of that. Well, I know it. And I can understand his doing that. Yes, I can! For men do such things.

'But I'll never understand, Sam, how he could turn his back on the Foundation! On his very life! Something is terribly wrong, Sam, and I am going to St. Louis to see what that wrong is.'

They tried to dissuade her. But she insisted that she must save Jock—and herself, too. She would go to St. Louis just as soon as she could get a reservation, pack, and leave.

'You may hurt yourself, Anna.'

She closed her eyes for a minute at the thought of further pain. 'I must have the "feel" of what is happening,' she told her friends.

'Could Frances go with you?'

'I'll be all right. Nothing will hurt me physically.'

She would not be dissuaded. Nor would she send a word ahead to Jock that she was coming. 'He wouldn't understand my need to go any better than you do.'

So she departed, a slender, grave-eyed young woman in her blue suit and an all-enveloping coat of pale cashmere. Dr. Applewhite drove her in to the city, and those left behind looked at each other in sadness and dismay.

'Askew's in a real spot,' said Sam Minter.

'Are you sorry for him?' demanded Dr. Keys.

'No. No, I'm not sorry for him. But he's in a spot, just the same.'

'What will she say or do?' asked Dr. Keys.

'I don't know. Perhaps Anna herself does not know.'

Anna did not. Grave-faced, she flew across half a continent, speaking quietly when it was necessary to speak, not reading, just staring ahead of her, seeming scarcely to move.

She had not reserved a room, but at the airport she called Jock's hotel, to see if she could get a room there. She could not. The West End hotels, said the answering clerk, were fully occupied by a convention of businesswomen. He suggested the name of a good downtown hotel.

Anna thanked him, and then called the Jefferson, securing accommodations immediately. Well—she would still be close to Jock.

It was night, and it was raining a little. The doorman could not shelter all the descending bus passengers with his umbrella. Anna scampered under the canopy, her white teeth flashing in a smile.

'Anna?' said a man's voice.

She looked up, amazed—and then went forward gladly. Jock's friend! Noah! 'Noah Green!' She held out both hands in happy greeting.

'What are you doing here?' he asked.

'Oh, I decided to come see what St. Louis had that California didn't. Doesn't.'

'Namely Jock?'

She nodded. 'Among other things.'

'Jock's staying at the Chase.'

'I know. I couldn't get a room there.'

'What's wrong with his room? Isn't he expecting you?'

'Oh, no.'

Noah stepped back and looked at her. She carried her hat in her hand. She looked small and defenceless in her big coat. 'Is anything wrong, Anna?' he asked.

'I hope not, Noah. I truly hope not.'

'Can I help you?'

'You already have. I'll check in, and call Jock—'

'Yes. Well—I'll give you a ring myself tomorrow. O.K?'

'O.K.!'

She watched him go out to a big and shining car that was waiting for him. He was kind. And he was Jock's friend. He would help, if she needed help.

Feeling encouraged—to have met a friend in

this strange place—she looked about for the desk, and crossed the great lobby. Few hotels had real lobbies these days. But this one was big and had a lot of couches and chairs, and lamps; she liked that. There were well-dressed people moving about, a teen-aged girl was taking a brace of dachshunds out on a double leash. Three men laughed uproariously at some joke. Several men in clerical collars came in through a side door.

'The Cathedral's just across the street,' the bell boy explained.

Anna nodded, and moved closer to the desk. A man was there, picking up his mail; he looked like Luke Fogarty from the back. Tall, slender, stooped— What was more, he looked like Luke from the front, too! He turned, saw Anna— and his arms opened wide.

The clerk and the bell boy, a porter, and two interested guests watched the reunion, smiling.

They both talked at once— What? Why? When ...?

Luke was playing in the Boulevard Room. But what was *Anna* doing here?

'Wait ...' he prevented her answering. 'You check in, and then eat dinner with me. We can talk. O.K.?'

Very much O.K. Anna did check in; she went upstairs to her room, swiftly freshened herself, and came down again. Luke was waiting, his eyes bright.

'Same girl,' he said contentedly as he led the way to the dining-room. 'Like a Dresden doll. I don't go on for a couple of hours—they have a string ensemble for the dinner hour. Here—we can talk here—'

Luke was known, and a few people came to them, though he had selected a table at the far corner of the candle-lit room.

'There's a girl singer with me,' he told Anna. 'Not anything like as good as you were. How about going on for me tonight?'

Anna shook her head.

'I'm working on a musical comedy,' he told her. 'Remember the one I was writing way back when? When I wanted you to be in it?'

'It was a hit,' she said gravely. 'What's this one to be like?'

'Oh—slightly costume. Teddy Roosevelt era. You wouldn't remember. But there's a place for you in it, and some songs, if you want the job.'

'Now that's loyalty for you,' said Anna, toying with her fruit cup.

He was watching her keenly, his concern evident in his homely face. 'You haven't changed a bit, Anna, sweetheart,' he told her fervently.

'Oh, Luke! Of course I have. It's been ten

330

years!' But she managed a small and grateful smile.

'How have things been with you?' he asked. 'Let's see. You married that doctor— What's happened to him? What was his name?'

Anna sipped water from the tall goblet. 'His name was—is—Jock Askew,' she said quietly. 'And nothing's happened to him.'

'Mhmmmn,' said Luke, leaning back to let the waiter put his dinner before him. 'I remember the guy. Tall, dark—are you still married to him?'

'Of course I'm still married to him! Why do you ask that?'

'Well—because I've seen the guy in here a couple of times. And you weren't with him.'

Anna leaned forward. 'Have you talked to him, Luke?'

'No. Of course he saw me. Had to, with the spotlight on the piano, and all. But I got the impression he didn't expect me to see him. And who is the cool blonde he brings here?'

The cool blonde. A *girl?* Anna had not, incredibly, thought that there might be a girl.

'He has a daughter in St. Louis, Luke,' she said uncertainly. 'He was married before— maybe you knew?'

'This dame isn't his daughter, sweetheart. She's a looker. Society. Money. You know? The expensive simple look. Pale, fragile-looking clothes—with a pastel mink, and a seven-carat clip on the shoulder of her dress. Blonde hair, almost silver-coloured, and cut just right. Beautiful figure, beautiful skin—but the woman's met up with forty, I'm sure. And what he sees in her—after you ...'

Anna sat stricken. Iris! She had not considered a girl, and she certainly had *not* considered Iris!

But of course he might—the children—a realisation of his obligation to their mother. In a great dizzying lurch, the whole world slipped away from Anna.

Luke was watching her in real concern.

'I'm sorry, kid,' he said gently. 'I thought you knew. I mean, I thought things had washed up between you and the doctor. I thought—when I knew you were here—that—well—'

'I did come to see him,' said Anna. 'But—'

'Maybe he only knows this dame, and—' His efforts were well meaning, and clumsy.

Anna smiled at him. A thin, unhappy smile. 'I hadn't considered her,' she said faintly. 'Jock—mentioned her. That he'd seen her. But when he'd phone me, he talked mostly about his son.'

'Hey, you married quite a family, didn't you?'

Anna shook her head. 'I don't know any of

them, Luke. He was separated from his wife, had been divorced for several years when I first saw him. He—he didn't see his family—and I've never met any of them. Well, this fall his father—he's a doctor, too—became seriously ill, and Jock was sent for. He came here to help—and he's stayed on, doing some of his father's work, and caring for his mother. Of course his parents are old. I suppose he had to see her. His wife I mean.'

'She's the blonde?'

'I've never seen her, Luke. I'm just guessing that's who the woman was that you saw.'

'Mhmmmn,' said Luke, breaking a salt stick. 'She's quite a dame. Not like you. She's cool, and poised, and very elegant. But she hasn't your excitement, dear. Though at one time this Jock of yours probably loved her.'

Anna looked at her friend, her dark eyebrows drawn together. 'But,' she cried, startled at the suggestion, 'that's been over for years.'

Luke shook his head. 'Are you sure?' he asked. 'Some men, you know, never get over a woman they have loved.'

Anna's hands fluttered, and her eyes were dark with distress. 'But, Luke!' she cried. 'He loves me! You know how he was—and *I* know that he's loved me! *I'm* his wife! She—that other one—'

'You're his wife now,' Luke agreed, filling his coffee cup. 'But have you been working at it lately, Anna?'

'Now, look.' She pushed back from the table, and tipped her head to see his face more clearly beyond the candlelight. 'Whose side are you on?'

'Yours, honey. I want everything right for you.'

She relaxed. 'If they can be,' she said softly.

'Yes,' he agreed. 'If they can be.'

CHAPTER FOURTEEN

When Anna left Luke she went up to her room, too hurt and bewildered to call Jock. She thought that she might not call him at all. She would go back to California without seeing him. She would not endure being placed in a position where she might seem to beseech and plead. Pride would prevent her from doing that.

She went to bed, thinking about those things.

But the next morning she awoke, having slept poorly, to remember that there still was Jock, and she knew that she must see him. Seeing him would make all the difference! She must learn what, exactly, had happened to him, and so to her.

Maybe he wouldn't want to see her, but she'd insist that he must. Maybe he wouldn't see her alone, and maybe someone would call her an Indian. So what? Even, what if she were one? Jock loved her. Or, he had used to.

With determination firming her chin, and glowing in her black eyes, she dressed and went downstairs to eat breakfast, sitting at a table by the window, and watching the busy traffic of Twelfth Street with genuine interest. Everything was decided, she would see Jock, talk to him—and know, then, what she must do.

She ate a good breakfast, and walked about the lobby for a few minutes, looking in at the shop windows, deciding that she would do a little shopping after she had seen Jock. She bought a newspaper, and went back to her room.

Her hands were shaking when she took the big telephone book and found the number of Jock's hotel. She wrote it down, and considered the trembling.

'I've been stalling for a time,' she said aloud. 'I'm afraid ...'

She got herself a drink of water, and came back to the desk. Firmly she picked up the telephone, and spoke the number into it. When an answering voice came to her, she firmly asked to speak to 'Dr. Jock—I mean, Dr. James Askew, Junior, please.'

There was a pause; Anna read the wine list under the glass desk top. And jumped a little when the operator spoke.

'I'm sorry, Dr. Askew is not in his room. Shall I have him paged?'

'No,' said Anna. 'Please leave word for him to call the Jefferson Hotel, Room 927. Mrs. Askew. Thank you.'

She put the phone down and looked at her watch. Jock would have gone to the hospital. She had forgotten how early hospital people started their days. Even at the Foundation everyone was busy by nine o'clock. Well, she could wait.

She tidied her clothes, washed out some stockings, turned on the TV, read the newspaper. She didn't want to leave the room for fear of missing Jock's call. She would just settle down and amuse herself. At noon she had some lunch sent up to her, and remembered that Noah had said he would call.

For a while she thought about Noah, and then about Luke Fogarty, both good friends, whom she liked and trusted.

After her lunch tray had gone away, she

roamed about the room, and tried fitfully to watch TV. She was tired, and sleepy, and finally she tucked up on the bed and took a nap; she awoke feeling confused. Where was she? What had happened that she should feel as if she had done something wrong, something foolish?

She stumbled to her feet, found her shoes, and went into the bathroom to wash her face, and comb her straight black hair.

The phone. It had not rung. Where could Jock *be*? Well, of course! He was at the hospital! And he had not returned to the hotel for lunch; he probably would not return all day. She should have called the hospital—hours ago. Here it was three o'clock, and she had wasted the whole day!

Again she tugged the heavy book out of its place on the shelf below the desk, and for a panicky minute she could not remember the name of the hospital.

'Now, take it easy,' she told herself. 'You'll recognise it ...' She flipped the pages with a flopping sound until, in the classified section, she found HOSPITALS. Her lips moving, she ran her finger down the list. What a lot of them there were!

Alexian. Barnes. Ah, there it was. Of course! Brownlee Memorial. How stupid of her!

She scribbled the number, put the book away, sighing at its weight, and then picked up the telephone. A pleasant voice answered immediately.

'Brownlee Memorial Hospital. Good afternoon.'

Anna asked if she might speak to Dr. Askew. It was Mrs. Askew calling.

'Just a minute, please.'

The voice came back. 'I'm sorry, Mrs. Askew, but doctor has checked out. He can be reached at the home of Mrs. Peter Henderson, the phone number is ...'

Anna wrote the number on the pad, said, 'Thank you,' and put the phone down. Mrs. Henderson would be Iris. Anna was sure of that. So what did she do now? Call there? Wait in this hated hotel room until Jock got back some time tonight, and called her?

No—

Again she stooped for the heavy directory. This time she cleared a space on the desk top; she would leave it there!

Again her finger traced down the column—there it was. The street address meant nothing to Anna. It could be ten miles away. But even if it was, she'd go see for herself who this woman was, where she lived, what Jock might be doing there.

She would dress and call a taxi—and go ...

She went over to the closet and considered the clothes that hung there. The blue suit; another one of small brown and white checks. The red jersey dress she was wearing. Which? She debated for several minutes—and when she had decided, she still fussed over the accessories she would use, the hat she would wear—if she wore a hat ...

All that fuss was not like Anna, and she knew it. The clothes she wore—or bought, for that matter—were usually a matter of quick decision, of instinctive combinations with the proper pin, or necklace, the right gloves and shoes and hat.

Finally, dressed in the brown check, with a small brown hat, a big brown bag, and the calfskin pumps, with gloves to match them, she hung her cashmere coat around her shoulders and went downstairs. The big lobby was busy, and she threaded her way through groups of hearty men wearing badges of some sort. Several looked appreciatively at the slender, dark young woman.

Anna did not notice them at all; she gave the address to the taxi driver, and settled into the seat, again interested in the city about her. She wasn't going to worry. She would see Jock within the hour, and she would be able to talk to him. Of course she would! She knew her husband; he had come back here to the city, to his home, and he had felt a strong sense of obligation to his family. He had, Anna knew, long suffered a feeling of guilt about his children, and about his parents.

'I did something wrong there,' he had told her once. 'Or we would not be so widely separated.' Now, that separation had ended. And his feeling that he could correct the wrong which he had done had probably overcome his sense of obligation to Anna. She would be able to talk to him ...

The drive took about twenty minutes, perhaps a little longer. Time enough, anyway, for Anna to gain her composure. When she got out of the cab, and paid the driver, she could stand for a minute and look at the street where Iris Henderson lived. There were tall, bare trees, terraced lawns, and handsome houses. There was a nursemaid with a child, an enchanting little boy on a tricycle. He said, 'Hi!' to Anna in the friendliest fashion.

'Hi!' she answered, and turned to go up the steps to the front door of the white-painted brick house.

For a second, she hesitated, then she lifted the knocker and let it drop. Would the sound be heard within a large house? She was curious about that problem, and bright-eyed, when a neat maid opened the door.

'Oh!' said Anna. 'I—I understand Dr. Askew is here? I would like to see him. Please?'

'The name?' asked the young woman.

'Mrs. Askew,' said Anna with dignity, and she moved forward.

'If you will wait in here ...' said the coloured girl, a bit uncertainly. Back-stairs gossip had not taken note of a present Mrs. Askew. So much for romance-making!

Anna walked into the den, struck at once by its comfort, and its rich air of serene quiet. The big red leather chairs, a bowl of red carnations—

The maid had left the door open, and the sounds of the house came to her. A baby cried, was stilled, and then could be heard making the small gurgly noises which a happy baby does make. Women's voices, and a man's laugh came from a distant room. And, finally, Jock's voice, richly firm and confident. He was upstairs, and—

Anna closed her eyes, and put her hand out for the chairback. Already she knew what had happened to Jock. She need not stay and ask him, for she knew! Here, in this house, was the one thing Anna had not been able to give him, a family. A son, a daughter—and the baby, the promise for the future. The 'obligation of

341

continuity,' Jock called it.

Feeling sick, Anna leaned against the chair, and tipped her head back. Her eyes fell upon the portrait that hung above the mantel. Life size, it was the painting of a young woman in a red hunting coat. She held a small black cap and a riding crop in one hand, her blonde hair clung to the velvet collar of her coat. Her eyes were blue, her mouth tender. A fragile girl, a sheltered flower.

The portrait confirmed Anna's conviction that she had lost this contest. Knowing that she had, she need not wait for him to tell her so. Biting her lip to keep from crying out in pain and defeat, Anna turned towards the door, wanting only to escape, and not see Jock!

But she had no luck there, either, for before she could take more than a step, Jock came in, walking fast, amazed to see her.

'Anna!' he cried loudly. 'What—?'

She held herself very still, her dark eyes steady. She said nothing.

'I thought it must be Mother,' he blurted. 'And I was worried. She usually comes right upstairs—and— What on earth are *you* doing *here?*'

He wore that familiar, inquiring look, so characteristic of Jock, though he seldom turned it on Anna. He had always seemed to know

342

what it was she wanted, what she had in mind.

She could have cried, and was so afraid that she would cry, and go to him, clinging, begging, that she stood wooden, not even moving her eyes.

'I came,' she said, speaking carefully and precisely, 'to see what had happened to you. I've found out—' She turned her head to look at the portrait, and her hand lifted a little to indicate those who were in the rooms above.

'I'm sorry—' said Jock, coming towards her.

She stepped back. 'You cannot be a bigamist, Jock Askew!' she said sharply.

He sighed, and nodded. That idea had come to him, too. That he was acting, and feeling, like a man with two wives.

He looked completely miserable, and Anna's heart went out to him. She had never before seen Jock look so.

'Look,' he said, 'let's go somewhere. We can't talk here.'

'Why can't we?' asked Anna, her face immobile. 'Because this is *her* house?' She tipped her head towards the blonde woman in the painting. 'And *she* wouldn't like it?'

'Now, look, Anna,' Jock cried in protest. Then he flushed, and looked miserable again.

'It is her house,' he admitted, 'and I— Oh, Anna, I am sorry for the whole thing. I haven't wanted to hurt you. It's the last thing I would ever want to do.'

Anna pulled at the cuff of her soft leather gloves. 'You have hurt me,' she said quietly. 'Now, what do we do? What comes next?'

He sighed. 'When did you get in? Where are you staying?'

She told him. 'It was a mistake to come, but I thought I had to see you, to talk to you.'

'Yes. I should have gone out and talked to you. I— Wait. I'll get my coat, and then I'll drive you downtown, and we can talk ...'

He went out of the room, and, after waiting a minute, Anna walked slowly to the front door, through it, and down the steps. On the sidewalk, she turned and looked up at the house, at the small-paned, lamp-lit windows, at the screened porch, and the garden behind the wall. A big, gracious house, and rich.

But Jock had plenty of money! More, probably, than he could earn by staying here in St. Louis and filling his father's shoes. For a swift instant, Anna wished that she could go to see that father! But, of course—

Then Jock brought a car up to the curb— Jamie's car, he told Anna. He would have talked more of Jamie, but Anna sat silent beside him, stony-faced, and frightened. Terribly, terribly frightened. So she would feel, caught helpless in an earthquake, with the walls of her home crashing and crumbling about her, and no way of escape open to her.

She sat very still in the low seat, and stared unblinking at the city streets. Dusk had fallen, and lights bloomed like bright flowers, yellow—red—blue—green—

Jock talked. She didn't listen. When they were, she knew, close to the hotel, she touched his hand, swiftly, withdrawing her fingers again. She would not trust herself really to touch him. She had never loved him more, nor wanted him so much.

'Can we park somewhere for a minute?' she asked; she could not endure any more of his fumbling for words.

He nodded, and within the next block he pulled against the curb. 'The hotel is only a block away.'

'I know. I want to talk here.'

He cut the motor. 'Anna ...'

'We must get a divorce, mustn't we?' she asked stonily.

He put his hand up to his face, shocked beyond words. The idea had never occurred to him. He would stay here and do what needed to be done. Then he would return to Anna, who would be waiting. But, of course— 'Is that what you want?' he asked stiffly.

She did not speak.

'I suppose it would be the honest, decent thing,' said Jock. 'For you, I mean. I feel that I have certain obligations here, and if I stay—'

'Which you intend to do.'

'Anna, if you could just understand!'

'I think I do understand.'

'I want to do the right thing!' He turned in the seat to speak earnestly to her. 'If, years ago, I had stayed here and done the things I should ...'

Again she straightened her gloves, and pulled her coat about her shoulders. 'You then would never have gone to Di Trapani's night club,' she said calmly.

He leaned forward to look at her in the faint light. His eyes were bright, and his mouth troubled. 'This isn't easy for me, Anna!' he blurted.

'Good!' She reached for the door handle.

'But I know I can count on you to be big-minded ...'

'You'd better not count on anything from me,' she said coldly.

He was shocked. He sat back in his seat and stared at her. 'You can make your own decisions, of course,' he said with what dignity he could muster.

'Whatever I decide, what I want, has seemed

to make no difference, Jock.'

Now his face was stubborn, and he stared ahead of him, not at her. 'I have to stay here,' he said tightly.

'Without me.'

His lips compressed. 'If you say so.'

She opened the car door. 'Well—good-bye, Jock.'

'Wait. I'll drive you.'

But she was on the sidewalk, and walking towards the corner. He sat where he was, watching her, slim, erect, sure of herself, not needing him or his help.

When she disappeared, he started the engine, turned the corner, and went back to the West End.

Anna was up in her hotel room, still shivering with the cold, and the emotion of the last hour, when the phone rang. It was Noah Green; he had not been able to locate Jock, he said, but would Anna ...?

'Wait.' Swiftly she told him what had happened. She had seen Jock; he wanted a divorce —and—

'I don't believe it!' shouted Noah.

'I don't either,' said Anna in a small voice. 'But I am going back to California as soon as I can get me a flight. I—I don't like your city, Noah.'

He protested. He offered to help her. He would punch Jock Askew in the nose.

Anna said that she would need no help, but that the punch might do Jock some good. A little. She thanked Noah, said good-bye, and hung up. After a minute she called the desk about air reservations. She could, she found, leave at midnight.

As for Noah Green, he decided that he would seek out that consummate fool, Jock Askew. He would find him, too, by all that was holy! And—yes—punch him in the nose.

So he did just that. He went to Jock's hotel, he sat down in one of the chairs beside the entrance steps, and when Jock came in, around eight, Noah stood up, laid his overcoat on the chair, grabbed Jock by his coat, and swung his fist hard. Jock staggered, and fell, the doorman sprung forward. Noah picked up his coat, gave the doorman a dollar, and walked out to his car parked along the curved drive.

By next morning, Jock Askew had the black eye his father had been waiting for. When asked about it by his family, and at the hospital, he said only that he must have had it coming to him.

Saying she would get the divorce was the easiest part of it, Anna was to find. There were countless details to handle, harrowing interviews in the lawyers' offices, conferences, arguments with her own lawyer. Things were to be her way, Jock had instructed his man, the Foundation's attorney. He would enter an appearance which meant that Jock would not contest the divorce action, said Anna's lawyer, one Troy McBride, whom Sam Minter had recommended. Once McBride had himself gone through the Foundation's tests and evaluation.

Anna stared unbelieving at him. 'Contest it!' she cried. 'He's the one who *wants* it!'

So McBride explained to her about collusion.

'I'm not colluding,' cried Anna. 'I'm doing what he's made me do!'

'She's a difficult client,' McBride told Dr. Minter. 'I hope she doesn't make trouble for us at the hearing.'

'She's a really fine person,' said Sam, in a troubled way. 'But so is Jock, for that matter.'

'Will you please tell me what goes on here?'

Sam tried to tell him. And the telling didn't make much sense, even to him.

'But I'll have to go on with it?' asked the attorney.

'You, or someone else.'

So McBride pursued the necessary course,

sorry for the slender, dark young woman who was so tortured every step of the way. The experience was leaving her with little but her pride. She was deeply hurt, and showed it. She would accept no alimony; she would not listen to the talk of a division of their property.

What did California laws matter to her? The Foundation was Jock's, and the car, and the house! Losing him, she must lose everything which she had had with him.

Of course she would get along! She would find work. She had done hospital office work before; she could do it again. No, not at the Foundation where she and Jock had lived together, and worked together. She tried doing that, for a few days, and knew that it was not the place for her to begin a new life. People watched her when they thought she was unaware, and she felt that they were asking each other what Anna must have done to make Jock desert her. She knew they asked such questions because she asked them herself. But the Foundation—Anna was loved there, all of the personnel had been her friends. But they had loved Jock, too. And he was needed—wanted. Anna was not. Jock would not return to the Foundation if she were there.

So she packed her clothes, and left. She told Sam and Frances that she meant to resume her career.

She knew many people in the world of entertainment, she said. Night-club owners, producers, actors, and singers; many had come to the Foundation, and several had maintained the friendship formed there with the Askews. So Anna went to Los Angeles, rented a small apartment, unpacked her clothes, and made a list of the people who might be able to help her.

She realised that she had lost her ability to think of herself as a single entity. She still could sing—but she no longer thought that people would enjoy seeing her or hearing her.

She did not want to be a café singer again! She wanted no man listening to her, watching her, applauding her! She would do better to get a job as a check-room girl, or behind some store counter. But that would be no good, either. Nothing was any good.

Trying to conceal this defeatist attitude, but not succeeding very well, she called the first man on her list, the owner of the big café where Jock first had seen her. George Di Trapani provided entertainment for his guests at all hours of the day. A floor show at night, dinner music, luncheon music—

Well, of course he wanted to see her, cried George when her call went through to him. 'What are you doing in town, darling? Look, I'll arrange a little party! Is the doctor with you?'

'No, George. Now, listen to me. I want to see you on a business matter ...'

He laughed heartily at the seriousness of her tone. That was Anna's line, he told his secretary when he hung up. 'She is as grave as an Indian, and she looks like a doll—and then she'll move her eyes, or flash her teeth—and you're just devastated, darling! You really *are!*'

'What does she want?'

'Business, she says. Probably a benefit or something. Anyway, she's a doll, so leave me two hours for luncheon with her. Can do?'

'I'll try.'

George Di Trapani was a big man; his clothes were meticulously tailored to conceal any bulges. His black hair was thinning; he wore heavy black-rimmed glasses, usually pushed up on his forehead, and he always carried a half-smoked cigar.

'I hope,' thought Anna, coming into his office, 'that when Di finally dies, they put his glasses up that way, and have a cigar in his hand ...' She smiled faintly at the conceit, and George came around the desk to greet her.

He pressed his cheek against hers, and assured her that her smile was worth a thousand dollars. He had ordered lunch sent to his office. Would Anna like that? Good.

He seated her in a chair at the corner of his great desk, and resumed his big leather chair behind it. Anna gazed at him gravely. What problems and emotional disturbances had Di brought to the Foundation last year? Had the unit helped him? He seemed supremely self-confident and in charge of his life. But, according to Jock, nearly every man had his conflicts. Some hidden frustration or sense of failure, perhaps hidden even from himself.

Perhaps Jock would say that those frustrations were evidenced in the size of this man's office, its richness, the great mahogany desk, and the thronelike chair behind it. His coat lapels were a thread more narrow, his cuffs seemed whiter than those of other men.

Anna shook her head. She had never been the psychiatrist of the family; why should she start now? She glanced at Di's face, and smiled faintly. He was watching her.

'What can I do for you, sweetheart?' he asked gently.

She—fumbling—told him. The best she could.

The man behind the desk listened, his lips pursed, and soon he began to shake his head. 'It doesn't make sense, darling,' he told her when she stopped speaking.

'That I want to go back to work?'

His hand, and the cigar, slashed through the air. 'No! That Dr. Askew should decide to go back to his mother and his first wife—and that you would let him do such a thing!'

'But, Di—'

'I suppose you are thinking that you have been a good sport about the whole thing. All right. Tell me this: why should you be any kind of a sport? You married the doctor, you were a good wife to him—that I know!—why did you let him even ask you to be a good sport?'

'Do you think all this was my fault?'

'Some of it, certainly. Of course that first wife—and that mother—they helped you.'

Anna had scarcely mentioned Jock's mother, and Iris only by implication. 'His family,' she had called Jock's obligation in St. Louis.

'But, Jock—'

'Oh, he is doing what he thinks he wants to do. But you know better; why didn't you make him know it, too?' He shook his head reproachfully at Anna, then turned to shout, 'Come in!' towards a discreet knock on the door. A waiter wheeled in a table containing their luncheon. He arranged the food, set chairs, and departed. Anna and Di Trapani moved to the table.

'Now, eat,' said Di, as a father would speak to a child. 'We can talk later. The fillet should not get cold.'

Anna tried to obey. She listened to his chatter about his restaurant, about his wife, and his new boat. The food was delicious—but after twenty minutes, Di gave in.

'All right, sweetheart,' he said sadly, 'so the food is no good.'

'Oh, Di—'

'I know. I know. A crust of bread where the heart is— So talk to Di some more. You want to sing in my dining-room. Is that it?'

'I just want work of some kind, Di. I know your performers—'

'They don't come better than you, Anna. But you'd need clothes, a band connection—arrangements— So let's start from the beginning, eh?'

'I still don't know why you think I am more to blame than Jock for what has happened,' she said dispiritedly.

'Because you *are* more to blame,' Di told her. He was slipping a fresh cigar out of its wrapper. 'Eat your *spumone*, darling. It is very good, and you are much too thin. Your eyes are too big.'

Anna tasted the green centre of the ice cream on her plate. It was very good indeed.

Di nodded with satisfaction to see her eating.

'It isn't that we blame you in the usual sense,' he said slowly. 'I mean, like we would if you had been unfaithful to the doctor, or something. But you did send him off; you told me that he didn't want to go when his father was first sick? Yes. Well, you sent him off—you should have gone with him. All right, all right! So his people had never welcomed you. But is there a law says you couldn't have stayed in the hotel near where Askew was? No, there is not such a law.

'So that is one thing you did wrong. Especially if there was another woman waiting for him in St. Louis. And, having done wrong to let him go off alone, you let him stay there alone. Why did you do such a thing, Anna, darling?

'I am sorry for you, but I am even sorrier for Jock Askew. I owe that man a lot. He set me straight with my life. And I would like to see his life set straight. It used to be a very good life. When I was in Tree Valley, one of the big items there for me was the way you were, and the way he was. His contentment, his assurance in you and in his home, and in his work. Remember that late afternoon on your porch—a big, airy porch it was. And we sat there talking. The doctor sat slumped down in his big chair, his hand rubbing his dog's ears. But if you spoke or moved, his eyes would always go to you, and he would smile a little. You two made life seem so simple, and possible for other men to have. It—well—it helped me.

'So now you have spoiled that life, and you have come to me, and ask me why I blame you for letting Dr. Askew be the way all men are. Even smart men. Maybe *especially* smart men, Anna. They need to have their one woman close, to be able to smile at her. When they are left alone, other things come into their lives.

'Oh, Anna, you should have stayed right with Jock, held on to him, and put up a fight if he showed any sign of leaving you and your good life together. Did you do that? Did you fight?'

Anna looked down at her hands and bit her lip. 'I couldn't,' she murmured. 'I was too hurt. I realised that he had never broken with his past. And he must do that, Di. He must do that himself!'

'He will do it,' Di said sadly. 'Perhaps too late, but—'

'What should I have done?'

'Not what you did do. Let the past take him back. He is a virile man, with his own ideas. And you lost him. That's the easiest kind to lose, even for you. And I cannot understand what you must have been thinking of, not to make a fight to keep him.'

He leaned back and regarded Anna, who was an exciting woman. She sat there across the table from him, her black hair smooth, her pointed, piquant face troubled. When she lifted

357

her huge black eyes towards him, Di's heart lurched. What has she lacked? he asked in wonder. What did she lack?

Now she smoothed the edges of her checked jacket, and looked pleadingly at the big man across from her.

'I thought I was doing the right thing,' she said sadly. 'I have been most upset. Puzzled. I didn't understand why he would want to leave me and his work— Just as you did, I thought Jock liked everything he had. I thought—I counted on his realising that he had made a mistake, and I thought that when he did realise it, he would come back to me, and that all this nightmare would be over.

'But he hasn't come back. He's gone out of my life, just as if he had died. But I must go on living—though I don't know how that will be done.'

George Di Trapani was kind to her. He said that she could have a job in his restaurant. She could serve as one of the hostesses, and line up some sort of programme, singing with the orchestra at the cocktail hour. There were details to be worked out, of course, but he would help Anna.

She thanked him, and went away, promising to call him. And she went back to the apartment to sit looking at the wall, remembering all that he had said to her. Everyone seemed to agree with Di. But what could she do? Now?

For one thing, she'd not use this man's pity. She meant to earn her way! To go back and do for herself as she had done before she married Jock. And to go that far back—meant—Luke.

Was Luke still in St. Louis? Should she phone the hotel and find out? Or—

She went out and bought a copy of *Variety*. She hunted—and found—the few lines she searched for. Luke Fogarty, and his 'combination,' was playing in Chicago. Luke was readying a new musical comedy. It was to be a costume piece. His past successes were—

Three days later, Anna was on her way to Chicago to see Luke. Now pride had no place in the things which she took with her. She was alone, she needed work, and where else should a woman in such a position look except to her friends?

Besides, Luke knew the kind of work she could do. She had worked with him, and successfully. They could dig up the old arrangements—he had mentioned a part for her in his musical comedy—Yes, Luke would be the solution.

Luke, too, told her that she had been a fool.

But of course he would help her.

'Will you marry me, Anna?'

'You're joking!'

'Not me.'

'Well, I wish you were. I came here—I want a *job*, Luke. Work!'

'But, Anna—'

She made a gesture of impatience. 'I know you love me, Luke,' she cried. 'Or think you do ...'

'I love you,' he said soberly.

'But— Oh, I am sorry, dear, but right now what I need is—'

'Yes. A job. Well—all right. There's one for you. A small part in the new play—I wrote it with you in mind. It has two good songs, and you'll be a smash. I know you will be. So— We go into production in April. I'll tell the producer. I'll bet many a nostalgic man will remember Anna Heath—'

But Anna's black hair was whipping from side to side. 'No, Luke,' she said firmly. 'I've been Mrs. Jock Askew for ten years. I'll be Anna Askew—and make *that* name famous for you. Oh, Luke, I am asking a great deal, I know.'

'You'll make the play,' he said gruffly. 'So I'm not giving you a thing!'

'Good. I'm glad you feel that way. But, don't

you see, darling, that I do still feel like Jock's wife? A piece of paper and some records back in California can't change that. And I'm just as sure that Jock, in his inner thoughts, considers me as he did during the time we were together.'

'Then the guy can be brought up for bigamy, I suspect,' said Luke angrily.

'If so, I'm agreeing to the crime. For bigamy is better than nothing, Luke. However many other women he has in his life, I am still Jock's wife, and I'll go on as if things would turn out all right for both of us.'

Luke shook his head. 'You beat the world, Anna,' he told her, gazing at the small, exquisite girl, wondering what it was she possessed that touched the hearts of all men, and made them want to shelter her, to help her, to—love her. All men but that prime idiot, Jock Askew. Had the man lost his mind? Or was it only that he had left Anna, and so her spell had faded ...

Well, his loss might be Luke's gain, given time, and patience.

'Tell me,' he asked Anna, 'is Jock going to marry the blonde?'

Anna shrugged. 'I don't know ...'

Luke leaned towards her. 'Don't you care?'

She smiled a little wryly. 'Oh, I care,' she said earnestly. 'But his marrying her or not doesn't make much difference. In the way I feel about him, I mean.'

Luke sighed. 'You're different, Anna,' he said slowly. 'You've changed.'

'Oh, Luke—'

'I still love you,' he told her. 'Maybe I love you even more—if that could be possible. But you *are* different!'

'It's been ten years. And people grow.'

'The strong ones do,' he agreed. He smiled at her, lacquered hair, small, perfect body, her face—the high cheek bones and the great solemn eyes.

The fragile, serene, though troubled, woman was looking up at him. 'Are you calling me strong?' she asked, in wonder—and hope.

CHAPTER FIFTEEN

It was a pleasantly warm spring evening, and Jock protested mildly at Jamie's wish to go into the hospital through the ambulance entrance.

'You have a fine taste in knick-knacks,' he told his son, only half sincere in his growl. Jock was happy that he could go anywhere with the boy.

'Don't you find the emergency rooms exciting?' asked the slim, eye-glassed youth at his side.

'Demanding, stimulating—' said Jock in a considering tone. 'And—yes—exciting, sometimes.' His brown eyes sparkled.

Jamie made a small sound of assent. 'I thought so,' he muttered.

Jock opened the door, and the two men went into the lighted corridor, on either side of which opened the treatment rooms. Just within the door was a desk, and the admittance doctor in charge. There were benches for waiting patients or relatives of patients, there were nurses about, and an extremely busy intern. Jamie sniffed the air of hurry and urgency, and a smile of pure contentment settled about his lips and eyes. Jock noted the expression—Jamie would work out well as a doctor. He spoke to the resident and to the intern, and turned his head at the *clang, clang* of an ambulance bell.

A stretcher was already going through the door. Almost as quickly it came in again.

'Baby's almost here,' called the ambulance driver, following.

That stretcher went straight for the elevator.

'Who is she?' whispered Jamie.

Jock shrugged. 'We get them from everywhere,' he told his son, speaking in his normal voice which was firm, and clearly heard, neither loud nor secretively soft. 'Bankers, burglars—people from all walks of life. She could come from Ladue or the Millcreek district.'

'Will she make it to Delivery?'

'I think so. Because the intern thought she would.'

'Is he a good intern? I mean, would he know?' Jamie was anxious on this point.

'He's a good intern. And I hope he knows. If he doesn't, he will have learned a good deal tonight. He—' Jock broke off, for the doors were flapping open again. This time a squad car stood on the ramp, and there had been neither honk nor clang.

Two uniformed men got out of the black and white car, and escorted a well-dressed, fortyish man who walked with a stumble, and had a dazed look in his eyes. Blood dripped across his eye and cheek from a cut on his forehead.

Jamie looked inquiringly at Jock.

'OBS probably,' said his father. 'Observation,' he added in explanation.

The man could not remember anything but his name. He thought the time was Christmas 1944—Jock went over to him after a glance at the resident, and talked to the chap quietly for a minute.

'Send him to Psycho,' he told the resident, who agreed, just as a car's brakes screeched in the driveway, and a man stuck his head through the doors, asking for a stretcher.

That patient, a woman, had passed out suddenly at home; she had come to on the ride to the hospital, but she was having hysterics. She turned and tossed and moaned as the bearers brought the stretcher inside. Behind her hovered three anxious relatives; they were asked to wait on the benches, and a doctor and a nurse followed the stretcher into room number 3.

Jamie's eyes questioned his father. 'We'll soon know,' said Jock. 'I can't make snap diagnoses.'

'You're pretty good at it,' said Jamie.

'A woman in labour, a man with a mental lapse,' Jock agreed. 'And sight unseen I'll bet this next one shows blood.'

'This next one' did. The ambulance clangs had been three, and the resident went out with the stretcher. As he came back he was saying 'get Barnaby.'

'Oh, oh,' murmured Jock. 'A hand's been hurt.'

'How do you know *that?*' asked Jamie.

'Tell you later. There's your blood.'

And, indeed, it was there, dripping in a trail

behind the stretcher going into room 4.

'We'll tag along when Barnaby comes,' Jock promised Jamie.

'Can you?'

'As Acting Medical Director, I'm supposed to know what goes on around here. Now here comes your diagnosis on the hysteria.'

Jamie reluctantly turned away from his fascination with room 4. The intern was talking to the relatives of the hysterical woman; her anxiety had lessened appreciatively once the doctor and nurse had taken charge.

'It's a simple matter of low blood pressure,' the young man was saying in the kindest possible way. 'When she came to she was frightened, and hysteria occurred. She's had a sedative, and will be all right, but our advice would be to enter her for tests and treatment.'

Jamie smiled at his father. 'It's nice when they turn out that way,' he said boyishly.

'Very nice. Here comes Barnaby.'

'Dad ...'

'Later, son. Now, let's just squinch into a corner and watch. Unless you don't want to?'

Jamie was into room 4, close behind the surgeon.

The injured man had a broken arm, and a mangled hand. Jock indicated that to Jamie.

'Keep your attention on the hand,' he said softly.

'What ...?'

'Trauma to the distal phalanx,' said Jock, loudly enough for Barnaby to catch the words, and turn to look at him.

'I'm teaching, doctor,' said Jock.

Jamie flushed.

Barnaby grunted something, and turned back to the hand under examination. 'Soak it in sterile saline and pHisohex,' he said gruffly. 'For fifteen minutes. Give toxoid—antitetanus— as required. You can question him. Demarol. And then bring him up to surgery.'

He glanced at Jock again, and went out.

Jamie and Jock watched for another five minutes or so, then Jock touched Jamie's arm, and they left the room. 'We'll sit in on the job upstairs,' Jock told the boy.

'Does Dr. Barnaby tend to just fingers?' asked Jamie, in the elevator. It was the one in which Jock had once been caught between floors.

'No,' Jock told him. 'But *just fingers* can be pretty damn important. And, to continue the lecture I started downstairs, trauma can include partial or complete amputation, avulsion of the tactile pad—I hope you're following me?— crushing with avulsion of soft tissue and bone, and avulsion or rupture of the nail base with exposure of the bone. There's already been involuntary amputation for our man, so we'll see some good surgery—and, to answer your question, Barnaby was called because Brownlee Hospital is especially sensitive just now to distal phalanges.'

They walked out of the elevator, and down the corridor to the locker room. Since Jock's activities as Medical Director in Brownlee, and his intensified campaign against staph infections, no one got past the heavy swinging doors of the operating rooms without being masked, shirted, trousered, booted and capped in faded green, sterile clothing that was as relatively germ free as human ingenuity could make it.

Jamie's eyes sparkled to find himself invested in the same wrinkled garments as Jock wore, and as did Dr. Barnaby, the Chief Surgeon. He was especially intrigued by the cloth boots.

'Put them on over your shoes,' Jock directed the boy. 'They have rubberised soles because of the static electricity hazard.'

'Aren't the floors ...?' asked Jamie.

'They're as safe as we can make them,' said Jock. 'But a gas explosion does some very nasty things. Come along.'

He led the way to the lower of the two benches which arced about the operating theatre. They found the surgical team waiting for the patient to be anaesthetised. Everything was in readiness. Dr. Barnaby was holding aloft a pair of scissors in his gloved hand. The nurse, her hair hidden under a surgical cap, and her face masked, stood with both her rubber gloves held high, as if in benediction.

'Dad, tell me ...' whispered Jamie.

'Not here, son. Watch the surgery. I'll explain that, and it will let you understand the rest of the story, which I'll tell you later.'

Three others—students—had come in to observe. The resident surgeon began to explain the procedure to them, and Barnaby said something to him. He glanced at Jock. 'Doctor, if you would prefer ...?'

'Not at all,' said Jock. 'Carry on. But keep it simple. My candidate has not yet digested the red dictionary.'

There were smiles, and the patient moaned a little.

'We have a matter of crushing here,' said the resident, then. 'Second and third fingers, with abrasion to the whole hand. There is also a simple fracture above the wrist. This will be cared for at a later time. Now the anaesthesia ...'

The anaesthetist took over, and mentioned the Demarol. 'Anaesthesia occurs at both ends of the anterior quadrant at the level of the proximal flexion crease—'

Jock was showing Jamie on his own hand, and one of the medical students moved to a place where he could watch them.

'1.5 to 2cc. of 1 per cent Procaine,' said the anaesthetist.

'Volar block of each digital nerve provides anaesthesia of the dorsum of the distal two phalanges. Since it is necessary here, a digital tourniquet is used to prevent bleeding.'

'Arm tourniquets are not used,' said the resident.

'Irrigation,' Jock explained to his small audience, 'normal saline. I suppose.'

'All loose bits of tissue, epidermis and keratin are removed,' said the resident, who was busy handing things to Dr. Barnaby. 'Skin edges are trimmed only if bad crushing occurs—it does here on one finger. Fragments of bone—are dissected out. Soft tissue is freed from the bone before trimming.'

'Technique,' spoke up Dr. Barnaby, waiting for the nurse to sponge his brow, 'must be gentle, and fine instruments are used.'

The resident held up a thin-bladed scalpel, and then pointed with it to the tray of 'fine' instruments.

The two men worked on for a few minutes, silently and absorbedly. 'After reconstruction,' said the resident when he resumed his lecture, 'the remaining defect is covered with a split-thickness graft from the upper medial forearm. Sometimes this graft is taken from the lateral thigh. Ligatures and sutures are—' He glanced at the nurse, and she murmured something. 'Yes! 5-0 silk. The fingers are dressed with two triple-folded 4 x 8-inch gauze pads, one covering the sides, and the other the front and back of the finger. Roller gauze and adhesive tape are used for compression. The arm is to be carried in a sling. Any questions?'

'What antibiotics?' asked the student on the upper bench.

'None!' said both Dr. Barnaby and the resident.

'The patient might go home at once, though this one has some shock, and of course the fracture. We'll attend to that tomorrow morning—let him rest tonight—and then send him home. The dressings from the graft will be removed in five to seven days, but the direct repair should wait ten to twelve days.'

The surgeons withdrew, and Jock touched Jamie's arm. 'We'll change, then go down to my office,' he said. 'And, yes, I'll tell you, down there.'

One of the students delayed Dr. Askew with a question; when he and Jamie did reach the elevator, Dr. Barnaby was coming along the corridor, still wearing his green robe. 'I've a superstition about taking this thing off,' he told Jock, smiling at Jamie, 'until I get beyond phone reach.' He stepped into the elevator.

'Were you in the house when that case came up?' asked Jock, nodding his head back towards o.r.

'Yes. On rounds. I've left a standing order that I be called for these little items.'

'I know. But lightning may next strike some place else.'

'Wish we could eliminate the lightning.'

'We know how to do it, doctor. Though, as I've told you before, I am quite sure the surgery did not feature in our case.'

'You've said, too, that your intent is to clear up other hazardous factors here in this hospital.'

'I've said just that.' Jock's chin jutted.

Saying no more, Dr. Barnaby got off on three, and Jock and Jamie rode down to first.

'It gets more muddled all the time,' said Jamie unhappily.

'That will soon be over. Come in here.'

He sat down and glanced at a memo on the blotter. Jamie sat in one of the chairs, and looked at his father. He shifted his position, and shifted again. His dislocated hip made sitting a matter of careful calculation, often. 'Now,' he said hopefully, a determined look in his eye, 'what is all this about distal phalanges?'

Jock grinned at the boy, and leaned down to draw a folder from his desk drawer. He placed the papers on his blotter, but made no move to open the cover. Jamie knew by now that records were kept, and stored, in such folders, labelled and clamped.

'This matter will probably get into the newspaper within days,' Jock said slowly, 'though your grandmother and the hospital would give a great deal to preven tit. But it will come out, and in any case you have a right to know about the thing. Perhaps, in telling you about it, I shall be continuing the lecture I began upstairs.'

Jamie looked interested, dismayed, and puzzled, all at once. 'Shall I take notes?'

'If you want to. But I think you'll hold these things in mind, for a time, at least. You see, Jamie, your grandfather is being sued for malpractice and injury after surgery much like that you saw tonight.'

'But—'

'Yes. The injury occurred two and a half years ago; this migrant fruit picker managed to get his hand caught in a conveyer over in the Illinois peach orchards. He was brought into the hospital here, and Dr. Jim operated before a class, because hand injuries are common, and any surgeon—any doctor, almost—needs to know how to do the job. Now there is some tendon trouble, and the man is suing for damages. Among other charges of malpractice, he cites things which he claims were said in o.r. while the operation was taking place. He was conscious, of course, and he claims that remarks were made then, and later, concerning his nationality to indicate that he was getting less than first-class care from the surgeon.'

'Oh, dear,' said Jamie, but still looking bewildered.'

'Yes,' said Jock dryly. 'Oh, dear. Now—this suit was filed just before your grandfather became ill last November; it was on his mind; he was angry about it, and determined to fight the charge. When I came here, it seemed up to me to do what I could to protect Father's name.'

'I see.'

Jock smiled grimly. 'I've tried, in every way I could. I have studied the case, and talked to lawyers, on both sides. I have tried to see the man. Now it seems that the case must come to trial, and I am afraid Father's case is not too strong.'

'But surely the surgery was all right?'

'There is some remaining tendon damage.

The suit claims that transplants should have been made, which may or may not be a point. But I am fairly certain that this suit has been brought not so much as a complaint against the surgery done as it is in retaliation for the manner used when the patient was in the hospital. Your grandfather had his prejudices; we all do. And in the past months, he has been emotionally unbalanced so that his feelings against the minorities probably were not kept well concealed.'

'You mean, he hated Negroes and foreigners,' said Jamie bluntly.

Jock glanced at the boy. 'That is known to you, too, isn't it?'

'Of course. He had a fit when they first allowed Negroes to go to the University, and he wanted me to go some place else.'

For a minute or two, Jock said nothing. He would not, he thought, advise putting Jamie on the witness stand when the malpractice suit came to trial. But of course the boy—

He sat forward, and leaned towards his son. 'Several years ago,' he said slowly, 'I did some work for a group of insurance companies inquiring into the causes and circumstances of damage suits for malpractice.'

'Grandfather was a wonderful surgeon, wasn't he?'

'He certainly was. Skilled beyond most men.'

'O.K. Tell me what you started to say.'

Jock smiled at the boy, but the smile was sad. 'We found,' he said slowly, 'that many suits arose from the emotional imbalance of the patient involved. But we found that just about as many showed involvement with a doctor who was emotionally ill.'

The boy looked ready to say something, but he did not speak, and Jock continued. 'We found that psychological reactions played a bigger part in malpractice suits than the quality of treatment, or the fact that the doctor made a mistake in medical judgment. We found that the breakdown in doctor-patient relationship could be traced, more often than not, to a twisted emotional attitude. On the part of the patient—or of the doctor.'

'And you're saying that Grandfather—'

Jock sighed heavily. 'You yourself just mentioned that Dr. Jim had voiced deep-rooted racial and religious prejudices.'

'Ye-es.'

'In these past months he has been a sick man, Jamie. How long that sickness was coming on, we do not know. It seems certain that he continued to work long after he should have stopped.'

'Then you think—'

'Jamie, I know my father very well. Twenty years ago, he and I decided mutually that we could not work together, and the causes for that decision were valid.'

'Was it his fault?'

'Not entirely. I was opinionated, and stubborn.'

'Grandfather was stubborn, too. I know that! If people didn't agree with him, or like him—' Jamie broke off, his young face distressed.

'Yes,' said Jock. 'Many people demand frequent gratification of their emotional needs, though often on a subconscious level. I do conclude, however, that many, many suits for malpractice would never be filed had the attitude of the attending physician been—well—different.'

'But you still think that Grandfather did a good surgical job? On this patient, I mean.'

'I do. I truly do. Hand injuries often leave tendon trouble. However, the quality of the surgery is not the real issue. Not with the patient, and it won't be with the jury if this thing comes to trial.'

'And will it come to trial?'

'Your grandmother thinks that I should, before this, have told the Corbett Insurance Company to effect a settlement out of court.'

'Wasn't that the company you conducted the

investigation for?'

'That makes no difference, Jamie. This man sued; Corbett held your grandfather's liability insurance. Routinely, the company would have tried to effect a settlement out of court, as favourably as possible. Instead, I've been exploring the possibility of fighting the charge. But now I recognise that there is justification for a "damage" suit.

'Now, understand me, Jamie, I would like to be able to defend your grandfather entirely in this matter. He was a fine man, but like all of us, he had his faults. And in this case his prejudices probably did make him somewhat guilty of malpractice. I mean, he gave less of himself than he should, and I find it difficult to defend him to you when I find so much on the patient's side.'

He broke off to consider the way Jamie was looking at him. 'What's wrong?' he asked, involuntarily.

Jamie shrugged, and scrubbed the back of his neck with his fist. 'Oh,' he said unhappily, 'I was wondering why, if you feel that way, you *do* defend him.'

'Well, for one thing,' said Jock. 'He is my father. You'd defend me, I think, if I'd need defence. Wouldn't you?'

Jamie's tongue ran across his lips. 'With my

fists, maybe,' he conceded. Then he grinned swiftly. 'For what that sort of defence would be worth. But I'd not defend you by compromising my sense of what was right and just.'

Jock still gazed at the boy. He could feel his cheeks going hot, he could feel the edges of the hot tide of colour, and shame, creep across his face and down his throat. He got up from the chair abruptly, and walked across the room. Where had he let himself be led? Where had he gone of his own free will and wish?

He turned and looked at Jamie, still seated in the chair beside the desk, a slender young man, not very strong—physically.

'We'll talk about this some more,' he said gruffly.

It was not any part of coincidence that, the next morning, Jock's secretary brought him the card of Floyd Groghan, District Claims Agent for the giant Corbett Insurance Company.

For a long minute, Jock sat holding the card in his hand. Then he smiled up at the puzzled young woman. 'Ask Mr. Groghan to come in, please,' he said quietly.

He greeted his caller in the friendliest fashion, and the two men sat down. Mr. Groghan asked about Jock's father, and Jock replied.

'I suppose you know what brings me here,'

said Groghan.

'Perhaps you should tell me.'

'The name Yglesias rings loudly about us.'

'I hear it. The case goes to court next month.'

Floyd Groghan was a full-fleshed man, his face was as pink as a baby's, his deep-set blue eyes were keen. 'I came,' he said, 'to ask you if we couldn't help in some way.'

Jock's cheeks reddened, and he leaned forward, his hands tight on the desk edge. 'No!' he said loudly.

Groghan nodded. 'I win five bucks on that answer.'

'Floyd—this has been the hardest job I have had put upon me by Father's collapse.'

'You should have let us handle the whole thing. It was our job, right from the filing of the suit.'

'Yes, I know. But there was no fault with the surgery; you must understand that it could be defended in court!'

'I do understand that.'

'Our man is sore about being a fruit picker, and a foreigner.'

'And because someone said so.'

'In the hospital—in the operating room—yes.'

'But you still think he has no case?'

'Oh, he has a case. But not the one his lawyers will prosecute in court, that of negligence and faulty surgery.'

'You've looked into this, we know. Now, Jock, from here on, why don't you let us handle things? I may as well tell you that, whether you like it or not, the Company means to try to settle out of court. We're going to try our damnedest!'

Jock stared at his visitor. 'I should have known that, shouldn't I?' he asked in an odd tone.

'You were busy as all get out, trying to save your father's name.'

'I'd still hope to save it.'

'So would we.'

Jock wiped his hand down across his face. 'I'd have done better to stay out ...' he said in a tone of wry wonder at himself. Then he glanced at Groghan. 'You know? I've spent a considerable amount of time, and I've sacrificed a considerable lot of my own interests—'

Groghan stood up. 'While we were waiting for you to come to us. We owed you some favours, though I knew you wouldn't ask for any. That's why I came here myself this morning. To tell you that we'll be doing you no favour, but we hope to get you out of your hole, anyway.'

Jock laughed, and shook his head. 'What kept you?' he asked shakily. 'What *kept* you?'

Jock Askew was not so naïve as to suppose that everyone in Brownlee Hospital had welcomed his assignment as Acting Medical Director. To him, the main decision had been over his own willingness to serve. He was prepared for some of his changes in the hospital to be unpopular—and they were. He thought, after four months, that he knew pretty well who approved of him, and who did not. Any Medical Director had his admirers and his detractors.

But so far as Dr. Barnaby was concerned, the relationship had been friendly, courteous, and never in any way indicative that Dr. Jim's former assistant resented the naming of Jock to fill the post. He was certain that the surgeon had never, earlier, spoken to Emma on the subject. It was only when it seemed that the malpractice suit might be going to court that Barnaby spoke to Jim's wife, and Emma then spoke to Jock.

Jock didn't know exactly what Barnaby had said—something, he supposed, about a proper Medical Director standing behind his staff men, especially in time of trouble. At any rate, that was the message which Emma brought to her son.

'I'm sure,' she asserted, 'that if Dr. Barnaby

had been named Medical Director, he would be taking a different stand in this matter. He would do everything he could to keep Jim's name out of a sensational court trial.'

Jock sighed. 'Mother,' he attempted, 'this is a hospital matter.'

Emma's white head went up. 'And since when can't I discuss hospital matters with you?' she demanded. 'If you would only listen, my advice to you would be good. I had hoped that your work at Brownlee this time would go smoothly, and it would go that way if you would profit by the mishaps of the past. Now I can tell you what you should be doing to smooth things out here—'

'I was not aware of any roughness.'

'You should be aware of it! And most of the trouble is over your ideas for changing things in the hospital. You must give up those notions, Jock! They are only ideas. They do not work out in practice, and the wise thing for you to do would be to abandon them at once!'

That pleasant spring evening, Jock had welcomed his mother's suggestion that they drive out into the country. She went few places and her wanting to drive ... Now he drove at a steady pace, looking at the road before them, and only half-listening to her charges.

'... no need to change things! The hospital

is a busy, well-run institution, and it's got that way through routines and regulations set down through the years. Most of them were developed by your father. His ways have worked, and the personnel wants to have the old ways maintained, knowing that they work.

'When you came home, I was happy for you to take over your father's job. That is the way things should be. Father to son. You couldn't do the surgery but you did take over the medical directorship. Now, why can't you get along with Dr. Barnaby, who is doing your father's surgical work?'

'I get along with Barnaby.'

'Not by suggesting that your father mistreated a patient.'

'Oh, Mother!'

'If you were a surgeon yourself you'd understand your father's work, and you could have persuaded that man—'

Jock pulled the car into a wide semicircle at the side of the road. Below them was spread the Meramec Valley, misty now in the falling dusk of evening. The distant hills were purpling with the shadows of night.

'Mother,' Jock said firmly. 'Father thought the case should be fought in court. He wouldn't have had a chance to win it, but—'

'Why wouldn't he?'

'Not because of any surgical failure, but because of other elements which I, as a psychiatrist, can understand and value.'

'Psychiatrist!' sniffed Emma.

'I am one. In time, I think you'll find that my being one has helped you and Father.'

'You'd better forget all that, Jock, and get the insurance company—beg them, if necessary—to settle this case out of court. You don't seem to know how to handle this job any better than you're handling the medical directorship. I'm bitterly disappointed in you, Jock!'

All at once, he could take no more! Suddenly, he felt like screaming at his mother. He *wanted* to scream. Never before in his life had he felt so—so—torn into little flying shreds. He bit his lip, and clenched his hands, wishing that he were alone, that he could get out of the car and walk—that he—

All he could do was to draw a deep breath, and a second one. Then he turned, planning to say again that his mother knew nothing of hospital matters, but he stopped to consider the patient smile upon her face. Well, of course. To Emma he was about ten, and not exceptionally bright for his age.

'Let's go back to the city,' he said gruffly, starting the engine.

Emma did not speak again until they had

reached her hotel, and Jock got out to help her descend.

She reached up to kiss his cheek. 'Good night, dear. Don't worry about things. I'll see what I can do.'

Jock did not answer her. He stood, stiff as a wooden Indian, and watched her enter the hotel, and disappear from view. Then he got into the car, and drove back to the garage, still feeling that he could scream, and pound his fists, and shout, and—

He surrendered the car to the attendant, and went up to the lobby, across to the elevator, and finally to his room. Once inside, he leaned against the door, and felt sick—sick as he had never before been in his life. He wondered—

Moving carefully, he turned on some lights. He went into the bathroom and stared at his face in the mirror. He went out to the armchair, and sat looking at his hands. Who was this man who sat here in a hotel room in St. Louis when he belonged ...?

Whoever this man was, what had happened to Jock Askew? What had he become, and why?

Feeling the pull of the puppet strings on his wrists and limbs, resenting the need to move and speak in ways other than his own will dictated, he could, just barely, realise how those strings had become affixed.

But beyond that knowledge, what had *happened to him, a man in his own right? What changes had taken place in Jock Askew? Had he now the courage to examine that?* Anna could tell him, and would, if she were here. Only—she was not here.

Anna.

With a groan, Jock leaned forward and held his head in his hands.

Probably Dr. Barnaby had said more to Emma Askew than she had repeated to Jock. For Dr. Barnaby knew that several forces were at work in the hospital organisation, and outside of it, too. There was, for instance, Noah Green.

Noah's interest, and his behaviour, fascinated Dr. Barnaby. He did not understand why the man should be so interested in Brownlee Hospital affairs—an interest that was certainly there. Beginning with that first call on Dr. Barnaby, the surgeon had had repeated indications of Noah's 'meddling.'

There was the spring late afternoon when Barnaby encountered Mr. Green on the street. Perhaps by accident, but Noah seized upon his opportunity.

'Hello, doctor! How are things with you? How is the hospital doing? Is Jock Askew still trying to fill his father's shoes?' Noah fired his questions at Barnaby, and scarcely listened to the answers. 'I've never believed in dynasties,' he swept on. 'Doesn't Madame Askew know that she can't hand a job like the medical directorship down from father to son?'

'Mrs. Askew ...' attempted Dr. Barnaby.

'Oh, yes, she has had a hand in it. And I expect Jock might even make you a good director, given a chance.'

'Very good,' said poor Barnaby.

'Of course he's not needed here. For you would make an excellent director.'

Barnaby blinked.

'You were in line for the job, weren't you? Dr. Jim's assistant?'

'Yes, but those things can go many ways.'

'They can, they can! Well, it begins to look as if I should really be seeing what I can do.' Noah started down the street.

'Mr. Green ...'

Noah stopped, turned, and came back to Dr. Barnaby. His blue eye was dancing. 'I may not be a match for the ladies,' he agreed.

'But what do you plan to do, sir? I mean—hospital ethics—'

Noah nodded. 'Oh, there are several ways to handle this, Barnaby, and still be ethical. Now take the Brownlee Memorial Fund—it's always on the lookout for endowments. Since I may have one or two in my pocket—'

'Mr. Green, I want no appointment except on my own merit!'

'Sure. And you would get it that way, doctor. Just as Jock would lose it by the same process.'

'He's your *friend*, Mr. Green!'

'And I'm his.'

'But—'

'Don't worry. My scheme may not work. But if it does, Jock won't know what hit him. I can promise you that!'

Unhappy about the ones he did know about, Jock would have been shocked to guess at some of the forces at work. The morning after his anger with his mother, Jock rose, dressed, and went to his desk to carry on the day's work. He read his mail, he kept appointments—and at two o'clock that afternoon, he went to the scheduled Board meeting.

There were various items to be discussed—interns who were about to move on, new ones coming in. The matter of more air conditioning to the hospital. Jock had a suggestion to make about medical records.

He made the suggestion, asking that the records committee meet every two weeks, rather than once a month.

'Why is this desirable, Dr. Askew?' inquired one of the laymen of the Board.

Jock explained the services of the medical records committee, mentioning that it commonly met only once a month, and that, in a large hospital, too many patients' charts accumulated to be adequately reviewed in one session.

It was the sort of thing the Medical Director might be expected to suggest at a Board meeting. Jock had expected no great debate on the matter. He had already mentioned the thing in staff meetings. But now—

'Did the committee meet once a month when your father was Medical Director?' asked someone.

Jock frowned a little. 'Yes, sir, I believe so.'

'Have you made many changes in the hospital since you've taken office, sir?'

Now Jock glanced around the table. What was this?

'Well,' he said slowly, 'there's a certain amount of activity expected from any new broom.'

The smiles were only faint ones.

'I think the question to be answered,' said Mr. John Brownlee, Jr., the Chairman of the Board, 'is whether, should you become Medical Director of Brownlee Hospital, you would carry on in your father's way, or not? I have heard some talk, for instance, that you think the Pavilion should be discontinued. We would be opposed to such radical changes. Could you assure us that they would not be made?'

Jock opened his lips to reply. Then he paused, and again looked around the Board room. When he came to Mrs. Brownlee Hudson, strangely it was not her plump pink face he saw beneath the blue flower hat, but the face of his mother, stern, self-controlled, and handsome. And beyond it he had a quick vision of Beulah Stone, standing on the back stairs, her arms filled with feather pillows, when she told Jock—

What *would* Beulah say to Jock now?

His head went up, his cleft chin thrust forward, his brown eyes shone. 'I could assure you of no such thing,' he said clearly and firmly. 'There are many changes that I would make!'

'Humph!' said the Chairman of the Board, and went on to discuss the matter of air conditioning; should they extend this to the residents' quarters?

Jock doodled on his pad until the meeting was over, but once it was, he rose swiftly, and strode out of the room without speaking to anyone. His step was firm, his head was up— he felt one hundred per cent better for having made that decision, and announcing it!

He filled the rest of the day with routine matters; he ate dinner alone, and that evening attended a symposium on mental health, at which he was announced as Dr. Askew, of the Tree Valley Foundation.

The next morning, when he reached his desk at Brownlee, he found on it, precisely centred on the fresh green blotter, a letter from the Chairman of the Board. For a moment he sat looking at it, tempted to throw the thing, unopened, into the brass waste basket. But he did open it; he read the three paragraphs.

The hospital had valued Dr. Askew's services to them in a time of emergency ...

The Board had, in a special session, voted to extend the position of Medical Director to Dr. John Barnaby, of the Staff Surgical Service.

The Board appreciated the long service of Dr. James Askew, Sr., and recognised the sacrifice which his son had made in remaining in St. Louis for the months it had taken to find a replacement.

The Board extended its best wishes ...

Jock then dropped the letter into the basket, and sat staring at nothing. The letter could have said, but it did not, that the ideas of Dr. James Askew, Jr., were too advanced for the Board at this time ...

Jock smiled wryly, and shook his head.

Would he have to reply? Yes, he must dictate a short, formal letter. Then he must clean out his desk and take his possessions back to the hotel.

He must—

His phone buzzed and he snapped a button on his desk.

'Yes?'

'Dr. Askew, could you see Dr. Dees?'

'Yes. Yes, of course.'

Dr. Dees came into the office before Jock could compose his face into calm unconcern.

But the young resident in orthopedics was not in any mood to judge the expression on another man's face. His own calm had melted like snow, his usual drawl had turned into a spate of words, protests, and threats. 'I've been waiting for you, doctor!' he asserted. 'From the minute I saw that asinine notice up on the bulletin board, I—'

'Hey, now, look,' said Jock firmly. 'Sit down, doctor, and let's not lose our respective heads.'

'Dr. Askew—'

'Yes, I know. You are surprised. But, from the first, let's not lose sight of the fact that you are a surgeon, that the head of the surgical service in this hospital has been made the Medical Director, and that you have about forty years' worth of career ahead of you, doctor.'

Dees stared at the man behind the desk. 'Not in this hospital!' he cried.

Jock shrugged. 'This hospital isn't too much different from many hospitals, Dees.'

'Well, it could be, and it should be, and I'm telling you right now what I'll tell Barnaby when I get the chance, that I am resigning, and what's more, that half of the staff is ready to resign with me.'

Was that true? Then—

Dees stood up, and leaned over the desk. 'This is purely a *Board* action, doctor,' he said loudly, his hand softly pounding. 'And it shouldn't be. The Staff Executive Committee should elect its own Director. And, believe me, you'd be *our* choice. So—we'll quit their damn hospital, and—'

'What's going to happen to your patients?' Jock asked quietly.

Dees frowned. 'Oh, there will be a hospital here to care for them,' he conceded. 'For a day or two, some adjustments will have to be made—but after six months, doctor, you wouldn't be able to tell that you—or I—had ever been here. The rat race will resume, pick up speed, and—'

Jock was nodding, thoughtfully. 'You could do much more for the hospital if you'd stay on here, and work.'

'And fight Barnaby, you mean?'

'Not Barnaby specifically. He's a good surgeon, as you know, and you can learn a lot from him. Besides, I'm not sure, Dees, that Dr. Barnaby had much, if anything, to do with this appointment.'

Dees snorted. 'He accepted the thing, didn't he? And all the time you've been here, he's acted as if he were your friend.'

Yes. Barnaby had acted that way.

'He was my friend,' said Jock. 'But he's a doctor, too, you must remember. And he has a family to consider. This appointment ...'

'Will he keep, or make, any of your changes?'

'Possibly not. If his job depends on conformity.'

'Expediency,' said Dees, slumping down into the chair again.

'Yes,' said Jock, sounding tired. 'A lot of people think that a worth-while motivation.'

Dees was shaking his head. 'He's young enough, and he is a good doctor.'

'Of course he is. But one can be young, and a good doctor—and expedient, too.'

Dees' eyes rolled upward to look at Jock. 'But not you.'

'No', said Jock, 'I've never seemed able to manage that whole combination.'

The news went out into the city in various ways; that same morning Noah Green saw Jamie and Jenny Woodham on the links of the Country Club, and cut across to ask Jamie about the development.

Jamie said he didn't know much about it, that he hadn't yet talked to Jock. 'I think it's perhaps a mistake,' he said uncertainly.

'Well, I sure hope *not,*' declared Noah, tugging at his glove. 'It's a good thing to have happen to the guy. He certainly doesn't belong here, working in that hospital.'

'Maybe not,' said Jamie. 'Only— We haven't been seeing you, Mr. Green.'

'Nor has Jock,' declared Noah. 'I gave him a black eye when I heard he was leaving Anna, and he hasn't come around for a second one.'

'Did *you* give him that shiner?' asked Jamie, awed.

'I hope it was a good one. Of all the crazy idiots! Have you ever met Anna?'

'No ...'

'Well, let's sit down under that tree, and I'll tell you all about her.'

CHAPTER SIXTEEN

For another hour, Jock stayed in his office, thinking, then trying to compose his letter of— resignation? Acceptance?

He asked not to be interrupted, and he was not. Before leaving, Dees had said something about this never happening if they hadn't sent the Administrator away early on a vacation.

Perhaps not. Perhaps the Board had planned to do this while Armstrong was away. Perhaps the hospital had heard that the lawsuit was being handled by Corbett, and had no further use for Dr. Askew, Jr.

Not that any of it mattered, now, except that Jock thought he would have liked to tell the Administrator about the relief he was feeling to have the Board decide things for him, and in this way.

They were right so to decide. The job was really Barnaby's, and it was good for Jock to know that his mother had not been able to 'work things' for him. She probably had tried; if not, when the word reached her, she would try.

But it wouldn't do any good. And Jock was glad.

He drew a sheet of paper towards him, and swiftly wrote his letter. He had been glad to fill in during the emergency created by his father's illness, he said; he was relieved to know that the position was now so adequately filled, and that he could return to the demands of his profession and his Foundation.

Slowly he folded the sheet of fine bond. Relieved or not, he *had* expected to be asked to be Director—and now, knowing that he had not been asked, and would not be, there was left a certain emptiness in his immediate life.

He must now move out, and on—and— What would he do?

Go back to the Foundation, as he had told the Chairman of the Board? Would he do that?

Could he do it? Tree Valley was his home. He had been able to work there as he had not been able anywhere else. His success in life had been there with the Foundation.

But could he go back? No. Not to stay. For Anna was there, and his hurt to her had been too great to hope for any healing.

He had put Anna out of his life, and with it his Foundation. He had done those enormous things in order to stay in St. Louis, to work in a hospital that did not want him, and to draw his family ties together.

Well—the family still remained to him. In fact, just at the minute, it seemed all that did remain. His parents, his children, and Iris. The wrongs he had done to Iris years ago seemed to be righted. Perhaps now he could go on— with her—and build a new life for them both. Perhaps they could start, and build, a new Foundation.

California had nothing to do with the sort of work he knew how to do. He could go out here into St. Louis County, and set up another Foundation—and Iris could help him! They would do some exciting work together, and—

He would go and talk to her about it at once!

Excited at the idea, his eyes shining, he strode out of his office, across the lobby, and out of the hospital, not doing one thing about clearing his desk; he did not even give his letter to his secretary, or tell her where he was going.

'You'd think he'd just inherited a million dollars,' that young woman told the Administrator's girl.

Jock did glance at his watch as he got into his car. It was eleven o'clock and he wasn't sure how Iris would take his breaking in on her at that hour of the morning. But he had to talk to her! About his idea, and about the help she could be to him. She knew everybody in the city, she had poise and grace as a hostess—

Yes, he had to talk to her!

If what Dees had said about 'half the staff' were true, he would have all the medical contacts he would need to start his project. The whole project was feasible, promising, and Jock was anxious to get to work on it. Perhaps some of the trained men from Tree Valley would come on here long enough to get the thing rolling. Jock had already done some preliminary speaking about it in this vicinity. He—

His face aglow, his manner eager, he ran up the steps, and lifted the knocker of Iris's front door. Months ago, Jock had stopped calling it Pete Henderson's door.

The maid welcomed him with a smile; Mrs. Henderson, she said, was out on the garden terrace— 'Just sittin', doctah. You know the way ...'

Jock did know it, and he went swiftly through the house, and out into the shadow of the screened porch. Iris sat on a long chair, all but her head in the bright sunlight. She wore a white dress, the skirt of it falling into full folds that were riffled a little in the small breeze. Her limbs and her shoulders were pale gold, and her hair— How was it the Psalm said it?

'... as the wings of a dove that is covered with

silver wings, and her feathers like gold.'

Yes. That described Iris's hair. Jock moved forward, and hearing his step, she turned her head, then reached out her hand to him. 'Oh, Jock!' she said softly, pleasantly surprised.

When he took her fingers in his, she drew his hand up and pressed it to her cheek, which was both warm and cool, the fragrance of her perfume rising like a soft puff of air, and her voice soft and murmuring. Jock had never seen her more lovely.

He sat down on the end of the chaise, his hand warmly upon her ankle. She lay back against the cushion, faintly smiling. 'You look as if you had news,' she said.

'I do. Big news.' He smiled at her.

'Tell me?'

'Of course. You see, this morning it was announced that Barnaby had been selected as Medical Director of Brownlee Hospital, so that sets me free to make other plans. And I thought—'

'But—' Iris had stiffened. 'When did you say?'

'This morning. I had a letter.'

'Tell me exactly what happened,' she demanded. So Jock told her again. Barnaby was in, he was out, and—

'But can they do that?' she asked, sitting erect.

401

He laughed. 'They can. They have done it.'

'But don't you care?'

'Not really. Their manners could have been better.'

'Jock, I don't think you are telling the whole story.'

'But I am, Iris.'

She was shocked. Her blue eyes narrowed, and her voice sharpened. 'Just *what* happened?' she demanded. '*Why* did they do this thing?'

He tried to tell her, and when he mentioned that his ideas of reforms and changes appeared to be the stumbling block—'They asked me if I would make changes in the way my father had directed the hospital's medical policies, and of course I told them that I would.'

'You are a complete fool!' she cried shrilly. 'I might have known you would be! You haven't learned a thing! What about the lawsuit? I hope you haven't bungled that, too!'

'That is to be as you and Mother want—it will be settled out of court.'

'Well, I'd hope so!' She said more, much more, scolding and berating.

Slowly, Jock got to his feet, still watching Iris, and listening. So she had sounded, and looked, twenty years ago. When Jock would not compromise his own ideas to please his father, when Iris had wanted Pete Henderson and his money.

Her voice still in his ears, Jock looked curiously around him, at the flowers, at the deep, cool shadows below the overhanging porch, and at the sunlit lawn, at the tall white house. Pete's house. His money had bought it all, had paid for the chaise longue, and the little ceramic-topped table, for the tall glass which stood upon it, for this woman's beauty—such as she had.

Yes, indeed, Jock Askew was a fool! A blind fool. A dreamer. And now the time had come for his awakening, for realisation— Had he been given the Directorship, would he have remained blind? For how long?

Feeling sick, he turned his eyes again on Iris. She was saying again that he couldn't seem to learn a *thing!*

'I've learned quite a lot in the past twenty years,' he told her, his voice low.

'Couldn't you have *done* something, Jock?' she cried in anguish, not able to bear seeing her dream-structure collapse into shreds of lathe and plaster and old bricks.

'Yes,' he said quietly. 'I could have done several things. I didn't. And I wouldn't.'

Perhaps Iris, too, recognised them both as the same people they had been twenty years ago. She rose from the long chair, gracefully, and composed. One never saw Iris with her hair or clothing awry! She came over to Jock, and put her hand on his sleeve. Her voice had quieted.

'Jock?' she said questioningly. 'I'd begun to think that you still—well—loved me, and would want to please me.'

He looked down at her. So close, he could see that there were very faint, threadlike lines about her eyes, and others spraying out from the corners of her mouth.

'If I did love you, Iris,' he said deeply. 'And if I felt that you loved me—I would have wanted to please you. Wouldn't I?'

She stepped back and looked up at him. 'I don't understand,' she said uncertainly.

'No. You don't understand. That's always been your trouble. For a time I thought you might have come to understand. I came to you here this morning, hoping that your understanding would let you—'

'I need you, Jock.'

He heard her. But, not answering, he walked away from her a few steps, then turned to look at her. He brushed his hands across his eyes, and looked again up at the house, and finally again at Iris.

Her need for him—for any man—perhaps her need for *anyone*—was to be able to show her power over them. Sometimes, as with her parents, that power was expressed by her own helplessness, sometimes it took the form of her silver-gilt loveliness, or her money, her will; but by some means she must control those close to her, and live their lives to the last detail. Not for them, nor for their sakes, but for herself, for the bolstering of her ego, which was her true, her only, love.

Jock's face crumpled, and he turned abruptly away from Iris.

There were many women like her. More like her than there were women like Anna. Outgoing, giving—and wise.

Without looking at Iris again, or speaking to her, he strode across the terrace, and out through the gate to the street where he stopped short in amazement to see Jamie seated behind the wheel of Jock's car.

'Hi, Dad!' said the young man.

'What are you doing here?'

'I was going to ask you. Me, I'm getting ready to borrow your car. Mine's in the shop for the rest of the day. I got the bright idea when I came home from the Club and found your heap parked here, and you inside talking to Mother. I thought I'd have to come in and ask you. Now, I'll just drive you back to the hospital, or wherever, and—'

'Oh, shut up the bright talk, will you?' Jock

growled. 'Take me to the hotel—and then you can have the damned car. If you want it.' He got in and slumped down in the seat.

'Can do,' said Jamie cheerfully.

Jock was tired. More tired than he had ever been in his life, more tired than he had ever been working at the Foundation, and working very hard.

Of course, there, Anna had been present to buffer for him, and—

He sat shaking his head. With Anna, he had been safe. Never, then, had he had this sickening sense of his foot slipping on the edge of a precipice. If he had been given that Directorship—he brushed his hand across his eyes.

They reached the hotel. Jamie parked the car in the circle and followed Jock into the lobby. Jock looked at him.

'I thought I'd come in, Dad, and talk a little.'

Jock went up to his room, his keys jingling. There he collapsed into the big chair, and Jamie moved about, opening the blinds, suggesting a cold drink. 'Or lunch, maybe?'

'If you like,' said Jock dispiritedly. Hands hanging at his side, he sat with his head back, his eyes staring at the ceiling.

The lunch came almost at once, club sandwiches, iced tea, wedges of Jefferson Davis pie. Jock picked up a potato chip and sat holding it.

Jamie studied him. 'What's wrong with you, Dad?' he asked quietly. 'I know about the Directorship.'

'Yes. Well—nothing is especially wrong with me, Jamie. Even about that. In fact, I am more than relieved not to have it. But—I was thinking of California, and my work there. You see, Jamie—'

For a half-hour he talked about California, about the Foundation, about the trees, and the tiny view of the ocean, and the little brown pool surrounded by ferns. He talked about the doctors, and the men who came to Tree Valley as patients, and in talking, his tiredness rolled away from him. He ate his sandwich, and drank the tea, then picked up his fork to eat his pie.

'You should go back there,' said Jamie, in a matter-of-fact tone.

'I—'

'It's yours, Dad. You made it. Even if you had been given the Directorship here, it would not have been your job in the sense that the Foundation is yours. Why, that place is like a book you might have written. No other man could have done it. And—oh, for gosh sake, Dad, don't let anything interfere! You look at things as they are; you go back there and be your own man.'

Beulah Stone on the stairs, her pillows in her

arms. This slender youth with his white tennis sweater, and his stubborn mouth. A mouth like Jock's own, and a chin with a cleft in it.

Jock stared at the boy.

'I thought,' he said uncertainly, 'that I was doing right to stay here.'

'Whose right?' asked Jamie. 'Certainly not yours!'

'But—'

'Oh, you were not needed!' said Jamie bluntly. Jock gaped at him.

'Of course,' Jamie qualified. 'Nana got some comfort and satisfaction in thinking you'd come back. Mother felt the same way. They've both been quite smug all winter. They got you home. They got you to stay here—to go to Betsy's. They used you to handle the malpractice suit. Of course you threw a shoe with me, but their loud and ringing theme song has been, and will be, "If we can get Jock to do such and such ..."

'They're both strong *women*, Dad! With strengths you and I can only guess at. They can get along on their own, I promise you. Though, for that matter, almost anybody can get along on his own. Barring babies, and some idiots, of course. But adults can manage, if they have to. You found that out when you left here before—that *you* could get along, and did.'

'Yes, but I had Anna to help me. I didn't write my book alone, son. She was with me all along. Not as my manager but—'

'I know. And I'm glad as all get out that you had her. For a time, there, you had me worried. I was afraid that you might go so far as to marry Mother again.'

Jock still stared at the boy.

'I knew you didn't want her so much as you did your family. You wouldn't want *her*. She gave you a very rough deal back there when she ditched you and married Pete Henderson for his money, and his clothes, and his house.

'When it was too late, she found out that Pete couldn't give her what you had, and would have. And that was the position of a good reputation in your profession.

'Pete wasn't reputable, you know. That's how he got his money. Mother soon found it out. I found it out in my first year at Country Day. And Mother recognised that the bargain she had made was not a good one, for you came to have money, too, along with that core of integrity which Pete lacked. Every time you used to come to the city and your name would be in the paper as speaker at some convocation or other, she'd give Pete a hard time. Grandfather and Pete would disagree with you, whatever was speeched about. And—well—I got to know the difference between you and Pete. That's what she wanted of you this time, your respectability and the prestige of the name you've made.'

'Jamie ...' Jock managed to say.

'How do I know about such things? Well, I'll tell you. I've figured some of them out only lately, but they're true. And they'll always be true. You see, Dad, I have fallen in love with Jenny, and I know what it is I see in that girl that's worth while, and what she'll be able to give me. From what Mr. Green told me this morning about your wife—Anna, I mean—she gave you those same things. And it just *must* be worth everything to a man to be able to find, and love, that sort of woman.'

Jock brushed his hand across his eyes. 'But, Jamie,' he said uncertainly. 'I decided that *you* needed me.'

Jamie nodded. 'I did. And I still do. But I am completely horrified to think that you would give up Anna for me and my needs. That was wrong, Dad. Dead wrong! It was not right to do that for me! She must be a wonderful woman. Noah Green says that she is, and just listening to him talk about her, I think I fell in love with her myself. And you *needn't* have lost her, Dad. You didn't need to do that!'

Jock sat back in his chair, limp with the

410

horror his son's words had put upon him. For Jamie was right. He need not have lost Anna! And the waste of it was enough to kill a man. The grief, the futility—the needless waste.

After a bit he managed to look up and meet Jamie's eyes. 'You've changed,' he told his son. 'This morning you're older than I am. Wiser, and stronger, too.'

'I know it,' said Jamie calmly. 'You did that for me, Dad, and I'm grateful for it. It's as if you'd put some sound bones into my flabby flesh. Well—anyway—you have done some very big things for me.'

'May I say that helping has been an item for me, too?'

'I'm sure it has been,' said Jamie staunchly. 'But not big enough to justify the sacrifice of your whole life. So—well, you should go back, Dad, to the things which are yours. Your Foundation—and Anna, if she'll have you back.

'Even I don't need you here any more. I'm well. I'll start Med School in the fall, and I have Jenny.'

'You could go to California with me.'

Jamie stood up. 'No, sir!' he cried.

Jock nodded, and got up out of the deep chair. 'You're right in that, too,' he said. 'You will, and should, make it on your own now. Don't *ever* let me feature in what you decide and do, Jamie.'

'Not ever?' asked Jamie.

Jock laughed, and brushed his hand across his face. 'I'm bushed,' he said, sounding as if he truly were. 'Not so much by what has happened today as by the realisation of what might have happened.'

'I have some personal thoughts on that subject, too,' said Jamie.

'Keep them to yourself. In time I'll sell myself on the idea that it didn't take failure to get the Director's job to show me the error of my ways. But I will point out to you, Jamie, that it is quite enough for any man to live his own life, without trying to live that of others. Now there's a profoundly wise truth, and one you can stay with.'

'I shall, if you don't mean he must live that life alone.'

'I don't. And I'm awfully glad you have Jenny, son.'

'Just as I'm glad you have Anna.'

Jock winced. 'I don't even know where she is.'

'Can't you guess?'

'I intend to guess.'

Jamie left then, Jock telling him to put the car into the garage when he was through with

412

it. 'I'm going to California on the first flight I can get.'

Jamie circled his thumb and finger, and went out, smiling. Jock called the airport, then began to gather his belongings. He had more clothes than his two bags would hold; the hotel probably would pack and send his winter things; he could throw out a lot of junk ... He wished he were not so tired. He must call the hospital—

He did, speaking to the Administrator's secretary. He had been called out of town, she said. Since Dr. Barnaby was probably ready to take over his office at once ...

He set the phone down, and called, *'Come in!'* loudly to whoever was knocking on his door. Probably the bellhop ...

He began to stack books and magazines. 'Jock?'

He whirled. His mother was standing there, just a few feet inside the room, her face and white hair, her printed silk dress, all in the usual good order, the usual triple strand of pearls about her throat.

'Oh—Mother,' he said uncertainly. 'I've been packing.'

'I see. May I come in?'

He cleared a chair, and she sat down. 'Would you have left without seeing me?' she asked, her voice cool.

'I'd at least have phoned you. This all came up unexpectedly.'

'Where are you going?'

Jock stacked a dozen issues of *Life*. What a mess this room was in ! 'Home,' he said tersely.

'Oh, Jock.'

'I am needed out there, Mother. I've been needed there for several months.'

'Iris tells me that you are very upset about the Director position going to John Barnaby.'

Iris! Well, of course. She would have got in touch with Emma, and Emma had come right over to see what could be done to— What was Jamie's phrase?—'get Jock to ...'

Jock smiled faintly, and dropped the stack of magazines into the corner.

'I was upset about several things,' he said calmly. Glad that he could be calm. 'But not about the job, Mother. Giving it to Barnaby was the best thing that ever happened to me.'

'Now just what does that mean?'

Jock rested one foot on the chair at the desk, and looked at his mother. 'It means that I can be my own man again. Remember? At Christmas you told me that was what you wanted, for me to be my own man.

'I thought I was my own man before I came home last winter, though I had no more than got here, Mother, but what you began to tie

414

strings to me. The family, your demands, Father's illness, the lawsuit, and the job of Acting Director of Brownlee Hospital.

'I knew it was happening, but I let it happen anyway. Perhaps I would have broken those strings in time, but today, when I was told that Barnaby had been named Director, and that you couldn't get that knot tied firmly enough around my ankle—why, I broke the rest of them. And now—I am leaving your puppet show.'

'Jock—'

He nodded. 'Yes, I know. It's not really a bad show. It just doesn't happen to be my show. Now I'd like to think that some of you will continue to be a part of my life. But it's got to be *my* life, Mother.

'You can share it if you like, and as much as you like I hope you will share it. But it must be on my terms.

'I want to respect you as well as love you. And I have to have respect from you, in my turn. Remember that! Always remember it!'

Emma said many things in reply. And Jock answered her, briefly, kindly. He also went on with his sorting and packing, and when the time came for him to leave, he did leave. He took his mother down with him to the desk; she stood and watched him get into the airport bus.

And her face was angry, not grieved.

So Jamie was right. Emma Askew was a strong woman, and she could take care of herself.

CHAPTER SEVENTEEN

Jock was glad that his mother was provoked at him. It made it easier to leave her, and turn his thoughts westward to the Foundation, and to Anna.

He had been thinking of Anna ever since Jamie had spoken of her. 'Noah Green was in love with her, and I fell in love with her, too.'

Jock was in love with her himself, and had been since that night when he had first seen her, a grave-eyed girl in white ...

Oh, and now he did want her desperately! Because he had failed?

Perhaps so. A man had a right to need his wife, and Anna was the sort of woman a man could need, and feel no shame. He must see her—at least that. He had no claim upon her, of course, but he must see her. Talk to her, if she would let him. Perhaps he would need to

416

court her again, and he would, as humbly, and as hopefully, as he had done that first time.

As the miles flowed past below the plane, his eagerness increased. He reached San Francisco, and rented a car to drive the seventy-five miles to Tree Valley, having always to watch his speed.

But at last the familiar wooded slopes opened before him, the winding road and the low buildings of the Foundation. He would have gone straight up to the house; he wanted to go. But he pulled into the gravelled parking space before the Main Building, and got out.

'Well, Dr. Askew!' cried the porter, who was raking gravel. 'It's good to have you back, sir.'

'Believe me,' said Jock, 'it's good to be back!'

Excitement bubbling in his blood, he went up the shallow steps, and into the shadow of the entry. A half-dozen people greeted him, and looked astonished to see him. But—there was something in the air. He was welcomed, but everyone seemed to be waiting for some other thing to happen. His coming alone was not just what they wanted, or expected.

Three lines furrowed deeply between his brows, he went down the corridor to his office, pushed the door open, and met the lifted eyes of Sam Minter who was seated behind the desk.

Sam looked surprised, and—yes, questioning.

417

Why had he come back? That was the question. Everyone wanted to know that. *Why* had Jock come home? And now?

Recovering himself at once, Sam got up and shook hands. He told Jock to sit down, man, sit down! And asked him how he was.

'Well,' said Jock, shaking his head a little. 'Just at the minute I feel like one of my own patients.'

If he had thought Sam would be surprised at such a statement, he couldn't have been more wrong. For Sam was sitting there, calmly nodding his head.

'I'm glad to know you haven't been yourself,' he said dryly.

Jock started to answer, then flushed. 'I'm glad to know that, too,' he said gruffly. 'I've been trying to believe it.'

'How is your father doing?' asked Sam politely.

'Cerebral arteriosclerosis? You know how he's doing. It's the way he was doing last November. Look, Sam—if you chaps don't want me here—'

'It's your Foundation, Jock.'

'You know better than that. We all built it. You men, and Anna.'

'Ah, yes, Anna.' Sam leaned back in his chair. Outside the window a branch bobbed up and down in the breeze.

Jock watched it, and chewed his lip. 'How is—Anna?' he asked tightly.

'So far as I know, she's all right.'

'So far as you— Isn't she here?'

'Of course she isn't here,' said Sam. Not looking at Jock, but the man was angry.

Jock sat stunned. He had come up a dead end. He should have expected it, he supposed—but he really had not. He had thought to find everything as usual at Tree Valley. The buildings, the patients, the doctors—and Anna up the hill, perhaps in her pink clamdiggers and striped shirt, working with her ferns, or just sitting, gazing up at the clouds, her face like something delicately carved, yet ready to break into life at sight of Jock coming up the path ...

But now—

Jock sighed, and shook his head, then got out his handkerchief and mopped his face. Sam was watching him.

'I feel more than ever like one of my own patients,' Jock confessed. 'Badly in need of counsel. I feel, Sam—these past months, I've felt as if a will beyond my own was forcing me, and guiding me.'

Sam pursed his lips. 'A will stronger than you,' he said thoughtfully. 'Yes, that could be the way it was.'

Jock noted the change which Dr. Minter had made.

'And maybe you do need help,' said Sam.

Jock sat on in the chair, thinking—trying to think—and Sam sat watching him; the stack of reports under his hand needed his attention. Jock knew that they did. But still Sam would let this troubled man talk to him—try to talk—

'I could attempt to make you see how it was,' Jock said once.

'If you like.'

No. Jock did not 'like.' Later he could, perhaps, talk to his staff men. Now—there was just this bruised, pulpy feeling of loss.

'Why ...?' he asked, looking up. 'Why did she leave, Sam? Her home, her friends ...?'

'Why shouldn't she leave, Jock? The home and the friends didn't matter. It seemed to Anna that all she had left was herself.'

'What can I do?'

'I don't know. But I would say that you should first accept her premise.'

That hurt terribly, but it was true. Heavily, as if his limbs were weighted, Jock stood up, turned and walked out of the office, and out of the building, his face like stone.

He walked slowly up the hill—to the house, and past it. He met patients, and spoke to them gravely, seeing them, but forgetting them the minute they had passed. He went to all the places where he best remembered Anna. The big, smooth boulder where she liked to sit in the warm sunlight, to the seat beside the chattering creek, to the bower of low, vine-covered trees where the stream ran brown.

He tried to think. And in no way could he imagine a life without Anna.

He spent hours in this fashion. Had he reached the Foundation at night, he still would have walked the woods and thought, and not noticed what time of day or night it was. This hard, tough knot of pain and regret—would he always carry it with him? Once he had spoken fatuously of a margin of error. Oh, dear God! Dear God!

For all that afternoon, he walked and walked; he sat for a time on this bench and that, and then walked again. Thinking, thinking, always thinking. Until, with blue shadows beginning to clot and thicken among the trees and the sky pale above their blowing tops, he went resolutely down the hill, past his house with no more than a tight-lipped glance at it, down to the Main Building and into Sam's office.

But the office was empty, and the desk cleared. Dr. Minter had gone home, said the girl out at the main desk. Jock nodded. He thanked her, and went into the staff lounge to refresh himself. He looked like the devil, tired and dusty.

He came out, and went, still resolute, up the path to Sam's house. Frances met him warmly, kindly, her eyes sorry for him. 'I'm glad you're back, Jock.'

'Yes. I should have come before this. Where's Sam?'

'Out on the terrace. He's taken up fly-tying. He says it lets him get mad at inanimate things.'

Jock's hand patted Frances's cheek. 'I have to talk to him.'

'I think he's expecting you. Go on out. I'll be busy whipping cream or something.'

Sam glanced up from the bits of bright steel, brighter feathers, and spools of thread he had spread out on the table before him; he was a big man, but his hands were incredibly skilled with a bit of silk.

For a minute Jock watched him. Then he sat down in one of the cushioned chairs, leaned forward and clasped his hands between his knees. 'Sam,' he said deeply, 'where's Anna?'

Sam glanced at him, struck with the drawn and weary look of Jock's face, and the glitter in his brown eyes.

'Well, tell me this,' said Jock. 'Is she planning

to marry—again?'

'It was an interlocutory decree,' said Sam, his voice kind. Askew was in torment! Deserved maybe, but it was not in Dr. Minter to inflict further punishment.

'She was opposed to the things I was doing, Sam,' Jock said. 'She wouldn't join me. I thought it only fair to offer her a chance to be free of me. She took it. But—now—I realise— Where *is* she, Sam?'

'Working. She would take no property settlement, Jock, as you know. We tried to persuade her. We tried to keep her here.'

Jock leaned forward. 'But where has she *gone?*'

'Well—to take up her own life again, Jock. Her old life.'

'You mean ...?'

'Wait.' Sam got up and went into the living-room; almost at once he came back with a copy of a news magazine, two or three weeks old. He flipped its pages, and then showed an article to Jock. It was in a section headed THEATRE, and the article indicated by Sam's finger had to do with a new musical comedy, *Spring Fancy,* which Luke Fogarty had written, and which was about to have its première in Philadelphia. The setting was 1904, the dance routines were by—the star was— Nowhere was Anna mentioned. Jock looked up at Sam and frowned.

'That's where she is, Jock,' said Sam, sitting down again, and picking up a pair of long-nosed forceps.

'But—why, she can't go back to singing! To stage work! Not after ten years!'

'Can't she?' Sam looked hard at a peacock's feather. 'Isn't that what you did? Or tried to do? Go back?'

Jock groaned. 'I suppose that was part of it. Look, Sam, I really don't know what I thought I was doing, or why I did as I did. Why I stayed on—'

'Anna thought that you preferred the old way to the new.'

'It wasn't that. If she would have joined me—'

'Could she? She had no place in your past.'

Jock sat desolate.

'I decided that there was probably some shock over your father's condition.'

Jock glanced at his friend. He was speaking honestly. 'There was a little shock,' he said slowly. 'And—I found myself reunited, by his illness, with my family, with my children. Then—I became busy. That explains something about the time I stayed. I was busy. I worked in my father's hospital as Acting

Medical Director, you see. I had always wanted to work there, and make certain changes—

'There were all those things, though I accomplished nothing.' He spoke sadly. 'The malpractice suit will be settled as it would have been if I'd never gone to St. Louis. My mother and father—two days would have taken care of them. The hospital—' Jock's lips twisted wryly. 'I accomplished nothing there. Jamie— But I could have had the children, and Anna, too! And if I couldn't— Nothing was worth what I did to her!'

'And to yourself,' said Sam quietly.

'Yes,' Jock agreed. 'Yes. To us both.'

'And now?'

'Now I'll try to find her. If I can. If I can't, I'll come back here and work, as best I'm able. If I'd still have a place here.'

'Good,' said Sam. 'We've been running short-handed without you.'

For a long minute, Jock sat silent, while Sam hunted for some yellow silk, found it, and began to wrap it around a tiny, barbed hook.

'To go back,' Jock said softly. 'To live the old life—I failed miserably if that was what I was trying to do.'

'Because the old life was wrong?' asked Sam, not looking up from his work. He had snapped on a crook-necked lamp; in the dusk, his hands and the lower part of his face were sharply illuminated.

'That was part of it,' said Jock. 'But only part. Of course it *was* what I was trying to do. To correct, to obliterate the failures I had made with my parents, with my—wife, and my children. But one can't go back, Sam! Not really. Did you know that? For life moves forward—'

'Then it must for all of us.'

'Yes. For Anna, too. Sam—' Jock stood up. 'I'm going to find her. You're right. She will be with Luke Fogarty—and perhaps she'll want no part of me. But I'm going to Philadelphia tomorrow.'

'Tomorrow, yes. But get a hot bath and a night's sleep first, eh? Some food.'

Jock turned only half-way to nod agreement; he was out through the screen door, and had started up the hill again to his house.

The next morning, Jock drove the rented car back to San Francisco, but when he bought his ticket at the air terminal it was for St. Louis. He would return there, gather up the loose ends he had left behind him—in short, he would stop acting like a blundering fool—a child.

He went first to Brownlee Hospital, and hunted up Dr. Barnaby. Then he emptied his desk, and claimed the raincoat he had left in the closet. He said good-bye to his secretary, and told her where to forward his mail.

'Tree Valley Foundation ...'

'Yes, doctor. I'm sorry you're leaving.'

'Come and see us sometime.'

'I may do just that!'

Smiling, Jock went out, and deliberately waited until he could use the elevator which somehow, in his mind, had started 'all this' back in November. He went up to his father's room, and as he had expected at that hour of the day, he found Emma there.

She was very glad to see him. Cheeks pink, she clung to him and chattered gaily.

His father extended a hand, and asked why he hadn't been to see him sooner. 'I've been sick a long time, Jock.'

'Yes, sir, I know. I thought maybe you and mother and I should make some plans about where you'll go to convalesce.'

'Now, Jock ...' said Emma, warningly.

'I have to return to California,' Jock said firmly. 'And I'll have to stay. I thought perhaps you two would like to come out there, and try the climate.'

'I don't expect you'll get Emma away from her grandchildren,' said Jim, unexpectedly firm and lucid.

Jock nodded. 'They're prettier than I am, I'll admit,' he said, and Jim chuckled.

But he soon drifted back into the half-sleeping, half-waking state in which his hours were generally passed, and Jock agreed when Emma indicated that they should go out into the hall.

Visiting hours were in effect, and the corridor swarmed.

'Let's go down to the coffee shop,' Emma suggested. 'Are you at the hotel?'

'No. I won't be staying. I have a flight out at three.' Jock shifted the raincoat.

Frowning a little, Emma went into the elevator.

'Mother,' said Jock, 'if I am to help you, we must decide immediately about where we'll take Father.'

'He can't go to California.'

'Then have Barnaby select a good nursing home near the city here. The hospital will move him.'

'You have it all settled, haven't you?' said Emma, smiling at the waitress. 'I'll have a glass of iced tea, Lucy, and some of the shortbread cookies, if you have them.'

The girl nodded. 'Dr. Askew?'

'Coffee,' he said. 'No cookies.'

'Now, Jock,' said Emma. 'What about *you?*'

'What about me? I said upstairs that I was going back to California.'

'I am sure that you should stay here, son. Work, and be near your family.'

'Mother, will you please relax and let me make my own decisions?'

'But, of course, Jock. I only—'

'You only want to guide me, protect me. I know. You've always wanted that. And there was a time when it was a good thing for you to do. But as the years have gone by, you've never faced the fact that I grew up, that I was—and am—a grown man.'

'You're grown,' said Emma, taking off her white gloves. 'But men stay children to their dying day. And,' she shook a finger at him, her rings flashing, 'you men like it that way.'

'Not I,' said Jock. 'I have a man's work to do, and I do not intend to do it, as a child, in St. Louis.'

'But, son—what about Iris? Don't you feel that she has a claim upon you?'

'I realise that you've tried to engineer things so that I'd feel obligated—'

'Any *engineering* I may have done,' said Emma, finding the word distasteful, 'was for your own good. And hers.'

'That may be,' Jock agreed. 'But Iris has no claim upon me, Mother.'

'Then what of the children?'

'I intend to keep in close touch with them.'

'Jamie really needs you. Your presence here—'

'I'll take care of Jamie. I'm going over to the house now—and, good-bye, Mother. Keep in touch with me, and tell me what you decide to do about Father.'

He kissed her, and Emma watched him until he had disappeared. Jock, she thought, looked older.

Iris, herself, opened the white front door, and would have embraced Jock. He shook his head, and her cheeks flushed pink. Jamie, she said hurriedly, was not at home.

Jock nodded. 'I'm leaving the city, permanently,' he told her, standing in the hall. 'I expect Mother phoned you?' He knew that she had. 'All right, then, there's not much need for us to talk, is there? Except that I have one word for you, Iris. It's advice, not a threat. And the word is this: Let Jamie alone, will you? Let him be a man. Let him do the things he wants to do. If he wants to enough, he can do them.'

Iris's lips quivered. 'You'd like to take him away from me, wouldn't you?'

'I couldn't do that unless he wanted to come. I wouldn't want to do it, unless—he wanted to come. Now, I'll write this to him, but you tell him, too. I'll pay his way through medical school—'

'But there's no need for that, Jock.'

'There's a need in me, and in Jamie, for me to do that! You tell him. I'll do that much for him, and the rest will be up to him.'

'Shall I tell him that, too?'

'He'll know it. Well—good-bye, then, Iris.'

He went out. And paused on the steps. Noah? Should he go see him, and tell him ...? No, he had nothing yet to tell Noah.

But maybe he should hunt up Dr. Dees, say good-bye, and offer him a place in California ...?

No. Again Jock shook his head, and got into the waiting taxi. Dees would go places on his own. I did, thought Jock.

'He'll have a few setbacks.' Jock grinned. 'I did.'

CHAPTER EIGHTEEN

It was good again to be a man on top of himself, and his affairs. Jock realised that he had not felt this way in months. When, having reached Philadelphia, the feeling began to thin some-

431

what, he clutched at it determinedly.

He registered at a hotel, asked about the new musical comedy. The opening was that very night, he discovered, and he was inclined to hesitate. He'd never get a ticket!

But he went on to the theatre anyway, glad that he had picked up his coat, for a light mist was beginning to fall; the lights of the theatre made long ribbons of gaiety on the street; the cars that pulled up to the marquee glistened with a rich and shining radiance.

Jock had been right; no tickets were available. He circled the lobby, looking at the pictures—Luke Fogarty's name was prominent. It had become the symbol of success in this particular world. There were pictures of the leading lady, of the baritone star—and finally, yes, there was a picture of Anna. Jock stood transfixed, gazing at it. A new picture, just of her head and throat—but she looked exactly as he knew her image in his heart. Shining black hair, close to her head. Level-gazing dark eyes, the merest promise of a smile upon her lips ...

And, in a slashing script, her name. *Anna Askew.* Anna—Askew. Feeling odd, Jock's finger traced the last name, and he again studied the picture of her, remembering her as he had first seen her. White dress, cool, remote assurance of herself as a person ...

432

The sound of music came to him, faintly, and the swell of applause; the chap in the box office was watching him with a strange expression on his face. Jock glanced once more at Anna's picture, turned on his heel and went outside. A woman in a blue dress and a fur shoulder wrap, a man in a black hat and a narrow-cut suit were getting out of a shining red car. They had tickets. They were the typical late-arrivers. Why couldn't they come early to see Anna? One would not want to miss a note of her deep-throated song!

Frowning, Jock turned and strode swiftly down the street.

Back stage, amid the usual confusion of a first-night performance, Anna Askew stood in the wings with Luke Fogarty, awaiting her entrance cue. Electricians, prop boys, and the prompter eddied about them. A dancer brushed past, and apologised for her hat's long feather.

Anna, in a long-skirted white dress, the neck of it demure against her throat, the sleeves long to her wrists; tucks and Valenciennes lace made the frock prettily quaint, and at least as provocative as bare shoulders would have been ...

'You look wonderful, honey,' Luke told her. 'Nervous?'

Anna shrugged. 'I could never be doing this

433

without you,' she said softly. 'Oh, I do thank you, Luke!'

For the peace she had found in work, for giving her a life to live, a life of a sort—

He patted her shoulder. 'There you go, sweetheart,' he said, giving her a little push, his eyes watching her.

She was all right. She walked with poise and assurance out upon the stage; she confronted the leading man, her chin tilted.

An older actor—a man of sixty, whose life had been the stage—stood at Luke's side. 'She went out there,' this man said, 'like a great actress about to make stage history. You'd never know it was her first play. She's a great lady, Luke.'

'She's a great woman,' said Luke gruffly.

'That's better?' asked the man.

'Oh, sure. Being a woman is lots better.'

Jock came hurrying back to the theatre, a long box under his arm. He would take the flowers to the stage door, and manage somehow—

The ten years he had had with Anna. They had been lived, those years and, as of tonight, Jock Askew meant to make use of them, not lose them.

Not being experienced in such things, he had a little trouble finding the stage door. A

434

friendly policeman helped him, after Jock had identified himself. He was late, he explained, he had flown in from the West Coast—he showed his identification—he was the husband of one of the actresses in the play, he said.

At the stage door, he must persuade the doorman, a shirt-sleeved chap who was suspicious of all comers.

'I'm Dr. James Askew, Jr.,' said Jock earnestly. 'My wife is in the play. Anna Askew. Look, you can verify that with Luke Fogarty. *He* knows me.'

The man got up from his chair. 'Shall I take them flowers in?'

'You can. But ask Mr. Fogarty to let me in, to see Anna—'

The man stumped off, committing himself to nothing.

Strange sounds came to Jock, feet pounding on iron stairs, a thread of music—voices—

And the doorman came back, down the narrow, brick-walled corridor. 'Mr. Fogarty says for you to come on in.'

'May I ...?'

'He jest said to let you in. You go right straight through there, and turn left. You'll find him—*if* you know him.'

Jock did find Luke. He was coming towards him, his homely face inquiring. 'What are you doing here in the East, doctor?' he asked, his twanging voice drawling the words.

Jock smiled. 'Mending my fences,' he replied in kind.

Luke's eyebrow went up. 'I thought you were back in the hospital. Back in several hospitals, as a matter of fact.'

'No. But I do mean to return to my hospital—my Foundation—in California, and stay there. After I've seen Anna.'

'Do you think Anna will go back with you?' Luke leaned against the wall, and took a cigar out of his pocket, studied it, and put it away again.

'I don't know what she will do,' Jock answered readily. 'I wouldn't deserve it, if she did consent to go back with me.'

Luke said nothing.

'But, then, I never did deserve Anna.'

Luke nodded, straightened, and started down the narrow passage. 'You come along,' he said over his shoulder. 'Stand right here. And don't make a sound. She'll be out—here.'

Jock stood where he was told. He could see a thin wedge of the lighted stage. Behind him a man pulled levers and flipped toggle switches. The light on the stage was incredibly bright, the shadows about Jock incredibly dark. He was aware of a webbing of ropes, of a spiralling

436

staircase some twenty feet away, of small signal lights on the switchboard—

But mostly he was aware of the slender, dark-haired woman out on the stage. She spoke, she laughed—and she sang. Something about the fancy of a girl in the springtime ...

About him, people moved silently, ghostlike; twice Jock stepped aside to let someone pass. The stage filled, but the spotlight was still on Anna in her quaint white dress and with her long-handled parasol—as any spotlight should be upon her.

'She's doing a grand job,' said Luke at Jock's shoulder again. 'Of course she has only a small part.'

Jock turned to glance at him, the light flashing in his eyes, shadowing the cleft in his chin. 'Anna,' he said tensely, 'couldn't play a small part if she tried!'

Luke nodded, and pointed his hand. 'Catch this,' he said. 'It'll be great.'

'In the spring,' sang Anna, her face a-light, 'a girl's fancy does, too!' The song was exquisite. Light, joyous, lilting. A Luke Fogarty specialty, such a song.

'She thinks of love,' sang the dark-haired sprite. 'Oh, she thinks of love—of love—of love!'

The last note hung, trembling, in the air, and then Anna was coming off stage, turning once to flash her rare smile at the audience, then to come—running—

Applause rose like waves of thunder, rolling, rolling—

But Anna heard none of it.

For she was in Jock's arms, safely, where she wanted to be.